Gilead had moved closer. Subtly his face changed as he studied hers. His pupils dilated, turning the irises near purple. Slowly a hand came up to cup her chin and he traced her lips lightly with his thumb.

"Ye want to be kissed, lass?" It really wasn't so much a question as a statement.

Dear God. She shouldn't. He had made it clear with his strict formality that he didn't want to have anything to do with her. This would mean nothing to him. She should pull away; she really should. He wasn't holding her forcefully, but the gentle touch of his fingers might as well have been an iron collar. Deidre shut her eyes and parted her lips.

She heard his sharp intake of breath and then his lips brushed hers, tantalizing her as he kept the pressure easy and gentle. It was slow torture, and finally she could stand no more. She thrust her tongue deep into his mouth.

He hesitated but a moment and then brought his arms around her waist, pulling her to him as he responded. . . .

Also by Cynthia Breeding

CAMELOT'S DESTINY

Published by Zebra Books

MY NOBLE KNIGHT

CYNTHIA BREEDING

ZEBRA BOOKS
Kensington Publishing Corp.
www.kensingtonbooks.com

ZEBRA BOOKS are published by

Kensington Publishing Corp.
850 Third Avenue
New York, NY 10022

All Kensington titles, imprints, and distributed lines are available at special quantity discounts for bulk purchases for sales promotion, premiums, fund-raising, educational, or institutional use.

Special book excerpts or customized printings can also be created to fit specific needs. For details, write or phone the office of the Kensington Special Sales Manager: Attn. Special Sales Department. Kensington Publishing Corp., 850 Third Avenue, New York, NY 10022. Phone: 1-800-221-2647.

ISBN-13: 978-0-8217-8031-2
ISBN-10: 0-8217-8031-X

First Printing: June 2007
10 9 8 7 6 5 4 3 2 1

Printed in the United States of America

Foreword

The Philosopher's Stone has always had an intriguing aura about it. What is it exactly? From whence did it come? What is its purpose?

Laurence Gardner, in his book *Bloodline of the Holy Grail* (Fair Winds Press, 2002), explains that Hermes Trismegistus (the Greek name for Thoth, the Egyptian god of alchemy and geometry) held special knowledge of the Lost Wisdom of Lamech, seventh in succession from Eve's son Cain. Lamech's three sons, who were a mathematician, a mason, and a metalworker, respectively, preserved the ancient wisdom of creative science on two stone monuments known as the Antediluvian Pillars. Hermes discovered one of the pillars and transcribed its Sacred Geometry onto an emerald tablet that was inherited by Pythagoras, who discovered the second pillar.

Hermes believed in the adage "as above, so below," meaning that the earth is the mortal image of the cosmological structure, and that a repetitive geometric law prevails through all matter and through all energy.

The emerald tablet became known as the Philosopher's Stone. On it lies the code for human existence, for those who have eyes to see.

Prologue

Deidre of the Languedoc leaned back against the sun-warmed rocks on the bank of the river Garonne and closed the ancient book, careful not to break the brittle vellum pages. Her fingertips traced the Latin letters tooled into the smooth, old leather. *Locus Vocare Camulodunum:* "A Place Called Camelot." Deidre's cornflower eyes lit with excitement. In contrast to Gaul, with the never-ending squabbles of the deceased King Clovis's four sons, Camelot was apparently a place of peace across the Narrow Channel, where courtly gentlemen honored and revered women as in the days when the Goddess fully ruled. If only Deidre could go there.

She frowned, remembering how furious her mother, high priestess to Isis, had been to find the book—or The Book—as Deidre liked to call it, lying in place of the Philosopher's Stone in the grotto deep inside a hidden cave. Her mother had accused the old magician who had ensconced himself near the shrine of stealing it. She searched his goods, only to find nothing. But the next morning he was gone. Deidre's burgeoning gift of Sight had not been able to find him. For the past two years, the magician had cloaked himself and the Stone well.

The Stone was one of Solomon's lost treasures: the symbols of the Sacred Geometry that defined all life and the sum of all wisdom were embedded in it. Deidre had not actually seen it, for she was too young, at two-and-ten, to be initiated into the Ways, but it had been her mother's duty and honor to protect the Stone, as it had been with her people since the Magdalen brought it with her when she fled Judea with her daughter, Sarah. The holy family's bloodline traced through the Stone as well, for in Goddess circles, the Magdalen was believed to be descended from Isis herself.

Now the Stone was gone and so was her mother, who, after two years, so despaired that the Stone would remain hidden forever that she jumped from a cliff high above the warm waters of the Mediterranean, never to surface from those lapis depths. And Deidre was being sent to her cousin Childebert, to the Christian king's castle in Paris. She wrinkled her nose and tossed back her long, blond hair defiantly. From what she had heard of the austere Christian court, there would be no ritual mating at Beltane—and this was to have been her first, at four-and-ten—nor any other festival that held true to the Goddess. Just her luck, when she was finally about to find out what all the young priestesses in her mother's care giggled about the morning after such celebrations.

Deidre had always dreamed that when she came of age, she would be allowed to choose her consort according to the Old Ways, as her mother had done with the Celtic-born Caw of Pictland. The Book had filled her adolescent head with even grander ideas. Her young man would be handsome and strong and pledge his faith completely, like the knights of the Round Table did.

Deidre hugged the volume to herself as she stood. She would hide it well within her trunk and reread the stories of honorable Arthur, courteous Gawain, steadfast Bedwyr, and the irresistible Lancelot. The book would be a symbol of hope that one day she too would find her true noble knight.

Chapter One

BELTANE

Scotland, ten years later

Scents of sex and musk permeated the cool night air, accompanied by deep grunts, soft moans, labored panting, and sharp gasps. Cautiously, Deidre pushed back the bracken and peered into the sheltered glade, canopied by a velvety black sky sprinkled liberally with diamonds. It had seemed harmless enough, but she'd lost both her escort and coin, and barely managed to escape abduction the night before. She wasn't taking any chances. To her right, a banked fire sent slow spirals of blue smoke curling lazily into the air, interrupted only by an occasional crackle of yellow flame when the breeze fanned unburned wood.

Deidre squinted beyond the light of the smoldering embers and detected movement near a shrub. A giggle accosted her from the left and she shifted her gaze. A naked young man, his erection huge in the dim light, was coaxing the shirt off a girl who lay writhing on the ground beneath him. Well, maybe he wasn't "coaxing" her clothes off. Tearing them off might be a better description. Deidre blinked. In her unfortunately still-virgin state, she'd never seen a naked man before. She gasped a little as he lowered himself over the girl and she heard the muffled shriek that told her he had not been gentle. Apparently, though, the woman was used to it, for she was bucking enthusiastically, begging him for more.

Deidre surveyed her surroundings. The remains of a huge bonfire cast shadows of the trees near the glade. A road or track led off around a bend. As her eyes grew accustomed to the light, she could now see more squirming couples beneath the low bushes that spread toward the tree line. Quite a bacchanalian sight.

Listening to gasps and groans of pleasure was really more than a reluctant virgin of four-and-twenty could take. She should have lost her accursed maidenhood and been wed long ago were it not for her gift of Sight, which kept her practically a prisoner at Childebert's court. Her cousin needed her talent, he said, even though his Christian mother, Clotilde, frowned on anything pagan. Sometimes Deidre thought the only reason Clotilde tolerated her was for the large dowry she'd inherited from her mother, which Childebert had access to as long as she remained a maid. Between her cousin and his mother, they'd managed to discourage any and all suitors.

Suddenly Deidre became aware of other noises. Boots. Male voices. Laughter. Drunken laughter, from the sound of it. She stepped back quickly, intending to seek shelter in the trees. Too late. She had been seen.

"Begorra! There's a fine lass," someone shouted. "Doona let her get away!"

Deidre tripped and picked up her long skirt. Dratted thing. Traveling clothes were always heavy. The skirt alone had to weigh near a half stone. Deidre hiccupped hysterically, stifling a scream. She ripped the headdress off; the ungainly thing was hindering her sight as she raced toward the trees.

A big, burly arm caught her roughly around the waist, expelling the air from her lungs. She gasped as she fought to free herself, kicking and scratching.

"Och, a feisty lass. I like that kind." The man laughed, and, with one huge paw on her shoulder, spun her around.

He wore a kilt and sash and his breath reeked of liquor, although he was not drunk. He was barrel-chested, big and bulky, with gray hair and a bushy beard, and his eyes glinted like steel in the moonlight. He grabbed her face in one beefy fist and leaned close, his mouth slack and drooling. As much as she resented her virginity, she was not about to lose it to this lecher. The thankful young stable lads to whom she'd slipped forbidden sweetmeats at Childebert's court had taught her a few things. Deidre brought her knee up hard to meet the lout's groin.

A surprised look crossed his face as he doubled over. She lost no time in pushing back and starting to sprint away, but the man lurched for her and she landed on the ground with a hard thud. He rolled her over, his considerable weight pressing her down, leaving no room for air in her lungs.

"Ye'll pay for that, lassie, but I like it rough," he said, grabbing her long, flaxen hair and pulling her head back painfully. He pushed her skirts up and thrust a knee between her thighs, the wayward kilt obligingly out of the way.

Deidre struggled, but her arms were pinned. She fought to keep her knees together, but he only laughed and spread her legs farther. All those years spent dreaming of giving herself willingly to one of the gallant knights from The Book were about to disintegrate into her worst nightmare. Desperately, she snapped at him with her teeth, drawing blood from his chin.

He raised a fist and she turned her head, bracing herself for the blow. Perhaps being knocked unconscious would be the best thing that could happen to her. As if he read her thoughts, he brought his hand down and roughly flipped her over.

"Ye can't do much damage like this," he said, "and I can go deeper."

Deidre tried to push against him, and then realized she was probably helping him more than herself. She gritted her teeth. *Bâtard.* Then, suddenly, the weight was lifted and she could breathe. She rolled to a sitting position, hands protecting her face, and gulped for air.

"I'm thinking the lass might not be wantin' to play yer game, Niall."

The voice of an angel. It had to be. A soft, rich Scottish burr, not menacing, but authoritative all the same.

Deidre opened one eye and peered up. *By the saints*. It could have been the archangel Michael himself, complete with flaming sword. Righteous indignation flashed across his face as he towered over her attacker, claymore at the ready. Relief flooded her and she couldn't help but notice the muscular, leather-clad thighs that were at nose level. She forced herself to look up past a flat belly and narrow waist. Firelight reflected off a finely chiseled face with high cheekbones, a straight nose, and a sinfully sensual full mouth. The wind rippled through her rescuer's shoulder-length dark hair and caused the flowing white shirt he wore to flatten against a broad chest and powerful arms. A whimper escaped her. Angels shouldn't look like this. If they did, she was definitely going to start attending more of those boring Masses she hated.

"It's Beltane, mon!" Niall said churlishly. "What's she doing out, if she doesn't want to be taken?"

Beltane. The ancient pagan fertility festival held on May 1. She'd forgotten, after last night's narrow escape.

Her personal god turned a discerning gaze on her. "I don't know why she's here, but I'll make sure the lass gets back to where she needs to go." Niall gave him a challenging look. "Safe and unmolested," he added, as he met the older man's gaze.

Niall stared at him sullenly and then gestured to his men that they were leaving. He looked down at Deidre ominously. "Ye haven't seen the last of me, lass. No woman gets the best of me."

She shuddered slightly as he strode off, straightening his sash. And then, her divine savior was offering her his hand.

She slipped hers into his. Strong, warm fingers closed over her hand, sending tiny tingles coursing up her arm. He put a steadying arm around her waist as she stood and those sparks ignited into full flames that shot deeply through her belly. She wanted nothing more than to press her suddenly achy breasts against that hard chest. Even her wildest flights of fancy about Camelot's knights hadn't evoked such passion.

"I'm Gilead. Are ye all right? He didn't hurt ye?"

Gilead. Perhaps the comparison to the archangel Michael

hadn't been such a stretch after all. Gilead was one of the names of the Bloodline that traced through Kings Solomon and David all the way back to Abraham. The original Gilead's father had been named Michael. Did this Gilead have aught to do with the Stone that she had come to find? Sometimes the Sight worked in strange ways. She wished her gift was more reliable.

For certes, he had the most brilliant blue eyes she had ever seen. Even in the near darkness, she could see they were fringed with thick, black lashes that any female would kill for. His clean soap and leather scent seared her brain; the man was intoxicating. He might have stepped right off the pages of The Book, even if he wasn't wearing shining armor. He *did* have a sword. Here he was, all six-foot-plus of solid, muscular, good-looking male—exactly the kind of man Childebert had kept away from her—and all she could do was stare at him like a dullard.

"I'm Deidre. Yes. I'm fine." *Entretien éclatant!* Brilliant conversation, that!

"Dee? Of Dundee?" He looked puzzled that her name sounded like a town.

Dee. She liked the Gaelic pronunciation, or maybe because it was coming from *him*. He really could make Adonis weep in envy. "No. My name is Deidre, but you may call me Dee if you wish." She added, "Thank you for rescuing a damsel in distress," hoping he'd respond in true knightly fashion. Even with all the personal defense skills she'd covertly learned, she *had* been in need of rescuing this eve. Like it or not.

He nodded curtly. "I'd best be getting ye to the Hall, then." He turned abruptly and headed back up the path.

Not quite the answer she wanted, but . . . "Wait!" She ran to the bush where she'd dropped the satchel that held The Book and a few other necessities. "I'll need this."

He gave the small bag a curious look but said nothing as he began to walk.

Deidre started after him and tripped again on her heavy skirt. *Merde!* Did her celestial deity have to take such long strides? She was a lot shorter than he was, barely coming to his shoulder. *And,* he seemed annoyed with her. Hurt swept over her and then she raised her chin defiantly. It wasn't *her* fault she'd nearly been raped by some brute. She inhaled quickly as realization hit her. *Certainement.* It was Beltane. Her fabulous man had probably been on the way to rendezvous with some wench and she'd ruined his plans. She felt a ping of jealousy toward her unknown competitor. He was *her* knight, right from The Book. *Mon Dieu,* to feel Gilead's full sensual lips on hers . . .

Her fantasy paused. "Are ye coming?"

Her mother, rest her soul, always told her she was a dreamer, but just looking at him and hearing that delicious brogue . . . hmmm. The scowl on his face brought her fanciful notions back to reality. Really, he didn't have to spoil the moment and be rude. Swains who rescued damsels were supposed to pledge faith or something. That's what it said in The Book.

She stuck out her chin, picked up the skirt, and hurried to catch up. "I'm sorry if I'm keeping you from an . . . appointment."

His glance swept down to her bared legs and she thought she saw his mouth twitch. "Ye are a Sassenach, an outlander. It's a strange accent ye have."

Deidre thought quickly. Her cousin was powerful and the Franks always a threat to the Isle. If Gilead found out she'd escaped from Childebert's clutches, no doubt she'd be returned for a ransom and incur not only the king's wrath, but his dungeon as well. She couldn't take that chance, not now when the mists surrounding the hidden Stone were finally lifting. If the Stone were found by the wrong person . . . Well, the fewer people who knew about her mission, the better.

Her erratic "gift" really was a curse, she thought again. Had the rumor not reached Paris that Bishop Dubricius of Britain claimed to have had a vision of a spectacular golden jeweled cup from which the Christos had drunk at his last supper—and had not that greedy holy man issued a reward for its discovery—Childebert would probably never have remembered the stolen Philosopher's Stone.

But he had, and he'd called Deidre in to question her about it. The familiar light-headedness that heralded a Sighting had engulfed her immediately. After more than a decade of the

Stone being hidden from her Sight, her senses stirred. An image of the sea and craggy hills spotted with heather had told her the Stone was no longer in Gaul, but if Childebert sent men to Scotland and he found the Stone, he would turn it over to the ever-needy hands of the Roman Church in exchange for Rome's powerful backing. The wisdom of the Goddess would be lost to history. When found, the Stone must be returned to its grotto in the Languedoc and the priestesses recalled. It was her duty to see that it was done.

She couldn't deny the Sighting, but she had misdirected her cousin's men toward Rome instead, while she made plans to visit Pictland, and the father she'd never met. When Childebert traced her escape—and he would—to a fishing vessel that left from Calais, he'd assume she had gone to the closest port in Londinium. He'd not, she hoped, look for her this far north.

But what to tell the darkly brooding Eros standing in front of her?

"I come from Armorica, across the sea."

He frowned. "Ye're a long way from home, then. How came ye here?"

What to say? Twenty to thirty red-cloaked cavalry, looking for all the world like a turma from the old Roman legions, had surrounded her small escort and taken them away last night. Dion, the sturdy captain of her loyal guard, had rallied their defense, but he had been wounded badly, slung over a horse, and taken, along with the rest of the men. If Deidre hadn't wandered a little too far into the cover of the trees to insure privacy for her personal ministrations, she would have been abducted too. She clutched her satchel with The Book inside; thank goodness it had contained items she'd needed to use and she'd taken it with her. It was all she had. She hated having to lie, but she had no idea whose troops those were . . . perhaps even her hero's. Until she reached her father's lands, her identity would have to remain a secret.

"I . . . uh . . . was traveling and our coach was accosted by highwaymen. I just barely managed to escape."

He raised a dark eyebrow. "My Da willna be pleased to hear that. Were ye coming to Culross? Do ye have family near?"

Culross on the Firth of Forth was close to her destination.
Or at least where she thought Caw's lands would be. "Yes."

Gilead stopped and was apparently waiting for her to continue. "My mother is dead." No need to tell him how long ago
or that she thought her father's holdings would be a good
place to search from. "I am kin to Caw of Pictland," she said.
"I was hoping he'd take me in. Do you know him?"

"Aye. His wife is a distant relative of my mother's." His
face softened momentarily. "But, lass, Caw was long banished to the West. He was killed in battle not long ago."

Deidre drew her breath in sharply. Since her visions of the
Stone had begun again, her goal had been to reach Caw. Childebert did not know who her father was, and she would have
been safe. She swallowed hard to keep the threat of panic from
bubbling up. She'd need food and lodging now that she was on
her own, and somewhere to start finding out what happened to
her escort. "I guess I'll need to find employment."

He looked skeptical as he turned back to the path. They
continued to walk even more briskly. Deidre hiked her skirts
up farther in order to match his stride, and again his glance
swooped down. A small smile flitted briefly across his face.
Enough to get that delicious tingle started again.

His voice was gentler when he spoke. "My mother will
find ye something. Mayhap as a lady's maid."

"A maid?" Deidre nearly bumped into him as they turned
a sharp corner and he abruptly stopped. They had left the
trees behind and the path they were on converged with a
wider road that led up a steep hill to a stone castle. Well, perhaps more of a fort, she realized as she studied it. She saw
how earthwork banks were laid out defensively as they
climbed the incline. It was steeper than she thought, and she
saved her breath for exertion, since Gilead had quickened the
pace instead of slowing it. Did that devastating bulk of
muscle never get winded? Apparently not.

Metal ratcheted wheels clacked, and chains rattled as the
massive, heavy oak gates slowly opened at their approach.
Gilead looked down at her as they waited and a corner of his
full mouth quirked up, giving him more the look of a *fallen*
angel.

"Ye might be putting yer skirts down now. It'd be best if the men dinna think ye a wanton."

She felt herself flush crimson. She knew that. Modesty had been drilled into her at the Frankish court under the strict tutelage of her prudish aunt Clotilde. Most of it hadn't stuck, to her aunt's frustration, but it was *his* fault she'd had to hike her skirt to her knees, anyway. Furiously, she shook it out, only to have the hem in back tangle itself. "If you'd adjusted your pace to meet mine like a proper courtier . . ."

The quirk widened to a slow, lopsided grin as he bent over to smooth the lower folds, his fingers just barely brushing her calf. The touch had been so light, Deidre wasn't sure if he'd done it intentionally or it was an accident. Either way, the unfamiliar warmth zapped right up her leg to pulse at the juncture of her thighs, setting her active imagination into spirals. What would a real caress from him feel like? His face was passive, though, as he straightened and gestured her through the arch.

Deidre stared up at the bowmen standing on the battlements as they passed through the thick curtain wall. The palisade had to be at least fifty feet high. Armed warriors stood five paces apart on the battlements. The place was impressively fortified. Ahead of them, across the bailey, sat the Great Hall.

"What does your mother do here?" she asked tentatively as Gilead stopped at the solid wooden door and knocked.

For a moment, he looked puzzled. "She's the lairdess," he answered, "of Cenel Oengus." When Deidre frowned, he sighed. "Cenel—a clan—my father is Angus Mac Oengus. Ye Bretons would call him a king."

"You're a king's son?" Deidre began and then stopped when the door swung open and a maid bobbed a greeting. She didn't have time to ask any more questions, for Gilead quickly explained that she was to be given a room for the night and his mother would see her in the morning. He gave her a slight bow and turned away.

Deidre stared after his broad, retreating back. Was he still so eager to meet his liaison? Her shoulders drooped. She had just met her knight—rightly a prince he was—and he thought she was a maid. Even worse, she couldn't tell him that she, too, had royal blood, her lineage going back through the Merovingians to the Sicambrians and Arcadians and eventually to the Magdalen herself. Still another reason Childebert discouraged suitors. He didn't want her to bear an heir more royal than himself.

Gilead dripped sensuality in that charming, unaffected way of acting honorably and seemingly not knowing he was the most erotic fantasy that ever trod through her fertile mind, thanks in part to the escapades The Book described of Lancelot and Gwenhwyfar. Had Gilead shown any interest at all? Her emerging libido conjured up the image of her sex god in a kilt. Those strong, well-muscled thighs exposed . . . she wondered what a "mon" wore under a kilt, anyway. Clotilde would need more than smelling salts if she ever knew that all her Bible-thumping chastity served was to whet Deidre's appetite for the forbidden pleasures a man might give. Now that she had broken loose from her aunt and cousin's restraints, Deidre was more than ready to find out exactly what those pleasures were.

Deidre giggled and then sobered. She'd have to show some decorum and act like a lady or she'd end up as a scullery maid instead. As she had seen this evening, those women were commonly tumbled. Somewhere on this side of the Channel was a land where knights abided by a code of honor and respected women. They were supposed to pledge themselves to a lady. Did Gilead already have a lady? She panicked a moment and then released her breath in a whoosh. Probably not, if he were out rutting like everyone else. How could she get him to notice her without behaving like a wanton he would not respect? She sighed. Judging from Gilead's hasty departure, she doubted she'd impressed the laird's son at all.

Gilead cursed softly as he quickly made his way down the road from the fort. For certes, his father's trail would be cold now. He'd lost him taking the lass back to the Hall, but what else could he have done? Clearly, Niall Mac Douglas was bent on raping her. He gritted his teeth. Their neighbor was a ruthless laird, but his lands were strategically located between Culross and the infernal, warmongering Fergus of Cenel Loairn to the northwest. His father needed Niall as an ally, not an enemy.

By the Dagda! His father courted more than enough trouble by being besotted with the Briton King Turius's wife. Ever since Gilead had come of age, nigh five years ago, he'd tried to keep them apart when the king and queen visited. It wasn't easy though, for Angus and Queen Formorian were like two long-drawn notes melding on a bagpipe.

He groaned as he left the road and ducked into the forest, following a deer path that led to a secluded clearing near the Firth. Why did King Turius and that siren queen of his have to arrive on Beltane? If they had waited just one more day, Angus would have had to host a proper feast for them, and Gilead could have made sure there was no opportunity for his father to slip away with the vixen. But no. On Beltane, men got drunk and whorishness ran rampant. And Angus had made sure Turius had plenty to drink, as well as the company of several curvaceous wenches.

Gilead cursed again when he found the clearing empty. What other niche could his father have taken her to? It would be dawn soon, and he wasn't sure either of them had enough sense to be back in their own beds by then. It was why he had tried to follow them. He shook his head. He would never allow himself to become besotted over any woman—look what it did to his otherwise intelligent father. Even though Turius had fathered a son on a pagan priestess years ago, Gilead doubted that he'd appreciate being cuckolded by his Scotti friend and ally.

As he stepped out on the road, a hearty voice slurred at him. "Aye, Gil. Huntin' yer Da again?"

He turned to see his friend, Drustan, walking toward him, an arm casually draped across the shoulders of a girl Gilead recognized from the kitchen staff. She giggled drunkenly as Drustan nuzzled her neck.

Gilead frowned. Did everyone know of his father's indiscretion? "Certes not. I was checking the grounds."

Drustan lifted an eyebrow and grinned. "Well, then. There're still plenty of lassies yonder that won't mind a wee bit of wooing from ye. Might even be a fresh one if ye look hard."

The thought of a woman with another man's juices inside her was not exactly arousing. Now the bonny lass he'd escorted to the Hall and the sight of her well-turned, slender ankle . . . He pushed the thought away. Unbelieving as he was of her story, she was dressed as a high-born lady and she needed to be protected, just like his poor mother, who pretended not to know what was going on. Still, he hadn't been able to resist that one brief brush against the lassie's flesh as he smoothed her skirt. Even now, he remembered how the heat of that touch had pricked his hand. *Better not think about it.*

"Not tonight, Drus."

His friend shook his head as he pulled his willing wench toward some gorse. "Beltane. Even ye're allowed to lower the barriers ye keep erected so high about ye."

Gilead turned to make his way up the incline. Those walls were in place for a reason. Relationships with women were trouble. If they cared too much, like his mother, they got hurt, and he had no wish to bring misery to a woman. What was worse, though, women used their wiles to befuddle a mon's brain and made him throw caution to the winds. Like his Da.

War with the powerful Briton king they didn't need. Not when the Saxons were raiding the northeasterly shores, much too close for comfort. Turius had managed to hold them to the fens of eastern Britain and was here now to help Angus develop strategy for the North. Formorian could very well ignite something more explosive than scrimmaging with Saxon invaders. Bah. Better to stick to women who willingly took silver coin for their services. Certes, he'd never let a woman addle his wits.

Unbidden, Deidre drifted into his mind again. *Dee.* The lass with the odd accent was most comely, with her pert nose, aquamarine eyes, and long, moonlight-colored hair. He had to admit, he liked the way her chin came up defiantly when he'd pressured her to keep up the pace. Not to mention having a glimpse of shapely legs . . . wee thing that she was, he could easily lift her and wrap those legs around his waist as he pressed her against a wall. . . . With some surprise, he felt his member thicken and harden, jutting itself against his trews. He had no right to be thinking such lecherous thoughts about the poor lass. She was orphaned and alone and—if her story was true—had been waylaid by bandits, not to mention nearly raped this eve. After what she'd been through, the last thing she'd want was for yet another mon to make unwelcome advances. No. He would not become his father. His duty as the laird's son was to be sure she was safe from such things.

He sighed as he headed home. The thought of her lush lips softly pressing against his, did nothing to diminish the bulge straining to be released.

"I think ye'll find everything ye need," the young maid said as they climbed the stairs and she opened the door to a small corner room off the main hallway. "There's peat laid in the brazier and the flint's there." She pointed to a tinderbox. "Chamber pot's behind the screen." She paused, looking curiously at Deidre, as though she was not sure if the young woman was a real guest or not.

Deidre smiled pleasantly and nodded. The girl sighed, apparently not ready to take the chance of insulting someone who might be important. She picked up the earthenware pitcher. "I'll fetch ye some hot water for washing, then."

When she had gone, Deidre looked around the room. Heavy tapestries hung along the walls, blocking some of the damp that seeped through the thick, grey stone. A small window was shuttered against the chilling breeze that came off the water she could hear rushing over stones far below. Next to the chest that held the Samian-ware chamber set stood an intricately carved wardrobe. A polished wooden table and two chairs were along the opposite wall.

Deidre went over to the tinderbox tentatively. She had no clue how to strike enough sparks to get the fire going, since her thin, waspish aunt was always cold and servants kept the fires burning at the Frankish court.

The little maid returned with the water and a bar of

scented soap. *Good. She thinks I'm an invited guest.* She smiled at the girl.

"Would you mind lighting the fire, please? I'm afraid I've never had to learn . . ." The maid bobbed her head and hurried to do her bidding. Deidre's smile faded as she remembered that Gilead thought she was a maid, too, and she'd probably be lighting these very same fires herself soon. Mayhap it would behoove her to pay attention.

"I know Gilead didn't tell you this. . . ." She stopped at the way the maid's eyes had widened. "What is it?"

"Well, mum, ye're to call him Master Gilead . . . that is, unless ye're . . . ye're . . ."

"I'm what?"

The girl colored deeply and looked away. "Unless ye're his leman."

Leman? Mistress? Now there's a thought. The idea of Gilead coming to her chamber, baring those massive shoulders and chest as he ripped off his tunic before taking her down on the bed, his weight pinning her beneath him . . . "*Yes, yes, yes,*" the eager rescued damsel whispered. "*No, no, no,*" her aunt's cold, authoritative voice rebuked her. The reluctant virgin pouted as her practical side took over.

"Ah. Forgive me," Deidre said to the maid. "Master Gilead saved me from a boorish man this evening. My name is Deidre. I was waylaid by bandits a day ago and have gotten quite a bump on my head." She forced a light laugh. "I seem to have forgotten my manners."

The maid looked her over, more curiously than before. "I'm Anna. If it's a bad bump ye have, ye should be seein' our healer in the morning."

"I'm sure I'll be fine by morning. I'm looking forward to the pleasure of meeting the laird and his wife."

A closed expression crossed the young girl's face as she walked to the door. "The pleasure?" she muttered as she closed the door behind her.

Deidre stared at the door. What did that mean? She was too tired to worry about it. She sat down on the coverlet, sinking into surprisingly soft feather down. The bed swayed slightly on its leather webbing.

She rubbed her temples, aware suddenly of how truly weary she was. With the news that her father was dead, she needed to find her escort and she needed to find the Stone before her cousin did. But part of her tension came from the fact that every nerve ending tingled in anticipation—of what, exactly, she wasn't sure—whenever she was near Gilead. The air around them vibrated with the sharp, clear tang that she had smelled once just as a bolt of lightning split a mighty oak tree near her. Her hair had stood on end that time, too.

She quivered with excitement, her energy suddenly renewed. She was on the other side of the Narrow Channel now, where Camelot should be. She pulled The Book from her satchel and soothed herself with fingering the rich texture of the soft, worn leather. Did Camelot exist? Was it here? Tomorrow, would she find an idyllic place of peace and prosperity, of courtly feasts complete with bards and jesters? Unlike the drab dreariness and stark, cold walls of the Frankish court, would there be colorful pageantry and chivalrous knights sallying forth in tournaments to win favors from their ladies? She had always thought her own knight would be as noble and peerless as the legendary Lancelot, and love her as fiercely as Lanceot did Gwenhwyfar. She wanted that with all her heart.

And she'd found him. Gilead was her knight. The only problem was that he didn't know it just yet.

Chapter Two

THE HANDFAST

Deidre was awakened the next morning by a brisk rapping on the door. Sleepily, she struggled to sit up in bed. The fire in the brazier had burned out, leaving the room chilly and nearly dark. By the saints, it was hardly light outside! What time was it? Was this not a civilized household?

She had no more time for thinking, for the door swung open and one of the largest women she had ever seen strutted through. The woman wasn't fat; she was just huge. Nearly six feet she must be, and solid. Deidre blinked as she came to a stop beside the bed, hands on her broad hips.

"I be Una, the castellan o're this keep. Well? Do ye think to shirk yer duties the first morn ye're here? A fine impression that'll make on Lady Elen."

"Duties?" Deidre asked as she swung her legs out of bed and then winced as her feet hit the cold floor. Where was that maid, Anna? She needed a nice, warm fire and maybe some tea.

"Aye." The woman handed her a modest gown of soft, blue wool. "Make quick with yer washin'. I'll be back for ye in a few minutes."

Deidre padded over to the pitcher, poured some water into

the basin and dipped her fingers. She flinched. "The water is icy. Could I send for some hot?"

The woman stopped halfway through the door and turned around, an incredulous look on her face. "If it's hot water ye're wantin', ye'll need to get up earlier and get it yerself. Master Gilead informed me that ye came seekin' work." Her eyes momentarily shifted to the well-tailored traveling dress that Deidre had tossed over a chair the night before. "I normally start newcomers in the kitchen or dairy or maybe as a chambermaid, but Master Gilead said to let ye attend directly to our lady."

"Attend . . . ?" Deidre thought. "You mean a lady-in-waiting?"

"Ye won't be waiting. Ye'll be doing . . . anything that Lady Elen wants."

Deidre frowned and then quickly smoothed her brow. The last thing she wanted was for this giant of a woman to assign her to scouring pots and pans. She hoped the "lady" would not be too snobbish or demanding. Deidre didn't know if she could handle that, but what choice did she have at the moment? She had no idea what had become of her escort, and the news of Caw's death had been a blow.

"Of course," she said as she turned back to the basin. "I'll be ready in a few minutes." What time was she going to have to get up in the days to come? She stole a longing glance at her warm, soft bed and sighed. "Where can I break my fast?"

The woman snorted. "*Tomorrow,* if ye're willing to haul yerself out of bed in time, ye can make ye're way to the kitchens. Make ready now."

Deidre stared as the door closed behind the woman. She wasn't going to be allowed to eat? Surely, there were others who were still breaking their fasts in the Great Hall. She could imagine sideboards overburdened with a surplus of food. Her stomach growled in anticipation and she groaned. Perhaps she had not found Camelot after all.

She wasn't prepared for Lady Elen. When Una opened the door to the lavishly decorated chamber, the stench of a sick room assailed her nostrils. Pungent herbs blended with the sharpness of eucalyptus, but both were overpowered by the oppressive smell of camphor that seemed to seep from every expensively woven tapestry. Deidre longed to throw open the shuttered window and let in some fresh air.

Elen sat plumped in a huge, overstuffed chair, bright tartans draped over her lap. She seemed lost in the chair, so small was she. Deidre was not much over five feet herself, but she wondered if Elen was even smaller. Her fragile body was wrapped in a fine ivory silk nightdress, matching her pale hair, but her blue eyes—so much like Gilead's—were kind as they watched her.

Two other women were in the room. One seemed to be Deidre's age, with dark hair and eyes; the other was several years older, with red hair and snapping ginger eyes. Both of them looked at her sullenly as Una brought her forward. She guessed they were ladies-in-waiting, too, since their dresses were similar to hers.

"This is the one yer son said to bring ye." Una's tone clearly mirrored the negative attitudes of the two women in the corner.

"Ah, yes," Elen started to say in a soft, whispery voice, but was interrupted when the curtains parted in the back of her chamber and a white-haired woman stepped through. She carried a cup that she handed to Elen.

"Drink this now, my lady. Ye'll feel much better soon."

At first, Deidre took the woman to be ancient, but when she turned to look at Deidre, her eyes were black as ebony and her face nearly lineless. She could have been any age. Deidre shivered a little, although the room was stifling, with two braziers burning brightly.

Elen wrinkled her delicate nose. "Do I have to have this horrible concoction every day, Brena? Ye know I hate it."

"I've told ye, Mistress, the brew will keep the soreness from yer joints."

Just then Deidre heard a timid scratching at the door and Anna pushed it open slowly, bearing a heavy tray laden with food. She set it down on the table beside Elen and dipped a curtsy. Deidre's mouth watered at the smell of still-warm bannocks and freshly churned butter. The steam from the cinnamon-scented porridge was heavenly and if she could just have a slice of that cheese . . . She put a hand to her stomach to keep it from rumbling.

Anna smiled at her and Deidre was relieved that at least one of the servants was friendly. Then Anna nodded toward Brena.

"This is the healer I told ye about last eve. She might take a look at the bump to yer head."

Deidre started. "No. That won't be necessary." Too late. The healer was already heading her way.

"I'll have a look." Deft fingers felt through Deidre's hair and when Brena stepped away, she gave Deidre a speculative look. "'Tis nothing that won't heal itself."

She knows I lied. Deidre tried not to fidget and then, to her embarrassment, her stomach gave a huge and hungry growl.

The women in the corner twittered and Lady Elen sent them a reproving look. "Sheila," she said gently to the older, red-haired one, "ye and Janet should know better than to make fun of someone in front of me. I wilna tolerate it."

"Yes, Mistress," they said in unison and dipped their heads.

Deidre was grateful that Lady Elen seemed kind, but feared that somehow those soft words had sealed the other maids' dislike of her. Seething resentment floated toward her from both of them.

Elen glanced at Una and then turned her attention to Deidre. "Have ye not broken yer fast, my child?"

Before Deidre could answer, the door was flung open wide, nearly hitting the back wall, as a man strode through, well-muscled thighs rippling beneath the tight leather of his trews.

His presence filled the room. Tall, even more broad-shouldered than Gilead, the man had well-developed biceps that bulged from the jerkin he wore with no shirt beneath it. The massive chest tapered to a narrow waist and taunt belly. His dark hair, pulled back with a leather thong, showed no signs of silver, even though Deidre knew without a doubt that she was looking at the laird of the castle. Everything about him roared pure, raw male.

Elen seemed to shrink further into her wrappings as Angus towered over her and placed a silver goblet of wine on the table.

"Drink this instead of that tea ye're so fond of. 'Twill put some color in yer cheeks." He wiped a band of sweat from his forehead. "Bel's fires! Why is it so hot in here? Someone open that window."

Sheila moved forward, slanting an upward glance at him and arching her back so her breasts thrust out. "Allow me, my lord."

He nodded and watched as she swung her hips provocatively on her way to the window. "All the way, my lord?" she asked.

He grinned appreciatively at the innuendo, giving her a slow, lopsided smile. "Aye. All the way, lass."

Deidre groaned inwardly. His voice was the same rich, soft baritone as Gilead's, and his smile was a lot like his son's, too, only there was nothing archangelic about him. The devil's own spawn, more like, judging from how mesmerized Sheila seemed by him.

As though he had heard her, he swung his dark-eyed gaze her way. His eyes were penetrating, the kind that could make a woman feel like she was not wearing any clothes. He turned, legs splayed, appraising her. Deidre forced herself to stand still and not fidget. But God, he was intimidating.

He crossed his arms over his chest. "Leave us," he said.

Sheila looked disappointed, but had enough sense not to question him. Deidre turned to follow the rest of the women out.

"Not you."

She paused in midstep. "What could my lord possibly want with me?"

He raised an eyebrow. A corner of his full mouth lifted as his eyelids lowered slightly, but he said nothing until the door had been closed.

She made herself meet his hooded gaze. "My lord?"

Still, he didn't answer, but he circled her, pacing slowly like a predator. Deidre willed herself not to pivot and keep him in her sights. The skin on her back crawled when he came up behind her. *Saint Brighid!* What did the man intend to do? His wife was sitting not ten feet away, her blue eyes wide in her pale face. Clearly, she was afraid of him.

Deidre brought her chin up defiantly. She refused to be cowed by him, laird or no. She whirled around to face him.

He looked surprised and faintly amused.

"I don't appreciate your stalking me like I'm prey," she said.

Elen gasped, but Angus paid her no mind. Something that looked almost like respect flashed through his smoke-colored eyes and then was gone.

"So ye're the one he wants."

He? Who? Gilead? Could Gilead possibly want her? The hopeful virgin perked up her ears.

Angus walked over to the table and partially sat on it, thrusting one long leg out in front of him. "Suppose ye tell me how ye came to be here? I dinna ken of highwaymen robbing coaches of late."

Deidre gulped. The laird must have patrols on his borders. Were those men in the red cloaks his? *Think quick.* "Bandits, my lord. Two days past. Perhaps before we came on your lands."

He narrowed his eyes, the predator back. "Ye speak strange. With yer yellow hair and blue eyes, ye could be Saxon. A spy, mayhap?"

She felt herself pale. She hadn't thought about being taken for a Saxon, intent on hiding who she really was. He needed to believe her story. If he turned her out, where would she go? She took a deep breath.

"No Saxon, my lord. My coloring is the same as your wife's. I doubt that she's Saxon. Is she?"

Elen shrank even further into her wraps as Angus cast a cursory look over her and then shifted back to Deidre. "Ye've a sharp tongue, lassie." He moved toward her suddenly, as agile as a cougar, and then grinned antagonizingly. "Mayhap ye would suit me, after all."

Suit? Did he mean "bring together"? Him and her? He couldn't possibly be making such an outrageous advance in front of his wife. And yet, something told her he could. She drew herself up to her full five feet and one half inch. Her nose came to his chest. "You insult me. You are a married man and I will not go to bed with you just to insure a place here." There. She'd said it. And she'd probably be turned out on her ear in the next five minutes.

Angus stared at her for what seemed a breadth of infinity. Then he threw back his head and laughed—a deep, full-bodied rumble.

For a moment, Deidre felt relief, and then her temper began to simmer. Really. It wasn't that funny. Why was he nearly howling like that? Suddenly, she felt herself flush to the roots of her hair. Perhaps he thought her so unimportant that such a proposition wasn't possible? The gall of him. He was toying with her like a kitten with a string.

He held up a hand, attempting to stop grinning. "Ah, lass, there be no need to flash sword points of fire through me with yer eyes, pretty as they are." He took a deep breath and cleared his throat. "I meant that I think ye're strong enough to stand up to the man. God help him." He squelched another chuckle.

To him? Whom? Gilead? Deidre's blood heated at the thought of being suited to him. *That* was something she wouldn't protest, not that she would want to *stand* up to him—*lie* beside him, maybe—could Gilead actually have asked his father for her? Mayhap this would turn out to be Camelot after all.

"I might consider that an honor, my lord."

"Would ye now? Then Gilead rescued ye for naught last eve?"

"I was grateful to your son for saving me," Deidre answered. "If you think we suit, I will . . ." She stopped, both because of the small cry that came from Elen and the look on Angus's face. For a moment she thought she saw—pity?—then it was gone.

"Och, no, lass." He sounded almost resigned. "Gilead has little time for women, even though many, like ye, are willing to throw themselves at him."

Deidre felt the heat break over her face and looked away. *Fool. I let myself get carried away again.* Gilead had only been a gentleman last night. Like any true knight of the Round Table would have been, she reflected ruefully. Had that meddling old magician somehow bespelled The Book so that she was forever enthralled in flights of fancy? Slowly, another thought emerged and she looked up at Angus in dread.

"Who, then?"

He hesitated briefly. "Niall has asked to be handfasted to ye."

Deidre's blood sludged to rivers of ice. Engaged? To be married? The thought of that man's burly body on hers made her want to retch. Except there was nothing in her stomach. Numbly, she heard Elen protest. Angus silenced her with a glance. Deidre took a deep breath and squared her shoulders.

"You can tell the man I said 'no.' He nearly raped me."

Angus frowned slightly. "I was told that he might have come on a bit strong last eve, but it was Beltane. Lasses that are about are fair game."

"I told you why I was out. I had nowhere to go after the attack."

"Aye. The bandits." He studied her, his dark eyes seeming to penetrate to her very soul. "Ye appear to be high-born, but ye have no coin and no clothes other than what ye're wearing."

She didn't have to be told she was a charity case. The one small trunk she'd managed to take was gone, along with the coin that her guard carried for her. Deidre shifted uneasily, refusing to think that she was at this man's mercy. But she would take to the roads and risk her luck before she'd let that . . . that monster near her again. She gritted her teeth.

"I thank you for taking me in and giving me shelter. I am quite prepared to work hard, attending Lady Elen, and earn my keep."

"Attending Her Ladyship is not hard work. She rarely leaves this room." He glanced at his wife perfunctorily. "Mayhap if she did, she'd be fit to bear me a son . . . or a daughter that I could marry off and bind the clans."

Elen's delicate features flushed with embarrassment and she ducked her head. "My lord knows the physician said . . ."

"Yes." He cut her off and turned back to Deidre. "Niall's been widowed nigh two years. He is a wealthy mon with holdings half as large as mine. Many a lass has gone willingly to his bed, trying to entice him into making her his wife."

"Fortunately, I am not one of those." *The man is twice my age!*

"Ye're a mite stubborn for a woman. Niall will be wantin' to cure ye of that."

What? He thinks to break me like a horse to saddle? Hardly. "I said 'no.'"

He continued as though she hadn't spoken. "'Twould be wise of ye not to provoke him thus. He has a bit of a temper."

She just wagered he did. "The man threatened me last night."

"Did he, now? In what way, with Gilead there?"

"He said . . . he said I hadn't seen the last of him . . ."

"He spoke true there, lass. But it's an honorable thing he's doing, asking to handfast. Ye should be pleased that he honors ye."

"Honors me?" Deidre shook her head, hoping to clear her ears. *Did this overbearing laird not understand a thing I said?* "He said no woman would get the best of him."

Angus stifled a grin. "No woman gets the best of me, either, lass. It's the way of things. No harm there."

What had happened to chivalry? The Book said men were supposed to treat women as fragile, delicate creatures whose virtue was always to be protected. Deidre nearly stamped her foot in frustration. She would try one more time.

"He would abuse me—beat me—for I would never stand down from him."

Angus took a step toward her and bent close, his handsome face inches from hers. "I don't know where ye're from, lass, but here 'tis a wife's duty to obey. A husband has every right to keep his wife in line."

Deidre's eyes shifted to Elen, whose face had gone pale as an Easter lily. She looked back at Angus, refusing to flinch at the overwhelming sense of power that sprang from him. "Do you beat Lady Elen?"

He drew back at that and stared at her. For a fleeting moment, Deidre was afraid he might strike her, so stormy had his eyes become.

"Nay. I've never stuck a woman in my life." He gestured at Elen. "Ask her, if ye'll not believe me."

Deidre looked askance at Elen, who seemed to be struggling to find her voice.

"'Tis true," she said in barely a whisper. "My husband has n'er laid anything but a gentle hand on me."

Deidre had a hard time envisioning this big, brawny male as gentle. Gilead, yes. His father, no. Why else was Lady Elen so frightened of him, then?

"Ye see? I'm no ogre, nor is Niall." Angus watched her intently. "'Twould be a good match, lass. Niall is the son of an Eire king— the second son, which is why he is here—but noble still. Ye could do much worse, being an orphan with no dowry."

"For once and for all, I'll not marry the man." Her prince was Gilead or none! Deidre's heart sank. Of course, Angus would require a noblewoman for his only son. And one with a huge dowry, no less.

His eyes turned dark again. Clearly, she was trying his patience, yet Deidre felt she was desperately fighting for her freedom, if not her life. Angus might not be cruel, but Niall certainly was. She didn't need the Sight to know that.

Angus sighed and began to pace, stalking the room like a lobo. Finally, he stopped and turned back to Deidre. "I don't ken why I needs must explain myself to ye, but I will grant ye that. We have three great cenels north of Hadrian's Wall. Mine own land, Oengus, stretches east to the North Sea. To the west, near the Firth of Clyde, lies Cenel Gabrain, an ally of mine, as is the smaller Cenel Comgaill to the northwest. Our great foe be Fergus Mor of Loairn who holds much of the North and ever seeks to take more lands from the rest of us." He stopped. "Are ye understanding aught of this?"

Did he think she was stupid? She had listened to enough war strategies at the Frankish court. "I'm not daft. Go on."

Angus began to pace once more. "Niall's lands lie between Fergus and me. It's of much import that he remains allied to me and not turn and serve Fergus. Do ye ken?"

Deidre nodded. "That would be good strategy, of course. What does it have to do with me?"

Dark eyebrows knitted together in a frown. "My son told Niall this morn that ye had been orphaned and sought our help because ye thought yerself to be a distant relation."

Gilead had said that? Bless him. He really was protecting her, like a real knight would. It was a much simpler explanation than trying to manufacture more stories. "I had no idea my father had lost both his lands and his life when I came here."

Angus's frown deepened and his eyes turned murky. "Caw ran afoul of the Lothian king and was sent to Gwynedd. He rousted the Scotti there and we accepted most of them. I dinna claim Caw as friend, even though his wife, rest her soul, was a distant cousin to Elen." He paused. "But there wasna blood shed between us."

So her stepmother was dead, too, not that Deidre would have expected her help. "Well, then. I have nowhere to go. I will serve your wife well; you'll be pleased."

Angus shook his head. "Doona ye see? Niall thinks ye are kin; a marriage would bind him to my clan."

"No." Had that answer not penetrated his skull by now?

"'Twould be a grand thing not to worry about Niall when we still have painted barbarians to the north and the blood-thirsty Saxons coming ashore." He narrowed his eyes thoughtfully. "'Twould keep Niall's father, Lugaid, in Eire as well, and not be raiding our lands. I'm beginning to like the idea of ye as kin."

"I won't do it."

"Ye will."

"Never."

Angus stomped over to her, stopping so close, she nearly had to bend backward to avoid being in body contact. A small whimper came from Elen.

He towered over her, fists clenched. "I am laird here. Ye will do as I say or find yerself in the dungeons." A stifled sob emerged from Elen's chair and he looked at her in irritation.

"Please, Angus," she said as she held out pale, shaking hands. "'Tis not the lass's fault. Let her stay with me."

His face turned dark and Deidre thought he would lash verbal abuse at his poor wife. She could feel him fighting for control. Deidre sensed this was probably the boldest thing the timid Elen had said to him in ages.

"I'll not let two women tell me what to do." He took a ragged breath and unclenched his hands. "A compromise, then. A handfast be an agreement to hold to each other for a year and a day, to act as husband and wife afore marriage. Niall dinna want to wait past Lugnasad to marry ye, three months hence. Said 'twould be enough time to tame ye." Deidre bristled, but he held up his hand. "I'll agree to that, but I will tell him there'll be no bedding ye until the wedding day."

He looked quite pleased with himself. Deidre opened her mouth to protest, but he held a finger to her lips. "It's settled, lass." With that, he turned and walked out.

She stared after him. Did he think he'd made some grand concession? What right did he have to control her life, anyhow? If only she could tell him who she really was, but that would throw her mission of finding the Stone into jeopardy.

With a horrible, sinking feeling that felt like a whole load of Welsh coal ore had settled in her stomach, she realized that he did have that right to control her life. Women were chattel. This was definitely not Camelot. A curse on the magician for filling her head with such dreams all these years.

Three months. August's festival of harvest. One of the ancient power nights of the Goddess. Not as strong as Samhain, when the mists between this world and the next could be parted and the sidhe emerged from their hollow hills to aid those who believed, but still, an energy force would emerge. She might be able to See where the Stone lay hidden. But could she wait that long?

She straightened her shoulders and lifted her chin. One thing *was* certain: she would not be marrying Niall. No matter what the dominating, forceful laird thought.

Chapter Three

THE LADY ELEN

"Come, child. Sit with me and eat."

Deidre turned from staring at the closed door and walked over to where Elen sat, wrapped in her plaids. "Are you cold? Do you want the window shut?"

She shook her head. "Angus would not approve."

"It's your room, my lady. I'll close it, if you like."

Elen hesitated, and then a small smile appeared as she nodded. "Ye are not afraid of my lord?"

Deidre latched the window and gratefully took the bowl of porridge that Elen handed her, sliding into the chair opposite her. She savored a bite of buttery bannock melting in her mouth before she answered.

"Should I be afraid of your husband, my lady? Does he hurt you?"

Elen's blue eyes widened. "Oh, no. I spoke true on that. Nay, he doona hurt me. . . ." She paused, looking wistful. "He doona touch me at all." She forced a laugh, but it sounded empty. "'Tis because I'm so fragile . . . I've not much strength."

Deidre looked at the breakfast on the table. Elen hadn't touched it. Guiltily, she put down her second bannock, covered in jam. "Maybe you need to eat more, my lady."

"Truth, child, my stomach turns at the sight of food." She picked up the goblet and sipped the wine. "I care not for this, but Angus insists I have a cup every morning."

Someone rapped at the door and, as it started to open, Elen glanced fearfully at the shut window. Deidre laid down her wooden spoon. This was ridiculous. If Angus were back to criticize . . .

She turned, but the frown on her face faded quickly as Gilead approached them.

"Good morn, Mother. How are ye feeling?" he asked as he leaned down to give her a kiss on the cheek and then settled between her and Deidre. He glanced at the bowl in front of Deidre and then back to his mother. "Have ye eaten?"

Deidre felt her ears burn. Only one bowl had been on the tray. Did he think she'd kept his mother from eating? She felt her face grow hot and bent her head so her hair would fall forward. Maybe she had. She had been so hungry, she hadn't noticed that Elen didn't have anything to eat with. A fine lady-in-waiting she was making; if that giantess of a castellan found out, she *would* be scouring pots and pans.

Was Gilead angry? She braved a glance through strands of hair to find him watching her. This morning, he wore his hair pulled back by a thong, too, and, like his father, he wore a leather jerkin with no shirt. *Do the men in this family have any idea of the effect they have on women? Probably.* Dark curls on his bronze chest teased her before they disappeared beneath the vest. How much hair covered him? She'd seen a wounded soldier once, his shirt stripped from his chest before Clotilde whisked her away. Did Gilead's hair form a neat little trail all the way to his waist and down inside his pants? Deidre forced herself to not look there. Not that it helped, for his hard, sculpted biceps were equally tantalizing. He wore a leather bracer on his left arm, leaving the strong right forearm naked. *How can just looking at a man's bare arm make my tummy quiver?* But as she looked at his hands, the long fingers tapping on the table, she remembered how strong and warm they had felt last night. The quiver vibrated deeper into her belly.

"I wasna hungry, my son," Elen said and broke into Deidre's

reverie. "And I suspect Una didn't give the poor lass a chance to break her fast."

Bless the woman. Already, Deidre felt a kinship for her. She hastily gathered the half-eaten bannock and empty bowl and put them on the tray. "I'll just take this to the kitchens," she said as she began to rise.

"Wait."

Before she realized what he was about, Gilead leaned over and ran a forefinger lightly across the corner of her mouth. The sizzling warmth his touch left made her lips all puffy. What did he think he was doing?

"Jam," he said as he held his hand up and licked the jelly off his finger. He gave her a lopsided grin. "Mind if I finish that?"

Deidre hoped she wouldn't start to drool. It was bad enough that she couldn't eat without making a mess. But his touch . . . did she still have jam on her mouth? Was he going to *kiss* it off? The idea caused a battalion of butterflies to flutter helplessly in her stomach.

"Ye can stay if ye like," he said as he reached for her half-eaten bannock. "I visit my mother every morn."

He was going to come in half-dressed like this every morning? Deidre wasn't sure she could take it. But Goddess, she wasn't going to miss it, either.

"Is it archery practice this morning?" Elen asked as Deidre settled into her chair.

"Aye," Gilead answered. "Ye know how Da likes to compete with Turius when he's here."

A cloud settled over Elen's fine features. "I heard that they arrived yesterday. I was sorry to be so ill I could not greet them properly."

He patted his mother's hand. "The king understood. Dinna fash."

Deidre thought Gilead looked like he wanted to say more, but did not. She wondered who this king was and why Elen didn't sound as though she was sorry at all.

The door opened and Sheila and Janet entered, giggling. They stopped when they saw Deidre and Gilead seated at the table and Janet narrowed her eyes. Deidre didn't need any interpretation of what that meant.

Janet ignored her completely as she approached the table, a small, sly smile playing on her lips. *Sweet Mary. Was she one of Gilead's wenches? The lover from last night perhaps? Sheila had openly flirted with Angus earlier; did the father and son tumble sisters?* A very green-eyed cat arched its back and hissed inside Deidre's mind.

"I'll just take the tray," Janet said as she leaned in front of Gilead, bountiful cleavage just inches away from his face. And then she slipped and fell, smashing her breasts against his hard chest.

Right where Deidre wanted to be. She'd never seen such bad acting in her life, even with what passed for entertainment in Childebert's court.

"Oh, my lord. How clumsy of me." Janet made a pretense of trying to right herself which only resulted in her clearly rubbing herself against him.

His father had been right. Women did literally throw themselves at Gilead.

Gilead took hold of her shoulders and set her on her feet. With a polite smile, he handed her the tray. "Una will be waiting for this. Tell her my mother . . ." His dark blue eyes met Deidre's as he paused. "Tell her my mother enjoyed breaking her fast this morn. Verra much."

For absolutely no logical reason, giddiness swept through Deidre. He was giving her a compliment. . . . *And* he didn't appear taken with Janet's tactics.

"I'll leave ye to yer bath now, Mother," Gilead said as he stood to leave.

"A moment," Elen said. "There will be a feast tonight? In their honor?"

He hesitated. "Aye. Da has ordered it."

She sighed and lifted her head. "Tell him I will be there. In my rightful place beside him."

He nodded and Deidre wondered why he looked so troubled. He reached out and picked up his mother's hand.

"Dinna fash. I'll sit beside Formorian myself tonight." He

kissed her forehead then and turned to Deidre. "See that ye attend my mother this eve."

"I'll be glad to, if she wishes it."

For a moment, she thought she saw the same spark of dominance that showed so clearly in his father's face, but he merely nodded curtly and left.

Deidre frowned. Who was Formorian?

The rest of the morning was taken up with new chores. Servants carried pails of hot water up to Elen's room, where a large wooden tub sat behind a fine mesh screen. Sheila scented the water with dried rose petals and Una brought a cake of perfumed soap that delighted Elen.

"A new batch!" she said, sniffing it.

"The chandler pressed more heather than he needed for this eve's candles, so I thought the oil would make yer skin softer," Una said with a pleased expression on her otherwise grim face. She glared at Deidre and Janet. "I'll not want to find ye using it. 'Tis for the lady only."

Of course. Lye soap for the servants, no doubt. She'd have to keep hidden the bar that Anna had brought her last night.

After Elen had bathed and dressed, she dismissed all of them. "I believe I'll stay in my rooms and work on my stitching for an hour or two," she said as she sank into a chair by the window where she picked up a delicate pale silk.

"Our lady does the daintiest embroidery in all the Isles," Anna said proudly to Deidre as they left. "Ye'll see tonight on the fine gown she'll be wearing."

And what will I be wearing if I'm to attend Lady Elen? Deidre smoothed the plain wool dress. It was simple, with no ornamentation. Well, it was the least of her worries. She'd keep her ears open tonight and listen for any news from the guests of what might have happened to her escort.

Since she had some time, she decided to find the kitchens. Not only would she want to break her fast in the morning, but she might as well get to know the staff. She hoped the chief cook would be friendlier than Una was.

She was not.

"Get out! One of Lady Elen's maids has already been in here! I've not time to be waitin' on the likes of ye." The woman, well past middle age, glared at Deidre as she waved an apron at one of the scullery maids. Two kitchen maids began chopping vegetables vigorously while another scurried around the irate woman.

Deidre stayed where she was, just inside the door. She was determined to be pleasant. "I'm new here. I just wanted to introduce myself . . ."

"Bah!" The woman's double chin shook as she whipped around to grab the scullion lad who was trying to get past her broad form. "See what's keeping the dairy girl; I've butter to be churned and cream to be whipped." She turned and shouted more instructions at the hapless servants, who were clearly terrified of her. She seemed surprised to find Deidre still there.

"If ye don't want to be spoilin' that fine dress by working in here," she said, "ye'd best stay out of my kitchen. We've a feast to prepare and it'll take all day to do it. Laird Angus will be most wroth with me if things aren't just so for the king and especially that wife of his."

Formorian again. Who was she?

When the cook picked up a wicked-looking knife, Deidre decided it was time to depart. She wasn't sure if she wanted to know what the cook's intentions were.

Stepping outside from the kitchen's back door, her attention turned to shouting and whistling. She followed the sound around the corner of the Great Hall and saw a group of men, Gilead among them. As she approached the handful of spectators, she saw that the men were competing in archery. Her sport! Her mother had insisted that, to protect the Stone, the priestesses first had to know how to protect themselves. If a man didn't respect the wisdom of the Goddess encoded in the Stone, maybe he would understand real weapons used in Her defense.

Niall also stood with the archers. He looked surprised to see her, then he winked and grinned. Deidre lifted her chin and looked away, hoping he'd recognize the insult.

She watched as Angus nocked his arrow, drew and released.

There was silence as the arrow took flight and then enthusiastic applause when it hit dead center on the target. He grinned and gestured to the man beside him.

Deidre watched with interest. This must be King Turius. He was almost as tall as Angus, but more wiry. He wore woolen trews over soft leather boots and a simple white tunic belted at the waist. A finely woven, intricately designed, purple cloak was the only clue that he might be a king. He tossed that back with a practiced hand as he calmly took his stance and sighted. Light brown hair fell free to his shoulders and even from where Deidre stood, she could see his clear hazel eyes steady and focused, a determined look on his face. A muscle twitched in his square jaw, the only indication that he might not be quite as confident as he looked.

Wrong again. His arrow landed neatly beside Angus's. The applause was spontaneous, but subsided quickly, as though everyone was holding a collective breath. Then Angus nodded and held out his hand.

"A tie, then. How shall we break it?" Turius asked.

"We'll each declare a champion," Angus answered. "Gilead will stand for me. How about Formorian for ye?"

Formorian? The mysterious queen was an archer? Deidre looked around. There were only two other women spectators and neither of them looked queenly.

Turius shook his head. "That green stallion she insisted on riding limped as we neared here yesterday. No doubt, she's in the stables assuring herself the stud is not lame. You know how she is."

An odd smile crossed Angus's face. "Aye. No doubt the horse is enjoying her company."

Gilead coughed. "Do ye want to declare someone, Lord Turius?"

The Briton king looked over his men. Deidre wondered why he hesitated. Was Gilead that good? A wicked little idea poked at her. Maybe she should find out.

She stepped forward. "Your Lordship. A word, if you please."

Angus looked at her sharply, as though noticing her for the first time. "What are ye doing out here? Ye should be with my wife."

Deidre smiled sweetly. She wasn't about to miss this opportunity to show Niall she was not someone he wanted to take to task. "Lady Elen gave us leave for a short while." She turned to Turius. "Perhaps I can be of help. Will you let me stand for you?"

Gilead stared at her, nearly dropping the arrow he had been fingering. "I don't think ye understand, lass. This is not practice. Gold coin rests on the one shot."

She looked up at him, willing herself not to get lost in those lapis eyes. "I am aware of that. What makes you think I can't shoot?" She smiled at Turius. "Your queen obviously does . . . and does it well, if Lord Angus thought her worthy."

Turius studied her thoughtfully, his eyes penetrating as though to read her mind. She had the oddest sensation that he really was checking her out as a soldier and not a mere female. She was even more determined to shoot.

"Nay." Angus stepped forward, not pleased. "Ye'll not make a laughing stock of Turius. Ye are such a wee thing, I doubt ye could pull the bow at all."

She squared her shoulders. She'd had to put up with her cousin's arrogance for ten years at court because she was small. They were about to find out what a "wee thing" could do.

Turius held up a hand to Angus and smiled at Deidre. "You could very well make a fool of me, my lady, but something tells me to take a chance. My hunches are seldom wrong. What is your name?"

"Deidre," she answered and noticed that Gilead had turned away, but his shoulders seemed to shake. Was he *laughing* at her?

Turius didn't seem to notice. He looked at Angus. "Deidre will stand for me."

Angus shrugged. "'Tis yer loss, then." He gestured to Deidre. "Do ye want me to fetch a child's bow for ye?"

"Do ye think to insult me, my lord?" she asked in her best imitation of his brogue.

He blinked and then grinned. "Nay, lassie. I'll let Gilead do those favors."

Gilead looked decidedly uncomfortable as he followed her

to where a collection of bows lay on the ground. "Are ye sure about this, lass?"

She bent down and picked up a polished longbow made of yew. It was slightly shorter than the others.

"A good choice," Gilead murmured, so close that she could feel his breath lightly in her ear. "'Tis Formorian's. Let me brace it for ye."

Deidre willed herself not to turn around. One look into his eyes and she'd not have any strength at all. Not to mention, that sensual mouth would be mere inches from hers. She took a deep breath. She needed to concentrate, and not on him. Gilead was probably doing it on purpose, to weaken her resolve. She muttered a curse she'd heard Childebert use when his mother wasn't within earshot. Win any way you can.

"That won't be necessary," she said as she bent the bow and attached the string to the bow nock. "I need to get the feel of it." She forced herself to move away from his body heat before she lay in a melted puddle at his feet. *I have to win this. I must show Niall I won't stand down from him. Ever.* She remembered the way Turius had scrutinized her and given her his trust. Suddenly, she wanted to win as much for him as for herself. She wondered if he inspired that kind of loyalty in all his soldiers.

She chose her arrow carefully. The bow shot was not long, perhaps a hundred yards. A slightly thicker arrow would be more accurate. She sighted two or three for straightness and made her choice.

"I'm ready."

They walked to the target range. "After ye," Gilead said.

She nocked the arrow and then a thought came to her. She lowered her bow. "I want you to go first."

He looked puzzled. "Why?"

"Because I don't want anyone—*anyone*—to think you let me win by perhaps misjudging your shot."

A corner of his sinful mouth turned up. "My Da would have my hide for that. I intend to hit dead center."

"Then do it."

He gave her a quick grin and took his stance, legs splayed. Some of his hair had come free of the thong and dark strands fell over his forehead. Deidre's fingers itched, wanting to brush it back for him. The muscles of his right arm rippled into ribbons of iron as he canted the bow and drew. The arrow spiraled upward, arched, and came down like a swooping eagle. Dead center, as he promised.

Loud shouting and whistling rent the air. Deidre glanced over to where Angus was laughing. Beside him, Turius looked calm. He nodded at Deidre and smiled.

Deidre took a deep breath, thankful again that the Frankish squires had a collective sweet tooth for the things she pilfered and let her secretly practice with them to keep her skills sharp. She cocked her arrow, making sure the cock feather stood up and sighted straight. She was a point-of-aim archer rather than an instinctive one like Gilead. *Draw now . . . slow and easy . . . pull to the right ear. . . .* She felt her left arm strain from the draw weight. *Merde!* The long bow was heavier than the one she used. She gritted her teeth. *If that Queen Formorian can handle this bow, so can I.* Just another inch and she'd have it. She always felt the exact second she shouldered her head . . . *hold . . . and NOW.* She loosed the arrow, watching its flight, straight and true. It seemed an eternity in the air, and then it knocked Gilead's arrow from the target.

There was stunned silence from the crowd. Gilead turned to her and bent low, bringing her hand to his mouth and letting his lips graze her knuckles. "Well done, lass," he said. "Where did ye learn that?"

A warm, fuzzy infusion wafted up her arm at his touch and she hoped her knees wouldn't suddenly give way. She managed a deep breath, wishing she could tell him the truth. She changed the subject.

"You're not angry with me?"

"Nay. Ye won fair. Come, now. I'll take ye to my father."

"I don't doubt that he will resent losing to a woman, whether it be me or the Queen Formorian."

A muscle twitched in Gilead's square jaw. "Ye'll be fine."

Deidre wasn't so sure. Angus's dark eyes bore through her as they approached. Maybe she had pushed it too far. She had wanted to prove to Niall that she would never subject herself to him, but if Angus started probing her origins, what would she do? She straightened her back and lifted her chin.

"I wish my wife had been here," Turius said as they approached. "She always likes to win, too." He smiled as he handed Deidre the sack of gold coin. "I believe this belongs to you."

Deidre held her hands up. "No, my lord. I stood as your champion. The money is yours."

"I've no need of it," Turius replied, "and neither does Angus. We're like to compete for anything for the mere sport of it." He held the bag out to Gilead. "You're younger than I am. Perhaps you can convince the lady to accept it. Come, Angus, I will be letting you take the edge off my thirst."

Angus gave each of them a long look before he turned. "Niall. Come with us. We have talking to do."

Niall gave Deidre a long, scrutinizing look before he left, but she ignored him.

"Turius is right," Gilead said as they left and the crowd dwindled. He pressed the bag into her palm and closed both of his hands over hers, enveloping her in a warmth that spread up her arms and coursed down her belly, invoking more than a fuzzy feeling this time. "'Twould be good for a lass to have some coin. Ye lost all in the robbery."

Deidre hoped he didn't feel her trembling. It was hard to think straight with her skin—and other parts—on fire. All she wanted to do was pull his arms around her and be lost in the resulting *feu de joie*. Safe from Niall. Safe with Gilead. He seemed genuinely happy for her.

What would he do if he knew the truth? And could she tell him?

Elen had been pleased when Deidre told her of the event over the midday meal, consumed in the lairdess's room. She told Deidre to spend the afternoon settling in and to arrive early to help her prepare for the night's feast. A look of trepidation replaced the happiness on Elen's face at the thought of the feast. Deidre wondered why.

It wasn't until late afternoon when Anna brought some

clothing that might fit Deidre that she had a chance to question her about the elusive Formorian.

"I met the king today and I looked for his wife afterward, but I couldn't find her. I wanted to thank her for the use of her bow. A finely crafted weapon."

"Aye." Anna busied herself taking gowns from a trunk that had been delivered. "Queen Formorian insists on only the best, 'tis said. I've heard His Lordship say she's quite skilled in swordplay as well."

Deidre raised an eyebrow. She had tried her skill a time or two, but the sword was heavy and she preferred the bow. "She fights?"

"Aye, although not to the king's liking, I think."

Deidre blinked. What man would want his wife in combat with him? Was chivalry just a myth from her mysterious writer? Well, Deidre wasn't planning to go to war with anyone except Niall. "Where did she get her training?"

The maid shrugged. "From her Da, I guess. She's the daughter of the laird of Gabrain. Lord Gabran ne'r had a son, so he taught his daughter to fight. She be a warrior queen like Boudicca."

The first-century warrior queen who had led an uprising against the Romans. Interesting. No wonder poor Lady Elen was intimidated. Elen was so fragile and feminine; to have to put up with a masculine, muscular woman who probably used the same rough field language that men did must be distressing. Elen was a lady—Deidre knew that much just from the time she'd spent with her—and she would be forced to endure the woman's crudeness at dinner tonight.

Well, Gilead had asked her to attend his mother. Now she understood it was to protect her. And Deidre would do it. Somehow, she'd pawn this female brute off onto Angus. He was the host, after all. Talk of battles and bloodshed she'd probably relish.

Then Lady Elen could sit back and relax and not be bothered with her.

Deidre smiled, thinking how pleased Gilead would be.

Chapter Four

QUEEN FORMORIAN

"What a beautiful dress!" Deidre exclaimed as she helped Elen with the pale blue watered-silk gown. It had a high lace collar and gathered delicately below the bosom, allowing the fine material to fall in soft folds to the floor. Long, fitted sleeves were trimmed with more of the expensive, imported lace from Eire. The color enhanced the translucent whiteness of Elen's skin.

Too white. Deidre looked more closely. Elen looked pasty. "Are you ill?"

"Nay." Elen sank onto a padded stool as Sheila started combing her hair. "These feasts just try my nerves, that is all."

"Shall I send to Brena for a potion, my lady?" Janet asked.

Elen shook her head. "They make me sleepy. I must needs be awake this eve."

"Don't you worry," Deidre said soothingly. "I won't leave your side."

Sheila raised an eyebrow. "Who invited ye to the high table?"

Deidre couldn't help a somewhat smug smile. "Gilead did."

Janet glowered. "And why would he be doing that?"

"You'll have to ask him," Deidre said and was interrupted as Brena came through the door bearing a goblet of wine.

"From my lord," she said as she handed it to Elen. "He wants ye to drink all of it before ye come to table."

"But why?" Elen asked plaintively. "Wine will flow when we eat."

"Aye. But he wants ye to have some color in yer cheeks when ye arrive." The healer tilted her head to one side. "Ye do look uncommonly pale. Wilna do to have King Turius and Queen Formorian think ye weak and spineless, will it?"

Deidre watched as Elen turned even more ashen. What a cruel thing to say! Fragile Elen might appear, but Deidre suspected there was strength under that exterior. She would just have to help Elen find it.

This Formorian would probably behave like a boorish man, but Deidre would be there to make sure she didn't affect Lady Elen. This was one feast the laird's wife would be able to enjoy.

Deidre caught her breath as they entered the Great Hall. Transformation had taken place since she had walked through it earlier that day. Fresh rushes, laced with heather and meadowsweet, covered the floor. Colorful plaids of the various visiting clans lined the walls, almost overwhelming the senses with their brightly interwoven reds, greens, and blues. Turius's standard, a black bear encased in the constellation of the Big Dipper, set on a field of blue, stood on the dais at the far end of the Hall next to Angus's red, pawing lion on a gold background. The trestle tables were laden with pewter and the high table, set perpendicular to them and parallel to the long wall, was set in silver and gold.

As she and Elen walked to the high table, Gilead caught her eye. He looked resplendent in a midnight-blue waistcoat, white shirt, and fly plaid pinned across his left shoulder. His dark hair glistened nearly black and the low light from oil lamps defined his features into a handsomeness that would have made even Apollo retreat in his fiery chariot. Deidre felt herself begin to pant and forced a deep breath. She longed to feel Gilead's full sensual lips on hers. The thought caused the hundreds of butterflies to rise from their roosts in her stomach. *And . . . dear Lord.*

Oh, Goddess, no. Yes. He was wearing a kilt! Three different shades of blue squares intermittently run through with red threading. Her glance lowered. Thin, off-white hose hugged well turned-out calves, the muscles bunching as he moved toward them. And under the kilt . . . ?

When did it grow so infernally hot in here? Even though Deidre's borrowed gown was modestly low-cut and had short sleeves, she could feel heat radiating from her in shimmering waves.

Gilead stopped a few feet from her and smiled, his sapphire glance sweeping over her neckline, inflaming her already aroused sensitivity. She had no idea—not in her most vivid dreams—that someone could affect her this way.

He stepped closer and she inhaled the scent of him, an intoxicating mix of soap and leather and a light spice.

"Come," he said and gestured for them to follow. He held a chair for his mother, next to the high-backed one that was for Angus, and handed her the rose from the plate. He frowned slightly as he noticed another rose on the plate next to hers.

Elen noticed it too. "Formorian," she said softly.

Deidre grimaced. How cruel to put that Amazon next to poor Lady Elen. She spotted Angus near the dais.

"I'll be right back," she said.

He was talking to Turius. Like his son, he was wearing a kilt, and again, Deidre was struck by how much they looked alike. Angus had to be near fifty, yet there was no flab on him at all and his legs were as heavily muscled as Gilead's. Well, better not think about Gilead. She had a job to do.

They stopped talking as she came near, Turius giving her a nod and a smile. He was dressed more Briton, in soft leather trews, a red woolen tunic, and a golden torque at his throat.

"Don't tell me my wife's not well this eve," Angus said.

Deidre hesitated. She had to take care with her words in front of Turius for she didn't want to insult him by calling his queen uncouth, although no doubt she was.

"Lady Elen is here, my lord, but you are right. She doesn't feel well and I fear won't be good company for Queen Formorian." She ignored his raised eyebrow and went on. "If you would allow me to switch the seating arrangements, I could take care of Lady Elen and I'll seat the queen between you and King Turius. You are the host tonight; I'm sure she won't be insulted."

The corner of Angus's mouth twitched. "Does my wife know ye're doing this?"

"No," Deidre said, "but I'm sure she'd want to have the queen entertained properly."

"Properly? Aye. I'm sure she'd want everything to be proper," he said.

"Sounds like a good idea to me," Turius added. "I wouldn't want to burden Elen. In truth, my wife can be a bit vivacious at times."

I'll just wager she can. Talking about weapons and war and killing strategies like a man would certainly be what I'd want to listen to! Deidre smiled sweetly. "Thank-you, my lords."

The herald called them to tables. With a grin, Angus pulled the chair next to Elen for Deidre. As she sat down, she whispered to Elen, "Don't worry. I've taken care of the seating. You won't have to listen to field talk and battles tonight."

Elen threw a startled glance to her. "What have ye done?"

Before Deidre could answer, Gilead took the seat on her other side. "I'm sorry, but this is for Queen Formorian," he said. "We always seat the king to my father's right and the queen to my mother's left."

"That's okay," Deidre said happily. "I've changed that for tonight. Queen Formorian can bore your father with her talk instead of your mother."

Elen gasped and grasped the table with a soft moan.

Gilead's mouth was a hard line. "Ye did this without permission?"

"Oh, no," Deidre said, puzzled by his expression. "I asked your father. He seemed all right with it."

Gilead's blue eyes turned dark. "Of course he would," he muttered.

Was he *angry* with her? Deidre couldn't fathom why. She'd saved his mother from a boring evening listening to wretched talk about bloodshed.

"What's wrong?" she asked.

Before he could answer, the room stilled. Chairs stopped dragging, cups weren't clacking, conversations dropped off. Deidre turned her head to see why.

At the main entrance, opposite the wall with the dais, a woman stood. "Stood" was not quite right. She reigned. Still as a Roman statue, she surveyed the room. She could have been the Huntress, Diana. Tall, she wore a simple white gown that bared slender golden arms. Cut low in front to reveal firmly rounded breasts, she had sashed it with a golden belt at her slender waist. Her hair was a blazing halo of fire. Thick and curly, it cascaded over her shoulders and down her back in shimmering strands of auburn, amber, and russet. Green eyes, slightly slanted over impossibly high cheekbones, began to twinkle mischievously as she surveyed the room. Her full pink mouth curved into a welcoming smile, revealing small white teeth as she walked to the high table.

"Who . . . ?" Deidre started to ask and then she knew. Formorian. Not some heavily-built mannish woman as she had imagined. Oh, no. This one was all graceful curves. More of a goddess than a warrior.

Both Angus and Turius leaped to their feet to pull her chair. She smiled at her husband and kissed him fully on the lips. Then, to Deidre's amazement, she turned to Angus and did the same thing, running her fingers languidly through his long hair. Elen averted her eyes.

"Sorry I'm late," Formorian said as she sat down. She smiled indulgently at the crowd seated below them. "I hope I haven't kept the meal waiting."

"Certes not," Angus said gallantly. "We were only about to start." He waved at the servants, waiting with full trays. "Bring the food."

As they quickly made their way among the tables, conversations resumed. Soon the high table was groaning beneath heaping platters of boar, venison, and mutton. Steamed salmon and pickled eel came next, accompanied by roast peacock and swan. A jellied broth was ladled into silver bowls and set before them. Puddings and warm bread were passed, and a tray of apples and pears appeared.

Deidre hardly ate. Elen looked wan and preoccupied and Deidre tried, in vain, to engage her in conversation so she wouldn't have to listen to the outrageous flirtation that was taking place next to her.

Formorian was a virtual maestro. Her light chatter and tinkling laugh had both men vying for her attention. She played them like harp strings, resting her hand on her husband's thigh while she listened attentively to whatever story Angus was telling. Turius couldn't see her face, turned away from him, but Deidre could. The queen's eyes smoldered and her gaze slowly went to Angus's mouth, and then she turned back to her husband. To Deidre's surprise, Angus seemed amused by it.

She sighed. The feast and entertainment were more lavish than anything Childebert ever attempted. There were acrobats entertaining the diners, and a lone harpist in the corner, and she couldn't enjoy any of it. Not with poor Lady Elen having to listen to the sounds of her husband's laughter over some jest that Formorian made.

Deidre turned her attention to the harper, a striking young man with golden hair that fell to his shoulders. Slim, yet well-proportioned, he gave the appearance of elegant gracefulness. Long, slender fingers plucked a haunting melody, soft and low, that slowly built to a frenzied pitch. Deidre envisioned heather moors and sky-colored burns weaving through the crags of the Highlands. The music lived with a soul of its own.

Gilead rejoined the table. She turned to him. "Who is the harpist?"

For a moment she wasn't sure he'd answer, for he still looked upset with her. All she'd done was try to help, for Heaven's sake. How was she to know Turius was married to someone Venus would envy?

Finally, he said, "That's Drustan. Turius brought him along on a trip here a few years ago and Mother took a liking to his music."

"I can see why. But if he's Briton, why does he stay here?"

Gilead shrugged. "At the time, he had no place else to go. Turius was fighting in the far South and found him stowing away on one of the ships. Apparently, his uncle had caught him . . . uh, in a compromising circumstance. Drus was inclined to want to keep his head attached to the rest of him."

Deidre was intrigued. "He looks more angel than devil."

That brought a mocking laugh. "Aye. The lassies fall for it ne'r every time."

She bristled. Just because Drustan could play the harp like Gabriel's trumpet, didn't mean she was some addle-witted wench. "I meant the music . . . it speaks to me. I can feel the entire rugged outdoors, smell the grass and heather, feel the sun warm on my face, the wind cool in my hair. . . ." She paused, for Gilead was watching her strangely.

"Aye, lass. Talent he has, but be thankful he's in a good mood, for the sound can turn blae when he's not. It be wild and mournful then, as dark and cold as the north wind that howls down the mountains in the winter."

"What makes him angry?"

Gilead grinned. "Women. Or more like the lack of one. Since Drus claims he lost his real love, he dinna like a cold bed."

Do you? Deidre bit her lip to keep from asking. They were finally having a conversation and she liked the direction this was heading. Definitely. "And who was his true love?"

He sobered suddenly. "His uncle's wife." He looked past her to his mother and then on to Angus. A scowl crossed his face and he abruptly stood. "Excuse me, I need to attend to something."

Deidre sat bewildered. One moment he had been friendly, and the next, cold as the depths of a loch. And now he marched off. With an effort, she turned her attention to Angus; he had ignored his wife throughout dinner, enthralled with the charms of the flame-haired queen.

"Would you like to leave?" Deidre whispered to Elen. "Dinner's over." Even as she said it, servants were carrying away empty platters while others were pushing trestle tables and benches to the side, clearing a wide space in the center of the Hall.

"I canna," Elen said. "My place is by my husband's side at such events."

A husband who's barely glanced at you. Deidre felt a lump rising in her throat. Poor Lady Elen. Did she think the men would stop vying for Formorian's favor if she stayed? Or worse . . . that Angus would take the next step if Elen left? She really wasn't looking at all well, but there was a determined look on her face as she ignored Formorian. Deidre nearly gasped at the insight. Elen might be afraid of her husband, but she still loved him!

Just then, Angus rapped his golden goblet sharply on the table and gestured to the pipers hovering in a corner. "Music! Let the dancing begin!" He looked at Elen with some reluctance. "Would ye honor me with the first dance, wife?"

Elen colored faintly. "Ye know it tires me."

Angus leaned down. "It would seem everything tires ye these days."

Deidre gaped at him, then narrowed her eyes. Anyone could see Elen wasn't up to dancing. "You've ignored her all night; why don't you leave her alone?"

He straightened, his eyes turning darker as he studied her. Then he abruptly grasped her hand. "Ye and I have some talking to do. Let's dance."

Deidre started to protest, but his grip was firm and the hand on her back propelled her forward. "I don't know how to dance like this!"

"Nay? Then I'll teach ye." Angus spun her around, an arm about her waist and nodded to the bagpipers.

They struck a lively tune and soon the floor was awash in a swirling pattern of bright plaid kilts and colorful gowns. Deidre stumbled once, on a turn, but Angus expertly balanced her. She had to admit that he was a good dancer and didn't hold her too closely either. Which was really good, since Formorian swept by with Turius and gave her more than a curious look. Deidre had no inclination to get tangled with *her*. She was thinking she could survive this dance when he spoke.

"I'll not be having ye criticize my relationship with my wife."

"You don't have a relationship," she started to say, and then bit her lip. His voice was flat and low. Deidre recognized the barely concealed anger. When she looked up at him, his face was impassive, but his eyes bore through her.

"Understood, lass?"

She took a deep breath, knowing she had overstepped her bounds. "Understood."

"Good." He swung her toward the sidelines and released her. "I'll leave ye in good hands then."

She turned and nearly bumped into the one man she didn't want to see.

"Did the laird warm ye up for me?" Niall asked with a smirk.

Deidre backed away from him. "I must tend to Lady Elen."

He grabbed her wrist and jerked her toward him, his other arm going around her waist and pressing her against him.

"Let go of me!" Deidre balled her fists and pushed at him.

"Nay, lassie. We will dance." He gave her a lecherous smile and moved onto the dance floor, pulling her with him.

"I told you. I have to see to Gilead's mother."

"His mother be attended. Look." He nodded his head toward the table where Sheila sat with Elen. He brushed his whiskers against Deidre's cheek and she drew back in alarm. He laughed. "No need to be shy, lass. We be handfasted."

"We are not!" Vainly she tried pushing away from him again, but only stumbled as he made a turn. He caught her, crushing her to him.

"Aye, we are. Angus agreed to it."

"Then he can marry you," Deidre exploded, "for I will not!"

Niall's eyes narrowed and he tightened his grip on her hand. She gasped. The pressure he was exerting was enough to break a bone. "Let . . ."

"Nay, I wilna." He grinned, but it looked more menacing than it did friendly. "Ye will wed me."

"Never!"

He twisted her wrist and Deidre bit her lip to keep from crying out in pain. She was sure it would be swollen tomorrow, if not worse. She looked around desperately for help. Angus was dancing with Formorian, oblivious to anything going on around him. Gilead was near his mother, but Janet was hanging on to his arm, looking up at him adoringly.

Merde! Not a chivalrous knight in sight. She was beginning
to think the magician had played a monstrous trick on her by
leaving The Book. She was definitely in need of rescue. *Now*
would be nice.

She forced a smile, hoping Niall would relax his hold on
her hand before she heard something snap. It worked, and she
bent her wrist slightly, testing it. "Angus told me you are the
son of an Eire king. I'm sure there are a lot of women who
would be happy to wed you. Women who would submit to
you willingly."

His eyebrows arched at that and he gave an evil chuckle.
"Aye. More than enough are willing. It's ye I want."

Deidre ground her teeth. This was becoming tedious.
"Why?"

He leaned closer and she could smell the whiskey on his
breath. She forced herself not to grimace. If he would just
loosen his hold a little more . . .

"Because I like breaking wild mares. Ye were feisty last
night and this morn's bit of shooting roused me fierce. Ye'll
do fine warming my bed."

"I've no intentions of warming your bed!" Deidre choked
back a whimper as he seized her arm, nearly wrenching it.

"Is that so? I let Angus talk me into not bedding ye until
Lugnasad, but he said naught about a wee kiss for my bride."
He rubbed his whiskers against her cheek again, seeking her
mouth.

Deidre whipped her head to the side and pushed at him
with all her might. "Stop it! Let me go!"

"Ye heard the lady."

Gilead. Deidre nearly collapsed with relief. Her knight had
come, after all.

Niall slowly released her and stared at Gilead through slit-
ted eyes. "Be wary, lad. This be twice now that ye've come
between me and what I wanted."

Gilead stood firm, his eyes locked with Niall's. "I don't
think it's what the lady wanted." He turned to Deidre. "Do ye
want to dance with this man?"

She shook her head numbly and then found her voice.
"I . . . I'd like some fresh air, I think."

He nodded. "Let me escort ye, then." Gilead took her hand and tucked it inside his arm, his fingers strong and warm and reassuring.

"Thank you," Deidre said as they stepped outside into the cool evening air.

He gave her a half smile. "Ye dinna seem to be having a good time."

She involuntarily shuddered. That was a slight understatement.

"Are ye cold?" Without waiting for a reply, he slipped off his jacket and pressed it about her shoulders.

The coat enveloped her, the clean, spicy scent of him filling her nostrils, burying her in a cocoon of safety. A warm glow spread over her.

"Would ye like to walk the battlements?" he asked. "The view is good on a clear night like this."

Deidre nodded and they climbed the stairs and rested their arms on the embrasure between two merlons. The full moon had risen, sending its silver light over a wide stretch of countryside. Her eyes followed the pale winding road as it led down toward the small path that twisted its way to the forest and last night's bonfire. She breathed in the night scent of pine and watched as an owl floated silently past them from a tower.

"It's so peaceful up here," she said.

"Aye," Gilead answered, gazing off into the distance. "I fear it won't be for long, if Fergus has his way."

"Your father mentioned him," Deidre said. "Is he so powerful, then?"

He looked down at her, his eyes like midnight sapphire. "My Da has received reports from our scouts that Fergus is amassing men. That means he plans to move soon. This summer, most like. 'Tis why Turius is here. He was most successful in clearing the Caledonian Woods of Saxons several years ago. The people there will rally to him, if not my father, for he let them keep their lands. And, he knows the best places to lie in ambush and the safest places to store weapons and hide campsites." Gilead smiled ironically. "Because of a greedy Scotti we have a Briton king abiding with us."

"And his queen," Deidre said softly.

"His queen," Gilead said with a trace of bitterness, "could very well launch another war."

"How so? Because she flirts? Turius seems to take that in stride." Indeed, Deidre had watched him rather closely, since Angus and Formorian made no effort to mask their interest in each other. Turius had seemed oblivious.

"For now," Gilead answered. "Turius values her skills as a warrior and the alliance with her father more than her . . . ah, other assets."

Deidre's eyes widened. "She really fights?" She had a hard time imagining that feminine physique pulling a bow or lifting a sword.

"Don't let her looks fool ye. She's a hellion in the saddle and nimble of foot and quick as a cat in swordplay. Those slender arms are like bands of steel." Gilead frowned. "Or so my father says."

Deidre hesitated for a moment and then asked, "Is your father's interest in her more than solicitous?"

"Aye." Gilead put his hands in fists and pummeled the wall. "They draw to each other like lightning to metal. I tried to talk to Da about it once and he told me it was ne'r my business and cuffed my ear to make sure I understood. Now, I just try to keep them apart when I can."

"And I made it worse by changing the seating arrangements. I'm so sorry." A sob caught in her throat and she asked softly, "How long has this been going on?" Poor Elen. Did she know?

"Eons it seems. They were keen to marry long before I was born, but it dinna happen."

Deidre blinked. Gilead was near her age. Twenty-five years or more was a long time to love another man's wife. "What happened?"

He sighed. "King Gabran's lands—her father's lands—lay directly to the south of Fergus Mor and north of the Wall. Turius's father, Ambrose, ruled most of northern Britain from Luguvalium. To hold off Fergus, Gabran needed the Briton's help, but he didn't want to put himself into a position to have his lands confiscated by Ambrose, so he offered a pact. Marriage of his daughter to the Briton king's son. Neither of them was happy with it, for Turius had designs on a pagan priestess, but it was done."

Deidre thought about it. Perhaps that was why Angus didn't listen to her when she said she would not handfast with Niall. He had lost his own love. She wondered how he'd met Elen or why he'd married her. They seemed to have little in common.

She placed her hand on Gilead's. "Your poor mother. Does she know?" She heard his quick intake of breath and then his hand covered hers, sending another heat wave coursing through her.

"She didn't, for years. I always wondered why my father paid so many visits to Turius. If my father was seeing Formorian, he had the sense not to bring her here. I think my mother knows now, although I try to shield her from it." Gilead looked back out into the night. "These visits go hard with her, especially since she has not been well."

"Has she always been so . . . fragile?"

"Nay. She's always had a gentle nature, but when I was a child, she was full of laughter; she loved playing Catch My Shadow."

It was hard to imagine Elen full of energy, lifting her skirts to run after her child in the sunlight, stepping on his shadow. "What happened?" Deidre asked softly.

"About two years ago, we started having trouble with the Saxons. Octa first, until Turius's army cleaned out the woods. Now other barbarians threaten our eastern shores. My father thought it wise to enlist Turius's help to hold them back. Conveniently, his warrior queen accompanied him. My mother fell ill shortly after that."

Deidre frowned. She could understand Elen's spirits falling if she suspected what might be going on, but her illness seemed more physical than in her head. "Did Formorian actually do something to her? Hurt her in some way?"

"Nay. Not that I know of. In fact, her healer gave my mother a brew that seemed to revive her quickly and took away the pain she sometimes feels in her joints."

Deidre remembered the concoction from that morning. "Brena? If she worked for Turius, why is she here?"

"She dinna like Britain. Said she was a Scotti at heart and asked to stay with us." Gilead shrugged. "Our own physician had died but the day before they were to return, so Da agreed to keep her. She has proved her worth." He laced his fingers with hers. "I think ye will be good for my mother. She likes ye."

Heat seared through her veins at that companionable touch. It felt so very comfortable—so right. *His mother. We're talking about his mother. Focus.* "I like your mother, too, and I'll try to protect her from having to put up with Formorian as well. Do you think they'll stay long?"

He sighed, his thumb absently tracing a pattern along the side of her hand, sending further tingles straight to the faint pulsation that was beginning at the vee of her thighs. "I hope not. They have the clan council meeting on the morrow. I tire of Niall's company, too. I don't like the way he presses himself on ye."

Niall. She'd forgotten about him while talking to Gilead. Somehow, she had to make Angus understand she would not marry the man.

Gilead tilted her chin toward him with his free hand. "What's wrong? Ye look grim of a sudden."

She didn't want to spoil the moment. Not when he was looking at her like this. Not when that sensual thumb was sending erotic messages to her brain . . . and elsewhere. "It's nothing," she said.

He bent closer, looking intently into her eyes. Lord, she felt like her knees might just dissolve into a mass of quivering jelly.

"Tell me," he said softly.

A girl really could drown trying to swim in the deep blue depths of his eyes. They mesmerized her. She was going down . . . sinking . . . She took a deep breath. "Your father wants me to marry Niall."

"What?" Gilead straightened in surprise, dropping her hand. "Why?"

Now she'd done it. All that closeness was gone. *Que le diable emporte, Niall. Damn the man.* "Your father will claim me as kin through Caw and bind Niall to his clan by the marriage."

Gilead looked miserable. "I mentioned that thinking to protect ye. I had no idea my father would try to do such a brainless thing. Well, he canna do it."

Deidre felt a little bit of hope. "He cannot? He says Niall and I are handfasted until Lugnasad; then we are to be married."

"Nay. I wilna let it happen." He put his hands on her shoulders, turning her to face him. He traced the curve of her cheek with one finger and she shivered. "Are ye cold?" Gilead wrapped his coat around her, pulling her closer. The moment hung suspended in time as his eyes searched her face and then lingered on her mouth.

He cradled her head in his hands, lifting her face toward his. His lips brushed hers lightly. And again, teasingly, not allowing Deidre time to kiss him back. And she wanted to. Her nipples tightened as her breasts filled. Gilead played with her lips, slanting his mouth across hers, exerting gentle pressure, sucking her lower lip between his lips. He licked an outline around her mouth, nibbling at the corner of it. A little mewling sound escaped her.

As if the sound had been a Saxon battle cry, he abruptly pulled back. Dazed, Deidre's eyes fluttered open. Why in the world had he stopped? Just when it felt so good?

He looked confused. "I shouldna have done that. My apologies."

Apologies? For kissing her when she had wanted a whole lot more of him? Her breasts ached to press up against him, to have him hold her tight and feel the hardness of that muscular chest. For a moment, she was tempted to grab his hair and pull him into her embrace. She didn't fully understand what was happening to her, but she knew she didn't want it to stop. Too late, she remembered the code of courtly love from The Book. Now wasn't the time to be worshipped from afar. Certes, that was a downside to chivalry.

"Will ye forgive me?" He still looked troubled.

"Of course," Deidre said and forced a smile. "Perhaps we'd better go in."

"Aye," he answered in relief as he helped her down the

steps. "I meant what I said to ye. I will find my father and talk to him. Tonight. He wilna force ye to marry."

This time her smile was genuine. "My thanks to you, Gilead. I will be forever grateful. Forever."

He nodded, but did not look at her as he opened the door and they stepped inside.

Angus was nowhere to be found, nor was Formorian.

Suddenly, that no longer mattered. Elen had just collapsed at the high table.

Chapter Five

BETRAYAL

The noise of the feast abated as Angus closed the door to Formorian's bedchamber and slipped the strap of her dress off her shoulder. He trailed a series of soft, wet kisses down her throat. *Bel's fires!* Her fingers were hot as they worked feverishly to divest him of shirt and plaid. His hands slid slowly up her ribs to cup her breasts as he pushed his hard erection against her and back-walked her to the bed in his chamber. Deftly, he unfastened the back of the gown and it dropped to the floor before they both tumbled onto the feather down.

"Ye get more beautiful every time I see ye," he murmured, his tongue laving lazy circles around her soft mound of breast. His thumb brushed across the other nipple, teasing its tight bud into a rock pebble.

Formorian moaned and arched her back into him. "Ye saw me just last night. By Dagda, Angus, suck on me. Hard."

"So soon, Mori?" Angus raised his dark head and gave her a slow, lopsided grin. "I think to torture ye a bit first." He pushed his knee between her thighs and lowered himself over her, dipping down to flay a nipple lightly back and forth with his tongue before moving upward to reclaim her mouth.

Her lips parted for him and he thrust inside, exploring the

sweet taste of her tongue, the spongy lining of her mouth. He tugged her lip between his and then pressed his open mouth across hers, their tongues battling for supremacy.

Her body wanted more. Angus nuzzled her neck, his big hands sliding over her torso, kneading both breasts, loving the feel of her squirming, lush body beneath his. A body made for hours of lovemaking. He nibbled her earlobe and then gently bit the hollow between her throat and shoulder.

With something that sounded like a feral growl, Formorian raked her fingers through his silky hair and brought his head down to her breast. He laughed and then mouthed her breast, rolling the nipple with his tongue. She moaned and slid her hands to his shoulders, feeling the hard biceps bulge as he kept most of his weight off her. Most. Just enough to have full body contact and feel his hardened shaft pressing hard against her belly.

Angus began to suckle and a bolt of fire seared directly to her already throbbing center. Abdominal muscles contracted as his mouth demanded more, the sucking hard and deep now. Just as she liked it. She shuddered.

"Nay, not yet," Angus whispered and slipped lower, the scorching touch of his tongue blazing its way downward. He spread her legs, slipping a knee over each of his shoulders and licking at her core in broad, flat strokes. Ripples of intense sensation rocked her. His mouth closed on Formorian's nub and she spasmed, wave upon pulsating wave surging through her.

He waited for her panting to subside and then in one long, sensual motion he eased himself over her and plunged his cock deep inside her, filling her completely.

Formorian wrapped her legs around his thighs, meeting his thrusts, bucking and flexing under him as he ground into her. Fast and hard, he took her past her limit, her breath coming in short gasps as her body throbbed, gathering itself for one enormous convulsion. She felt his tension a split second before she felt his seed explode and then her body shattered.

They lay, sweaty and exhausted, arms and legs entwined.

"Is the door locked?" Formorian asked musingly.

"Damn." Angus raised his head to look. "Yes." He looked

back down at her, flushed and sated beneath him. "That's what ye do to me. I take leave of my senses."

Formorian gave him a smile that almost caused another erection. By Lugh, what effect that woman had on him! He was nigh fifty and in less than five minutes . . .

She trailed lazy fingertips down his arm. "Stop looking at me like that. Ye know we have to get back before we're missed."

He sighed and rolled off her. "Fate should never have separated us, Mori. We belong together."

She draped his arm around her and settled onto his shoulder. "Aye. And I love ye. But the marriage to Turius made sense. Even my old nurse—half-crazed though she was—thought Ambrose would have confiscated Da's lands if I were not his son's wife."

Angus sighed. "I always liked old Cailyn, even though folks claimed she was part fey."

Formorian's fingertips grazed his chest. "And Cailyn was near mad about ye. She always told me that one day the Great Mother would bring us together. But I think her sister be more fey than Cailyn."

"Our Brena?" he asked, teasing a nipple to hardness again. "She be a good healer, nothing more." He bent his dark head and mouthed her breast. "Let's not talk about either of them."

Formorian closed her eyes with pleasure and then popped them open again when he stopped suddenly. "Why are ye frowning?" she asked.

"It blinds me white to think of ye with Turius, doing what we just did."

"Hush." Formorian propped herself up on her elbow and brushed damp strands of hair off his forehead. "Don't think on it." She traced his lips with a finger. "It doesna happen that often; Turius would rather wage war than love."

Angus caught her hand and kissed the palm. "Still, if ye were free . . ."

She arched an eyebrow at him. "Even if Turius were killed in battle, ye would still be wed. Have ye forgotten that?"

He frowned. "How can I? I was duped into the marriage, as ye well know. I had no more choice than ye."

A small sigh rose from Formorian. "I couldna have abided my father losing title to Ambrose. Ye know how we Scotti love our land."

Angus knew. He felt the same. But he wasn't interested in logic just now. Not when he already wanted her again and they weren't even out of bed yet. He stroked a path across her hip and over her buttock.

Formorian laughed. "Ye know we've not the time. . . ."

His dark eyes smoldered as he took her shoulder, drawing him to her until he could take her full swollen breast into his mouth again. He sucked forcefully.

She gave a soft cry and he pulled her over on top of him. "Yer turn, my lady. Ride me hard."

With half-lidded eyes and a slow, knowing smile, Formorian impaled herself on him, leaning forward to brush her breasts across his chest. Angus groaned and swept his hands down her back, rocking beneath her.

Something crashed outside in the hall, followed by voices and footsteps. Lots of them. For one moment, Angus and Formorian remained frozen and then they both moved. Fast.

"Turius?" she whispered as she hurriedly slipped into her gown and turned for Angus to fasten it. "Surely he wouldn't be so stupid as to clamber up to my guest chamber with all yer guards about."

"Shhh. Nay, I don't think so." Angus flung on his kilt and threw over his plaid. "I hear no armor or weapons." He paused, listening. "It sounds like servants. Ye stay here; I'll see what it's about."

He took a deep breath and opened the door.

Deidre quickly opened the door to Elen's chambers and Gilead carried his mother through and placed her gently on the bed. Behind them, a whole retinue of servants followed, hovering anxiously in the doorway. One of them righted a potted plant that had been overturned on the procession up the stairs. Sheila and Janet were subdued for once. Una armed her way through, barking orders at the gawking servants for cold water, fresh towels, and hot tea. They scattered like dandelion silk on the wind.

"It hurts," Elen moaned and clutched her stomach, wincing.

Deidre undid the laces to Elen's bodice and loosened her lacy collar. "There, there. You need some air." She glanced at Gilead. "Find a fan."

He returned as Brena bustled in with her basket of herbs. Quickly, she sat down on the edge of the bed and placed a hand to Elen's forehead. "No fever. Did ye faint?"

"My stomach. It burns dreadful, like a snake is twisting inside."

The door burst open and Angus strode in. He looked disheveled and his fly plaid was crooked. "What goes on here?" he demanded and then saw his wife on the bed with Brena standing nearby. "What's happened?"

Gilead's eyebrow arched as he took in his father's appearance, but he said nothing about it. "Mother collapsed."

Elen groaned again, her body beginning to shake. "I feel so cold," she murmured weakly. "There's a dirk in my stomach. I swear it." Cold sweat appeared on her face and she curled herself into a ball as another cramp struck her.

Deidre remembered a time when she'd eaten fish that hadn't been properly cooked and she'd had painful cramping. They'd had salmon tonight. She moved forward past Angus.

"Lady, perhaps it was something you ate. If fish is undercooked—"

"I hadna fish." Elen grasped a handful of bed sheet and gasped in pain. "A bit of venison and a pear."

Deidre had the venison herself and felt fine. But a pear . . . She remembered a story from The Book about one of King Arthur's knights being poisoned by an apple. There had been a very fine pear at the top of the fruit plate and Elen had been offered first choice. She looked around. "Did anyone else have a pear?"

No one answered. Gilead wore a puzzled expression, but Angus looked thoughtful. "What are ye getting at, lass?"

Deidre took a deep breath, hoping she wasn't letting her fertile imagination get away from her. Mayhap she was obsessed with the legends and mayhap the magician had bewitched her somehow. "Is there a possibility that pear could have been poisoned?"

Angus went pale beneath his deep tan and Brena looked at her sharply. "Nonsense," she said. "Who would want to kill our gentle Lady Elen?"

Who, indeed? Deidre couldn't imagine that Elen could have any enemies, except perhaps Formorian. But the queen could hardly have wandered through the kitchens—not with that hellcat of a head cook—and drawn no attention. Deidre shuddered. She'd have to brave the woman tomorrow and find out. Still, if it were poison . . . Deidre lifted her chin determinedly.

"I don't know. But if I'm right, she should be made to vomit and then fed lots of fluids to dilute whatever it is." She could thank Clotilde for that information; more than one attempt had been made on Childebert's life.

Brena visibly bristled. "A healer now, are ye?"

"Do it." Angus said in a voice that left no room for argument. "It can't hurt her, can it?"

With a sniff, Brena shuffled through her herbs and lifted out a mandrake root. She took a small, sharp sickle from a concealed fold of her skirt and carefully scraped some of the root into a glass half-filled with water, warmed it over the brazier, and added a pinch of salt. She handed it to Elen.

Deidre moved forward with the empty water basin from the dresser, but Gilead took it from her.

"I'll hold it," he said.

Una dismissed the few servants who remained and shut the door behind them. Angus raked a hand through his hair and began pacing. Deidre was about to tell him he was driving her mad when Elen began retching. The boots stopped their incessant pounding and Angus went to the window to gaze out.

Deidre poured some cool water onto a cloth and bathed Elen's face between heaves. "You'll feel better soon. Just get it all out."

Elen grasped her hand weakly and squeezed before she was sick again. Eventually, she lay back on the pillow exhausted.

"I'll fetch ye some wine," Brena said as she covered the fouled bowl with a cloth.

"No!" Elen made an effort to sit up, but Gilead placed a re-straining hand on her shoulder and she slumped back again. "No wine," she said again. "I've not felt well since I drank the cup before dinner."

Angus turned away from the window to stare at his wife. Deidre jumped up and ran to the goblet still standing on the table. She started to sniff it and then set it down, disappointed. The cup had been washed; no residue remained. She looked up to find Angus watching her.

"I poured that wine myself," he said sardonically.

Deidre felt herself flush all the way to the roots of her hair. She was practically accusing the laird of poisoning his own wife! A statement like that could really get her thrown in the dungeon . . . or worse.

"I'm sorry, my lord. I didn't mean to imply . . ."

He simply raised an eyebrow and went to the door. "If my wife is going to be all right, I'll return to the festivities and see to my guests. As ye reminded me earlier, I am the host."

"She'll be fine now, my lord." Brena seemed anxious to please. "I'll steep a little snakeroot in some goldenseal tea and make sure she drinks it." She turned to Deidre. "If ye have any more suspicions, miss, ye and I will drink the tea also."

"Aye. Do that," Angus said and slammed the door as he left.

Deidre bit her lip and looked at the closed door. Either Angus was righteously indignant because he was innocent or he was diabolical enough to have covered his own tracks with a big red herring.

Gilead rubbed his eyes. By the saints, he was tired this morning. He'd stayed at his mother's bedside until the wee hours, making sure her sleep was normal and undisturbed. The idea that poison might have been involved shook him. Deidre had come in once, offering to relieve him, but she had dark circles under her eyes and he'd told her to go to bed. Once she'd left, he felt even more torn.

She confused him. He had a feeling she wasn't telling the truth about herself, or at least, not all of it. How had she known what to do last night? She'd seemed perfectly competent and at ease helping his mother. Was she a healer? Most of the women who healed in Britain and Pictland were pagan and often studied on the Druid's Isle. But her accent was strange. Mayhap his father was right; she was a Saxon spy sent to get the lay of the place before they invaded. Mayhap he needed to keep more of an eye on her.

He smiled in spite of being exhausted. As beautiful as she was, keeping an eye on her was no hardship. The hardship was in his trews; he wanted to do much more. Why he allowed himself to fall into temptation last eve on the battlements he didn't know. He hadn't intended to kiss her. Not at all. But when she placed her hand on his, his blood pulsed furiously through his veins. Her hand had felt so small and soft that he'd allowed himself a brief kiss. It wasn't supposed to be more than that. He was always in control of his emotions when it came to women. Always. Then the taste of her sweet full lips pressing against his—answering him, for God's sake—ignited a fire that surged directly to his groin. He moaned a little, that even now in broad daylight he felt an active urge inside his pants. He'd wanted to slide his fingers beneath her coat and run his hands along her back, snugging her tightly to him so that her breasts would be mashed against his chest. Bloody hell. He'd wanted to tear their clothes off so it would be bare skin he would feel against his own. He shook his head and drew a shaky breath. *This won't do. I'm as bad as my father.*

He paused at the door to the solarium in the east wing, hoping his father was inside having his morning cup of watered wine. The gods only knew where he and Formorian had gone off to last night before his mother's collapse, but they were running him ragged. It was only a stroke of fortune that Niall had been in his cups and Turius had decided to stay close to him, lest a brawl break out.

Gilead pushed the door open, relieved to find his father sitting in an easy chair, absorbing the morning sun.

"Don't ye knock?" he asked.

Gilead ignored the question and poured himself some wine. He preferred goat's milk in the morning, but Angus didn't keep any in the solarium. His father was not looking his fittest. Although his clothes were clean, he had not shaved and he looked tired. Or maybe worried? He should be. And where had he been that he appeared so quickly once they'd taken his mother to her chambers?

"Mother's better this morning," Gilead said as he took a seat.

Angus nodded. "I'll have ye take her wine to her this morn, lest there be any more rumor of my tainting it."

"No one would think that," Gilead answered.

Angus arched a brow. "Our bonny Deidre did."

Gilead toyed with his goblet. Had Deidre really thought his father capable of murdering his mother?

"We don't know that there was poison at all," Gilead finally said. "Mother's not been well. Mayhap putting up with . . ." He stopped. "I mean, these visits always seem to take their toll on her. She's delicate."

Angus snorted. "Yer mother snivels. I've not time for waiting on her hand and foot. Would that she developed a back-bone and stood up for herself."

"Like Formorian?"

His father gave him a long, dark look. "Have a care. Ye tread on boggy ground."

Gilead reined in his temper with an effort. Drat that woman. It was fine that Turius treated her like an equal and actually preferred she ride beside him, but was he blind to what was happening? Gilead wasn't sure if that was a bless-ing or not. He sighed. Formorian was like a Highland burn, rushing to meet the sea, tumbling down falls, slipping around rocks, merging the energy again to pursue the relentless jour-ney, destroying any obstacle in her path or taking it with her. His mother was probably another obstacle, which made him angry again. He clenched his jaw. He'd get nowhere arguing with his father and he was here because of Deidre.

Gilead chose his words carefully. "I meant that I ken ye re-spect the queen for her independence."

Angus gave him a suspicious look. "That I do, as does Turius."

"Aye. Mayhap, then, ye could also have respect for Deidre's wishes."

"And what would those wishes be?"

"The lass does not wish to be handfasted to Niall."

His father sat back. "The lass is in no position to make demands. She's an orphan—or so she says—with no dowry. Niall has both money and lands. She should consider herself lucky."

"She should be allowed a choice," Gilead said stubbornly.

"Why?"

"Because . . . because it is her life, Da! Ye know Niall. He is not a kind man. He'll try to break her spirit, just like he did his last wife."

"Bah! Rhea was mousy to begin with. I wager Deidre's sharp tongue will give Niall a turn or two. 'Tis one of the reasons I think they'll suit. A man likes a challenge now and then."

Gilead didn't think Niall would appreciate a "turn or two." More likely, he'd beat her. And he couldn't see Deidre going willingly to Niall's bed. A dagger twisted in Gilead's gut. Deidre, naked and vulnerable, her soft, satin skin mottled . . . those lusciously round breasts bruised . . . her full lips split and swollen . . ."

"Nay. She will stand up to him."

Angus tilted his head and studied him. "Ye seem to know a great deal about her. Have ye tupped her?"

"Certes not!" Not that he hadn't wanted to. God knows, he'd not felt urges like this since he was a lad and had dreams that left him wet in the mornings. He could well imagine what it would feel like to have her warm, pliant body beneath his, opening herself to him . . . He struggled to push those thoughts away.

"Da. Ye ken that Niall craves power and must needs feel he is in control—"

"Exactly." Angus leaned forward. "It is a frightening thing in a man given to weaknesses like liquor. If I claim Deidre as kin, I bind Niall to me. *And* I bring in powerful allies from Eire, should we need them."

"She will deny she's kin, then."

"Hmmm. Not unless she wants to tell us who she really is," Angus answered. "I doona believe her story. But mayhap ye should try to find out. Now go. I have preparations to make before the council meeting."

Aha! His father was inadvertently giving him permission to be with her! Gilead stood and walked to the door. "She'll be free of the handfasting until I find out who she really is?"

"Nay. I canna do that. Niall has already agreed to terms."

"But handfasts can be broken," Gilead answered.

Angus hesitated. "Aye. Under certain circumstances. Find out who she is, lad." As Gilead turned to the door, Angus spoke once more. "Don't even think on tupping her, son. I doona need war with Niall."

Gilead's back stiffened and he didn't turn back. His father was a fine one to talk.

The council meeting was not going well. Niall sported a massive hangover and was surly, snarling at nearly every suggestion Turius made. Comgall, the laird of Cenel Comgaill, could barely contain his fury at Niall's boorishness. Not that Gilead could blame him. He stood more to lose than any of them, since his lands were to the west of Niall's and actually bordered Fergus Mor's. He was likely to see the brunt of the summer attack.

Turius threw down the quill over the map on the long, rectangular table and stood. "I'll wash my hands of all of you if you won't listen to reason! If you keep bickering among yourselves, Fergus will pick you off as easily as ripe berries from a bush. I won't send my men in to die because you can't unite."

Gabran frowned and looked at his daughter. Formorian laid a hand on Turius's arm. "Remember, my father's lands are vulnerable as well."

Turius paused and then sank into his chair. "What would you have me do?"

Gilead had long ceased being surprised at Formorian's presence—the only woman allowed—at these meetings, but it was the first time he'd actually heard Turius ask for an opinion. He glanced sideways at his father, but Angus appeared to be waiting for an answer, too. Gilead shook his head. What was it with that woman?

This morning she was dressed like a man, in boots, trews, and an overlarge linen shirt that was probably Turius's. A leather cuirass hung over the back of her chair and her hair was pulled severely back, no doubt because Turius and his guard would be wanting her ready to ride directly after the meeting. There was nothing feminine about her attire, yet with just a touch, she had managed to bring her husband into line and his own father looked mesmerized.

Formorian picked up the quill and used it as a pointer. "I think Fergus will move northeast rather than southeast through Comgaill."

"He'd have to fight the Picts, then!" Comgall exclaimed.

"Mayhap. But if he could ally with them temporarily— promise them even more land just for passing through— Fergus would have a formidable force to press down on us from the north. And," she added, "he wouldn't have to bludgeon his way through all of ye first."

"Blethering foolishness from a woman!" Niall muttered. "Who ever heard of the painted barbarians willing to talk truce with anyone?"

Angus gave Formorian a thoughtful look. "If ye're right, Fergus could march to the eastern sea and squeeze us in from three sides."

"Exactly." She gave Angus a wide smile and then turned to Turius. "I suggest this: One. The lairds fortify the northern borders to Pictland and track any movement. Two. Ye send an envoy to treaty with the Picts first."

"Ye be taupie!" Niall yelled.

Angus brought his fist down on the table. "Formorian is *not* stupid . . . and ye best watch yer mouth if ye want teeth left in it." He turned to Turius. "I'll send the envoy from Oengus. We be the closest clan to Pictland."

Turius nodded, looking relieved. "Then it's settled."

"Are ye daft?" Niall leapt to his feet, overturning his chair.

"Nay," Angus replied. "And if ye don't keep a civil tongue, the handfast we spoke of may be made null. I'll not subject my kin to such rantings."

Niall narrowed his eyes and glared at Angus, but he kept his mouth closed.

"What's this?" Formorian asked with interest. "A handfasting? To your *kin?*"

Gilead's gut felt like it had received a solid kick from an ornery mule. Why couldn't his father have kept still? So far, no one else had known. Now the news would spread like wildfire throughout the clans.

"Aye. Elen's new handmaiden . . ." Angus glanced at Gilead and then back to Formorian. "The lass, Deidre, would appear to be distant kin."

Formorian turned her green, catlike gaze to Gilead. "Isn't she the one who bested ye with the bow?"

He squelched a sudden grin. He ought to be upset about that, but truth was, he was looking forward to a rematch. He would ask Deidre to try a larger bow and then he could stand behind her, one hand supporting her bow arm, the other helping her with the draw weight, bringing her close against him. . . . He stopped. No, that was something his father would do. Not him. "Aye. She did."

Gabran leaned forward. "I, for one, think it's high time ye chose a wife, Niall. A good woman to keep ye on the straight and narrow." *And sober,* the message left unsaid.

Camgall fixed an eye on Gilead. "Aye. A fine wife can bring out the best in a mon. When do ye plan to wed, Gilead?"

Gilead started. Marriage was the last thing on his mind. His parents' match was a farce and Turius and Formorian seemed oblivious to each other. Drustan's heart had been broken by a woman who toyed with him. Gilead wanted no part in such disasters. "I'd not thought on it."

"Well, my daughter, Dallis, is of marriageable age," Comgall answered and glanced at Angus. "I'd not mind binding my clan to yers, either, Angus."

"Mayhap the lad fears he can't control a woman," Niall sneered. "He was just bested by one. I'd not allow a woman to best me."

Formorian threw him a sharp look. "Ye might not have a

choice!" She tossed her head and walked out of the room. Silently, the rest of the men followed her.

Niall was still muttering under his breath when Gilead reached the hallway and looked up. The other hoof of that ornery mule kicked him hard, causing him to take great gulps of air.

Deidre stood at the far end of the hall and Formorian was talking to her, one hand on her shoulder. Gilead didn't have to hear what was being said to know Formorian was asking about the handfast. Deidre's face had gone ashen and her blue eyes had dilated to appear nearly black in her chalky face. A hand flew to her mouth and then she spotted Gilead. She turned and ran from the hall.

Gilead started to go after her, but instinctively he knew she wouldn't see him. He had never felt so miserable in his life. He had failed Deidre.

Still trembling, Deidre leaned against the windowsill of her small room and watched as Turius's troops fell into rank in preparation for leaving. She was surprised to see that Roman discipline had been ingrained in the men. Archers lined up in maniples of twenty men across, five maniples deep. Next came the spearmen, followed by the sword and mace holders. Each row was so precise that from her upstairs window she could see even spaces horizontally, vertically, and diagonally. They moved forward out the gates in the same formation to make room for the cavalry.

Deidre gasped as she watched the half century of men emerge from the stables. Each of them wore a red cloak identical to the soldiers who had abducted her escort. They had been Turius's men.

She let the curtain fall back and sank onto the bed. It wouldn't take long for Turius to find out who her escort was once he returned home. She hadn't even had time to begin searching for the Stone. Her guards were loyal men, not given to easy confessions. But would Turius torture them? And if one talked, what would happen to her?

Chapter Six

TREACHERY AFOOT

Deidre avoided Gilead for the next three days, managing to vacate the room on one pretense or another moments before his morning visits to his mother. She huddled now near the small table in her room, hoping Una didn't come looking for her. Even though Niall had taken care to leave no bruises, her wrist was still swollen from the wrenching he had given it when they danced. Only the lightest tasks caused her no pain. Fortunately, Elen was not demanding and seemed not to notice her quick disappearances prior to Gilead's visits.

The handfast news had spread like fire on dry grass. Janet openly gloated at her, no doubt relieved that she was no longer competition for Gilead's attention.

Ha! As if I ever had been. He'd told me he'd talk with his father so that I wouldn't have to marry Niall. Apparently he forgot to do that! She didn't mean anything to him at all. And the kiss? Clotilde had warned her over and over about letting men make advances. Gilead had just taken advantage of what she'd freely given. Well. She wouldn't make that mistake again.

Nor was she going to marry Niall. She touched her wrist protectively. She'd have to take care not to anger him further while she sought escape. The mere thought of being pleasant to him nearly made her retch.

She didn't know how much time she had if Turius managed to make her men talk. She must find a way to escape and she must find the Stone. She had been here a sennight already and had not been able to start searching, since she had no way to leave the castle. Her Sight had remained maddeningly elusive. Too bad she couldn't summon it up at will or, in lieu of that, conjure up Merlin from The Book. Sadly, magic was not one of her talents.

A thought tripped over the last one and she sat up straighter. Allegedly, Merlin had moved the huge stones that formed Stonehenge. Scotland had its share of standing stones. Those ancient circles were supposed to contain power. If she could locate one close enough, perhaps her Vision would return to her once she stepped inside.

But first, she realized, she'd have to have access to a horse. She'd need one to explore faerie mounds, sacred springs, and other ancient sites where the magician might have hidden the Stone, although she wasn't sure how she would be able to slip away. Mayhap she could convince Angus to let her learn to ride. She knew how, thanks to the stable lads, but if she pretended that she wanted to learn to please Niall—she forced herself to swallow the bile that rose in her throat—well, it might work. Formorian rode. It wasn't that unusual.

She rose determinedly. Now that she had a plan, she felt brave enough to confront the cook about whether Formorian had been seen in the kitchen the day that Elen took so ill. After that success, she'd find Angus.

For the several hundredth time, Gilead felt like kicking himself. He had let Deidre down. Worse, he hadn't seen her in three days. He stabbed a forkful of manure and tossed it outside his horse's stall. He'd expected her to be angry with him, and had even been glad he didn't have to face her wrath the day Turius and Formorian left. But now Deidre was openly avoiding him. He'd seen a wisp of her skirt disappearing around the corner of the hall one day and just this morning he'd heard her door close as he came up the steps. He'd thought briefly about knocking on it, but he didn't really know what to say. Being sorry was no good. He'd have to find a way to make good on his promise. Breaking his word was unthinkable.

Angrily, he pitched another load out the door and nearly hit his father.

"Why are ye mucking out yer horse's stall? We've stable hands enough for that." Angus leaned casually against the frame, one foot crossed over the other.

"It gives me something to do," Gilead said as he scooped more soiled straw.

His father folded his arms over his chest. "It seems to me, ye have been 'doing something' a might strong these past two days."

"I don't know what ye are talking about." Gilead scraped the last remains together. "Malcolm likes a clean stall."

Angus glanced over to the chestnut stallion tethered nearby and then back to his son. "And would Malcolm also be insisting that ye spend hours at swordplay, tiring our best warriors, or even more time with the bow, wearying the archers?"

Gilead brushed past him to gather fresh straw. "Fergus will make his move soon. I thought ye wanted us fit to fight."

"Aye. But men fight better not wounded. Yesterday ye drew blood twice."

"Hardly a nick. Young Calum misstepped." Gilead threw the straw down and went back for a second armful.

"And Adair?"

"Slow. 'Tis all."

Angus raised an eyebrow. "My Captain of the Guard is *slow?*"

Gilead hesitated. Adair was second only to his father in skill. He had simply not expected Gilead to unleash hell's full fury on him yesterday. And Gilead didn't quite understand it himself. He just knew he had to release the anger that was raging inside of him. He did not like to fail and he had failed Deidre. Memory of her bloodless face when Formorian spoke with her—and the gods only knew what she said—haunted him.

"Mayhap I was a bit fashed."

"Being fashed can get ye killed in battle. Ye were lucky that Adair was lax; I will speak to him about it."

Gilead groaned inwardly. The captain already delighted in making workouts strenuous for him. Only preparing him to be laird one day, Adair would say. After Adair had received a tongue-lashing from his father, Gilead would be in for more misery. "I doona think there be a need, Da."

"I do. Neither of ye focused on yer weapons like ye should. Ye've so much pent up energy, it's nigh to steaming out yer ears." Angus tilted his head and studied his son. "I think ye need a woman. Seeing as ye have fresh straw, why not fetch a willing maid for a tumble?"

His father's answer to everything. Deliberately, Gilead pushed back the tempting image of a satin-skinned, naked Deidre writhing beneath him, begging. . . . *Bah! Deidre would probably rather rake her nails over me like sharp daggers, until my blood runs.* Gilead sighed. "I doona think that would help."

His father looked at him incredulously. "How can it not?"

Gilead shook his head. "It just wouldn't." He untethered Malcolm, led him into the stall, and picked up a brush to curry him.

His father stared at him for a moment and then turned to go. He stopped abruptly. "It's that wench ye brought home, isn't it?"

Gilead felt his ears turn hot. He remembered her lips against his, warm and moist and soft like the light zephyr on the battlements that night. Yielding. Her hair had felt so silky in his hands and her skin so smooth beneath his fingertips. Even now, he could smell the subtle fragrance of heather soap that clung to her.

"I told ye, lad. That is one wench ye'll not be tupping."

He lifted his chin and looked into his father's eyes. "I told ye I wouldn't."

Angus held his gaze and then he snorted. "Bloody hell, son. There are plenty of women who would come to yer bed. Bonny Janet, for one. Ye have aught but to lift a finger and she'll strip for ye before ye can take her to the floor."

No thanks. He'd made that mistake once, years ago when he barely knew what to do with his new erection. One of his mother's older maids had seduced him, and, once he'd gotten over the wonderment of spilling his seed, he'd not been able to get rid of her. She trailed him like a mooncalf until Elen had finally sent her home to her father.

Gilead shook his head. "What ails me, Da, is that I told Deidre I would talk to ye . . . make ye understand she has no will to be handfasted to Niall."

"That again. Ye did what ye said ye'd do. Ye talked to me. I said 'no.'" When Gilead did not respond, he added, "It's the way of things." He turned to get his own horse. "She belongs to Niall, or she will. Ye keep yer hands off her."

Gilead clenched his jaw as he turned back to Malcolm. "It would be nice if he followed his own advice, wouldn't it?" he asked his horse.

The stallion nodded his head sagely.

Deidre took a deep breath and walked through the door to the kitchen. The big cook, whose name was Meara—Deidre had to chuckle at the irony of a name that meant "merry"—had her back to her. A tantalizing aroma of mutton stew and warm oatcakes filled the room.

"That smells delicious," Deidre said, causing one of the scullery maids to look up in panic.

The cook turned around, meat cleaver in hand. "I thought I spoke with ye earlier about staying out of me kitchen."

It would be nice if she put that huge knife down. Deidre fought the impulse to turn and run. She forced a smile that made her face hurt. "I . . . I came to ask your help."

The woman eyed her suspiciously. "What kind of help? I'll not be making something special for ye, not unless Lady Elen asks."

"Oh, no, it isn't that," Deidre hastened to say. "But it's about Lady Elen."

Meara's eyes narrowed. "Are ye complaining? Naught is right for the mistress?"

Deidre shook her head quickly. By the saints, the woman was bristly. "No. The lady is fine. At least, she is now."

"Now?"

"Yes." Deidre let her glance slide over the still-panicked maid and the scullion boy who stood gaping at her. "Could we speak privately?"

The cook waved the big knife at the two and they collided with each other, trying to get out the door. Deidre stifled a smile. Probably better not to laugh when the woman was brandishing a meat cleaver.

"Well? Speak yer piece. I've work to do."

"Yes. Thank you. The night of the feast, Lady Elen became deathly ill—"

"Are ye saying something be wrong with me food?" the cook roared.

Deidre kept her eyes on the fist that yielded that weapon. "No! No. I didn't mean that . . . I meant that I thought it might be poison. . . ."

The woman's face mottled. The color grew from red to maroon and veins began to bulge at her temples. This was not going well. Deidre took a small step backward. "I didn't mean you! I vow! Just stay calm."

Meara threw the cleaver down and the blade bit into the floor planks, leaving the wooden handle vibrating. Her fists clenched and unclenched and her mouth worked silently as a nasty storm brewed in her eyes.

Deidre glanced toward the door. Two steps. Maybe three.

"Ye wee bitch! Master Gilead is kind enough to bring ye here and feed ye—with *my* food—and ye accuse me—"

"No! Not you." Deidre swallowed hard. She had to know if Formorian had been in the kitchen that day. "Were you in the kitchen all day? Could someone have come in without your permission?"

The scowl on the cook's face became scudding thunderclouds. *Now what have I done?*

"Only ye. I let no one in here, except the laird or Master Gilead." She stooped to retrieve the knife. "Now get out and dare not to darken my door again!"

Deidre nodded and backed away, only to collide with something soft.

"Goodness! What is going on in here?" Elen asked. "I could hear the shouting up the stairs."

To Deidre's utter amazement, the cook metamorphosed in front of her. The giant woman became a blubbering blob that puddled itself on the floor at Elen's feet. "My lady," she said in a shaky voice, tears streaming down her face, "This stranger—that ye have shown naught but kindness and mercy to—accuses me of poisoning ye! Me! I have been with ye since ye were a wee bairn—"

"There, there." Elen soothed her, stroking the older woman's hair as she knelt. "I'm sure she didn't mean it." She lifted troubled eyes to Deidre. "Mayhap ye best leave us. We'll speak later."

Deidre nodded and fled. *Mon Dieu!* Not only had she botched the whole thing and not gotten any information about Formorian, but now Elen was displeased with her. And somehow, that shamed her. Standing up to Angus, all six and a half feet of raw, domineering male that he was, was nothing. Let him rant and roar. Let Niall try to intimidate her. She could take it. But a softly spoken implied word of rebuke from Elen humiliated her. She stifled a sob. Could she make any more of a mess of things?

She found Angus a few minutes later in the stables, saddling his stallion. Better she get this over with before he found out about the fiasco in the kitchen. While she now knew that his lust lay with Formorian, Deidre still didn't think he'd take kindly to her upsetting his wife.

Good place for a meeting, the stables. Especially since she wanted a horse.

The black tossed his head and stamped his forehooves as she approached. Angus gave him a smack on his withers and he calmed.

"He's beautiful," Deidre said. "May I pet him?"

Angus turned, surprised, and looked down at her. "Donal doesna like strangers. Careful there, lassie!"

But Deidre had already offered the big horse an apple, one she'd pilfered from the sideboard of the Great Hall when Meara wasn't around. Donal's eyes rolled and he laid his ears back, but she didn't move, her hand just inches away from those big teeth. Angus gave the horse a sharp reprimand and jerked Deidre out of harm's way.

"What the hell do ye think ye're doing? One bite and yer bones be crushed."

Deidre gave him a wide-eyed look. "Don't all horses like apples?"

"Not this one. He's war-trained and taught to obey only my hand."

"A destrier," she breathed, her mind reeling back to descriptions of the horses the knights from The Book rode. Her cousin's cavalry rode smaller horses. This stallion stood nearly seventeen hands at the withers, with a full chest and massive hindquarters. In her mind, a procession of heavily armored warriors rode, colorful standards held high in front of them, baldrics supporting swords at their backs. Knights off on a quest . . . She gave herself a shake. *There I go again, letting my imagination take over. Have I not realized yet that this is no Camelot?*

"What are ye doing here, anyway?" Angus asked. "Should ye not be with Elen?"

"Ah . . . she gave me some free time."

He tightened the cinch and then wrapped an arm around the pommel, leaning against the horse, and gazed down at her. "And ye decided to come to the stable. Looking for anyone in particular?"

"You," Deidre said.

Angus raised an eyebrow. "Ye surprise me, lass."

She flushed bright scarlet at the implication. Good Lord! Did he think she was throwing herself at him like Sheila did? "It's not that."

He gave her a lopsided smile. *Merde!* Did he have to have the same smile Gilead did? Only with Gilead, it was a charmingly disarming smile, making her all warm and mushy inside. A teasing smile that hinted at pleasures to be shared.

His father's smile was purely sexual and left the impression that a woman was meant to be ravaged. Deidre shivered a little. No doubt, he and the warrior queen were well matched.

"Well?" he asked. "What would ye be wanting me to do for ye?"

Thank goodness he had not reached for her. She would have run screaming like a banshee. She stepped back a little, safe from any predatory move he might make, but he remained still, looking more amused than anything.

"I . . . I would like to learn to ride."

"Why would ye be needing to ride? I cannot imagine my very fragile wife being up to such outings."

"Perhaps not, my lord." Best to be as formal as possible. They were alone in this area of the barn. "But Queen Formorian rides . . ."

"Aye. She's ridden since she was a wee bairn. How does this matter to ye?"

"Well." Deidre lowered her eyes demurely, trying to look contrite. She really wasn't good at conniving, but she was desperate. "I think it pleases her husband that she rides beside him." When he was silent, she looked up to find him gazing absently into space. Mayhap she should not have mentioned Turius. "I mean . . . well, if I *am* to be wed, I would think it would please my husband to have me ride by his side." *Only that husband will never be Niall. Never.*

Angus looked surprised. "Ye'll agree to the handfast then?"

Only until I can find a way out. "What choice do I have, my lord?"

He didn't answer directly. "The idea of running yer own household, with servants of yer own, sets well?"

"I suppose I could get used to that." Deidre grasped one hand with the other to keep it from trembling. Here she was, merely evading the truth. She would never understand how anyone could be a bold-faced liar.

"So ye've come to yer senses, then?"

I've come to my senses. Gilead let me down. I can only depend on myself. "Yes, my lord."

Angus nodded. "I knew ye would; it just took a mite to adjust to the idea. Niall is not so verra bad. If ye treat him well, he'll do right by ye."

For a moment she was tempted to show him her wrist, but the swelling was not so bad that he'd believe her. She had no doubt that Niall would be a wife-beater, but she wasn't going to be here to find out. She swallowed hard to keep the bile down. "Yes, my lord. Do you not think it would please him to find out I can ride?"

"Aye. Ye can tell him tomorrow night; he'll be coming for a meeting on sending our envoy north."

She nearly panicked. "Ah, no, my lord. I wish it to be a surprise. Please. Not a word until I'm good enough to show him."

Angus studied her silently. Finally, he nodded. "Give me a day or two. I'll arrange it."

From behind her, she heard movement. Gilead appeared in the doorway of the stall to her right, a curry comb in one hand, an odd expression on his face.

Her skin heated at the sight of him and then her blood ran chill. He had heard everything. For all practical purposes, she had just agreed to marry Niall.

Merde. She didn't think things could get worse after the kitchen mess. Apparently, they could. They just did.

This time, Gilead wanted to kick himself for being such a fool. He had actually believed Deidre. She had looked into his face that night on the battlements, her big blue eyes brimming with tears, silently begging to be rescued—a second time— or so he thought. And the kiss . . . what a clever little wench she was to reel him in like a spawned salmon. "Forever grateful," she'd said and he'd swelled with pride, thinking that once he'd protected her from Niall, they might share another kiss. *Fool*. He kicked the stairs to his mother's room hard with his boot. *Fool. This is what happens when I let my emotions get in the way of my good sense.*

Oh, he had no doubt Deidre had been scared witless on Beltane, but obviously the idea of wealth and title overcame that fear. She was penniless. She might still not think Niall desirable, but that hardly mattered. She was ambitious. She had probably thought to use him, too.

Fool. Fool. Fool.

Gilead planted a smile on his face and opened the door to his mother's chambers. And then froze in his tracks.

Deidre sat beside his mother, weeping. His mother was comforting her, patting her on the shoulder. *Bel's fires! What, was the little minx trying to coerce his mother into believing her now?*

"There, now," Elen said. "We'll not speak of it again. 'Tis in the past."

"I'm just so sorry," Deidre said as she wiped her eyes with a linen cloth that Elen handed her.

He'd wager she was. Whatever it was. Convincing little vixen, just like Formorian. And look where that had landed his father, not to mention his poor mother. He should thank the Dagda for keeping him from such folly. He. Should. Thank. The. Gods.

Strangely, though, he was not comforted.

"Mother? Are ye all right?" he asked as he approached, ignoring Deidre, and gave his mother a kiss on her cheek.

"Aye. Except for this potion." Elen wrinkled her small nose and finished the thick brew that Brena provided. "Deidre had a wee problem, but it's been taken care of."

Janet arrived then with the breakfast tray. As she set it down on the table, her ample bosom brushed Gilead's shoulder. With a bit of annoyance, he noted that Deidre apparently did not notice the gesture.

He considered Janet, thinking about what his father had said. She was comely enough and seemed eager to please. Certes, she touched him as often as she could. Mayhap his father was right, much as he hated to admit it. A good tupping might just be what he needed.

He smiled at Janet, his hand brushing hers as he took the hot mug of tea and handed it to his mother. "Won't ye join us this morn, lass?"

Janet quickly flounced down beside him, giving Deidre a triumphant look, but Deidre seemed suddenly devoted to sprinkling just the right amount of sugar onto Elen's porridge. She set the bowl down in front of Elen as Angus burst through the door in his usual brusque manner. Elen cringed slightly.

"Good morn, husband."

Angus nodded and removed the mug of tea, replacing it with the wine goblet he'd brought. He looked at Gilead. "Adair will be wanting a rematch this morning. I hope ye'll think with yer head today."

Gilead clenched his teeth. "Aye. I will." His father no longer had to worry about which head he was thinking with. He was back in control of his emotions. It felt good, too. It really, really did. So good that he handed Janet a warm bannock, letting his fingers linger on hers for a moment.

Angus' mouth quirked at that and he sat down between his wife and Deidre. "I've decided who could best teach ye to ride," he said to Deidre.

Elen looked surprised. "Ye want to learn to ride, child? Like a man? 'Tis not what a lady does."

"She wants to learn," Angus replied with more than a bit of sarcasm, "because she wants to please her husband. Some wives do, ye know."

Elen looked down, a pink flush covering her face and neck. "Ye know I'm afraid of the big beasts."

"Aye. Ye've told me before." Angus sighed and turned back to Deidre. "I think it best if a woman teach ye. I'll send for Formorian."

Gilead stared at his father. That was a clever bit of maneuvering. *Formorian without Turius. Here. For weeks.* He wondered just how many minutes it had taken his father to formulate that plan. Probably less than one.

"Not a good choice," he said.

His father arched a brow. "Why not? Formorian has a way with horses."

Formorian had a way with everything. Gilead was not about to subject his mother to a prolonged visit. "I believe the discussion yesterday was that Mistress Deidre wished to surprise her . . . her fiancé," he managed to say. "It would seem odd to have Queen Formorian here for any length of time."

Angus eyes darkened and Gilead caught something that looked like respect. His Da loved mind games; only Gilead wasn't playing one. He plodded on. "We've enough fine horsemen here."

"Certes, we do." Elen sat up, her voice surprisingly strong. "Ye, for one, Gilead." She turned to Angus. "Does our son not always win the trials of horsemanship? Do ye not always brag on him?"

Angus looked wary and Gilead silently groaned. He hadn't wanted to push the issue this far. "In truth, I was thinking of Broderick." Gilead flinched a little as Deidre looked at him steadily for a moment and then looked away. "He is our Master of Horse."

"As such, I need him to ready the troops for the march

north," Angus answered and then eyed his son thoughtfully. "Mayhap, ye would be best at that."

Now what was his father crafting? He'd been told in no uncertain terms to leave Deidre alone . . . and then he remembered. His father had wanted him to find out where she really came from. He had not done that. Now that Deidre had declared her intentions for Niall, his father knew she was safe from him.

Absolutely, totally safe. Clever of his father. He nodded stiffly. "As ye wish, then." But he didn't have to make this easy for either of them. He turned to Deidre. "I'll expect ye at the stables at dawn's crack. We've both other things to do during the day."

He was somewhat gratified to see two rosy spots grow on her cheeks as she turned away. Fascinating, though, the way that pink glow spread all the way to the neckline of her dress. . . .

"Gilead!" he heard his mother exclaim. "Where are the manners I taught ye? Ye'll certes do nothing of the sort. I can spare Deidre in the afternoon." She folded her hands in her lap, looking more determined than he'd ever seen her. "I'll not have it any other way."

He glanced at Angus, only to find him looking at his wife with something close to awe on his face. Disconcerted, Gilead nodded and turned to walk away.

Somehow, he had the feeling that this was not going to go the way he wanted.

The man is a bloody boor, Deidre thought at the evening meal. Her stomach churned as she watched Niall's thick fingers tear a strip of venison from a shank and stick the whole thing into his mouth, the grease sliding into his beard. And they were seated at the high table!

She forced a smile and picked up the small bowl of water the laverer had left. "Would you like to dip your fingers, my lord?"

"Why should I?" Niall broke off a chunk of bread and wiped the lard from his fingers with it before he shoved the wad into his mouth, chewing noisily.

Deidre's plastered smile remained in place as she set the

bowl down. "As you wish, my lord." She thought she just might regurgitate her own food if she had to say "my lord" one more time, but Angus was seated within earshot and she wanted that horse. *Had* to have that horse.

The meal wore on. Not even Drustan's harp could soothe Deidre's emotional turmoil. Gilead had not presented himself at the table and Deidre alternated between wondering where he was and reminding herself that she was angry with him—and not only for avoiding her earlier. If he had kept his promise, she wouldn't be sitting here now with this oaf.

Suddenly, she felt the oaf's hand on her knee. Her skin nearly crawled in revulsion. As unobtrusively as she could, she shifted her weight, moving her leg away.

Niall's eyes narrowed. "Ye'll not be avoiding me once we're wed, lass."

She tried not to grind her teeth. "We aren't wed yet."

He leaned close to her, the odor of his rancid breath overpowering.

"I'm going to enjoy taming ye. The more ye fight me, the more ye rouse me."

His hand slipped under the table again and this time he gripped her thigh and squeezed hard until she gasped in pain. She was sure to have bruises tomorrow, but she could hardly show Angus her thigh.

Niall gave her a malicious smile. "One way or another, ye'll be trained to my hand. 'Twill be up to ye how much pain ye can bear."

Deidre took a deep breath and bared her teeth in what she hoped Angus would take was a smile. "Never," she hissed.

He pinched a little harder and then laughed as he turned his attention to his wine. He drained the cup and poured another. Deidre shuddered to think of what life would be like married to a cruel man doused to his gills in spirits. Well, she would not be here to find out. She would not.

Niall watched as Angus poured whiskey for the three of them in the council room after dinner. Gilead, he noticed, didn't partake. Prick. Sniffing around Deidre's skirts like she was a bitch dog in heat. He'd put a stop to that once they were wed. Pity that

Angus had made him agree to wait on bedding her. Little Miss High-and-Mighty needed a hard rutting to show her a woman's place. He intended to spear her with his cock until she was raw. Until she begged for mercy. But for now he would abide by the pact; it served his other ambitions.

"I'll send the envoy to Gunpar," Angus said as he sipped his whiskey.

Niall snorted. The man was really taking that Briton queen's idea seriously! The idea that a woman knew anything about war strategy was ridiculous. "Ye really think Fergus will take the north way?"

Angus slid a map across the table to him. "It would make sense. If he can reach the eastern shore, we would be fighting on three fronts."

"Nay. 'Tis just like a woman to come up with something like that."

"Formorian, I may remind you, has been battle-trained," Angus said somewhat coldly. "Why would she not understand an army's maneuvering? Turius listens to her. She knows what to do."

Aye. No doubt she knows what to do in yer bedchambers, too. The woman made no attempt to hide her interest. Niall always wondered why Turius overlooked it. He, himself, certainly hadn't, when Rhea had looked longingly on Angus at a feast one night when she'd had a bit of wine. He'd waited until she was stone-cold sober the next morning before he'd whipped her with his leather shaving strap in the privacy of their chambers. His servants knew not to question screams coming from his rooms.

Nay, if Formorian were *his* wife, she'd soon learn where she belonged. She'd be giving him a bairn every year, too. The Briton king was a fool for not keeping his wife pregnant. *That would cool Angus's lust. But, mayhap, I can use his lust against him.*

Niall shrugged and set his empty cup down. "'Tis late and I don't care to argue. Could I be seeing my sweet-intended before I leave?"

"Certes she is already abed at this hour," Gilead said.

Niall raised an eyebrow. "And how would ye be knowing that? Have ye been trying to sample my wares?"

Gilead clenched his fists, but Angus intervened. "My wife retires early and she expects her maids to be in attendance when she rises. I'm afraid ye'll have to wait."

Aye. Wait, Niall thought, as his horse was brought and he and his men started home. *I have waited a long time.* A second son doesn't inherit his father's kingdom and Lugaid always kept his brother, Carlin, too well protected for Niall to try to kill him. Not that Niall hadn't tried. In fact, it was that last fight that had got him sent here. Oh, Lugaid had made it sound like he would be equal to a king in status in this new land, but when he'd arrived, over half the lands his father said were to be his had been confiscated by Angus. No matter that Angus showed him papers with proper title. No doubt they were forged. This land was *his.*

And Elen should have been his. To bind the powerful Mac Erca to him and his father, uniting Eire, and once Mac Erca was dead—not too hard to accomplish by hiring mercenaries—he could have ruled in his place. Timid Elen would never have confronted him on anything.

But Fate had smiled when Deidre played right into his hands. Since Beltane night, when for that brief moment he had felt her under him and almost got his shaft driven home, he'd wanted the little bitch. If that damn, honorable Gilead were more of a cad like his father, Niall would have had her, too. He had become obsessed with seeing her naked, staked out in the bed, his to do with as he pleased, however he pleased. For as long as he pleased.

That she was kin to Angus was a stroke of Eire luck. Binding the clans would only give him more authority to claim the lands when he brought Angus down. *His* lands, he reminded himself. And for his trouble, he'd take all of Angus's remaining lands, too. He would totally and completely destroy Cenel Oengus. Niall smiled. *Oh, yes.*

Chapter Seven

A TANGLED WEB

Nearly a week passed and Niall did not make another appearance. Deidre didn't ask any questions. She was just grateful she didn't have to put up with him at dinner. He turned her appetite with his crude manners.

But she hadn't seen Gilead, either, and she was frustrated, eager to start her riding lessons. How else was she ever going to begin searching for the Stone? The day after their discussion in Elen's chambers, Deidre had waited for Gilead in the stables. She'd even skipped the midday meal, only to find he'd ridden off to check on a crofter that was having trouble with sheep being stolen. The next day he'd gone to Culross to settle a dispute over a game of chance one of their soldiers had engaged in with a villager. On the third day, he had a different excuse, and on the fourth and fifth as well. Deidre had no idea there were so many things that only Gilead could take care of. Well, this was one morning that he wasn't getting away.

"Good morn," she said, stepping out of the empty stall next to Malcolm's as Gilead led the stallion out.

He looked startled and the horse tossed his head. Gilead calmed him by stroking his neck. "What are ye doing here?"

Deidre widened her eyes with a look of pure innocence. "Why . . . you are supposed to be giving me riding lessons, remember?"

"Ah. That. Well, ye see, I need to go—"

"Nowhere," Deidre said sweetly and smiled. "Your father told me he'd send for Formorian if you can't help me."

A muscle twitched in Gilead's jaw as he stared over her head for a moment. Deidre could almost hear him battling with himself over which would be worse . . . having Formorian here or having to work with her himself. Apparently, she was the lesser of the two evils, for he sighed.

"Verra well." He looped Malcolm's reins around a hitching post near the stall. "Let me find ye a gentle nag, then."

Deidre followed him down the row of stalls. She was still angry with him, so why were her knees trembling? And her tummy butterflies all swooshing around erratically? Lord, she had no idea she could still be so intoxicated by him. His legs were encased in soft, doeskin trews that clung to his thigh muscles as he strode swiftly ahead of her. Did the man always move so fast? She could hardly keep up, but then, who was she to complain, with the sight of those tight buttocks shifting with each step? Her anger only seemed to whet her appetite for him. She almost giggled at the apoplectic fit Clotilde would have if she knew her niece was harboring such thoughts, but the woman in Deidre had awakened, and she didn't want to stop.

Engrossed with the fantasy of what he'd look like without the trews on, she ran full into his back when he stopped abruptly in front of a stall. She inhaled the freshly laundered scent of the crisp linen shirt that stretched over his broad shoulders. His back felt like smooth rock.

He jumped at the contact and turned around, looking down at her.

"Ouch," she said and rubbed her nose as she stepped back. "You might warn me when you intend to stop."

He raised an eyebrow. "I thought saying, 'Here we are,' to be enough."

Oh. Whoops. Sometimes her woolgathering did go a bit far.

But it really wasn't her fault; he had a fantastic arse. "Well. Sorry, then."

Gilead nodded and pointed to the stall. "Nell is a wee pony a lot of our bairns have learned to ride on."

Fantastique. A horse that probably wouldn't make it beyond the gates. Deidre stepped past him to look into the compartment. It was empty.

"How wee is this pony?" she asked as she looked up.

Gilead frowned and stepped closer, glancing over her shoulder. His body's heat enveloped her like a warm blanket and she forced herself to stand still. She'd already made a fool of herself once.

He turned and walked away, shouting for a stable hand. Broderick came running from the tack room.

"Aye, my lord? What's amiss?"

"Where have ye taken Nell?" Gilead asked.

"Doona ye remember? Ye said to take the old horses to the higher pastures for the summer, since we wouldn't be needing them."

"All of them?" Gilead asked.

"Aye. We've only the warhorses, the colts, and the brood mares. Why?"

"Mistress Deidre has convinced my father that she wants to learn to ride." Gilead didn't look at her. "She wants to surprise her . . . her fiancé."

Ouch. That hurt. Did he have to be so formal? If only I could tell him why . . . Deidre sighed. He would think her totally mad if she told him about the magician and the Stone, or worse, send her back to Childebert and a life of confirmed spinsterhood.

The Master of Horse was looking at her with interest. "Any chance that ye can persuade Lady Elen to join ye? 'Twould do our lady good to take some fresh air. I can send for a couple of the ponies to be brought down—"

No! That will take too long. She needed to find a circle of stones and she needed a good horse to do it. "Lady Elen is scared of their size," Deidre said apologetically. "Couldn't I ride one of the brood mares?"

"Ye could," Broderick agreed, "were they not either ready to foal or already have the young ones by their teat."

Gilead looked relieved. "Well, then. I guess we'll need to cancel the lesson."

Oh, no, you don't. Ummm. Deidre gave him a sorrowful look, turned, and walked away. She was next to Malcolm before he realized what she was planning to do.

"Wait!" Gilead sprinted after her. "Don't . . ."

But it was too late. Deidre gathered the big destrier's reins and quickly led him to a stoop. She had one foot in the stirrup and was trying to swing a leg over, hindered by the full skirt, when she felt Gilead's strong arm around her waist, lifting her off.

The horse sidled away and Gilead pulled her close. She could feel his chest heaving against her back, and for a moment, he laid his head atop hers and then he stepped away, spinning her around.

"Are ye daft? Malcolm would have tossed ye right out the door and broken half yer bones while he was at it!"

She could see now that the heaving of his chest wasn't due to exertion or concern, but to anger. She lifted her head in defiance. "Then get me a horse I can ride!"

He made a sound that sounded like a Gaelic curse, but she wasn't sure. "There are only warhorses here, trained for battle!"

Deidre shrugged. "Well, then. I guess I could always use the horse Formorian rides. When she comes to give me lessons, that is."

He uttered the same sound, his blue eyes blazing. "Ye are a stubborn lass."

Deidre folded her arms across her chest and tapped her foot.

They stared at each other, engaged in a silent battle of wills. Finally, Gilead gave a big sigh. "All right. If ye are that certain ye must impress Niall." For a moment, a look of hurt crossed his face and then his expression became impassive again. "But if ye break yer neck, doona blame me."

Gilead stomped off and Deidre had to run to keep up with him, not even having time to admire his backside. She didn't dare ask him to slow down; she had just barely managed to hold out on that clash of minds. She was sorry he was angry and even sorrier that he thought she wanted to impress Niall. The man wasn't worth impressing, except with a boot imprint somewhere, maybe.

With all her heart, she wished she could tell Gilead the truth.

Deidre really wants to impress Niall. Gilead pounded his fist on the polished table in his room several hours later. So. He had been wrong about her, after all. Watching how stiffly formal she had been with Niall, Gilead had thought she couldn't possibly have meant what she said to his father. He was almost sure that she cared nothing for Niall, but the only other motive left was greed. How disappointing. Somehow, he hadn't thought Dee—Mistress Deidre—would stoop to that level. Mayhap greed was what her interest in him had been, too. She was penniless. A laird's son had wealth and goods to offer a woman, and a lot of women had tried to latch on.

He sighed, remembering how the soft lushness of her full breasts had felt pressed into his back when she'd run into him. The sly wench probably did it on purpose. But she had felt so good in his arms when he pulled her off Malcolm and held her against him. The faint trace of heather soap had lingered in her hair and he couldn't help burying his nose in the silky strands for just a moment. *Fool.* Why couldn't he stop reacting to her now that he realized she hungered so much for material gain that she would agree to marry Niall?

Mistress Deidre was ambitious enough to rival Formorian. She had almost gotten Gilead wrapped around her delicate, well-cared-for pinky. He'd caught himself in time. He wasn't besotted like his father was. He was not Angus. He would never be like him.

Fergus Mor motioned for his guards to leave and close the door. He poured another whiskey for his guest and slid it across the table in the map room.

"Now what brings ye so close to the Highlands, Niall?"

Niall didn't answer right away, his cold, flinty eyes taking in the trappings. Fergus had done well for himself. Heavy tapestries with intricately woven hunting scenes lined three of the walls. A rock fireplace with a hearth large enough for a man to walk into took up the fourth wall. The heavy oak table was polished to a sheen and the equally solid chairs had thick cushions of leather. A comfortable man's room, and the whiskey was smooth as well.

"I'm waiting." There was mild reproof in Fergus's voice.

"I've come to offer my services," Niall said.

"Why would I be wanting yer service?"

"Word has it that ye are amassing men from Eire and that ye'll be seeking more land soon."

"And if I am?"

"The Angus held a meeting three sennights ago. The lairds of Comgaill and Gabrain were there, as well as the Briton king, Turius."

Fergus pale blue eyes lit up. "Was Queen Formorian with him?"

Niall clenched a fist under the table. What was it with that blasted woman? He wasn't here to discuss her; he had more lucrative matters on his mind.

"Aye." He laughed suddenly. "The land may be yers for the taking, at that, if Angus can't keep his hands off her."

Fergus's bushy red eyebrows knit together in a frown. "That's the way of it? Turius came close to claiming Caledonia once; does Angus think he won't confiscate Oengus if he's provoked?" He leaned back and studied Niall. "Aye. Is that what this is about? Ye think to lose yer lands, too, close as they are?"

"Nay!" Niall fingered his empty glass and looked hopefully at the bottle. "I came to warn ye about the plot."

Fergus straightened. "What plot?"

"The lairds think ye will not raid direct through Comgaill, but that ye are likely to move through Pictland to reach the eastern shore."

"Through Pictland? The painted people care not for intruders."

Niall nodded. "I said that, too, but Turius listens to that fool queen of his."

"This was *Formorian's* idea?" Fergus asked in surprise.

"Aye. Daft woman—"

"Nay. She be not daft. Gabran trained her well. Go on."

"She thinks ye would treaty for passage with the Picts. If ye reach the eastern shore with enough men ye could attack from three directions."

"Hmmm. An interesting idea," Fergus mused.

Niall stared at him. Couldn't anyone but him see the foolishness of listening to a woman? Did every man think with his cock when it came to her? He shook his head. "Angus has already sent an envoy up to ask for King Gunpar's help in staying ye."

"Then what is yer point? I'd not thought to move through Pictland."

"That's just it. They *think*—based on that bit—the queen's idea—that ye will. They plan to align their troops along Pictland's border to wait for ye." Niall leaned forward. "Doona ye see? Send some of yer new men as decoy troops to Pictland to let the lairds think they're right. If the troops die, they die. Comgall's army will not be watching its own borders. The way will be clear for ye to sweep it and invade Oengus." He paused. "Ye will have to pass through my lands, too, but ye'll find the passage clear."

Fergus raised a brow. "Where will Turius be? I have not a death wish to take on the British army, too."

Niall grinned wolfishly. "Think ye Turius would defend the man who cuckolded him?"

"Nay. Can ye prove that, though? Angus canna be such a fool."

"Aye. He can. Ye can trust me to make certes Turius finds out." He eyed the bottle again. "Wouldna ye like claiming Comgaill and Oengus?"

Fergus's eyes glittered. "'Twould be a boon. Mac Erca took my lands in Eire. 'Tis his daughter that is married to Angus." He leveled his gaze on Niall. "What's in it for ye, then?"

"I want the half of Oengus that was promised me by my father. 'Tis all." *No need to let him know the whole truth.* "Ye would have the other half and Comgaill. Together, we could crush Gabrain as well. Everything north of the Wall would be ours."

Fergus unstopped the bottle and poured two whiskies. He lifted one in salute. "We have a pact, then?"

Niall's hand shook as he took his drink. "Aye. A pact," he said and drained the glass. Whiskey had never tasted so good.

Gilead had managed to take himself south to Lothian again, costing Deidre nearly another sennight of instruction. Winger, the sorrel gelding that she'd been given, was a good horse, solid and docile. If only she could just saddle him and ride out! The solstice was approaching. She'd heard Janet and Sheila giggling over "Litha," the festival of fire. Her mother had observed it as well. Held on the summer solstice, it included the symbolic dance of the Oak King taking over the growth of new life, while the Holly King gave up his hold on the past year. Energies would shift on that night and the power in the stone circles would be stronger. She had to find one by then.

She had asked Elen if she knew of any nearby, but Elen rarely left the castle, so she didn't know. Brena had looked at her curiously when she'd asked, but had remained silent. The young maid, Anna, had left the castle to return home and care for younger siblings when her mother became ill. Deidre didn't want to arouse suspicion by asking anyone else.

Gilead had arrived home late last night, and this morning Deidre waited for him impatiently in the barn. When he arrived, he didn't seem particularly surprised to see her.

"Ye'd be wanting yer riding lesson, I suppose?"

He sounded so cold. "Yes. You've kept me waiting a week," Deidre said. "At this rate, I'll never learn to ride."

His face was impassive as he nodded and walked to the stall where the sorrel was stabled. Deidre followed him, wishing she could get him to give her his lopsided grin, or at least, *look* at her.

"Let me saddle him," she said impulsively as he led Winger out.

"Nay. The saddle is too heavy for a wee lass." He spread

the blanket over the charger's back and lifted the saddle off its tree.

"I'm stronger than I look," Deidre said and held out her hands.

"Suit yerself, then," Gilead answered and placed the saddle in her arms.

She staggered under its weight. It was made of solid wood beneath the leather seat and had to weigh near to four stone. Winger stood a good sixteen hands, which meant she'd have to lift the blasted thing over her head. *Merde.* Gilead stood there patiently, watching her. She didn't know what was wrong with him, but she *would* show him she could do this.

Deidre bent one leg and balanced the saddle against her thigh, tossing the cinch and right stirrup leather back and over the seat. With an effort, she got hold of the pommel in one hand and the cantle in the other. She squatted, about to push up, when Winger turned his head, caught the blanket between his teeth, and tossed it to the ground.

"Would ye like me to get that for ye?" Gilead asked languidly.

She glared at him. Did he think she could stand here holding this beastly thing forever? She didn't dare put it down for fear she wouldn't be able to pick it up. She gritted her teeth and forced a smile. "If you don't mind."

He bent over to retrieve the blanket and she thought she saw the corner of his mouth draw up. So now he was laughing at her? She saw nothing amusing in trying to be helpful.

Gilead smoothed the blanket over the horse's withers with agonizing slowness. "Ye must always be careful the pad is smooth," he said as he adjusted the corners carefully. "Otherwise it irritates the horse."

Like *he* wasn't irritating her? First the aloofness and now condescension? *Just look at that mocking expression on his face!* "I know that," she huffed out, short of breath. "Now please stand aside."

Gilead bowed slightly and stepped back. With a supreme effort, she hoisted what felt like a couple of bags of sodden peat up and over Winger's back. She almost made it. The saddle was half on and she braced it with her shoulder, but the gelding sidled away.

"Hell's fire and damnation!" she said and then found herself trapped between the horse and Gilead as he brought his arms around her to lift the saddle and settle it easily. Enclosed in his spicy scent, mingled with the smell of horse and leather, her blood heated and sent waves of pulsation racing deep into her groin.

Gilead's chest brushed her back as he reached around her to throw the cinch and stirrup over. Her nipples budded instantly at the slight touch of hard muscle and she fought the desire to turn around and press herself against him.

He placed his hands on her shoulders and she closed her eyes, hoping he would run those strong, warm fingers down her arms or dip his head and nibble her nape. *Mon Dieu,* she loved that! Involuntarily, she tilted her head a little, giving him access.

She felt him hesitate, his breath warm on her neck. Then, abruptly, he lifted her like a bag of feathers and set her aside. Silently, he finished saddling the horse and handed her the reins.

"I didna know a lady to curse so," he said as he looked into her eyes. "Is it the way of things in Armorica?"

Amorica? Oh, yes. Where I'm from. "Ummm. Yes, as a matter of fact. We do have that freedom."

He arched an eyebrow. "A lady does not, I think. Where did ye say ye lived?"

Deidre squirmed. Gilead had asked other questions about her past, but she had always managed to hedge them with vague answers. Now he wanted a place. "Benoic," she said quickly and then groaned inwardly. In The Book, it was Lancelot's home. Only it probably didn't exist, either.

Gilead looked confused. "Where exactly is that?"

She sincerely hoped that whoever had written the stories had based the legends on some sort of fact. "Just on the edge of Brocéliande."

"The dark forest?" he asked with narrowed eyes. "And is that where yer mother was killed?"

"Ah, yes. She fell into the lake and drowned." Part of that was true. Her mother *had* drowned. *I'm not good at this lying.*

Before he could ask any more questions she turned and walked toward the mounting stoop.

"Are we going to get on with the lesson? I really do want to learn."

Gilead's expression hardened. "Certes. I had forgotten that ye are most eager to impress your betrothed."

Deidre bit her lip as she walked Winger over to the corral that served as a paddock. Better that Gilead should think that than ask her any more questions. She was spinning a web like the proverbial spider, only she felt as though she was the fly.

Gilead was not in the best of moods. After their riding lesson—at which Dee seemed very adept, and he was beginning to wonder about that—he'd taken Malcolm out for a hard gallop. Feeling the strength of the huge horse under him, his powerful haunch muscles bunching as his legs stretched flat out, always soothed Gilead. The wind whipping, the course mane stinging his face as he leaned low, served as a wake-up call.

He'd almost let himself become a fool again. What was it about the wee blond lass that stirred his blood so? He had only meant to catch the saddle before it spooked Winger and yet, her body had felt so yielding, so soft, when he enveloped her. And he could have sworn she was waiting for a kiss. The temptation to succumb, to brush his lips across the smooth skin of her neck, to run his tongue over the sensitive hollow below her ear, was overwhelming. He'd felt her tense, knew she wanted him to do just that. But she also wanted to impress Niall. God help him, he'd never understand why.

What kind of games was she playing? He was pretty sure she was lying about her past. Today's hesitation over the place called Benoic only strengthened that theory. What the bonny lass didn't know was that his father's mother lived in the dark forest, at the very edge of the Black Lake itself. She would know if someone had drowned there. On the morrow, he would send an emissary to find out. He should have done it before, but in truth he had wanted to believe Deidre. The alternative, that she might be a Saxon spy, made him shudder. His father would have no mercy if she were.

Gilead's mood did not get any better at dinner when he found out that Niall had arrived. He scowled as the man took a seat next to Deidre.

"Our envoy has returned," Angus said, as the servants set down the heavy platters of roast boar and steaming bowls of sauces and gravies.

Niall looked up from his plate, juice dripping off his fingers. "Aye? And what did Gunpar have to say?"

"He's given us permission to amass at his borders, but not cross them," Angus answered, "and he's agreed to block any passage that Fergus may make."

"Hmmm. And what if Fergus offers him money?"

"The Picts care nothing for coin. They barter." Gilead said. "Sheep would be more to their liking."

Niall looked thoughtful. "Then do ye think Fergus will still attempt to do as the queen suggested?"

Angus gave him a hard look. "I do not think we can afford to ignore that risk. I've sent for Turius's relay runners to keep us posted."

"Relay runners?" Niall asked casually.

Gilead lifted his head. Did Niall seem overly interested? "Aye. Ye know they're very effective. Faster than our own scouts."

"What are relay runners?" Deidre asked.

"Turius posts a well-trained man every five leagues or so between his headquarters and the place he wants to watch," Gilead answered. "They're lightly armed and ride smaller, swift horses. The first rider hands off his message to the one waiting with a fresh horse at the next post. We will know within a day and night's time if Fergus moves."

"Gunpar also mentioned that longboats had been sighted on the horizon," Angus said. "Turius thought it might be wise if he positioned some of his troops to watch our eastern shore for Saxons while we are away in the North." He glanced toward Elen. "He and Formorian should be arriving within a few days."

She turned pale and quickly reached for her wine. Gilead

groaned. An extended stay from that huntress his mother didn't need, and he would, no doubt, exhaust himself keeping an eye on his libidinous father.

His mood blackened further when he noticed that Niall was running his fingers up Deidre's arm. He thought he saw her flinch, but then she caught him looking at her. She smiled at Niall as she withdrew her hand and reached for her wine. She *smiled* at him.

Bloody hell.

Deidre watched the Briton king and queen's arrival two days later from Elen's chambers, nervous that Turius might have found out who she was. But none of her escort was with him and she thought he might have brought them if the truth had come out.

Even from this distance, she could see Angus's hand linger on Formorian's arm as he helped her dismount. Deidre had serious doubts that the woman needed any help dismounting, trained for battle as she supposedly was, but no one would know by looking at how she slowly slithered down the front of him. Her horse shielded her from Turius's sight, but he wasn't paying attention anyway, already engrossed in conversation with Gilead.

She heard Elen's barely audible sigh and turned her attention away from the scene below. Poor lady. How she managed to find inner strength enough to maintain a gracious façade, Deidre didn't know. To have her husband practically flaunt his interest in Formorian was humiliating enough, but Deidre knew that Elen still loved Angus. How absolutely heart-wrenching that must be. And now, Turius and his beguiling queen would be here for weeks. Maybe months.

"You mustn't fret, Lady Elen. You'll only make yourself ill," Deidre said gently and led her away from the window.

Elen sank into her chair, seeming to fold into herself like a sack of squashed feathers. "I suppose 'tis no more than I deserve."

"Deserve?" Deidre could hardly conceal her outrage. "You deserve to be treated much better! Your husband—and I don't care if he *is* the laird—should show you some respect and contain himself."

Elen patted her hand. "Dear child. It would not change how he feels."

"Still," Deidre said stubbornly, "he married you, didn't he? He must care for you. You're the mother of his child."

"That, I am." Elen managed a weak smile. "It's probably the only reason my husband doesn't hate me."

"Hate you? Why should he hate you?"

"I did a bad thing. I was young and foolish and Angus paid the price for it." Elen looked up at Deidre. "There is honor in the man, child. Please believe that."

Deidre squelched an unladylike snort, but held her peace. Whatever Lady Elen had done, she had the refined class to act like a real lady. Too bad Angus couldn't act like a true knight.

Bah. There she was, still hoping for chivalry. Lady Elen was married to a man who didn't love her and Deidre was desperately trying to avoid another loveless marriage. Time to stop daydreaming and face reality. No courtly hero was going to ride in and rescue either one of them.

Gilead heaved a sigh of relief as he sat down at the high table for dinner that evening. He had managed to seat Formorian between Turius and Niall. She would, no doubt, take her hidden irritation of Gilead's maneuvering out on Niall, which suited Gilead even better. Check and checkmate. In a pique of almost childish delight, he had managed to seat a loathly matron on Niall's other side.

They were waiting on Elen's arrival to begin serving the meal. His mother had stayed withdrawn most of the day with Dee—Mistress Deidre, he reminded himself—in attendance. Whatever schemes the wee blond lass harbored, he had to admit that she was good for his mother.

His thoughts were interrupted by a shriek, followed by a scream and something clattering down the stairs in the hallway behind the dining area. He jumped to his feet as a breathless Deidre rushed through the door.

"Come quick!" she said. "Lady Elen has fallen down the stairs!"

Gilead reached his mother first. She lay in a crumpled heap at the foot of the stairs, moaning softly, her left leg drawn up under her.

He checked his mother for broken bones. Her ankle was already swelling, but it appeared to be sprained, not broken. As he started to pick her up, he noticed Deidre on the stairs above him.

"What are ye doing?" he asked.

For a moment, Deidre didn't answer and only ran her fingers along the side of the woven cloth that had been attached to the steps. When she finally looked at him, her eyes were clouded with worry.

"The rug was loose on this step. Your mother hooked a slipper on it."

"I'll have it repaired at once," Angus said and nodded toward Gilead. "Take yer mother to her chambers and I'll send for the medic." Turning, he cleared the hallway of onlookers. Formorian looked curiously up at him and then she, too, moved away.

Deidre was still sitting on the step. Gilead shifted his mother in his arms. "What is it now, lass?"

"It was deliberate," she whispered hoarsely. "The nails are nowhere to be found and the wood is fresh around the holes." She tugged the rug up, revealing a big slash in the middle. "Someone wanted your mother dead."

Chapter Eight

THE RIDE

"What do you mean, deliberate?" Angus narrowed his eyes as he looked up at Deidre from behind the table that served as a desk in the map room.

Deidre had just come from making sure Elen was settled for the evening. The medic had wrapped Elen's ankle in linen swaddling soaked in hot chamomile tea and Brena brought a sleeping concoction, laced with a wee bit of motherswort, the healer had said.

Deidre glanced at Gilead, seated across from his father. "That tear was not there yesterday."

"How can ye be so sure of that? 'Twould be an easy thing to miss in worn cloth. Angus scribbled a note to himself on a bit of vellum. "I'll have it replaced."

Deidre shook her head. "I know for certain. Lady Elen lost a small stone from her brooch yesterday afternoon when her cloak snagged on the railing. She sent me to look for it. I covered every single stair. There was no tear."

"Even so. Anyone could have tripped. What makes ye think someone wants to murder my wife?"

"Well, there was that poisoning attempt," Deidre said.

Angus raised an eyebrow. "If I remember, ye thought there

was something wrong with the wine I poured. Did I slash the rug, too?"

Deidre bit her lip. Would Gilead's father actually try to kill his own wife?

Angus obviously took her silence as an accusation, for he threw the quill down and rose angrily. "Bel's fires! I should have ye put in the dungeon." He gave her a disgusted look and then turned to Gilead. "See if ye can talk some sense into the lass before I do just that." He stomped to the door, slamming it hard behind him.

Gilead took a deep breath. "I should warn ye, my Da keeps his word. Ye'd most likely catch yer death in the damp and cold, if the rats didn't bite ye first."

Deidre shuddered. Dungeons they had; chivalrous champions they did not. From the impassive look on Gilead's face, he would not rescue her again. Did she dare risk his anger, too? Still, she had to ask.

"Do you think your father capable of murder?"

He stared at the glowing coals in the brazier for a long time before answering. "Certes, my father has killed in battle. The clans live by the sword. I don't think he would commit murder. What would his purpose be? Formorian is not free to go to him. It's much safer for my father to hide behind his marriage and not arouse Turius's suspicions any further than they may already be."

Strangely, Deidre felt relieved by that. She really didn't want Gilead's father to turn out to be a deliberate killer. "I owe him an apology, then."

Gilead looked relieved. "Aye. That would be a start."

Another thought burst into her brain. "What about Formorian, though?"

Gilead frowned. "What about her?"

"She was here when your mother was poisoned. She arrived yesterday. And didn't you say that your mother had her first illness strike just after Turius and Formorian had arrived that day two years ago?"

"Aye," Gilead answered thoughtfully.

Deidre pressed on. "The queen carries a dirk; it wouldn't have taken much time to rent the carpet and pull the nails. You said yourself that she is stronger than she looks."

"That I did." He toyed with the quill his father had tossed

down and sighed. "I've tried to keep them apart by trailing my father. Perhaps I should be following her."

Deidre couldn't help but smile. "She'd probably think you another conquest."

Gilead grimaced. "Hardly. But it would rouse my Da's suspicions, I suppose."

"Then let me follow her," Deidre said. "I'll befriend her as a way of apology to your father. It'll be a way to watch her and keep her away from your mother as well."

He nodded and rose, coming to stand beside her. He touched her shoulder briefly. "I should thank ye for being so concerned over my mother."

Her resident butterflies fluttered all atwitter as that slight touch sent quivers straight to her tummy. She took a ragged breath. The touch meant nothing to him, just a friendly gesture, perhaps a way of his apologizing to her for being so cold. Her reaction—wanting him to tear her clothes off right there—was unwarranted.

"Ye don't want Da to wonder about ye, either. What will ye say to him?"

Deidre thought about it. So far, Turius seemed not to have mentioned capturing her escort—or if he did, Angus had not connected the two incidents—and Deidre didn't want to attract too much attraction to herself. The obvious answer was to let Formorian take over the riding lessons, but that meant Gilead would probably disappear off the horizon for her. And, as much as the attraction was one-sided, as far as she could tell, the foolish romantic in her didn't want to let go. At least, if he continued to give her lessons, she could look and fantasize.

"I'll tell him I admire her talents and skills and want to learn from her."

Gilead gave her a lopsided grin. "To my father, her numerous 'talents and skills' lie in the art of seduction."

"There's an idea," Deidre quipped and then felt herself blush. She had been thinking of weaponry, but maybe if she observed the queen she'd find the secret of her ability to enchant men. And maybe it would work on Gilead. . . . She closed her eyes, only to have a searing image of a naked Gilead rising over her, muscular arms straining, chest glistening with sweat . . . and that bulge. What did Gilead look like *there?* She gasped, her breath catching in her throat—dear Lord, what was she thinking?—and forced her eyes open.

He had moved closer. Subtly his face changed as he studied hers. His pupils dilated, turning the irises near purple. Slowly a hand came up to cup her chin and he traced her lips lightly with his thumb.

"Ye want to be kissed, lass?" It really wasn't so much a question as a statement.

Dear God. She shouldn't. He had made it clear with his strict formality that he didn't want to have anything to do with her. This would mean nothing to him. She should pull away; she really should. He wasn't holding her forcefully, but the gentle touch of his fingers might as well have been an iron collar. Deidre shut her eyes and parted her lips.

She heard his sharp intake of breath and then his lips brushed hers, tantalizing her as he kept the pressure easy and gentle. It was slow torture, and finally she could stand no more. She thrust her tongue deep into his mouth.

He hesitated but a moment and then brought his arms around her waist, pulling her to him as he responded, probing her mouth. Then, abruptly, he pulled away.

Startled, Deidre's eyes flew open. Gilead looked furious.

"Mayhap ye and Formorian are a pair. Ye think to entice me for sport? As a wanton would practice, so ye'll please Niall? Or mayhap to make him jealous?"

Deidre felt like a bucket of frigid water from the fort's well has just been sluiced over her. Make Niall jealous? *Kiss* him? She would have laughed if every nerve in her body had not been benumbed by Gilead's outrageous accusation. Then, a raging heat melted the ice in her blood as anger and hurt took over. How dare he accuse her of being a slut?

She felt the tears well up, stinging her eyes. She would *not* let him see her cry! Pressing the knuckles of her hand against her mouth, she turned and ran out the door, slamming it behind her.

Deidre found Formorian waiting for her the next afternoon by the stables, dressed in trews and an oversized shirt, a dirk

in her belt, and a sword by her side. Somehow she managed
to look female in spite of the clothes and weapons.

"Angus told me that ye talked with him this morning. That
mayhap I could give ye a few tips on riding?"

Deidre nodded, her eyes searching for Gilead. He probably wouldn't show, not after their conversation. Better that
way, after all. She was still angry with him.

"He went to get yer horse," Formorian said drily.

Deidre feigned indifference. "Who?"

The queen arched a delicate brow just as Gilead led Winger
into the paddock. Deidre avoided looking at him, studiously
studying the horse. She ran a hand along the sorrel's neck and
spoke soothingly to him. He nickered softly in response.
Maybe she should stick with talking to male horses and let
the human ones alone, she thought dejectedly.

Gilead handed her the reins and their fingers brushed as
she took them. Both of them jumped back as though they'd
been bitten. Winger shied away, tossing his head and pulling
free of Deidre's hand.

"Easy there," Gilead said as he grabbed the straps before
the big horse could bolt. "The lass doona understand to move
slow around ye."

Deidre glared at him. He had jumped, too. She snatched
the reins from him and turned to lead the horse to the stoop.
It wasn't there. Now, how the devil was she supposed to
mount in full skirts?

And Formorian was watching. Out of the corner of her eye,
Deidre could see her standing by the fence, arms folded along
the top rail, her head tilted slightly, a partial smile on her lips.
Merde. Trying to keep the queen away from Elen was one
thing, but Deidre would find her insufferable if she started
laughing.

"Are ye not going to mount, Mistress Deidre? 'Twould
make the lesson easier," Gilead said with strained patience.

Deidre glowered. "If you would be so kind as to fetch the
stoop, my lord, I shall be happy to do so." She ignored his
surprised look. Fine. If he wanted formal, she could do
formal. She tapped her foot.

He said nothing, but went into the barn and returned,

rolling the tree stump in front of him. He set it upright and gave a slight bow. "Do ye need assistance?"

"I can manage quite well, thank you." Deidre stepped up and got her balance before putting her left foot in the stirrup. The blasted skirt billowed around her knees, making her feel clumsy. She tightened the right rein, holding the horse in check. She wasn't going to disgrace herself mounting this time, not with Formorian watching. She swung her leg over the saddle and, to her mortification, heard a rip that sounded like rolling thunder.

The skirt had caught on the rough bark of the stump's rim and now half of it billowed around her like a dense cloud, baring her well to the thigh. Gilead stared at her leg and then she saw him frown. What? Did he think she'd done this on purpose? That she was trying to lure him to her by exposing flesh? Angrily, she tried to gather the ballooning material. As if she would stoop to a Janet tactic!

"Mayhap ye should wear trews for this," Formorian suggested as she opened the gate and came toward them. She glanced at Gilead. "Are ye just going to stand there? Help the woman dismount."

He moved stiffly forward and Deidre willed herself not to react when she felt his big, strong hands at her waist, lifting her as though she were light as a pillow. For a brief moment she was pressed to his chest and inhaled his soapy, spicy scent, but he stepped quickly back once her feet were on the ground, as formal as ever. Formorian gave him a curious look.

"Wait here," she said to Gilead. "I'll lend Deidre some trews and then we'll go for a real ride, instead of prancing around in circles."

He opened his mouth to retort, but she had already turned away. The last thing Deidre wanted to do was borrow clothes from Angus's leman, but she had promised Gilead that she would help protect his mother. She would stick to that promise and that meant being friendly to Formorian.

Gilead had Malcolm and Formorian's white Arabian mare saddled when they returned a short time later. The trews really did feel good, freeing her legs of those cumbersome skirts. Formorian was tall and slender where Deidre was short and curvy, so she'd had to roll up the legs, but the buttery soft leather clung to her, hugging her hips and thighs.

Gilead stared at her and then quickly averted his gaze. He cupped his hands to give her a leg up. For a moment, she almost refused. He probably just wanted to see her rear end when she turned. Well, let him. She might as well enjoy what little sexual power she had, not that it was going anywhere.

Formorian mounted with graceful ease, fitting herself into the saddle even as the mare spun, eager to be off.

"Have a care," Gilead said gruffly as the horse pranced in place. "Dee—Mistress Deidre—be a beginner."

"Aye. I always walk the first mile out and the last mile in. Unless," she added with a mischievous grin, "I'm under attack by unscrupulous men."

Gilead grunted. "I dinna ken ye thought any man unscrupulous."

Deidre cringed, waiting for a sharp retort. Gilead might not like the queen, but insulting her might not be the wisest thing to do.

Formorian laughed. "Ye think to wound me with that barb? Ah, lad, ye misjudge me based on yer own misconceptions." She turned to Deidre. "I canna teach ye anything at a slow walk. Are ye game for a run?"

Deidre managed to hide her own grin. She'd been wanting to feel this charger's power under her since the first day. She looked appropriately apprehensive, however, as she gulped and nodded.

"Good. We'll start with a sharp trot," Formorian said and touched her heels to her horse's flanks.

Winger, being a good hand-and-a-half higher than the dainty mare, jogged along contentedly. Deidre made an effort to bounce around so she wouldn't raise suspicion and only hoped the poor animal would forgive her.

"I've not been off the castle grounds," she said between bumps. "Are there other castles or ruins or anything?"

Formorian furrowed her brow. "Ye have not been to Niall's place yet?"

"No." Not that it was a place she wanted to see or ever intended to go to.

"We could ride that way," Formorian said. "It's but two leagues in that direction." She pointed toward their left.

"Not today," Deidre said quickly. She would be seeing Niall at dinner tonight, unfortunately. He'd invited himself, stating some sort of business with Angus. Not that she listened to him prattling on. She pointed right. "What's in that direction?"

Formorian shrugged. "Woods. Streams. Probably a good place to avoid unless ye have a well-armed guard." She winked. "Or unless ye want to meet unscrupulous men."

Behind them, Deidre heard Gilead snort. If they were to succeed in protecting Elen from Formorian, he really needed to stop being churlish. She glanced back at him, only to find him glowering frightfully at both of them. She shook her head slightly and turned around. She might as well make use of the situation to see if there was a place the Stone might be.

"Would there be any ancient relics around? Historical ruins? Standing circles of stone maybe?"

Formorian gave her a slanted look. "Ye mean like the priestesses use in their rituals on High Days?" When Deidre nodded, Formorian considered her thoughtfully. Finally she said, "'Tis strange. When Turius and I returned home, we found we had . . . er, guests . . . from Gaul. They asked the same question."

Her escort! The men had not been killed. Careful to sound nonchalant, Deidre asked, "Why would Franks be this far north?"

Formorian shrugged, but her eyes never wavered from Deidre's. "They said Childebert had sent them looking for Bishop Dubricius's cup."

Deidre stymied the sigh of relief. Her loyal guards had not given her away! Were they even now looking for her? "Did your husband allow them to search for it?"

Formorian shook her head. "Turius thinks the cup exists only in the bishop's dreams. And he was not fond of the idea of allowing Frankish soldiers to roam and get the lay of the land. We never know who might be a spy."

Deidre ignored the comment, although she saw Gilead glance her way. She had to ask one more question, though. "Did . . . did King Turius kill them?"

Formorian gave her another thoughtful look. "Nay. He offered them the dungeon or escorted passage to the docks. They really dinna want to go, but eventually they took the ship to Calais."

Deidre took a deep breath. Dion and her men were safe then, although they would not be able to return to Childebert's court without her. Deidre's mother had lands in the Languedoc, well away from Childebert's clutches. Dion would go there, no doubt. They'd probably try to send word to Caw, but her father was dead. A small chill ran through her as she realized that she was truly alone now. "That was kind of the king," she managed to say.

"Aye. Turius sees no point in shedding blood needlessly. To answer yer question, though . . . There be a circle, but to get to it and return home before Angus sounds an alarm, ye'd have to gallop that brute."

"I don't think that's a good idea," Gilead said as he rode alongside.

Deidre ignored him. "Show me the way," she said.

Formorian grinned and leaned over and whispered in her mare's ear. The horse took a huge leap and stretched out in a full gallop. Winger didn't wait to be prodded.

Behind her, Deidre heard a muffled Gaelic curse and then the pounding of Malcolm's hooves as he strove to overtake them.

Deidre could hardly conceal her excitement that evening during supper. The stones existed and they were within a few hours' ride! She wished there had been time to go down into the valley where they stood, but Formorian had stopped on a hilltop some distance away to rest the horses, and Gilead had been firm that they were turning around and heading home. Nothing Deidre could say would sway his mind. He was as obstinate as his father, but at least now she knew where the circle was.

She relaxed and noticed for the first time that Drustan was not in his usual place. Instead a visiting bard was strumming his harp, and telling stories of his travels throughout Britain and across the Channel. An idea began to form in Deidre's head. If the bard were to return to Gaul soon, maybe she could slip him a note to take to Dion, to let him know she was well.

"Ye have a dreamy look in yer eyes this eve," Niall said beside her at the table. "Could ye be thinkin' o' our wedding night?"

Not hardly. Not now with the possibility of finding the Stone and leaving. Still, she must keep up the charade so she wouldn't lose access to the horse. She'd caught Formorian watching her more than once during the meal and she had a hunch the queen didn't miss much. If Formorian suspected anything, she might tell Angus about their conversation today. Deidre planted a smile on her face. "I might have a surprise for you by then."

Niall leaned forward, a lecherous smile twisting his face. "Would it have to do with pleasing me between the sheets?"

Mon Dieu. The very thought was repulsive; the man's breath was fetid and his body soft and fat with too much drink. "You'll have to wait and see."

Apparently he thought that meant "yes," since his chest expanded visibly and he smiled broadly.

"Let's have a wee dance, then!"

"Ah, no. I'm really tired," Deidre said quickly. "In fact, I was about to ask that I be excused to retire."

"No such thing!" Niall pushed back his chair and yanked her out of hers, his fingers around her arm in a death grip. "We will dance."

Deidre held on to the back of her chair and glared at him. "I don't want to."

He narrowed his eyes. "I do." He jerked her hand loose of the chair and brought an arm around her waist, strongholding her to the cleared floor.

He held her much too close and Deidre struggled to gain some space between them. She saw amused looks from some of the men who danced by with ladies held at an appropriate distance. Damn them all. Would no one cut in and rescue her from this ogre? Probably not, since they were handfasted. She glanced at the high table. Gilead had escorted his mother upstairs and she doubted that he would interfere again, anyway. Angus was involved in a discussion with Turius. Only Formorian was watching, her green eyes slightly narrowed.

"I want ye closer, lass." Niall's arm tightened around her waist, drawing her toward him.

She tried to push away. "No! Release me."

His fingers bit into sensitive skin just below her ribs. "Nay."

She felt his shaft harden against her stomach. To hell with decorum. She'd find another way to get the horse. Deidre brought her knee up.

He'd anticipated that, and, for all his weight, was surprisingly agile. He turned and thrust his hip into her, the handle of the dirk he wore on his belt jabbing sharply into the soft flesh of her abdomen.

Deidre nearly doubled over from the pain, a wave of nausea descending on her.

Niall laughed as she landed against him. "Aye, now, lassie. Isna this better?" He crunched her fingers in his big paw. "Tell me ye like it."

She swallowed the rising bile and tried not to cry out. He held her too tight for another try at his groin and she couldn't slide her foot down his instep the way the stable lads had taught her to do. His boots were too sturdy. He squeezed tighter and she gave a slight gasp. The bloody fool was going to crush her ribs if she didn't say it.

"I . . . like . . . it," she rasped through clenched teeth.

Niall spun her around and relaxed his hold on her hand. "The sooner ye learn to obey me, lass, the easier things will go." Deidre glared at him and he laughed. "Aye. If ye want to fight me, I'll enjoy the breaking of ye." He smiled as the music stopped and stepped back to bow formally, but his eyes were hard and cold. "Either way, ye *will* be attending to my pleasure, however and whenever I tell ye."

Deidre stroked her sore hand, realizing that to argue the point would be stupid. The man was sadistic, but he took care to hide it. Bruised ribs would heal. No one watching would have seen the cruelty; it was too subtle. Gilead actually thought she wanted this man! She felt tears welling up and fought them. Even if Angus would believe her accusations, which she doubted, he would not risk alienating Niall.

She would not allow this man to take her. Even though she felt the cold blade of fear pierce her, another part of her brain detached itself. She was sure being bedded by Gilead would be beyond her wildest fantasies, and by Niall, nothing less than brutal rape. Strange that such an act could either take a person to heaven or straight to the Christians' hell.

She prayed that the Old Power still lingered in the standing stones, for it was her only hope. The solstice was next week and she would need a horse for that. Deidre took a deep breath and smiled at Niall.

"Whatever you say, my lord."

As soon as she was able to detach herself from Niall, Deidre went to the solarium, where she knew Angus kept parchment and quill. The large windows that let in the sun's warmth during the day were pitch tonight, since there was no moon. Only a few embers still glowed in the brazier, but it was enough for her to make her way to the desk. Quickly, she penned a note to Dion saying she was visiting the laird at Cenel Oengus and she would continue onward toward her destination. Dion would know what she meant.

She approached the hall carefully, keeping to the back wall until she could see that Niall was no longer present. Then she realized that the bard was no longer playing and her gaze swept the room anxiously, only to find him standing near to where a serving wench was pouring tankards of ale.

Quickly, she made her way toward him. He arched an eyebrow and grinned when she asked if she could see him alone, but his face turned serious when she pressed the note along with several silver coins from the bag she had won into his hand.

"It's important to me that the man receive this," she said.

The bard slipped the note and coins into his sporran. "It will be done."

She nodded gratefully and moved away, unaware that Angus stood in the shadows not far away.

Angus awakened immediately at the slight sound on the other side of his door. Nothing more than a light scratch and then the latch slowly lifted. His hand found his dirk lying on the floor beside him. He eased it under the covers and lay perfectly still, feigning sleep.

The figure slipped silently into the moonlit room and he heard the door close quietly. The bolt slid in place with a muffled click. The figure paused, adjusting to the light, and then padded quietly toward the bed. Angus watched from beneath nearly closed lids and made a small snoring noise.

The person leaned over the bed and laid a firm hand on his cock.

"I know yer not sleeping," Formorian said.

In one fluid movement, Angus pushed back the sheet, pulled Formorian down and then rolled over on top of her, his hands fisting her hair.

"Ye might have gotten yerself killed," he said as he hastily undid the laces at the front of her shift.

"Doona tell me ye weren't expecting me." She laughed as she wrapped her legs around his. "Else why would ye be lying here, naked and hard?"

He growled and took an exposed breast into his mouth, his tongue circling the soft flesh before flicking across the hard nipple.

Formorian arched her back and ran her fingers through his thick hair, pressing his head to her. Angus began to suckle hungrily and she moaned softly.

His large hands slid down her ribs and under her back, lifting her hips to accommodate him. "Do ye want slow and easy or fast and hard?"

Her eyes glittered in the pale light. "Deep. To the hilt."

Angus plunged into her, feeling the hot tightness of her sheath encasing him even as he withdrew and thrust again, grinding his hips into hers. Formorian bucked wildly under him, her legs locked around his waist, urging his penetration still deeper. Her fingernails raked the straining muscles of his back as he rammed himself into her again and again. She bit back her cry as her entire body convulsed in spasm after spasm. Angus gave a great shudder and she felt him explode inside her.

They lay quietly panting for several moments, Angus still buried inside her.

"Yer son suspects me of harming Elen, ye know," Formorian said into his ear.

Angus lifted his head. "Och. The wee lass he brought home suspects me, too."

There was amusement in her voice. "Did we do it?"

Angus grunted and slowly withdrew from her, lying on his side. He propped himself up on an elbow. "Nay. 'Tis no need. We took the sacred blood vows a long time ago. The Old Ways are more binding than anything the priests mumble about."

"Aye." Formorian brushed his hair back gently. "Bound for eternity, one soul not complete without the other."

He caught her hand and kissed the fingertips. "Are ye ever sorry ye made the pact? 'Tis why there is no happiness for ye with Turius."

"Nay. Never sorry. I love ye, Angus."

"And I love ye, Mori. In this world and the next. Ye be my true mate." He leaned over to kiss her forehead and then stopped. "Ye are frowning."

"Sorry. I was thinking."

Angus raised a brow. "What ye think about in bed usually brings a smile to yer face . . . and mine, as well."

Formorian nodded. "It should. I doona think the lass, Deidre, will fare as well."

A trace of annoyance crossed his face. "Fash not. The lass may not lust after Niall, but his title and wealth should bring her comfort."

"Ye know that isna true. I have both."

"Because we took the vow, Mori, in the stone circle. Bonny Deidre has done no such thing."

"The stones. Funny thing. Deidre asked about that today."

Angus stopped playing with a ringlet of her hair. "Why?"

Formorian shrugged. "She was asking about the countryside. What lay in each direction, if there were other castles or ruins or standing stones. We rode to the hilltop only, for Gilead was in a hurry to return."

"They did not enter the circle then?"

"Nay."

He breathed a sigh of relief. "Good. She must be kept away

from it." Then his brow furrowed. "Why were ye riding that far? She's naught but a beginner."

Formorian smiled. "Is that what she told ye?"

His frown deepened. "She said she wanted to learn to ride to please Niall. It was to be a surprise."

She burst into laughter. "To please Niall? Hardly."

"I doona like to be misled. Why would the lass pretend to need riding lessons if she knew how to ride?"

"Oh, stop glowering. Think. To spend time with Gilead, most like."

"She be handfasted to Niall."

"Niall is an oaf. Your son, for all of his honorable intentions, attracts women like the Horned God himself."

"I doona think my son would care to be compared to Cernunnos," Angus said drily, the thunderous look on his face vanishing.

"Mayhap not," Formorion answered impishly, "but he might learn from his father. Have I not told ye a thousand times ye would put even the god of the wild hunt to shame with yer skills?"

Angus grinned and traced her lips with a finger. "Come here then, wench."

Formorian gave his shoulder a little push, flipping him onto his back. She rolled between his legs and then slid her body slowly upward the length of his, flesh on flesh, her breasts pressed against his chest.

"As ye wish, my lord. As ye wish."

A fleeting thought brushed Angus just as Formorian's tongue assaulted his mouth. If the Breton lass were a spy, she would need access to a horse. Angus had been a fool.

No one made a fool of him.

But for now, there was only Mori.

Chapter Nine

THE SOLSTICE

"I doona like being made a fool of!" Angus thundered at Gilead the next morning in the solarium.

Gilead set down the cup of goat's milk he'd brought with him. "I doona like being made a fool of either, Da! I dinna know the lass could ride."

His father stared at him. "Ye have been giving her lessons, have ye not?"

Gilead bit his lip. In truth, he had been more interested in watching her rounded arse bounce up and down. Even now, as furious as his father was with him, he kept returning to that stolen kiss, savoring the softness of her as he held her in his arms, feeling the warm fullness of her lips, tasting her probing tongue . . . she didn't act like an innocent maid; she'd known what she wanted. He squared his shoulders. Who was she, really? Why had she come here?

"I kept the lessons to a walk and trot within the fence," he said, "and Winger is fifteen years, a solid, tolerant horse."

"Bah!" Angus reached for the watered wine and poured some into a goblet. "Ye are a horseman! Ye should have been able to tell. Formorian did."

Only because Formorian went galloping off recklessly, not

caring whether Dee could ride. He wondered when the queen had told his father.

"Are ye that besotted with the lass, son?"

"Nay," Gilead denied. "I told ye before."

"Ye did." Angus looked at him suspiciously. "I won't risk making an enemy of Niall. Not now. Fergus is bound to make his move as soon as his crops are in. I would say, just past the solstice. We need Niall's alliance."

Gilead sighed. He'd heard all this before. He knew his father was right. The alliance was needed. He wouldn't play with fire like his father did. Best just to stay away from the wily lass. Yes, that was it. Cancel the lessons; they were obviously not needed. And, for certes, he didn't need to see her in those trews again. By the Dagda! Every line of her form could be seen, plain as if she wore nothing at all. He was just thankful Niall hadn't been anywhere near.

"Are ye listening?"

Gilead's head snapped up. "I'm sorry, Da."

His father gave an exasperated snort. "I was saying that, in all probability, we have a Saxon spy in our midst. Remember the longboats that have been spotted along the coast?"

Dee, a spy? Mother likes her. She couldn't be. "I doona think so, Da."

Angus began to pace. "Think. Ye 'found' her on Beltane, with no coin nor baggage. Her accent is strange. How did she get here? I had the area searched. There were no reports of attacks by bandits or highwaymen within five leagues. No trace of a broken carriage. No fresh corpses. The lass couldn't have walked more than two or three leagues without her slippers wearing out." He paused. "And she slipped a note and coin to the bard last night."

Gilead frowned. "Did ye search him?"

Angus turned to face his son. "Nay. Word of such inhospitality would travel quicker than a fire through dry brush. Bards are protected everywhere, as ye ken. Even with the Saxons. Yer Deidre might very well have sent information to one of them."

Gilead hoped his father was wrong. But what other reason would she have? "Mayhap she sent word to relatives in Armorica."

Angus snorted. "The man ye sent to Armorica returned

saying my mother knew of no drownings at the Black Lake, nor had she ever heard of Deidre. I ask again, how did the lass get here?"

"I doona know, but I doona think she is a spy. Mother thinks well of her."

"Elen wouldn't think a man holding a dirk to her throat a murderer." He stopped suddenly and narrowed his eyes. "These 'accidents' that yer mother keeps having . . . they've only started since the lass has been here."

Gilead's temper flared. "Ye can't think Dee—Mistress Deidre—capable of hurting my mother?"

Angus arched an eyebrow. "I can indeed. Has she not always been at the scene?"

"That makes no sense! It was the lass who suggested it might be poison!"

"Aye. And if she is a spy, she'd be clever enough to come up with the idea first. She dashed quickly enough to make sure the cup had been washed, didna she?" He resumed pacing. "And she could easily have torn the carpet. There's always a knife on the morning tray for Elen."

"Bah! The nails were missing. 'Twas plain they'd been pulled out."

Angus wheeled on him. "Mayhap that is what she was doing instead of looking for a missing jewel from a brooch! Mayhap she intended to put them back to make it look an accident truly."

Gilead stared at his father. "Why would she kill my mother? I know she cares about her. She really does."

Angus slammed a fist on the table in front of Gilead, slurping the contents of both goblets unto the cloth. "If she's a spy, she would need to ingratiate herself with someone. Yer mother is the most gullible person I know."

"Stop insulting my mother!" Gilead leapt to his feet. "She's kind and gentle, generous and forgiving—"

"Stop there." Angus held up his hand. "I know ye hold yer mother in high esteem. As ye should. Doona expect me to do the same, for ye know not what she did."

That again. Elen had once admitted she'd done a grievous wrong to Angus, but she wouldn't tell him what it was. Only that the results had been worth it.

"Still," Gilead insisted, "there's no reason for . . . a spy . . . to kill my mother."

"No?" Angus motioned for him to sit, and pulled up a chair himself. "Consider this. If this woman, Deidre, is a spy, these accidents create good diversions. She wants to 'learn' to ride so she'll have access to a horse. If another incident happens, my bet is that she'll try to leave under cover of chaos."

"I'll cancel the riding lessons," Gilead said, "then she will have no access."

"No," Angus answered. "I want to find out what she's really about. Why she's here. We doona want to let her know we suspect a thing. We play along. Continue the lessons. Take her past the gates. See which direction she wants to ride in. More than likely, that's where her contact waits. Have a care, though. Don't wander more than a league. Ye doona want to be caught in an ambush."

Gilead groaned inwardly. The best thing he could do—should do—was avoid all contact with the treacherous lass. Every time he saw her his blood heated, but she was hand-fasted to Niall. Whether she actually liked Niall, Gilead didn't know, but the doubt still lingered that a penniless, although obviously high-born woman, might be ambitious enough to marry the old goat. He wasn't sure if that was worse than the fact that she might indeed be a Saxon spy. Either way, he was still attracted and felt oddly protective of her as well. But playing with fire was his father's game, not his.

"Why not let Formorian give her lessons?" Gilead asked. "That was yer original idea, wasn't it?"

Angus looked at him as though he were daft. "I canna have two women riding alone beyond the castle walls!"

Formorian was better armed than I was yesterday. "Then send an escort."

"Are ye not thinking at all, lad? With an escort, there is not much chance the lass will show her true colors. Too many people."

Gilead tried one more time. "Doona ye think Niall will be much jealous if he sees Deidre and me riding out without a proper escort?"

"I've sent Niall back to ready his army. He won't return

until the festival for Litha. That gives ye nigh a sennight to find the lass out. Ye are dismissed."

Gilead set his jaw as he stood to leave. A sennight. He had to resist temptation for just a week. He could do it. Angus's strict military training—something borrowed from the old Romans, which Turius had suggested—included resisting torture. Gilead had gone through a grueling fortnight of starvation, sleep deprivation, and painful techniques that had stopped just short of broken bones. He'd made it through that; surely he could resist one wee woman, however tormenting her company might be.

For whatever reason, Niall had disappeared and Deidre was grateful. Not having to run into Niall or put up with his foul hands at dinner freed her mind to plan her escape to the stones on the solstice, less than a week away.

"How are you feeling this morning?" she asked Elen after Janet had brought in the tray and left.

"The ankle is better," Elen said as she plumped the pillow under her foot on the stool, "but I've been waking in the mornings with such nausea."

Elen did look a little more peaked than usual. Deidre frowned. One of her mother's young priestesses had that symptom and a child followed several months later. Surely, Elen couldn't be pregnant! "How long has this been happening, my lady?"

Elen's delicate eyebrows came together as she thought. "It started shortly after my collapse at dinner that night."

After the poison incident. Had Angus stayed with his wife that night? I can't very well ask! "Do you have any other symptoms?"

Elen looked puzzled. "I don't think so. Just that I feel tired much of the time."

Deidre tried to cover her concern. If Elen were pregnant from a rare visit by her husband, she'd be in even more danger when Formorian—or maybe Angus himself—found out.

Much as she dreaded confronting Gilead's coldness again, he needed to know. She would have to seek him out.

* * *

Surprisingly, he was in a friendly mood when she found him in the stables after the midday meal.

"Well, Sassenach, are ye come for yer ride?"

Deidre looked around. "Will Formorian be joining us?"

"Nay. My father and Turius are working out battle plans; she'll be with them."

That was good news. She certainly didn't want to voice her suspicions in front of Formorian, of all people. She'd led Winger to the paddock when Gilead touched her shoulder. She tried to ignore the warmth that spread down her arm.

"Since ye have caught on to riding more quickly than I thought, would ye like to ride outside the walls?"

When she nodded eagerly, he cupped his hands to give her a leg up and she could have sworn the brush against her thigh was intentional, although he dropped his hands immediately and his face was impassive.

Once they were out the gate, Gilead turned to her. "Which way would ye like to go today?"

Why was he being so polite? Well, whatever the reason, she wasn't about to miss an opportunity to further study the road to the stones. "That way," she pointed.

As they rode along, it seemed to her that Gilead was tense. His targe, the rounded leather shield favored by the Scotti, hung from his pommel, and he had a dirk at his belt as well as his boot. Leather straps crisscrossed his chest supporting the baldric on his back, from which two swords protruded. His glance kept sweeping the sides of the road, even though there was only gorse and lichen-covered boulders that weren't very high.

"Are you expecting trouble?" Deidre asked.

He gave her a sideways look, but only shrugged noncommittedly. "Best to be prepared, riding without an escort."

"Could we gallop?" If she were going to get anywhere close to the hill from where she could see the circle, they would have to go faster that a slow trot.

"Ye seemed to take to the gallop right well yesterday for a beginner."

Did he suspect she knew how to ride? She smiled demurely and petted the big horse's neck. "Winger has a smooth gait, easy for anyone to ride, I'd think."

"Aye. Well, hold him to a slow canter, not that harebrained run Formorian took ye on yesterday. A horse running flat out is hard to control."

Deidre nodded and nudged Winger lightly. He responded so quickly she almost found herself behind the saddle. Mayhap Gilead had a point.

They stopped to rest the horses in a small, shaded grove of spindly scrub oaks. Gilead had ridden round the small copse before he'd let either of them dismount.

"Are you expecting someone to pounce out at us?" Deidre asked teasingly and was disconcerted when he didn't smile.

"We've come a fair ways from the keep," he answered. "We'll give the horses a wee break and then head back."

They weren't even halfway to the stones! Deidre was about to protest, but thought better of it. Something was on Gilead's mind and she doubted he could be persuaded to keep on going. She might as well address the other issue.

"There is something I want to talk to you about, Gilead." He looked suddenly wary. "Not about us," she added hastily. She thought she caught just the subtlest hint of relief on his face, but his bearing was still stiff.

"It's about your mother."

"What about her?"

"I think . . . I think she may be pregnant."

Gilead stared at her in total bewilderment. "What?"

She held up a hand. "Hear me out. Your mother has been having bouts of nausea in the morning and her appetite is gone. She looks pale and drawn."

Gilead pressed his lips into a thin line. "Just who do ye think the father is?"

It was Deidre's turn to stare. "Your father, of course. Her husband." Gilead was certainly having a strange reaction. Surely, at his age, he wouldn't resent a brother or sister? He was already the heir. "The night that Lady Elen was poisoned . . . your father showed real concern. I thought maybe he . . . that they . . . well, you know."

He almost smiled as he looked down at her. "My father has had his own bedchamber since I was a bairn. As far as I know, once I was born, he's never visited my mother's chambers for . . . ah, companionship."

"But Lady Elen could have died. Emotions were running high. Maybe he decided that it was his duty to stay with her and one thing led to another . . ."

Gilead laughed. "With Formorian in the castle? Hardly."

"But—"

He took her hands in his and looked into her eyes. "I appreciate yer concern. I even think ye are being honest, but it dinna happen. I stayed with my mother all night." He released her hands as quickly as he had taken them and walked over to the horses. "We need to be getting back."

Confused, Deidre rode beside him in silence. He didn't believe her. But if Elen weren't pregnant, then something else was causing her problems. Poison that worked more slowly perhaps?

And what had he meant, anyway, that he "even thought I was being honest"?

Niall leaned back in his chair at the Litha feast and studied the Great Hall. Servants cleared the trestle tables of empty platters that had held mutton and boar and hart. Other maids brought in steaming puddings and sweetmeats. He watched as the wench named Sheila carried a bowl of fruit toward the high table. His hard mouth twitched as she wedged herself between Formorian and Angus, her ample bosom brushing against the laird's shoulder. Mentally, he made a note of her interest and Angus's returning grin. Mayhap he could use the wench later.

Niall almost smiled. Maybe *he* would truly use the wench later. Catch her in the hall, press her against the wall and heave up her skirts. A few hard, rutting thrusts that would spill his seed deep inside her was all he needed to dispel the ache of his cock. An arm to her throat would cut off any scream she'd attempt to make. And mayhap he'd press harder, cut off her air a little. He liked to see fear in a woman's eyes. He inhaled sharply as he felt his groin tighten further.

He narrowed his eyes as the wench moved toward Elen and turned the tray slightly. He could see a highly polished apple inviting itself to be picked. Bel's fires! He'd told his accomplice not to use that trick again! They might have been caught with the pear incident if it hadn't been for Deidre's blundering assumption that something had been wrong with the wine. He allowed himself to grin at that. Doubt had been cast on Angus and Niall hadn't even had to lift a finger to bring it about.

Ah, his wee Deidre. She hovered over Elen, whispering in her ear. He saw Elen's hand hesitate as she reached for the apple and then she declined. The lass was smart, he had to admit. Mayhap, if she learned to obey him, he could use her in his more grandiose plans, once he had destroyed Angus.

Aye, she would learn to obey. He probably should thank Angus, he thought ironically, for making him swear to wait to bed her. The wait had only increased his obsession to possess her. Beautiful, with just enough flesh to make those curves round and soft. Spunky, not afraid of Angus or intimidated by Formorian. He sincerely hoped Deidre was a virgin. Taking her fast and hard the first time, splitting her wide while she was still dry. Having her cry and beg him to stop would go a long way toward salvaging his pride, wounded from her rebuffs.

Niall declined the fruit as it came around and poured another cup of wine from the flask on the table. Ah, yes. It would be good to hear her screams. All he had to do was wait a little while longer. Lugnasad wasn't that far away.

Dusk was settling as everyone converged in the bailey after the meal. A light mist hovered in the air, blending lavender and pink hues of light with the deepening blues of twilight, casting an eerie sense of surrealism over the atmosphere.

"Where is everyone going?" Deidre asked Elen as she watched nearly the entire staff of servants lining up and accepting torches from some of the soldiers.

"The blessing of the fields," Formorian answered for Elen as she and Angus joined them. "The people will walk around the fields, praying to the Goddess to encourage the crops to grow."

Elen pulled her woolen arisaid tightly about her shoulders and shivered slightly. "We have Christian priests now. Mayhap these pagan ways should be forgotten."

Formorian shrugged. "The Old Ways are important to the people. Litha celebrates the life that is in the Great Mother, implanted at Beltane." She glanced sideways at Angus and a small smile twitched on her lips. "It's said this is the night the god is at his peak."

"He rules the world until midnight, when he is slain by the upstart Oak King," Angus replied with a hint of amusement. "Best for the Holly King to make his moves before then."

"Aye," Formorian agreed, "the more strokes he can make, the better."

Deidre didn't think either of them was talking about the pagan ritual any longer. But so much the better. If they were going to carry on, that would be two fewer people she had to watch for when she rode out tonight.

The gloaming darkened into almost night. Deidre had to procure a horse fairly soon if she was going to reach the stones by midnight. The veil between the worlds was thinnest then. She might get a glimpse of where the Stone lay hidden.

She had been trying to avoid Niall all night by hovering and fussing over Elen. Angus insisted that his wife remain present while the ritual bonfires were lit and young men leaped over them in a show of physical prowess. Symbolically, the bravery merged with the peak-of-the-god, height-of-the-growing-season, and the longest day. But, as Formorion added wryly, most of the young bucks wanted to impress wenches who might be willing to couple with them later.

Deidre would have laughed if she hadn't been so anxious to retire for the evening and go steal a horse. Finally, Elen begged to take her leave. Angus absently nodded, no doubt already planning his own rendezvous. Deidre lost no time in helping Elen to her room and settling her for the night.

She hurried back to her own room and slipped into the trews and shirt that Formorian had lent her. She wished she had a black cloak, but the Angus plaid with its dark blue shades would have to do. She tucked the satchel with The Book and her small bag of coin beneath it. If she had a Sighting, she would not be returning.

Poking her nose out the door to make sure the corridor was clear, she carefully made her way to the back stairs. She would have to pass through the kitchen, but she hoped Meara was celebrating with the rest of the servants.

She wasn't. She was scolding some hapless scullery lad about not bringing in enough firewood and then Deidre heard her box his ears. The sound of her voice faded as she led the boy outside, no doubt holding on to his sore ears, Deidre thought. She dashed through the kitchen quickly before the woman could return.

Although the bonfires burned low, festivities were still going on in the bailey and Deidre kept hidden in the darkness of the back wall of the Hall as she made her way to the stables. She heard footsteps approach and stepped quickly back into shadow, but it was only a somewhat drunken soldier with his arm around a kitchen wench. Deidre probably could have danced a jig and they wouldn't have noticed.

Deidre hesitated when she came to the corner of the Hall. She would have to leave security behind and cross open space now. Luckily, the moon had not yet risen and the dim light from the fires would make her nearly invisible. She covered her head and pulled the cloak closer and stepped out.

Inside the stables, the warm smell of sweet hay and horse greeted her. The stable lads had joined the revelry and she quickly made her way to Winger's stall. He snuffed her hand for the apple she always brought.

"There you go, boy," she said as she struggled with the heavy saddle. "We're going on an adventure." The horse crunched contentedly as though he understood.

Deidre led him to the door and peered out. The gates were still open for Niall's men, who were camped outside the walls. A horseman leaving wouldn't be that unusual. She checked that her tight braid was still tucked into the back of her shirt and tied the bandanna around her head. Too bad she couldn't wear a leather helmet, but that would attract attention. Why would any soldier returning to a safe camp wear one?

She mounted and forced herself to walk the gelding sedately toward the gate. She glanced around the bailey. Neither Angus nor Gilead was to be seen. She had no doubt that Angus was bedding Formorian somewhere, but she wondered what had happened to Gilead. He had not really been near her all night, but whenever she looked up she'd find him watching her. Probably trying to analyze why she was treating Niall so well. If the circle gave her any clue where the Stone might be, it would be the last of Niall that she would have to see. Still, she felt more than a twinge of regret that she couldn't explain herself to Gilead or say good-bye. He had rescued her, after all. For one, brief moment he had been the knight in shining armor that she'd always wanted. She felt tears sting her eyes.

Deidre took a deep breath and straightened her shoulders, sitting tall in the saddle as she rode through the gates. She would not look back. Resolutely, she put the horse into a canter as soon as they passed the bend and lost the castle from view.

The stones loomed tall and dark and otherworldly, silhouetted against the pale wash of the full moon, now high in the sky. A low fog had formed in the valley, its tentacles swirling upward, licking at the stones, sweeping around the horse's hooves.

Deidre dismounted, dropping the reins, but leaving Winger unhobbled. She approached the circle and hesitated. The air felt different, heavy and warm like a blanket. She thought she heard a faintly haunting melody, soft and low like the strumming of a harp that she couldn't quite catch. It enveloped her, its elusive chords not real, yet permeating her mind somehow. Deidre shivered, though the night was mild. She half expected to see Merlin himself emerge from the mists.

She glanced up. The moon was directly overhead. It must be near midnight. Taking a deep breath, Deidre stepped inside the circle. Instantly, she could feel a magnetic pull toward the center where the Cromlech, or altar stone, stood. The soft sound of the music was more audible now, vibrating from the stones themselves.

Deidre swallowed hard and knelt beside the altar, trying to remember what her mother had taught her about summoning Power. So many years at Childebert's Christian court had faded her memory. She closed her eyes and concentrated. "I now draw the quarters to me: Cernunnos, king of Forest; Lleu, king of Wind; Belinos, king of Fire; Llyr, king of Water.

Gather unto me from the North and East and South and West. Let the Forces open a portal between the worlds." Deidre raised her face, letting the moon's beams wash over her face. "I call on you, Isis, Mother of us all, let me see where the Stone lies hidden."

The elusive music heightened in pitch and rhythm, drawing Deidre to her feet. Lifting her hands toward the moon, she began to sway.

She felt dizzy as the stones seemed to tilt in front of her and fade away. There was a slight rustle, as if a wind had suddenly sprung up through trees that were not present. A crackling sound like flames from dry timber doused by a stream of rushing water, carrying away all other sound. The air pulsed with energy. A shimmering haze began to stir, forming itself into a young woman with long, red-gold hair, dressed in a gossamer gown of white. It floated about her translucent shape as she hovered in the air. She smiled at Deidre.

Deidre struggled to stay calm. Her Sight had conjured up . . . something. This was not the time to lose her nerve. The apparition seemed benevolent enough.

"I seek the Philosopher's Stone," she whispered.

The spirit smiled and nodded. "Gar-al," she said, and then inclined her head gracefully. Even as Deidre watched, the image began to fade into nothingness.

The stones came back into focus and Deidre shook her head as though to clear it. Whoever, or whatever, the phantom was, she had sounded real enough. But what was a "gar-al," and what did it have to do with the Stone?

She shivered, despite the humid night air and stepped out of the circle. Thank goodness Winger was still there, contently grazing beside another horse.

Deidre's blood chilled and goose bumps rose. Another horse? So she had been followed, after all. Taking a deep breath, willing herself to stay calm, she turned slowly, knowing whom she would see.

Chapter Ten

TIME FOR TRUTH

"Would ye mind telling me what the bloody hell ye are doing out here?"

In the pale moonlight, Gilead's eyes glittered like black sapphires. Deidre could feel the heat of his anger even though he was several paces away. He stood, legs splayed, arms folded across his broad chest, unwavering.

She gulped. How much had he seen or heard? Suddenly, she felt like a fool, sneaking away to talk to thin air at midnight. What possible excuse could she give him? "I . . . had heard . . . that is . . . some people say stone circles have magic in them, especially on festival days." Deidre tried a nonchalant shrug that only caused her arm to shake as her shoulder jerked. "I . . . ah, I thought I would see for myself."

"It's not a wise thing to practice magic," he said grimly as his eyes bore into hers. "Witches burn at the stake here."

Her skin crawled at the thought. "I . . . I wasn't going to hurt anyone."

His expression didn't change and he looked around, scanning the area. "Whom did ye expect to meet?"

Deidre frowned. "Meet? No one. I told you, I was just going to see if there really was any magic. Silly of me. I didn't realize it was dangerous. We probably should be getting home." She turned and walked toward Winger.

He was beside her immediately, a hand on her arm, spinning her around.

"The truth, Sassenach."

She tried to pull her arm away, but his fingers were like steel. "You're hurting me." Instantly, he relaxed his grip, but not enough for her to move away. "I told you. I'd heard Janet and Sheila talking about Litha. Someone mentioned standing stones—"

Gilead tightened his hold slightly. "I doona like being lied to, Sassenach. Who are ye here to meet?"

"No one! Why won't you believe me?"

He stared at her for a moment and then he lifted his head and scented the wind, eyes scanning the horizon for any signs of movement. Deidre watched him, trying to ignore the feeling of warmth that always flooded her at his touch. Right now he looked like an alert panther ready to pounce. What was he looking for? The valley floor was flat, the meadow grass just knee high. A crooked little burn meandered through it and continued past the circle. The hill that she had ridden down was craggy and spotted with scrubby gorse, hardly anything a man or a horse could hide behind. The forest, where it picked up on the other side of the circle, was at least fifty fathoms away, well out of arrow shot. A lone rowan tree stood a few feet away, near the horses. "Whom do you think I'm meeting? Niall?"

Gilead grimaced and he released her. "He'd not have let ye get more than a quarter mile from the gates before he'd taken ye, lass."

Intent as she was on making her escape, she hadn't even considered that Niall might have followed her. Deidre shuddered, knowing Gilead was right. Niall would have waited only long enough to make sure no one heard her screams. Still, since she'd need a horse to try an alterative escape, she couldn't afford to admit that. "I was just testing my skill at riding and . . . well, when Formorian showed me the circle, I was curious. I didn't think I was taking that much of a risk."

"But ye did take a risk. A big one, riding alone at night, hours from help. Did the friends ye're meeting get the night wrong?"

Deidre rolled her eyes, exasperated. "I've not got any friends outside of your people. What do you think I am, a spy?" When he raised an eyebrow, she gasped. "You can't really believe that!"

He took a step toward her. "Ye are an outlander, yer accent more Saxon than Briton. Ye arrive in the middle of the night without baggage or coin. A good way to gain entry, asking for charity."

"I didn't ask! I told you we had been waylaid—"

Gilead moved closer, his face inscrutable. "Nay, I doona think that happened."

Deidre stepped back involuntarily. She had never seen him look so determined. "I'm no Saxon! I told you where I'm from."

He shook his head. "I sent inquiries to Armorica. Neither ye nor yer family has ever been heard of and no drownings reported."

She had to think quickly. If Gilead really believed she was a spy, she would be in big trouble when they got back. What did they do with spies here? Hang them? Stone them to death? She swallowed hard. "Brocéliande is a huge forest. Your messenger probably went to the wrong place."

"I doona think so. My grandmother—my father's mother—resides in the middle of it, by the Black Lake. She would know." He looked at Deidre steadily and inched closer. "I really doona like being lied to."

Deidre moved back and struck the tree. Before she could turn away, Gilead had braced an arm on either side of her, locking her in, his body inches from hers.

"I will have the truth from ye, lass."

His breath was warm on her cheek and she could smell his clean scent of soap and light spice, mixed with leather and horse. Her body started to tingle, her hopelessly romantic mind inclined to quite willingly acquiesce to any persuasion he might attempt.

"Perhaps I didn't tell you *all* of the story." Deidre kept her eyes fastened on Gilead's broad shoulders. That wasn't exactly making the tingles go away, but she knew she couldn't lie if she looked him in the face. "I . . . it was true that I had been in Brocéliande before I came here, but my family is not *from* there." She paused, trying to think, but he remained quiet. *Funny that I never noticed . . . the most fascinating dusting of black curls is visible where the top part of his shirt is unlaced . . . oh, yes. The story. Back to that.* How much "truth" could she tell him?

"My mother was a kind of healer," she said. "She traveled the land from Rennes to Carhaix. We moved about quite a bit; your grandmother would not have heard of us."

Deidre watched Gilead's chest slowly expand as he took a deep breath. He put a finger under her chin, lifting her face up, forcing her to look at him.

"Ye are a bloody poor liar, Sassenach."

"No! It's true."

He sighed and released her. Walking to his saddlebags, he rummaged through one and took out a length of cord. He looked troubled when he turned back to her.

Deidre eyed the rope warily. "What are you going to do with that?"

"Ah, lass. Ye leave me no choice. I will bind ye to the tree until ye tell me the truth. Who ye are, where ye are from, and why ye are here."

Deidre sprang away from the tree, trying to judge the distance to the horses. Gilead stood between her and Winger. She would never make it.

He moved toward her, the rope dangling in one hand. Deidre backed away.

"I doona wanna do this, ye ken. Tell me the truth, lass."

"I . . . did." She took another step back and sideways. Maybe if she could somehow circle around him . . . put the horses between them, she'd have a chance.

He stepped sideways, too. "Ye know ye canna escape me."

Deidre angled away, alert for any sudden lurch on his part. A few more steps and she could dart around the tree, put Malcolm between them and make a dash for Winger.

He followed her movements, an eyebrow lifted. "Ye want to make a game of this?"

Some game. She stepped sideways, eyes watchful.

The edge of his mouth lifted and he mimicked her. Deidre took a step back; he took a step forward. She took two more steps and so did he. *Merde! He's playing cat and mouse with me and enjoying it. Of course, he's not the one who's going to be tied to the tree.*

Then she realized what he'd been doing. As he was letting her move backward, he had been slowly and subtly herding her away from the horses. More distance parted them now. Deidre swore silently and then her eyes caught the moon's reflection on the stones. The circle! There had been some sort of energy there. She knew she had felt a magical pull. Maybe she could elude him by zigzagging through the menhirs. She turned and ran.

He caught her before she was halfway there. One strong arm circled her waist and before she could fall, he had picked her up and tossed her over his shoulder. One hand caressed her rump while the other arm held her calves firmly against his stomach. So much for making his crotch sore. She couldn't get a kick in. He knew so well where to hold—how many women had he carried like this?

"Let me down!" She pummeled his back with her fists and received a sharp slap to her behind. It stung through the thin leather of the trews and, for once, she would have been grateful for the hated full dresses with the layers beneath them. "Ouch!" She redoubled her efforts, only to receive another stinging pop.

"I doona want to hurt ye, Dee," Gilead said as they approached the tree and he slid her down the length of him, catching her hands. She struggled briefly, only to have him press her against the trunk, pinning her body with his. She felt his hard erection brush the softness of her stomach, but he swerved his hips away. Deftly, he wound the rope around one wrist and spiraled the cord around the tree, catching it easily in his hand and securing it to her other wrist. There was enough slack that she could raise her arms somewhat, but not enough for her fingers to touch.

Deidre glared at him as he unsaddled the horses and tethered them. He dug through one of the saddlebags and brought out a flask of water.

"Are ye thirsty?" he asked.

After all that exertion, she was, but she wasn't about to let him know it. "No, thanks. I'm fine."

He cocked an eyebrow and then took a long drink himself. Deidre could almost taste the water, but she averted her eyes when he held out the flask questioningly.

Gilead shrugged and put the water away. He spread out the horse blankets and laid his bedroll on top. He looked at her. "It will be cool by morn. Would ye like me to wrap my plaid around ye?"

Deidre stared at him. "You don't mean to make me stand here all night, do you?"

Gilead yawned. "Only a few hours until Prime. Unless ye want to tell me the truth now, I plan to get some sleep."

"I've told you the truth." Lord, how was she going to sleep standing up?

"Och, well. Mayhap ye'll think differently in the morn," Gilead said. He unwrapped his plaid and draped it over her breasts and shoulders, reaching around her neck to fasten it with his brooch in the back. He tucked the sides in behind her. "There now. If ye doona move much, ye'll stay all warm."

"How can I move at all? Gilead, untie me. Please. I promise not to run away."

He laughed. "Aye. I'd not wake up due to a dirk in my heart, I think."

"I would never kill you!"

"If ye are a spy, ye might."

Deidre stamped her foot in frustration. The plaid came loose on that side, allowing the cool night air to invade her cocoon. "Keep me tethered to you, if you must."

Gilead retucked the edge of plaid around her thigh and straightened. "If I did that, neither of us would get any sleep." For a moment, his glance fastened on her lips and he bent his head slowly toward her.

Deidre glared at him. He was going to kiss her now? She

was furious with him. She really was. Her breath quickened and her traitorous lips parted.

He hesitated, only an inch from her. Then, slowly, he cupped her face in his hands and leaned forward to kiss her lightly on her forehead.

"Good night, Dee. We will talk again in the morning."

It took Deidre less than an hour to decide that cooperation might be the better part of valor. Spirited defiance wasn't working. Gilead was asleep, blast him, and she was getting tired of shifting her weight from one foot to the other. Determined as he was, they could be out here for days unless Angus sent a search party. She'd racked her brain for another believable story, but came up with nothing. Well, if he wanted the truth, he'd have it. She just hoped she could convince him she wasn't a Frankish spy.

She pressed her back against the trunk and bent her knees, sliding down the scratchy bark a few inches. It was as far as she could go. Balancing her weight, she stretched out one leg and pointed her toe, trying to push at Gilead's boot. Just out of reach. She muttered a string of expletives that would have made Clotilde swoon, and painfully pushed herself another inch lower. There. Just barely. She nudged him.

Gilead groaned and rolled over, his leg sprawling over her foot. Aha. Deidre kicked him as hard as she could.

He let out a roar and sprang to a crouching position, dirk in his hand. He glanced around wildly and then looked at her. "Ye woke me?"

Deidre bit back the splendid retort that she wanted to make. "I've decided to tell you the truth."

He looked wary. "If this be another story . . ."

She shook her head quickly. "It isn't. Please untie me."

"I should make ye stand and tell it." He muttered something in Gaelic and moved toward her, sliding the dirk between her wrist and the rope. "Doona make a fool of me."

Deidre rubbed her wrist and sank to the ground. Grass had never felt so soft. "May I have some water first?"

Silently, he handed her the flask. Deidre tried not to guzzle it, but she was parched and some of the water dribbled down her chin. She wiped it off with the back of her hand and handed the flask back.

Gilead laid it down beside him. "Talk, Sassenach."

Deidre drew the plaid around her. His scent was somehow comforting. She took a deep breath.

"I am cousin to King Childebert of Gaul."

Gilead's eyes narrowed. "Not Saxon, but still a spy."

"No spy. My mother, King Clovis's sister, was descended from a royal bloodline dedicated to keeping the truth and wisdom of the Goddess alive." She paused.

"Go on."

"The code to that wisdom lies embedded in something called the Philosopher's Stone. It was my mother's duty—and that of her priestesses—to guard and protect it. It was stolen years ago by a magician."

Gilead looked puzzled. "And ye have searched for the Stone all this past?"

Deidre shook her head. "At first we did, but the magician was more powerful than we thought. Mayhap he was a Druid, for their powers are strong, and even our oldest seeress could not discern where he had hidden the Stone. Then my mother killed herself. The priestesses that had been under my mother's care found their way to Provence—to Rennes-le-Château—and I was taken to Childebert's court."

"I still doona understand. Why are ye here?"

"When news reached Childebert that one of the Briton bishops had launched a search for a grail that the Christos had used, my cousin remembered the Stone. He wanted it found so he could turn it over to Rome and be rewarded."

Gilead looked skeptical. "And he sent a woman to find it?"

"No. He wanted to use my gift of Sight—"

"Ye have the Sight? 'Tis not wise to admit that, with the Christian zealots eager to find such people."

"I know." Deidre tried not to sound impatient. "That's why I didn't want to tell you. I sent his men searching in the wrong direction. The Stone is here. I can feel it." She went on to tell him the whole story and then finished softly, "Over the years,

I always thought the magician would keep it safe, since I had his book."

Gilead's eyebrows lifted. "Ye practice magic, too?"

"No! The book is about . . ." Her voice trailed off. How could she tell him about knights in armor who rescued damsels and pledged their faith? He'd think her totally mad or worse, laugh at her whimsies and for having her head in faerie clouds. Well, she could tell him of some of the problems laid out. "The book says that descendents of a man named Cerdic will conquer Britain—"

"Cerdic?" Gilead asked in a shocked voice. "He is a Saxon plague already in the far south. Ye *are* a spy."

"*No!*" Deidre racked her brain about how to convince him and then she had an epiphany. "Didn't Turius say that Gunpar has spotted Saxon longboats?" At his nod, she went on. "The Saxon who leads them is named Ida." She hoped she was correct; she had skimmed the parts in The Book that didn't really interest her, looking instead for romantic interludes between Lancelot and Gwenhwyfar. "Ida will claim land near Lothian and bring more families." She wrinkled her forehead in thought. "Soon."

Gilead looked troubled. "Ye must not talk like that, Dee. Witches burn."

Tears welled in her eyes. "I'm no witch. All I'm looking for is the Stone, which must be returned to its grotto, safe from the wrong hands." She moved away from him and brought her fist to her mouth, trying to hold back the tears. "I knew you wouldn't believe me. That's why I made up the story of bandits. My real escort was overcome by Turius's men and I didn't know if they were friend or foe." The tears spilled over and she sobbed. "I was afraid you'd lock me in a dungeon or send me back to Childebert."

She felt comforting hands on her shoulders as Gilead turned her around and brought her against his chest. Deidre put her arms around his waist and buried her face in his shoulder as he stroked her hair, speaking soothingly as he would to calm a skittish horse. No doubt he thought she was a stark, raving lunatic who danced to no music and spoke to thin air.

"There now, lass. Cry yerself out," he said as he rocked her gently. "Ye've nothing to fear from me. Yer secret's safe. I doona believe ye are a spy."

Deidre raised a tear-stained face. "You . . . you don't?" she asked doubtfully.

"Nay." He took his thumb and wiped the tears away from one side of her face and then the other. "I doona think ye a witch, either." His fingers trailed lightly down the side of her face and traced the outline of her lips as he looked into her eyes. For a moment, the two of them were suspended in time and then he slanted his mouth over hers as he drew her tightly into his embrace.

Gilead kissed her softly, his warm lips tantalizing hers as he teased them, tugging at her lower lip, then nipping at the corner, and applying easy pressure against the fullness of her mouth. From somewhere deep inside her, Deidre emitted a primal groan and moved closer, pressing her aching breasts into his broad chest. Gilead ran his hands across her back, and slowly down her hips, cupping her buttocks and pulling her hard against him. He growled low in his throat as his tongue gained entrance to her mouth and he plunged inside that warm, wet orifice. His kisses were hot and demanding now, nothing teasing about them, his tongue only a promise of what his manhood, pulsating against her mound, could do. Her body prickled as though a thousand tiny flames burned her skin.

With a great shudder, Gilead pushed himself away from her. He stood there gasping, his hands on his knees. Deidre stared at him in bewilderment. How could he bring her so close to the brink—of what it was exactly, she didn't know, but her very core was throbbing—and then suddenly stop?

"Ye did it to me again," he ground out. "Mayhap ye are a witch after all."

Her face flamed and she was grateful the moon had gone behind the shadow of a cloud. He probably thought she was leading him on again, to "practice" her skills for Niall. Damn the man's pride! She was going home. She walked over to Winger and picked up his saddle.

"Let me do that." His voice was shaky as he took it from

her and flung it over the horse's back. He didn't speak again as he saddled Malcolm and adjusted the saddlebags. Once she was in the saddle, he looked up at her.

"I told ye earlier ye had nothing to fear from me," he said in a low voice, "and I almost lost control. I respect ye more than that." He handed her the reins. "I willna let it happen again."

Deidre bit her lip in frustration, wishing that he had inherited a little more of his father's lustful urges. Every nerve ending cried out to be satisfied, but Gilead was the perfect gentleman on the way home.

Merde.

Gilead finished putting both horses up and moved the saddles to their racks. He and Deidre had arrived back at the castle just before dawn and he'd sent her to her room before anyone was astir. The last thing he wanted to do was explain to anyone, let alone his father, what had transpired during the night. Better that no one knew either of them had been gone.

He didn't know what to make of her story. A cult of priestesses hidden in the Languedoc, guarding a lost treasure from Solomon's temple? How long before Frankish soldiers would be sent to find her? He would keep her secret, but if they came looking for her, his father would turn her over. They didn't need to add war with Gaul to their list of problems. But what concerned Gilead right now was her prediction of future events, either from the magician's book or from her Sight.

That had to stop. Deidre was already under suspicion because she looked Saxon and had an accent even Turius couldn't place. Easy now to know why, since they had few dealings with the Franks. Sassenachs were not easily accepted by the Scotti simply because they were outlanders, but if Deidre started telling people what was going to happen—and it did—that uneasy balance could quickly shift into an accusation of witchcraft.

Even their own priestesses had to be careful with the pagan rites these days. The Romans had introduced Christianity into Britain, but it wasn't until Saint Patrick swept through Eire that the Scotti had begun accepting the religion. Some of the more zealous priests were ready to cry heresy against their Lord for the most mundane of reasons and the Sight—or fortune-telling as they called it—was certainly a work of their devil, at least in their eyes. Even the gypsies had gone to ground.

Gilead didn't want Deidre to come to any harm. In spite of his honorable intentions, he was drawn to her like a bee to the first bloom of spring. And he'd almost taken her last night! He tried to block the memory of how plush her breasts had felt crushed on his chest or how inviting her full lips were or the sweet taste of her tongue tangling with his. His shaft began to throb just as it had when he'd pressed himself against her soft stomach.

He gritted his teeth. Even pushing aside the very important fact that the alliance with Niall must be kept intact, Gilead had no right to make her break her oath. And that's what it was, like it or not. She was handfasted to Niall. She had told his father she accepted that, and Gilead would not act like his father did, turning her into a leman for his pleasure.

Still, his father did expect him to watch her. It was the least he could do . . . just to keep her out of trouble, for certes.

With a lighter heart, he went in to break his fast.

Chapter Eleven

SHATTERED DREAMS

Over the next week, Deidre's attempts at finding a new escape plan were overcome by her concern for Elen. Gilead's mother seemed to be getting weaker with each passing day.

"I'm worried, too," Gilead said when she mentioned it to him one morning after he had visited his mother. He opened the door to the kitchen and Deidre stepped through with Elen's hardly touched breakfast tray.

"The only thing I can think of to do is taste everything that your mother eats," Deidre said. "If I get sick, then we'll know someone is trying to poison her."

Before he could reply, an immense wad of gray homespun and white linen hurled itself across the floor, shouting Gaelic curses.

"Ye sorry Sassenach!" Meara screamed, wielding a butcher's knife. "I'll not be having ye accuse me of hurting the laird's poor wife!"

Gilead pushed Deidre behind him and grabbed the cook's massive arm. His thumb found the pressure point between the knuckles and she dropped the large knife and glared at him.

"I'll not have mayhem here," he said calmly. "Is that verra clear?"

She sniffled. "It be her fault, accusing me of such."

"Dee wasna implying that."

"That's true," Deidre said, stepping out from behind his comfortingly broad, strong back. "I know how much you care for Lady Elen. In fact, you could help us."

Meara looked at her distrustingly. "How so?"

"I think someone is purposely trying to dispose of our lady and trying to make it look like an accident. Tainting her food would be easy. If you could make certain that her food comes to her directly from you, there'd be no chance of someone putting something in it, would there?"

"An interesting theory," Formorian said as she entered the kitchen with an empty cup in her hand. "Do ye really think someone is trying to kill Gilead's mother?"

"It's obvious something is wrong with her," Deidre answered. "It seems to me that Elen has not been well for some time."

Gilead eyed her stonily. "She seems worse when ye are here."

Formorian stared back at him for a long moment and then she gave a little shrug as she poured fresh goat's milk from the ewer on the counter. "I know ye won't believe me, but I doona wish yer mother ill." She lifted the cup in a mock salute as she went out the kitchen door.

Meara turned to Gilead. "Aye, my lord. That one bears watching, but she's ne'r been in my kitchen." She stared at Deidre. "I doona welcome anyone here but Himself and Her Ladyship." She reached down and picked up the knife and Deidre involuntarily took a step back. "But I will be bringing the lady her food myself from now on."

"Thank-ye," Gilead said and took Deidre's arm and led her to the hall.

"I'm glad Formorian heard that," Deidre said once they were out of earshot of the kitchen. "If she knows you suspect her, maybe she will stop."

Gilead shook his head. "I should have kept my mouth shut. If she is behind this, I'll just have driven her to ground."

"These accidents happen when she's here," Deidre reminded him and then hesitated before adding, "Do you think she acts alone?"

He gave her a level look. "Do ye mean my father may have to do with this?"

She felt herself redden. "I don't want to think so."

"Then doona." He headed toward the door and then turned back. "There may be no love lost between my parents, but I don't think him capable of murdering my mother." A muscle tightened in his jaw and he straightened his shoulders. "But ye'll have a chance to test yer idea. Da and I leave tomorrow for Pictland."

Deidre was surprised. "Didn't your father already send an envoy?"

Gilead nodded. "But Turius wants to talk to Gunpar about the Saxon longboats and Da thinks it would be good if we went with him as a show of unity. Niall is going, too. If my mother gets better while we're gone . . ."

"It doesn't mean your father is at fault," Deidre said gently. "Remember, Formorian has been warned, too."

Gilead gave her a small smile. "Aye. We will have to wait and see."

Deidre watched as he walked out the door and headed toward the stables. Wait and see indeed. She just hoped she and Lady Elen would both be alive and well when he returned.

Deidre tried to ignore Niall at dinner the night before the men were to leave. As usual, she was seated beside Elen, but tonight, Niall had managed to secure the seat on her other side. His hand kept roving to her thigh and she was tempted to permanently pinion his hand to the chair with her meat knife, but she doubted that anyone would believe stabbing him was an accident. She shifted away from him and closer to Elen.

His face turned dark and his smile only gave him a sinister look. "Ye won't be able to get away from me for long, lassie. 'Tis only a fortnight plus a sennight until Lugnasad. Think on it."

She was spared an answer by Formorian's exclamation of surprise from the other side of the table.

"What do ye mean, my father will not join with ye?"

Angus shrugged. "He's had a change of mind. Comgall's messenger arrived two days ago. His men are already deployed to wait for Fergus's advance along the border. My own troops will leave with us tomorrow. Yer father's scout came this morn."

Formorian tapped her tapered fingertips on the wooden table and looked thoughtful. "Did he say why?"

"Only that he thinks it foolish to leave both his and Comgall's lands unattended."

"Hmmm. He suspects a ruse, then." She turned to Turius. "What think ye?"

He was silent for some moments before he answered. "I think yer idea that Fergus would prefer to squeeze Angus in from three sides a sound one. To reach the eastern sea would be a boon for him and I doubt that he'd split his army. A show of force would be needed to persuade Gunpar to oblige him. Right now, he doesn't know that Scotti troops await him. However," he paused and then continued, "if we're wrong, we leave Fergus a clear southern path to Oengus. He would find some of my troops awaiting him here, but he would claim all lands he passes through and it would be the devil to get them back. All in all, yer father is probably a wise man to hold back."

"I agree," Angus said, "especially since we've already treatied with Gunpar. If Fergus moves northward, we can stop him without your father. If he moves south, he'll have Gabran waiting for him."

Niall had gone very still. At first, Deidre was just grateful he had stopped making his lewd remarks and kept his hands to himself, but now she noticed he was pale beneath the weathered skin.

"My lords," he said in a strained voice, "I fear I've eaten something that doesna agree with me." He got to his feet unsteadily. "If ye will excuse me, I think I'd best ride for home."

Deidre was relieved that he wouldn't be spending the night in the guest chambers as planned. At least she wouldn't catch him lurking in the hallways.

Angus looked up sharply, eyes narrowed. "Will ye still be riding with us on the morrow?"

Niall hesitated, as if undecided, and then finally nodded. "Aye. I'm sure I'll be fine in the morn."

Deidre caught Gilead's eye. He looked worried and then she realized why. With Turius, Angus, and Gilead all gone, who would protect her if Niall was the only one who stayed behind?

Gilead was relieved when Niall actually showed the next morning. There had been nothing wrong with the food, nor had anyone else, even his mother, gotten ill. He had been prepared to dig his heels in and stay if Niall remained, but now there was no need for a confrontation with his father.

The ride north through the Ochil Hills was uneventful, the rolling hills green with high summer. Shimmering waves of purple heather swayed in brisk breezes that crossed the moors and as they drew closer to the old Roman town of Bertha, the scent of sea salt blowing in from the Firth of Tay filled the air with its tang.

Gunpar waited for them several miles up the river where it converged with the Almond. Mounted bareback on shaggy mountain ponies, painted blue with woad, his near-naked warriors were formidable. Not to mention the wicked-looking spears each one of them carried.

He grunted at Angus's introduction of Niall and motioned for them to follow him. As they progressed toward his campsite, Gilead was amazed at how his band burgeoned, with more of the short, dark Picts joining him. They seemed to materialize silently from nowhere, and Gilead knew that was one of the things that made them so dangerous. Being nomadic by culture, following their herds of sheep from high pastures to low, they had developed the ability to blend in with what nature had to offer. The unsuspecting traveler would find himself relieved of transportation, goods, and clothes, lucky to be left alive. Usually they weren't.

Gunpar's woman, a comely lass with amazingly white teeth

in a swarthy face, served them a strong drink that tasted of honey, once they were seated in the main tent.

"Mead?" Angus asked in surprise. "How come ye by a Saxon drink?"

A corner of their host's mouth turned up in what was almost a smirk. "The light-hairs are an arrogant race. They sent only one longboat to scout the firth." He shrugged. "They almost made it."

Turius leaned forward. "How long ago was this?"

Gunpar's forehead wrinkled in thought. "Less than a sennight."

"They're close, then," Turius said softly. "Have you seen more since then?"

"Nothing on the horizon," Gunpar answered, "but the captain of the vessel was kind enough to give me the information I wanted."

The grim set of his mouth and the hard look in his eyes belied the benign tone of his voice. Gilead willed himself not to shudder about how that information had been so "kindly" given. The Norsemen were fearsome fighters; he'd never known one to surrender, and certes, not willingly acknowledge anything. But then, being slowly butchered alive may have had some influence on the man's tongue. At least, while he still had it.

"So what did you learn?" Turius asked.

"Famine has ravished their lands these past two years. They are looking to settle along the coast." Gunpar allowed a faint smile. "The one survivor took back the message: 'Not along my shore.' That leaves yours, Angus. You are wise to guard it."

"We intend to do that," Angus answered. "If we can count on you to block any move that Fergus might make."

Gunpar made a guttural sound. "I'll not allow him a hide of land. Or you, either," he said to Angus in warning.

"Fair enough. If ye hold fast, I can concentrate on keeping the northern barbarians from invading. Did yer man say how many of them were coming?"

"Near to five thousand is what I finally got out of him."

Angus sucked in his breath and even Turius looked disconcerted. "That would be over five hundred ships," Angus said.

"They'd be hard to hide," Turius replied. "They'd have to wait over the horizon until dark and then invade unknown shores."

"No doubt 'tis the reason they sent the scouting keel," Gunpar replied and motioned for another round of drinks.

Angus sent a questioning look to Gilead and he knew that his father was thinking that mayhap they already had a spy in their midst who was sending information back to them. But Gilead was more convinced than ever that Deidre was no informer. He shook his head slightly.

Angus turned back and accepted a cup from Gunpar's pretty wife and, to Gilead's relief, thanked her respectfully with hardly a glance. Observing propriety was a wise choice, given their tenuous circumstances. Even with their heavily armed guard, they were sorely outnumbered and, at best, their alliance with the Picts was dubious.

Niall, however, was leering at the woman and managed to brush her hand as he accepted a tumbler that he drained in record time. Gunpar's eyes narrowed slightly, his hand sliding casually to the knife he wore in his belt. An image of Niall, lying on the floor with his throat slit, flitted through Gilead's mind. Dee would be spared a marriage. He sighed. Tantalizing at the thought was, they could not risk raising the Pictish king's ire, or for that matter, Niall's father, either. Gilead reached for his cup, accidentally knocking it over.

The contents wet Niall's crotch. He leaped up with a roar. "Ye bloody fool!"

"Sorry," Gilead said as he righted his cup. "Clumsy of me."

Angus's glance swept across Gunpar's hand and he looked quickly at his son. Gilead could have sworn he almost smiled.

"Mayhap ye need to take yer leave, Niall. We can finish up here."

Niall gave Angus a surly look and drained his fourth cup before setting it down with a clatter. "I'll be back."

"There's no need," Turius said evenly. Niall glared at him for a moment, but Turius gave him the penetrating, bald stare that made even his seasoned commanders not question him. Niall sputtered for a moment and then turned on his heel and stormed out.

"Well, now," Turius said pleasantly as he turned back to Gunpar. "Where were we? Ah, yes. Do you know who the leader is?"

"A man called Ida," Gunpar answered.

Gilead felt a chill run through him and the hair on his arms pricked up. Ida? That was the name Dee had given him. His stomach roiled and he put down his goblet. It couldn't be.

Dee couldn't be a witch. Could she?

Niall cursed all the way back to the Scotti campsite. That loutish son of Angus had spilled the mead on purpose. He was sure of it. And just when he might have been able to grab a little free feel of Gunpar's wife. And who knows? Maybe the wench would have welcomed him later, once her husband was asleep. He'd heard that Pictish women practiced thigh freedom. He'd never swived a Pict before. The woman was fine-looking to boot. He doubted whether she'd had a strong, braw Scotti like himself, either. He might even think on being gentle with her, at least at first. He let out a string of Gaelic oaths. He'd not had enough time to judge her reaction and he couldn't take a chance on surprising her. Damn Gilead, always thwarting his plans.

He hoped the messenger he had sent to Fergus late last night when he'd feigned food poisoning made it on time. No sense sending a decoy to the North now. Fergus would need all his men to meet Gabran's defense.

Niall would hold back his men, as well. To defend Oengus, he would tell Angus. What a stroke of luck that the Saxons would be engaging both Angus and the overbearing Briton king with his calculating mind. It would make it easier for him and Fergus.

With a self-satisfied smirk, he quickly penned another letter to Fergus and dispatched it with one of his most loyal retainers. As loyal as silver could buy, anyway. And his messengers knew that, if they returned with no reply, he'd murder either their wives or children. In this case, the man was newly married and quite besotted with the young girl. A pretty thing with hair the color of a copper pence. Hmmm.

Niall uncapped a wineskin and took a deep drag. For everyone's sake, the man had better bring a response. Niall would enjoy using the sweet matron if he didn't.

By the time they returned, less than a sennight from when they'd left, Elen was looking better and feeling stronger. Deidre was glad to see that she even managed to engage her husband in conversation at dinner that night, though Formorian was sitting on his other side.

"What did ye do while we were gone?" Gilead asked in surprise as he slipped into the chair beside Deidre. "My mother has some of her old energy back."

She shrugged, pleased with the compliment. "Perhaps the right people know I'm tasting her food. She's not been ill at all."

Gilead smiled at her. "I wish ye could cure our troubles with Fergus Mor and the Saxons as well. 'Twould be nice to have peace in my lifetime."

Turius leaned across the table to Gilead. "A lofty idea, to be sure, but peace is as elusive as that damn treasure cup that some of my best men have been hunting for nigh unto a year now, instead of soldiering."

Gilead cast a wary eye at his mother's priest sitting at a nearby table. "Mayhap, it would be best if ye not curse the cup in front of the holy man."

Turius snorted. "Bishop Dubricius thinks the blasted relic to be one of King Solomon's lost treasures. No doubt, he put out the rubbish that it belonged to the Christ to put fear into any man who finds it. It must be returned to the Church, he says." Turius refilled his own goblet. "Any man who quests for the cup will find the journey a spiritual one as well, the good bishop says." Turius allowed a small smile. "I suspect the reason he wants it is because it's worth enough to make him a rich man. *If* it exists."

Just then, Drustan strummed a series of notes that halted the conversation. The hauntingly beautiful melody hovered in the air, seeming to quiet even the most lively of conversations.

Turius turned back to Formorian and Elen reached for Gilead's hand, a gentle smile on her face.

Deep in thought, Deidre hardly noticed. The lost cup again . . . one that had belonged to Jesus Christ. Could it be . . . no, of course not. So much else of what the unknown author had written in The Book hadn't happened. She was letting her overactive imagination run amok again. But she felt her heart quicken and her blood started to race through her veins. But what if . . . just what if it were? What if the Holy Grail really did exist? And what if that path were to lead her to the Stone?

The thought was still on her mind the next morning when she sought out Gilead. She found him grooming Malcolm.

"Tell me more about this treasure cup that King Turius mentioned."

He looked up briefly and then continued brushing the stallion's mane. "I don't know much about it. 'Tis a Christian relic that has been lost. Some say it's made of pure gold. No doubt that's why men chase after it."

"Could it possibly be the cup that Christ drank out of at the Last Supper?"

Gilead straightened and looked at her. "I suppose that if he did own it, he used it. Why do ye ask?"

Deidre hesitated and then said, "There is a story in the book I told you about of something called the Holy Grail. Have you ever heard of it?" When he shook his head, she continued. "Supposedly, Jesus did drink from it, and, after he was crucified, Joseph of Arimathea brought the cup with him when he sailed for Britain. He established a monastery at Ynys Gutrin, near Aguae Sulis, but the cup disappeared shortly after."

Gilead frowned. "That be far in the south of Briton. How is it ye know so much about the lay of the land, Sassenach?"

"I'm not a spy," Deidre said in exasperation. "I thought you believed me. I'm trying to tell you that the cup has healing powers. Certainly, those who drink from it could only feel goodwill toward others, even their enemies. Don't you see? If the Grail was found, there would be no need for war. Peace could be established."

Gilead smiled. "That would be worth questing for, indeed, lass, but probably more elusive than the Stone ye seek. At least ye know that it exists."

"Hear me out, please. The legend says that only a man pure of heart may find the Grail. Percival, who many thought to be a fool, was one. Galahad, Lancelot's son, was another. Lancelot was allowed to see it, but of course, he wasn't—"

"Stop! Who are these people? I've ne'r heard of them."

"Lancelot was King Arthur's best warrior and most trusted friend," Deidre began and was interrupted by Gilead once more.

"King Arthur? The only Arthur I know is the prince of Dyfed. Are ye speaking of him?"

Deidre stared at Gilead, excitement building inside her. Were the stories in The Book true, after all? Mayhap she just had the wrong area. "Possibly," she said, trying to hide the tremor in her voice. "Does he live at a place called Camelot?"

Gilead looked confused. "Do ye mean Camulodunum?"

The Latin name of the place from The Book's title! She felt her chest tighten and her breath came in shallow gasps. It existed! "Yes!"

He furrowed his brows. "Camulodunum is an old Roman town, now well within Saxon territory in the southeast of Britain. Across the country from Dyfed, lass."

She frowned. Not the same, then, but she would not let Gilead burst her bubble. "Maybe it isn't the same name. Tell me about Arthur."

"He regularly led raids into Gwynedd and Powys," Gilead answered. "Amassed a bit of land in the doing."

This might be it! "Can I meet him, do you think?"

Gilead shook his head and smiled. "Not unless ye plan to answer Janus's call to the Otherworld. The man was killed south of Dinas Mawddwy more than five years ago."

King Arthur was dead? And not at Camlann either. Deidre felt the air whoosh out of her lungs like a deflated balloon. Did Gwenhwyfar live? She had to ask. "Did King Arthur have a wife?"

"Prince, not king." He thought a moment and then shook

his head. "If he did, I pity the woman. He was a tyrant and more troublesome than anything."

Deidre's crystalline image of the myths was shattering like delicate, imported Phocaean slipware hitting Roman tiles. Shards of the romantic pictures she had held in her mind for years were flying everywhere. She was surprised she wasn't actually bleeding from the tiny slivers of imaginary glass. No Camelot. No knights. A ruthless Arthur and no Lancelot or Gwenhwyfar to keep her hopes up that true love would win one day. How her foolish heart had wanted to believe in that dream. The Book was nothing but falsehoods, just a cruel trick played by a deranged magician.

She had to get away from Gilead before he saw her cry. He would never understand. "Just as well that he's dead, then," she said and tried to keep the quiver out of her voice. "I'd better be getting back to your mother." She turned and stumbled from the stall.

How stupid and silly she had been. In spite of the stark reality of life in Gaul and the same ruthless, scheming, greedy men she had encountered here, she had hoped to find her noble knight. War and bloodshed were real, yet she had clung to the wisps of hopeless fantasy, which were now dissolving like tendrils of fog in bursting sunshine.

But there was no sunshine in her life. Only the bleak prospect of a forced marriage to another tyrant. Lugnasad was just over a fortnight away and the Stone remained as elusive as ever.

Chapter Twelve

SAXONS

Deidre had taken care to seat herself between Gilead and Elen as Angus and Niall joined them, along with the Briton king and queen, for the midday meal. She was getting mightily sick of seeing Niall day and night and wished he'd go attend to his own lands. But no, since their return from the meeting with Gunpar, he'd stuck around like a fly to manure.

They had just begun eating when a messenger was shown into the Hall. He looked dusty, as though he'd ridden hard, but his face burst into a big smile as he approached.

"Fergus has retreated!" Angus read the note that Broderick had sent. "I guess the sight of painted Picts not willing to treaty persuaded him."

Deidre thought Niall looked almost angry, but he quickly masked it by draining his wine and pouring more. She shook her head. *Sot.*

Gilead looked at Turius. "If Fergus isn't likely to attack, ye'll be able to return to Britain, I suppose."

Formorian arched an eyebrow. "Ye'd be happy to see us go?"

"He dinna mean that." Angus glared at Gilead who simply stared back at him. "We still have the Saxon menace to contend with."

"And that is Turius's specialty," Formorian said with a smile and turned to her husband. "Isna it, dear?"

Turius shrugged. "Dealing with Cerdic and Aelle has given me some insight into how their minds work. They crave land more than anything. This Ida is no different."

"Ida?" Niall looked up from the piece of venison he'd pulled from the haunch. "That be the gob's name?"

"That's what the scout said before Gunpar killed him," Angus replied.

"They'll move soon," Turius added, "for they'll want to establish themselves and harvest what they can before the weather turns cold. Since they know the Picts await them, they'll move farther south. My wager is the northern tip of Lothian."

Gilead threw a startled look at Deidre and she gave a little shrug.

"That would make sense," Angus agreed, "and King Loth will need our help covering the shoreline."

Gilead gave a little groan that only Deidre heard. That meant King Turius and his queen would be staying on. She sighed a little and then realized that Niall had been unusually quiet. Briefly she wondered what his problem was and then shoved the thought aside. As long as he left her alone, she didn't care.

Later, she would wish that she had taken more careful note.

Niall took his leave the next morning and Deidre breathed a sigh of relief. She turned to go back in to see to Elen and nearly bumped into Formorian. Where had she come from? The woman could move with a cat's stealthiness when she chose.

"It would seem that ye are less than impressed with yer intended," Formorian said as she slanted a sideways look at Deidre.

Deidre gave an unladylike snort. "That's somewhat of an understatement." A thought occurred to her. If anyone could persuade Angus to break this handfast, it would be Formorian. Would she help? "There is no love lost between us; Niall sees me as a challenge . . . something he can bend to his will."

Formorian's green-eyed glance strayed to Deidre's wrists and, reflexively, Deidre pulled the sleeves down.

"I've seen the swelling," Formorian said softly. "It's not good when a man treats a woman like that."

Deidre looked at her hopefully. "Then will you help me? If you would talk to Angus—I mean the laird—surely he would listen and call off this atrocity."

"Ye seem to think I have influence over the laird."

"Certes, you do! It's obvious," Deidre said and then felt herself flush as Formorian raised an eyebrow. This was not going well. "I mean . . . well, he respects your opinion."

Formorian seemed amused. "Aye. My opinion." She paused. "I already mentioned to him that I dinna think ye'd fare well with this union."

Deidre was touched. As much as she wanted to dislike the woman for the grief she caused Elen, Formorian could show surprising empathy. No doubt that charm was even more evident when it came to men.

"And?"

Formorian shrugged. "Some things are beyond my persuasive abilities."

She doubted it. At least where Angus was concerned. "What did he say?"

"That he needed Niall as an ally, not a foe."

Deidre groaned. "So he'll throw me to that wolf because he's scared of Niall's retaliating against him?"

Formorian took a step closer, her voice low. "Angus is not scared of anything, least of all Niall."

Deidre caught the warning note, but she was too angry to care. "Then why is he forcing me into a marriage that I do not want?"

For a moment a faraway look appeared in Formorian's eyes. "Wanting has nothing to do with it. When Fergus Mor was ousted by Mac Erca, he swore he would make all the land north of the Wall his. The only thing holding him back is that all four cenels are united—three of them by intermarried blood—to stand against him. And Fergus wants Oengus most of all, for Elen is Mac Erca's daughter. Niall's is the only cenel not bound by blood. If he turns, we would have a traitor right in the midst of all our lands, and Fergus would have an easy invasion for Oengus. Ye doona understand the clans. They would all be at each other's throats if it werna for the marriage bonds."

"Is that why you married Turius?" The question was out before Deidre could stop herself.

The slightly glazed look returned and Formorian became so quiet Deidre was about to leave. Finally she nodded. "Aye. Had I not been given to Turius, Ambrose would have laid claim to my father's land. It would have been his right. I couldna let that happen."

Again, Deidre was amazed at Formorian's forthrightness. She hadn't thought the woman had had a single altruistic thought in her entire life. Deidre ventured a bit further. "Is that why Angus—the laird, I mean—married Lady Elen?"

Formorian's full mouth tightened into a thin line and then she forced a smile. "Mac Erca would make a formidable enemy, but he had no desire to invade this land, not after ousting Fergus onto it."

"Then why did Angus marry?" Deidre pressed. For the life of her, she'd never seen two people so completely incompatible as he and Elen were.

But Formorian's face became guarded. "Ye'll have to ask Elen that." She shook her head a little as though to clear it. "I came out here to offer my help."

"Your help?"

"Aye. Ye may not be able to prevent the marriage, but ye can prevent the bruises and being beaten."

Deidre had every intention of preventing the marriage, if she had to steal a horse to do it. Better to be hanged than raped by Niall. Still, she was curious. "How so?"

Formorian gave her a genuine smile. "A man develops a certain . . . uh, respect . . . for a woman who can yield a dirk well. If he knows yer aim is deadly, he'll think twice about turning his back on ye when yer mad. And," she added as her smile widened into a grin, "a sharp blade pressed to hot balls will cool any advances ye doona want." She paused and studied Deidre. "As long as ye aren't afraid to follow through with it. A man will know if ye aren't."

The thought of castrating Niall was definitely appealing, but Deidre didn't want to get that close. A knife in his black heart would be fine. And she'd do it, too, if there was no other way out. She took a deep breath and nodded. "Let's get started."

"Your mother seems to be getting weaker again," Deidre said to Gilead a couple of days later as they rode along a southerly route toward some ruins in the forest he was taking her to see.

He looked worried as he nodded. "Yes, I noticed. I think the stress of having Formorian around all the time takes its toll."

"Mayhap," Deidre answered doubtfully, "but they do try and stay away from each other. Formorian has even stopped the blatant flirting at dinnertime."

Gilead raised an eyebrow. "Are ye defending her?"

"No. It's just that . . ." She wasn't sure how to put it into words. It was as though, since Angus and the queen were in each other's company much of the day, they had fallen into a sort of comfortable routine. Or they had come to their senses with Turius always at hand. In either case, Elen seem resigned to the woman's presence. She did what any lady of breeding would do. She ignored her opponent. Not that Formorian seemed to notice. "Well, how would she get any kind of poison to your mother? She knows we're watching. Meara and Brena are the only two who serve her." She didn't want to add that Angus still brought the morning wine.

Gilead seemed to read her thoughts. "But since my father's been back, she's grown weaker again. Do ye taste the wine?"

Deidre nodded. The first time she'd done it in front of Angus, his eyes had turned stormy and if looks could bore holes, she'd have been pinned to the wall. Then, suddenly, he had smiled and told her it was good to know he would not be a suspect anymore since she was obviously still alive. But his voice had had an ominous tone to it.

"What troubles me, though, is I have found empty wine goblets in her chambers in the morning. Lady Elen says it's only something that helps her sleep."

"I'm grateful for yer concern, Dee," Gilead said as they

entered a small clearing and stopped the horses. "We'll have to keep vigilant."

He dismounted and came around to help her off Winger. His strong hands around her waist sent a familiar spiral of warmth flooding her body and she longed to throw her arms around him and have him hold her close. She resisted the urge. Since their passionate kiss at the stone circle, he had kept himself at a proper distance. She knew if she tried to move closer, he would retreat behind the wall of formality. She sighed.

At least he wasn't angry with her anymore. Although he was obviously skeptical about The Book, she thought he might believe that she really was searching for the Philosopher's Stone. He had already taken her to a holy well and she had spoken to the doire who kept it, to no avail. They had ridden to a Druid's grove that was no longer used, but the energy of that place was long gone, probably thanks to half of the oak trees having been hewn down. She had pointed out a faerie mound on one ride, marked by its singular hawthorn tree, and they had stopped, but no sidhe magic lingered there either. This was the last place Gilead could think of that might have ties to the ancient past where a mad magician may have hidden the Stone.

They walked up the slight incline and Deidre looked at the few stones left to mark the foundation. The building had been rectangular and probably could hold no more than ten people. There was an opening where they stood, which had probably been the entrance. At the far end stood a marble slab, no more than four cubits long by a cubit wide and three cubits high. Deidre slid her hands across the smooth, cool surface.

"This looks like an altar of some sort."

"Aye. It was a hermitage built by one of St. Patrick's monks."

Deidre was puzzled. "If this was a Christian place, no magician—or Druid, if that's what he was—would set foot in it. Besides, they didn't believe in worshipping in man-made structures."

"True, but this chapel sits on top of a pagan burial ground." Gilead smiled. "I think it was a way for the Christians to think they were doing away with the old religion."

Deidre scoffed at that. "They couldn't quite kill off the

Goddess, though. Even in their religion, one aspect of Isis remains as the Holy Mother and another aspect in the Magdalen." She looked down and probed a loose stone with her foot. "Will you help me dig?"

"Aye. We'll have to be careful, though, because this will be difficult to explain. I'll bring some shovels and hide them in that small shack there."

She regarded the remains of what must have been attached to the chapel at one time and nodded. He was going to help her! She smiled happily and reached up to hug him, but he stepped out of reach, his face impassive.

"We'd best be getting back," he said.

She stared at his broad, retreating back as he went to get the horses. And then a thought came to her as clear as the Sight. *He's afraid of me. But why?*

Niall wished he had his sword. It was comforting keeping his hand on the hilt, even though he had no chance of escaping if his plan didn't work. But the Saxon brutes who met him on the muddy shores of Loch Leven disarmed him before he'd even fully dismounted. And then they blindfolded him and made him walk, instead of ride, since they'd brought no horses. It was nearly a league to the hidden camp along the river that led to the port of Leven on the Firth of Forth. By God, Ida's mead had best be strong to make up for this indignity!

If Fergus had been willing to come south and take on Turius and Gabran's armies, Niall could have saved himself this encounter. He'd had a devil of a time convincing a select few of his men to try and treaty with the Saxons. He'd sent three scouts to the northern shores to watch for longboats. That fool, Angus, may be willing to take troops to Lothian, but Niall didn't think the Pictish king had quite scared off the Saxons as he thought he had. Sure enough. It didn't take long to spot another keelboat wedging its way into the narrows along the southern peninsular of Fife Ness.

His men had almost been killed. Even now, Ida held two of them hostage and had let only one return.

The guards removed Niall's blindfold and shoved him

through a flap in a tent. It took a moment for his eyes to adjust, and he blinked in the candlelight.

Ida sat on the edge of his cot, a wolf-hide cloak about his shoulders, his yellow hair hanging down in two thick braids. He motioned to a tree stump that served as a chair and picked up a skin of mead from the floor. He poured hefty amounts into two wooden cups and handed one to Niall.

"You vant to talk, *ja?*"

Niall swigged a good draft, letting the mellow liquid slide down his throat before it lit a fire in his stomach. "Aye. I think we have a common goal."

The Saxon looked at him, unblinking. "Vat vould that be?"

"Land." Niall pulled a parchment from his sporran and handed it to Ida.

Ida spread it out on the cot beside him. A large area had been circled.

Niall leaned forward and pointed. "This land belongs to Angus Mac Oengus. Part of it is rightfully mine. The other half could be yers. Ye wouldna even have to fight the Picts for it."

Ida ran a thick finger around the radius of the circle. "A fine piece of land. Fertile. Shoreline for fishing and shipping. I doubt that the man vould give it up."

"Aye. He wouldna," Niall agreed. "But the clans expect ye to sail on south to Lothian. Angus has already sent forces there so he is but half-manned at his fort." He waited and was pleased at the reaction on Ida's face. Greed was always a good motivator. "And my troops wilna resist ye. All I ask is for my half when it's over."

"Culross is a good distance in," Ida said. "Ve'd be spotted vell before ve could attack. I'll not sacrifice brave men needlessly."

Sacrifice! By the Dagda! What were a few hundred men for such a reward? Niall never could understand that softness in Turius and here was a supposedly fearless Saxon spouting the same garbage. Well, perhaps once they'd taken Oengus, he'd overthrow Ida as well. It shouldn't be hard. Niall struggled not to sneer.

"Certes. Ye divert their attention. Ye have smaller boats attached to yer keels? It is not so verra hard to paddle the river to Loch Leven and then 'tis but a few leagues overland to Culross. They'd never be expecting Saxons to attack from the land. While their attention be turned, yer main force can sail right through the Firth and launch a full attack from the water side."

Ida stroked his chin thoughtfully. "It's risky splitting my men."

Bel's fires! Did the man think war was sitting down to tea? Niall wondered how the Saxons had ever gained a foothold in the south if they were all so hesitant to fight. Och, Turius with his undying hope for peace probably welcomed them!

"Then we need Fortune on our side." Niall eyed the skin of mead meaningfully and Ida shoved it toward him. He poured himself another good serving. "What if I told ye I know a hidden passageway that leads directly to the lairdess's chambers? Mayhap abducting the laird's wife would make him more willing to bargain with ye in the end."

Niall doubted that stealing Elen would bother Angus at all, but the laird would not want to incur the wrath of Mac Erca, either. And if Niall could manage to "rescue" Elen back from the fierce—ha!—Saxons, Mac Erca would have to look favorably on him. And if Angus were killed, he might even marry his widow! Although not until he finished breaking that bitch, Deidre. Och, he'd ravish her first. More than once. And then he'd arrange for an accident when he was through thoroughly humiliating her.

He pulled another, smaller, piece of vellum from his sporran. "A map of the castle. The postern gate lies here." He indicated with his finger. "Once I unlock it, yer men can slip inside from there and cause the distraction needed." He turned the paper slightly and pointed to a spot near the Forth River which flowed directly beneath the south wall. "There is a cave here, inaccessible at high tide but easy to maneuver at low. There's a stone passage that leads underground and into the keep. A good way for the lairds to sneak in and out if the fort were under siege." Niall had discovered it quite by accident several years ago. He'd suspected that Angus and Formorian were trysting and he'd followed Angus one day, only to see Formorian emerge from a shallow pool of water near the cave like some water sprite. He'd waited until they'd gone into the wood and then discovered the hidden stairwell. Aye, he'd expose that rutting too. If Angus survived, Mac Erca wouldn't take kindly to his exposing the adultery. Especially when Niall would promise to take such good care of the gentle lady.

With Mac Erca behind him, he could even take on the Picts. Fergus Mor wouldn't gain another league of land. Niall liked the idea.

From the corner of her eye, Deidre watched as Gilead heaved a shovelful of dirt from the chapel ruins. He had taken his shirt off with the heat of the July sun, and his body glistened with a light beading of sweat. The muscles in his back bunched and expanded as he lifted the heavy shovel, his well-defined biceps bulging as he threw the dirt. If only she were the swooning sort. She'd love to fall right into that strong embrace and smell the sun-freshness of him.

Suddenly, he dropped to his knees and began pawing the ground. "I think I've found something."

Deidre was on her knees beside him, her lustful fantasy momentarily forgotten. They'd managed to ride out twice before and dig, but found only grave markers.

Gilead pried at the stone until it came loose. Raising it, he scraped the dirt off and handed it to her. She looked at the symbols scratched on it. Only another marker.

He must have seen the look of disappointment on her face, for he took her hand and stood, lifting her with him. He leaned on his shovel. "That's probably all we're going to find, Sassenach. Markers of those who lived and died here."

She knew he was right. They had cleared almost half of the small area. Once they'd dug skeletal remains, which they carefully reburied to keep the shade from rising. But that was all. Still, she wanted to finish the job.

"I just have to know. I feel that the Stone is close."

Before he could answer, the bell in the little kirk in the village near the castle started clanging, followed by a ferocious screeching of bagpipes and the blowing of sheep horns.

"What on earth is that racket?" Deidre asked, but Gilead was already running for the horses.

"We're under attack!" he said quickly and plopped her unceremoniously into the saddle. "We'll try to head back through the postern gate."

They took the precaution of stopping well within the protection of the forest. Gilead narrowed his eyes, squinting. "The postern gate is open. Strange. We'll leave the horses here and approach on foot."

It seemed to take an infinity to reach the shadow of the stone wall and Deidre could hear the ruckus long before they slipped unnoticed through the unmanned gate. Still, she wasn't prepared for what she saw in the bailey.

There were Saxons everywhere, their light hair matted with blood, the saexes clanging against the shields of Turius's men. Angus's warriors countered the Saxon battle-axes with their own heavy claymores. The archers on the battlements were firing furiously at the front of the fort, no doubt holding back more invaders. She saw the stable boys hauling buckets of pitch and boiling water up the ladders. Some of Turius's men had formed a turtle shell, guarding the massive gate to keep it from being opened by the Saxons already inside the walls. Their spears stuck out between the front shields, as well as the side panels. Warriors in the center of the formation crouched and held their shields over their heads, protecting all of them. A classic Roman strategy. Deidre had heard Childebert discussing it more than once, but she had never seen it used. And she hoped she never would again.

She caught a glimpse of Angus and Turius fighting back to back, both of them strangely calm, even though they were surrounded by the fiendish barbarians. They both moved with determination, circling slowly, eyes wary.

Gilead pulled her toward the back wall, out of sight, and drew his sword. "Come, I'll get ye into the keep. Find my mother and bolt her door. Doona open it for anyone."

"Aid yer Da, Gilead," Formorian said as she dashed toward them, long sword in one hand and dirk in the other. "I'll take her inside."

Gilead hesitated only a second. "Ye stay inside, too. I'll not have my father fashing about yer safety while he's in battle."

For a moment, Formorian's eyes narrowed. She was dressed for battle, her hair pulled under a helmet, smears of blood on her hauberk. Then she nodded. "Aye. I'll watch over yer mother. Go to him."

Gilead gave Deidre one lingering glance and then he was gone.

Formorian thrust the dirk into Deidre's hand. "Don't be afraid to use this if ye have to." She peered cautiously around the corner. "Ye havna been spotted yet. A pity ye're in that dress, though. We have to make a dash to the kitchen door." She reached down and pulled a sgian dubh from her boot. The black handle on the knife glistened ominously in the shadow. "If we're attacked, pretend to swoon. Get in close, slash the groin. Thank Boudicca, the brynies the Saxon wear are short and their privates unprotected." She grinned. "Arrogant of them, isna it?"

Deidre stared at her. How could she laugh at a time like this? They might very well be killed in the next few minutes. She wanted nothing more than to clam her hands over her ears and shut out the clamor of steel against steel, and the screams of the wounded and dying.

"I'm scared," she whispered.

Formorian gave her an appraising look. "We doona have time to be scared. Ye must keep yer wits about ye until we're inside." She cocked her head and listened. "The noise is lessening, it shouldna be long now."

Deidre gathered up her skirt, not caring if her legs showed. She was going to run like the horned god himself was after her. "It shouldn't be long for what?"

"Until we win." She smiled wickedly. "I doubt that the barbarians knew that Angus's troops were reinforced with Turius's. Else they would not have been so stupid as to send in only a small contingent and leave their main forces outside." She looked around the corner again. "Let's go!"

Deidre had only a whirlwind glimpse of the devastation as they raced toward the back entrance to the kitchen. The bailey was littered with bodies, but Angus and Turius were still on their feet. She saw Gilead's sword flash in the sun.

"A woman!" she heard someone shout and she drew on an inner strength she didn't know she had and darted forward.

"Two of them," another voice shouted from close behind. Far too close. She felt rough hands on her arm jerking her backward and then the hand went slack. She turned briefly to see the Saxon face down, a dirk in his back. Looking up, she saw Gilead nod toward her before he returned to the battle.

Formorian was wielding her sword against the second man. "Get behind me," she ordered, and Deidre moved blindly, realizing that they needed to inch toward the door before someone else spotted them. She held her dirk a bit more firmly, wishing she had more skill. *Please, Goddess. If I survive this, I vow to practice with the dirk for hours, just as Formorian had told me to do. Just let me live!*

Formorian deflected the shorter saexe easily with her sword, her footwork as graceful as a dancer's. She feinted to the right and then the left, the heavier warrior trying to match her light steps. With his fur cloak tossed over his shoulders, he looked like a big lumbering bear.

Deidre's back bumped against the door. They had made it. She tried to pull the door only to find it locked. Bolted from the inside. She turned and pounded on the door, trying to shout above the din.

Formorian never took her eyes off her opponent, concentrating her efforts. If it seemed as though she had been playing with the man before, she was serious now, with the door locked. She parried quickly, careful to keep enough space between them so she would not press her sword against his. She disengaged suddenly, passing her blade beneath the saexe, and lunged in a blur of movement.

Deidre heard the soft swishing sound as the sword drove home, impaling the man. Funny, she thought, that death would come so quietly amid the battle. And then the door opened behind her and she nearly fell through.

Formorian leaped over her and Meara slammed the door shut again, sliding the bolt with one hand. In the other, she held her meat cleaver. Deidre didn't think she'd ever been so glad to see the cranky cook. No Saxon would live to get past her.

She rushed up the stairs, Formorian at her heels. They found Elen cringing in a corner, holding her little paring knife that she used for eating in front of her.

Formorian gave it a cursory glance and shook her head as

she fastened the bolt. "Did ye not even think to lock yer door?"

Elen's eyes were huge in her white face. "Get out of here!"

Instead, Formorian pulled up a chair next to the door and laid her bloodied sword across her knees. "I canna do that. Yer son asked me to take care of ye and Deidre."

Elen looked at Deidre, who nodded. "Formorian saved my life just now."

"Well, then," Elen said in a calmer voice, "I suppose I must put up with her." She straightened her shoulders and walked toward the table where she sat daintily on the edge of a tapestry chair. "Would ye care for some wine?"

Formorian's eyes glittered and Deidre was afraid she would start laughing. Not a wise thing to do. Elen might have a gentle nature, but the steely glint in her eyes showed Deidre that there might just be a bit of something much stronger in Elen. She just hoped, when the battle was over in the bailey, that another battle wouldn't have begun in here.

Angus stripped off his bloody and torn shirt and sank down on a stool in the infirmary. "See to him first," he told the medic. "I can wait."

Gilead clamped his jaw tight as the medic poured whiskey into the deep cut on his thigh and then began the painful stitching together of the ragged flesh. It hurt like hell, but that didn't matter. If he hadn't turned in time, his voice would have been noticeably higher in a week or two. The man had just finished binding the leg in linen when the door burst open and Deidre, his mother, and Formorian all came through at once.

Deidre and Elen rushed over to him. "How badly are ye hurt, son?"

Gilead managed a smile. "I'll heal."

"He needs to stay off that leg a few days," the medic said as he poured clean water into the basin and handed Elen a cloth. "If ye'll see to the cuts and bruises on his chest, I'll tend to the laird."

"No need," Formorian said. "I'll do it." Already, she had cleansed Angus's shoulder wound and was winding the needle through in tidy little stitches. She tied a knot and bent her head to bite the thread.

Gilead hoped he was the only one who noticed Formorian's tongue flicker to lick the skin near the wound, but then he saw how pale his mother had grown. Could the queen not contain herself even when his father was wounded and his mother was present? Formorian's hair was plastered to her head with sweat and she was covered in grime. Blood splattered her clothes, but Angus was looking at her as though she'd just stepped out of a hot bath. Gilead shook his head. "Playing with fire," he muttered under his breath.

Elen's mouth set in a tight line as she turned away, but she grew even more pale at the sight of Gilead.

"She's never been able to handle the sight of blood," Angus said.

Deidre took her arm to steady her. "Maybe you'd better leave," she said as she took the cloth away. "I can finish here."

Elen put a hand to her mouth and bolted to the door.

Gilead watched in silence as Deidre added warm water to the basin from the kettle hung over the brazier. She dipped the cloth in it and began to dab gently at the abrasions on his shoulders. By the Christian God, she had a touch softer than an angel's. He tried to get her to look at him, but she kept her eyes averted, tending to her task. He gasped a little when she dribbled the alcohol over the cuts, not so much in pain, but to see what her reaction would be.

She was instantly contrite. "I'm sorry. I didn't mean to hurt you, but the gashes must be clean or they'll fester."

"I can bear it." Gilead purposely avoided his father's incredulous stare and Formorian's amused smile. If he wanted to bask in a little attention, it was his due, wasn't it? Deidre was not often this docile. She was even more careful as she finished her ministrations and stepped back.

"That should do it," she said. "Formorian and I should be going."

He wasn't ready to let her go and caught her hand. "I think I'm going to be really stiff tomorrow. Would ye mind rubbing my back a bit before ye leave?"

"An excellent idea," Formorian said with an impish grin as

she looked at Angus. "Do ye think ye may be stiff tomorrow, too, my lord?"

He grinned back at her. "Aye. Mayhap I'll even need a stroking in the morn."

Gilead ignored both of them. There was magic in Deidre's fingers as she slowly spread them over his upper back and lightly kneaded his shoulders. Her hands traced a path down either side of his spine and up along his ribs, then circled his back again. Her touch was both soothing and arousing. Maybe there was a touch of witchcraft in the lass after all, but he wasn't about to complain. The pain of his wounds was definitely worth the attention he was getting.

Abruptly, though, they were interrupted as the door swung open and Elen stood glaring at them. "If it's not too much trouble, husband, Turius would like a word with ye." She nodded stiffly to Formorian. "I should think ye would wish to clean up a bit before yer husband sees ye."

Formorian gave Angus's arm a final pat before stepping away. "He's seen me far worse, but aye, a bath would be wonderful."

"I'll go, too," Deidre said quickly. "Lady Elen, you've had quite an upsetting day. Maybe a quiet dinner in your room this eve would be good." She turned back to Gilead. "I never did thank you for saving my life today."

"Ye repaid me already," he said and smiled at her.

Angus reached for a clean shirt after the ladies left and pulled it over his head. "That was quite an accomplishment," he said.

Gilead straightened his own shirt. "'Twas nothing. The brute intended to rape her. I put a dirk in the man's back. Anyone would have done the same."

"Certes," his father answered. "That wasna what I was talking about."

"I doona know what ye mean."

Angus chuckled. "Ye acted verra brave, only groaning a little from the deep pain ye must have felt from those wee cuts she tended for ye."

"It was the pain in my leg that I groaned about," Gilead said evasively.

"Then why dinna ye make a sound when the medic was sewing ye up?" He held his hand up as Gilead started to protest. "Doona worry, son. Yer secret is safe with me." He walked to the door and then turned back as he was about to leave. "But who is it, exactly, that's playing with fire?"

Deidre pushed aside the linen bedsheet and turned over. She had been tossing about for well over an hour. It had been a long, stressful day with the Saxon fighting and she should be sound asleep by now, but her thoughts kept returning to Gilead.

Had he actually been flirting with her? Seeing him nearly naked with only a plaid strewn across his loins had nearly taken her breath away. The snowy bandage had only served to accentuate the bronze color of well-developed, corded thighs. The skin on his back had felt satiny smooth over hard muscles and she had liked the way he involuntarily caught his breath when she softened her touch to brush lightly down his ribs and along the lower curve of his spine. If only she'd had the courage to sweep across his buttocks. She wondered what his reaction would have been then.

She rolled onto her back. She was never going to get any sleep if she kept thinking about him. The tips of her breasts were tingling and the pulsating throb had begun again between her legs. If she felt like this now, what would she feel like if he actually touched her *there?* Fleetingly, she thought of how the parlor maids had giggled about being tupped at the Frankish court. At the time she had been appalled, thanks in large part to the stern admonishments of Clotilde. But now she was beginning to envy those wenches their ability to make free with their favors.

She raised and punched her pillow, then sank back down into its depths. She must get some sleep.

Just as she was finally beginning to get drowsy, the air was rent by Elen's bloodcurdling scream.

Chapter Thirteen

THE ABDUCTION

Deidre threw on a robe as she rushed out the door. The stone floor was cold on her bare feet, but that scream had sounded fatal. She caught a wisp of dark skirt disappearing at the servant's stairs at the far end of the hall, but had no time to pursue it.

She flung the door open and rushed in. Elen stood in the middle of the room, pressed back against a huge Saxon. He had one burly arm around her waist and a hand over her mouth. Her dilated eyes contrasted with the bloodless white of her face.

Deidre turned to run for help and met the cold, blue eyes of another warrior as he silently slid the bolt on the door. He smiled wolfishly.

"It seems ve have a bonus here, Eric," he said as he advanced slowly toward her. "Ida vill be pleased vith two for ransom, I think."

Deidre eyed him warily. She couldn't step back much or she'd bump into Elen and the Saxon kept himself between her and the door. She wished she had the dirk she'd been practicing with. Formorian had told her to learn to sleep with it, but she had dashed out without thinking to pick it up. Still, she had to do something. She made a leap for the bed and scuttled across it, hoping to make it to the door.

The Saxon caught her legs and hauled her back across the bed, pinning her body with his while his hand gripped her hair, lowering his head to capture her mouth.

"Henrick! Ve don't have time for this," Eric snarled. "Let's go."

Already, Deidre could hear boots thundering up the steps. Thank God. They'd be rescued soon, since there was no way out.

Eric dragged Elen with him and pressed something near the small table that sat by the wall. Deidre stared, in stupefied horror, at a panel opening behind a tapestry. A passageway!

Henrick ran a thick finger across her mouth and sighed. "This vill have to vait." He rolled off her and grabbed her arm, yanking her upright and close to his side. "Move."

Deidre struggled against him and he cuffed her on her chin, causing her to stagger. For a moment, she saw sparkles in front of her eyes.

"I'll knock you out, voman, if you don't stop fighting."

Deidre decided that keeping her wits about her would at least give her a chance to escape. And someone had to look after Elen. She needed to stay conscious to do that. She went deceptively limp. "All right."

He cast a wary glance at her, but there was pounding on the door and Angus was shouting angrily. Henrick pushed Deidre through the opening in the wall and pressed something that caused the panel to slide shut.

She had never been in such total darkness. It felt thick and suffocating and she had no sense of balance. She felt herself teetering.

Henrick gave her arm a jerk. "Hold still. I don't vant you breaking your pretty little neck until I'm done with you."

She heard flint striking and then a torch flared, illuminating the area. Deidre squinted; the light seemed blinding after the pitch black.

They were standing on a small landing and she could see stone steps leading steeply downward. Eric held the torch with one hand and pulled Elen along with the other.

Henrick put his hand on the small of her back. "Unless you vant to go headlong, move. Now. Ve've not much time."

The pounding on the door was muffled in the tunnel and grew fainter as they descended. Deidre tried to calculate how long it would take Angus to get an axe and hew through the solid oak door.

They finally emerged in a small cave, not large enough to stand up in. Icy water swirled around Deidre's bare feet and soaked the hem of her nightgown as they crouched and crawled out of the hole.

"Are you all right?" she asked Elen worriedly.

To her surprise, Elen seemed calm. She smiled and patted Deidre's hand. "Whatever happens, save yerself if ye can."

"Not without you," Deidre whispered back.

"Stop the jabbering!" Eric pulled a small coracle hidden in some reeds near the bank of the Forth. "Get in."

They did as they were told. As the lightweight round boat bobbed up and down, caught in the swift current, Deidre thought it highly likely they might not survive the journey to wherever the longboats waited.

She was surprised then, when Eric poled away from the deepening water and headed for shore. Henrick released his hold on the two women to grab another pole and pull against the tide.

Elen made her move. Whether from panic or some random thought that suicide was better than capture, Deidre would never know. Elen stood up suddenly, causing the coracle to spin dizzily. Both men cursed as they fought to steady it, and, before Deidre could release her own hold on the side of it, Elen had fallen into the frigid water.

Deidre leaned over, trying to grasp a foot or part of the gown, only to find herself yanked backward by her hair. She didn't even notice the pain. Elen was fast being sucked out into the ever-widening expanse that led to open water.

Eric cursed as he leaned over with the pole extended in an attempt to catch Elen, but she was beyond his reach.

Deidre watched helplessly as the fragile arms flailed in an attempt to swim, and then Elen disappeared below the surface. Deidre strained her eyes, but could see no more, even with the moon's beams on the water. No screams or cries for help filled the air, only the sound of waves breaking over each other in their eternal rush to the sea.

With one last, massive stroke, the door splintered and Angus, Turius, and Gilead nearly fell into the room, swords drawn.

"Where is she?" Gilead asked. "I know the scream came from here."

"Aye. I heard it too," Angus said grimly and then went over to the small table. He touched something along the wall and, to Gilead's amazement, a passageway opened.

"I dinna know that was here!" he said.

"It goes down to the sea," Angus said. "The laird who built the castle wanted a sure escape if he needed it."

Turius sheathed his sword. "We'd better get going. Whoever took her already has a good start."

A short time later, they waded through the shallow water of the cave onto solid land. Angus bent down. "Something's been dragged here," he said as his hand scraped the mud.

"A boat, most like," Turius agreed, "and small enough to be hidden."

Angus stood up. "A small boat only big enough for one or two men and a woman. They'd likely not fight the ebb tide, fast as it is."

"They'd be headed for sea, then," Gilead said. "Do ye think the Saxons didn't learn their lesson today with the slaughter?"

Turius snorted. "They don't fear death. If they die in battle, one of their Valkyries escorts them straight to Valhalla." He turned to Angus. "But how would they know about the passage?"

"I don't know," he answered, "but I'm going to find out. Turius, go back and rouse the men. Tell them to skirt the coast and look for any signs of longboats. I'm going to follow the shore for a way."

"It might not be wise by yourself," Turius said. "If you come across a band . . ."

"I know this shoreline well," Angus replied. "There's a

rocky jetty less than half a league from here. The water behind it remains still enough to swim in. If Saxons didn't take Elen, whoever it was would most likely have horses waiting there."

Gilead knew the place and suddenly he wondered if this was another trysting spot of his father's. An image of a naked Formorian and his father splashing water at each other rose unbidden in his mind. And then another image imposed itself. Deidre, not quite submerged enough to cover her breasts, her nipples hard . . . He shook his head to clear it. His mother was missing, for God's sake.

"I'm coming with ye," he said.

For a moment, Angus looked like he might argue, but then he nodded. They moved into the wood, out of sight of any hidden men who might be waiting to pick them off, and followed the shore as closely as they could. They didn't speak, keeping their eyes peeled on the coast, and their ears open for any unusual sounds, but the forest was silent. Even their footsteps made no noise on the damp, fallen pine needles atop a cushion of moss. Not quite an hour later, they cautiously left the trees and headed toward the water.

Gilead could see the jagged edge of the jetty looming up ahead and then a cloud scudded across the moon, dimming the view. When the waning light returned, he nearly stumbled over a sodden bundle.

He looked down and then gave a low cry that caused Angus to turn around sharply. "What is it?"

But Gilead was already kneeling on the ground, holding the crumbled heap that was his mother.

Dawn broke, streaks of fire rending the dark sky as Deidre's captors led her into the Saxon camp.

They'd ridden most of the night, following deer paths and sometimes treading their way through dense underbrush in the deeper recesses of the forest. Deidre's legs were scratched and her feet cut from where they had to walk and lead the horses, but it was her wrists that hurt most, rubbed raw from the rope that bound her hands.

As glad as she was to slide down from the saddle and Henrick's grasp of her, she muffled a scream at the sight of some twenty barbarian warriors in various stages of morning undress.

A huge man with a brushy beard lumbered over. "Did you bring us a fair piece of sport, Henrick?" He reached for her breast with a leer on his face.

Henrick glowered at him and brushed his hand away. "I've not had her yet. You'll have to vait your turn."

Deidre shuddered involuntarily. How long could she keep from being raped? And, by the interested looks of the men now forming a circle around her, she wondered if she might even survive, once the pillage started. This was not the way she wanted to lose her virginity, and she didn't want to die being torn apart by savages.

What she wouldn't give to have had military training like Formorian, but she didn't even have the sgian dubh the queen had given her. Clotilde had kept her too protected, afraid her virtue would be compromised, and Deidre had been happy to immerse herself in stories of a perfect world in which knights rescued damsels in distress. She squelched her fear. According to that blasted book, when Gwenhwyfar was abducted, the legendary Lancelot rescued her. But there was no Lancelot in this world, nor any other gallant knights, either. Gilead came close, but he was wounded. And would anyone think to look for her, anyhow? They'd be far more concerned over Elen's disappearance. She'd have to fend for herself and the odds weren't good.

Another man stepped up and dangled a bag of coins in front of Henrick. "This is yours if you'll let me be first."

Others moved forward, too, rummaging through their clothes for coin. "I'll pay more than him," one said, only to have another yell over him, "Knucklehead! I've more money than the rest of you!"

Someone pushed Henrick aside and grabbed Deidre's arm. She tried to kick him, but with bare feet it made little impact on his shin. He merely laughed and pulled her toward him for a kiss, but she was jerked away before he had the chance. Suddenly, she was being jostled from one man to the other, each vying for first rights, it seemed. She stumbled and would have fallen except that there was always another pair of arms waiting to grab her. Anywhere. Places that she wanted only Gilead to touch.

"Hold!"

The persecution stopped and the men dropped back abruptly. The man who'd issued the command glowered at his soldiers as he strode through the now-silent ranks and came to a stop in front of her.

He was shirtless and his blond hair hung wet and loose to his shoulders. He had obviously been in the midst of morning washing and did not look pleased to be interrupted. He was nearly as tall as Angus and Deidre tried not to notice the many battle scars that crisscrossed his broad chest and heavily muscled arms. She had no doubt that he could swing one of the deadly battle-axes easily with one massive hand.

His eyes were the light blue of glaciers and nearly as cold. Deidre shivered slightly, in spite of the nearby fire that broke the morning chill. The man's voice was civil, though, when he spoke.

"My name is Ida. Velcome to my temporary quarters. I trust you vere not harmed coming here?" When she did not answer, he narrowed his eyes. Then he caught her chin with his thumb and forefinger and turned her head to the side.

"How did you get that bruise?"

Trying to think of a way to escape, she had almost forgotten the cuff that Henrick had given her. Now she was aware of the swelling and she winced at the pain. "I turned down your kind invitation to visit," she said, with more bravado than she felt.

His eyes glinted, either in anger at her sarcasm, or in humor. She couldn't tell.

"Vich one hit you?"

She caught the look of sheer terror that crossed Henrick's face. Well, too bad.

She pointed to him.

Ida dropped his hand and turned. Not a word was said, but Henrick stepped forward, his face pale. Ida hardly appeared to move, but the crunch of fist meeting bone sounded like thunder and then Henrick was on the ground, holding his bloody nose.

Ida looked at his men. "You can rut yourselves raw vith any other voman ve capture, but I'll not have this hostage harmed. Not vhen I can exchange her for land title. Does anyone vish to dispute me?"

The men shook their heads quickly and moved to other tasks. Eric gave Deidre almost a pleading look as he helped Henrick walk away.

Ida looked down at her. "You'll have nothing to fear vhile you're here. Once your husband agrees to turn over enough hides of land to allow us to settle, you'll be freed."

Her husband? Lands? Deidre stared at him as comprehension dawned. He thought she was Elen! The abduction must have been fully planned, the scrimmage yesterday a diversion. But Elen had drowned. No wonder Eric had given her that look. If Ida knew they had failed to bring back the right woman, they'd be in for worse than a bloody nose.

Angus wouldn't be paying a ransom for her. He wouldn't even look for her if they found Elen. What would Ida do when he found out she was only a maid?

"I want to know what happened," Angus said from where he was sitting at the table in Elen's chamber.

Gilead looked up, tucking the blanket around his mother's chin. "She's been through an ordeal, Da. Let her get some sleep."

Brena clucked disapprovingly at Angus as she slid the warmed clay bricks under the covers at Elen's feet. "Aye. My lady should rest."

Angus ignored her protest. "It's near dawn. We need to be battle-ready. Why don't ye go and get us all some wine?"

He waited until she'd left and then walked over to the bed. "I need to know, Elen. We could be under attack soon."

Her voice sounded strained and he bent to hear. "Brena had set down my sleeping potion on the table. Just as she left, the wall opened . . . Saxons . . . two of them . . ." Her voice drifted and her eyes closed.

Gilead felt for a pulse and then sat back, relieved. "She's still alive."

Angus cursed to himself. Who could have known about that secret passageway? He and Mori had used it long ago, after she was married to Turius, but he was still single. His father had revealed it to him before he died, and cautioned him not to let even the most trusted servant know. And he had held to that. He hadn't even mentioned it to Gilead, knowing that his suspicious son would assume the worst of him and Mori.

Elen opened her eyes again and gestured feebly to Gilead. "Deidre . . ."

He took her hand. "Do ye want me to get her? She's probably awake by now."

She looked distressed. "Nay. She's . . . gone . . ."

Angus frowned. "What do ye mean, gone?" If that wench somehow discovered the passage . . . if she were a Saxon spy, by the Dagda, he'd hunt her down himself.

"They took her, too," Elen whispered.

He leaned closer. "Where?"

"I don't know. We were in the boat, headed for shore . . . that's when I fell in."

Gilead jumped up. "The jetty probably." He gave his mother a quick kiss and headed for the door.

"Where do ye think ye're going?" Angus asked.

"I'm going to go look for her. With the tide out, the mud should show tracks."

"Ye are in no condition to ride," Angus answered. "Ye already opened the wound with the walking ye did tonight. Turius's men will be ready as soon as they break their fast. We'll look then."

"I'm not waiting," Gilead answered. "I can make better time on my own."

Angus watched him leave and then looked down at his sleeping wife. Her color was coming back. Brena's potion must be working. Wearily, he went to the door.

Formorian waited for him in the hall, a goblet half-filled with whiskey in her hand. "How is she?" she asked as she handed him the drink.

He took a healthy swig and put an arm around her shoulders. "She'll live." He hesitated. "Have you ever told anyone about the passageway?"

"Our tryst tunnel?" she asked in surprise. "No."

"Well, someone found it. That's how the Saxons entered. I'll have it boarded up this morning." He sighed. "They took Deidre, too. Gilead, the fool, is chasing after her, which means Turius and I will have to follow him."

"Certes," Formorian said. "Why wouldn't ye?"

He pulled her close to him and laid his head on top of hers. "Because I'm not sure she didn't go willingly. There's a chance she's a Saxon spy."

She twisted in his arms and looked up at him. "Ye doona believe that!"

"Why not?" he asked with a smile as he swept a finger along her cheek. "I never have believed her story of bandits." His hand drifted down to brush across her breast.

Formorian caught it. "I doona believe it either, but I think it's something else. The lass has a secretive air about her sometimes, as though she sees things that we don't."

Angus raised an eyebrow. "Ye think she's a fey?"

"Nay. But I think she's searching for something. The circle of stones, the digging that she and Gilead have been doing—"

"What digging?"

"By the old hermitage," Formorian said. "Two of Turius's troops saw them."

"But why?"

"I don't know," she answered, "but I think ye need to find both of them before Gilead's captured too. Ida would not be kind."

"Ye're right," Angus said with a sigh and gave her a kiss on the forehead. "But when we get back, ye'll reward me for rescuing the fools?"

Formorian smiled. "I'll think of something."

Gilead dismounted and bent down. The tracks were there, all right. Two sets of boots and a pair of smaller, bare feet. *Deidre had no shoes!* If she had already been in bed when his mother screamed, then that meant she was wearing little except a night shift and maybe a robe. She would be cold, and he prayed whoever had taken her hadn't raped her. No woman deserved that, and Deidre had been trying to help his mother.

He followed the traces where the boat had scraped against the muddy bank. The coracle lay hidden behind thick gorse. A short space away, the mud was churned by horses' hooves. Two, from the looks of it. That meant one of the men would be carrying Deidre and that would slow them down.

Gilead remounted and edged along the deer trail. As the ground grew harder, the tracks disappeared, but there were enough broken branches and bent bracken for him to follow. The fools had been clumsy and made no effort to hide their trail and he wondered why they were headed north over land. Could it be a trap? Or had his mother been wrong and they weren't Saxons at all?

And who could have known about the passageway? His Da had said the secret was only passed down from father to son. Something niggled at the back of his mind, just below the surface. And then he had it. Formorian. That room had been the best guest room before his father married. No doubt she was given that room. The passageway would have made a perfect way for her to visit Angus without being discovered. The hair prickled on his arms. Could Formorian have been behind his mother's abduction? No doubt, Elen's disappearance would have made life easier for her, even if she were still married to Turius. She and his father could just use the tunnel again. It would make sense, if she'd hired mercenaries, that they'd travel over land and not by sea.

He must be near Lake Leven, he thought, as he proceeded deeper into the forest, on foot now, leading his horse. Low branches caused him to duck and pull Malcolm's head down as he fought his way through the underbrush. Where in the world were they taking Deidre? Brambles tore at his clothes, spiky thorns digging into his hands as he brushed the stuff away. He spotted a patch of brown on a bed of pine needles and dropped to his knee. Dried blood. Was Deidre hurt or were her feet cut?

He moved on. A short time later, he came upon a bit of

cloth snagged on the trunk of a hemlock. A piece of white linen, no doubt from her night shift. The sticky sap did not hide the bloodstain. Gilead rubbed at it, his fingers turning slightly red. Fresh. That meant they weren't far away. But Deidre was hurt.

He clenched his fists and gritted his teeth. He hoped he'd reach her in time.

Deidre felt like a rabbit far from its burrow and that the badger watching her was only biding his time. She pulled the overlarge woolen tunic more closely to herself and tucked her legs under her as she sat by the midday cooking fire with a chunk of roasted hare in her hand. She forced herself to eat. She would need her strength if she had a chance to escape.

Across the fire, Ida studied her with calculated slowness.

"I thought you vould be older," he said.

There it was again. He'd been throwing odd questions at her all morning, as if to ascertain that she really was Elen. She'd racked her brain coming up with what she hoped were reasonable answers.

"I was but a moon from still being a child when Angus married me," she said.

"Hmmm. Do you not have a grown son?"

"He's just barely reached his manhood." Deidre just hoped he hadn't seen Gilead. If he had, he'd know she was lying. She didn't think she'd seen Ida in the bailey that day fighting, but then, she'd scarcely had the leisure to observe anything.

He narrowed his eyes, considering. "I also heard you vere not vell. You look healthy to me."

How did he know this? He must have gotten the information from someone who knew the situation. Who could the traitor inside the fortress be? Her first thought was Formorian, but she couldn't quite see the queen negotiating with Saxons, even if it meant getting rid of Elen. No, Formorion had agreed to marry Turius to keep her land free, even though she loved Angus. She would never let Saxons overrun it. Who, then? Who could the filthy villain be?

"I made a complete recovery just recently," she said.

"So it vould seem," Ida said and let his gaze wander over her full breasts and rounded curves.

Deidre crossed her arms, trying to hide her obviously well-fed body. Ida might protect her now because he thought she was a valuable hostage, but he had said his men could ravish any other woman. The predatory look in his eye told her he'd probably take her first if he found out the truth.

"I'm grateful for your protection," she said, "and I'll make sure my husband hears that you've treated me well."

He inclined his head. "More blood need not be shed unless Angus vishes it. I sent a messenger that I vill trade you—unharmed—for title to land. All he needs to do is agree."

Deidre's heart sank. Angus would never agree. If Formorian had been captured, she knew both Turius and Angus would have brought full armies down on the Saxons. And, because Elen's father was a formidable Eire king, Angus would have had to make some showing of trying to get his wife back. No doubt, Elen's body had washed up on shore by now, and why would Angus send anyone to look for a Sassenach, especially one he didn't trust? Deidre figured that, if she were lucky, she might have two days before the Saxon scout returned with the news that they had the wrong woman. She forced herself to smile.

"I'm sure your man will bring good news in a day or two. I'm quite ready to go home and be reunited with my family."

"You von't be returning home just yet," Ida answered and tore off a hunk of meat from the haunch he held.

She tried not to notice how powerful those hands were. "What do you mean?"

He finished chewing and swallowed before he spoke. "I think Angus vill be more villing to negotiate if you're safely tucked away vhere he can't reach you. One of the keelboats vill take you to my homeland. The rest of us vill vait offshore until ve get a response."

Deidre hoped her voice wouldn't give away the despair she felt. "You don't need to do that. My husband would never attack if there were danger to me involved."

Ida grinned. "I'm no fool. Until I get enough men settled

to combat any raids that your husband might try to make, you'll be my guest . . . across the North Sea."

His prisoner, more like. And the Stone. She still felt strongly that it was near, or the clue to it was. She'd never find it where he was sending her. In fact, she'd be lucky if he didn't have her killed once he found out he'd been duped. She must stay here, and somehow, she must escape. Tonight.

"Of course you're no fool. But my husband will want to *see* that I'm well before he'll agree to anything."

Ida regarded her frankly. "As you may have noticed, this var band is rather small. Ve von't be vaiting here like sitting ducks for your husband's army to surround us. The longboats vait for us at the mouth of the Leven. Ve sail at high tide."

High tide? The water had been ebbing last night. Deidre did a quick calculation. The next high tide would probably be near dawn and they had several miles of the river to navigate. Not much time to plan her flight. She needed time to think.

"May I be excused? I should like to rest."

Ida nodded and motioned for one of the men to lead her to one of the tents. "And stand guard," he said.

Deidre was surprised to find the inside of the tent to be rather roomy. A cot stood along one side and two tree stumps provided a makeshift table and chair. On the "table" stood a tin ewer and basin, along with a washing cloth, soap, and a razor strap. She must be in Ida's lodgings, and, for a moment, she panicked. Would he expect to share them with her? Probably. One more reason she had to get away.

She washed some of the grime of the night's journey away and lay down on the cot to think. It wasn't long before she heard voices outside.

"Vhat do you vant?" her guard asked the visitor.

"I'm to relieve you so you can go eat," the second voice answered and she recognized it as Henrick. Just what she didn't need. She'd seen the murderous look he'd given her when Eric led him away. Like it was her fault Ida broke his nose. She jumped from the cot to tell her guard not to leave her alone with Henrick, but by the time she pulled the flap, he was already whistling his way toward the cooking fire.

She backed away, but Henrick followed her into the tent.

His grotesquely swollen nose only exaggerated the bared teeth that no one would call a smile.

"You're going to pay for this," he said as he pointed to his face.

Deidre edged around the table, hoping to keep it between them. "Ida told you to leave me alone."

The leer broadened. "Ida vent to the river to check on the coracles. By the time he gets back, I'll be done." He unlaced his trews. "You owe me a good swiving. It vill go easier for you if you're villing."

Willing? He was about as appealing as Niall, although not as old. Warily, she circled away from him, careful not to leave too much distance between herself and the table. She needed that obstacle in front of her.

He moved to the right; she did the same. He moved left and she mimicked him. He feinted then, to the right and back to the left. Deidre bolted for the flap.

He caught her around the waist and threw her onto the cot. His body was on hers, pressing her down. She struggled, pushing against his chest with her fists, her head turned away from his kiss. There wasn't any way she could kick him so she wrapped one leg tightly behind the other. He laughed and pushed her tunic up, one hand grabbing a breast and squeezing hard. Deidre gasped in pain and slapped at his face. He grunted a curse and yanked her hands over her head, holding the wrists together with one hand while the other pried her legs apart. He managed to get a knee between her thighs and was about to release himself from his trews when there was a commotion outside.

"I gave no orders for you to be relieved!" Ida bellowed.

In one fluid motion, Henrick rolled off Deidre and shoved his swollen member inside his pants, lacing them with a shaky hand. "If you breathe a vord of this, I'll kill you."

With astonishment, Deidre watched him take a seat on the stump as Ida stormed through the door, followed by the red-faced guard. The redness wasn't from embarrassment; Deidre could see the welt Ida had left.

"Vhy are you in here?" he asked Henrick suspiciously.

Henrick looked at the guard's face before answering. "I

thought to let him get something to eat." He glanced at Deidre. "I vanted to apologize to the—lairdess—for any fear I may have caused."

His emphasis on "lairdess" told Deidre quite plainly that he'd keep her secret only if she kept his.

"Is that true?" Ida asked.

She hated having to give in to Henrick. "I've accepted his apology, but I'd prefer to have another guard, if you don't mind."

Ida dismissed both of them with a curt nod and then moved to the flap and shouted for another guard. The man—hardly more than a boy—had the fresh-faced look of one who hasn't seen much fighting.

"Carr," Ida said, "I vant you to guard the lady. *No* one passes through that flap, for any reason. The cook vill bring your supper and hers, tonight. Can I count on you to be vigilant and not let me down?"

"Yes, my atheling," he answered with a slight tremor in his voice.

From the worshipful expression on his face, Deidre could see he clearly thought this an honor. She wondered why she hadn't noticed him before.

He settled himself in front of her tent, legs splayed and arms folded across his chest, looking more like a puppy trying to be ferocious than an armed guard. The saexe attached to his belt, though, was real.

Deidre sat down on the stump and tried to think. The tent was situated toward the edge of the camp. If there were some way she could tear a hole in the back of the tent, she might be able to escape. There had to be a way she could get that knife. She looked around for a club or something that could be used as a weapon. Ida had removed anything lethal and no doubt had his battle-axe and sword with him, not that she would be able to yield either one of them. The saexe was her only hope.

She lifted the pitcher and the basin. Both were too light to do any damage. Her eye fell on the chamber pot, tucked into a corner. It was of solid brass and would be heavy. Deidre went and picked it up gingerly, glad to find it wasn't full. Quietly, she moved it near the flap and then lay back on the cot to wait for supper. She wished she could doze, but her body was too tightly wound to relax. This was her only chance. It had to work.

The shadows deepened into the fading Northern twilight by the time she heard the cook arrive. The stew smelled good and she ignored the rumble in her tummy. There would be no time to eat if her plan worked.

"Your meal's here," Carr called.

"Would you bring it in, please? Bring yours, too, and eat with me," Deidre answered, in what she hoped was a beguiling voice. If the young guard had both hands full, so much the better.

She saw his boot push through, separating the flap, and then he shouldered in, a wooden bowl in either hand.

"Right there." She gestured toward the table. As he bent to place the bowls down, she picked up the chamber pot and swung it at the back of his unsuspecting head. The thud it made as he fell forward was sickening, but she forced herself to swing the pot again. He moaned in pain and then lay still.

Deidre pulled the saexe from its sheath. For a moment, she stared at the side of that youthful face, flattened against the stump. She knew she should finish him, but she couldn't bring herself to do it. Goddess help her, she couldn't slash his throat.

Quickly, she stepped to the canvas and ripped an opening. It was stronger than it looked and she was in a light sweat by the time she had enlarged it enough to crawl through. She glanced once more at Carr, but he was still unconscious.

Once outside, she clung to the shadows of the tent. There was another guard making his rounds and she waited until he was past and then she bent and scuttled to the shadow of safety provided by the next tent. She held her breath as she heard footsteps approaching and two men stopped at the front of the tent. Deidre couldn't understand what they were saying and eventually they moved on. She let out the breath she had been holding.

Stealthily, she moved to the next tent and cautiously peered around it. Men were seated in a circle around the fire, some drinking mead, others already reclining. She didn't see Ida. Lord, she hoped he hadn't gone to her—his—tent yet.

There was no more cover for her now and the protection of the tree line was a good twenty paces away. The men who had their backs to her were no problem unless she made some noise. She hoped the fire would blind the ones facing her.

She fought the urge to bolt and run. Sudden movement might be noticed. She got down on her stomach and began to crawl painstakingly toward the security of the forest.

About halfway across the space, there was movement from the campfire. Deidre froze, her body flat and head pressed to the ground. Amid loud gaffaws, a man stumbled off toward a different set of trees, probably to relieve himself, and Deidre forced herself to move forward. She was shaking so badly, she was sure they would hear her bones rattle.

The distance seemed to stretch into infinity, but finally her hand touched the rough bark at the base of an oak tree. She forced herself to stay on her belly until she was well within the inky blackness of the tree cover. Still quivering, she pulled herself up and leaned against the solid trunk, trying to quell her ragged breathing.

She had made it, undetected. She was free. And she thought she knew what direction she needed to head in. She took one final deep breath and straightened. The forest was still and there were no sounds yet of discovery from camp.

She smiled a little as she turned to slip farther into the darkness. She had taken only two steps before a strong arm circled her waist and a hand clamped over her mouth.

Chapter Fourteen

THE RESCUE

"Shhhh. Don't make a sound," Gilead murmured in her ear.

Deidre's knees buckled, whether from fright or relief that he was here, she didn't know. All she wanted was to stay in his arms, safe from the rest of the world. She turned and wrapped around her arms around his neck.

Gilead's kiss was insistent as he drew her closer. His hands kneaded and massaged her back as his tongue plunged deep into her mouth and then, abruptly, he stepped back. Deidre moaned.

"No time—"

A roar erupted from the camp and brought them both back to reality. The young guard Deidre had hit staggered out of the tent, holding his head and jabbering in the Saxon tongue. Ida rushed past him into the tent.

"Come on," Gilead whispered and took Deidre's hand. "I've got Malcolm tethered not far away."

She didn't need to be told twice. They'd both be dead if Ida found them. Even as they crashed through the underbrush, she could hear Ida shouting orders for a search.

Malcolm nickered a greeting and then stamped an impatient hoof as he caught his master's tenseness. Gilead lifted

Deidre quickly and then mounted behind her. As they set off on the narrow deer trail, they could hear horses behind them.

The trail was so twisted they had to keep the stallion at a jogging trot. Deidre only prayed that Ida's men could go no faster, either.

A damp, grey dawn was breaking when they finally reached something that might be called a road. The clouds hung heavy and low and the air was thick with the mist that was rising off the nearby loch.

Gilead dismounted and led Malcolm to the water's edge for a drink. "At least we're on the other side of the loch now," he said. "With luck, they'll think we went due south to get home."

Deidre strained her eyes to see through the rapidly developing fog. They had not heard anything for the past hour and Gilead had chanced this clearing for Malcolm. And then, just as she was about to relax, she saw them.

"There!" She pointed toward the tree line they had just left. At least ten riders appeared. She heard Gilead mutter something Gaelic as he led the horse quietly away from the bank. She didn't really have to guess at what it was.

"Aren't you going to ride?" she asked.

"Shhh. Keep yer voice down," he whispered. "If they havna spotted us in the fog, I doona want them to hear us." He had no more than finished that sentence when a shout went up. Gilead cursed again and sprang into the saddle, pulling her up behind him and giving the stallion his head.

Malcolm thundered along the road that circled the loch, his powerful haunches propelling them forward. They rode at a full gallop for nearly a league until the big horse began to slow. Deidre knew he was a stronger horse than the ones the Saxons rode, but he was also carrying two people.

Gilead reined him in and turned off the road. Ahead of them stood a copse of oak trees and beyond that, hills broken only with jagged pieces of granite. Gilead stopped behind one of the bigger boulders.

"I've got to let him rest," he said as he surveyed the road they had come on. It didn't take long before they could hear their pursuers. Gilead pulled Malcolm's head down as they came closer and wrapped his arm lightly around the horse's muzzle. "Steady there, boy. Not a sound."

They watched as the Saxons galloped past. A light rain had started, dispelling the fog that had protected them.

"Come, we'll walk," Gilead said as he led Malcolm toward a gap between two hillocks. "We can't stay here. The road is muddy; they'll double back when they realize there aren't any tracks." He looked up at the ominous sky. "It's probably going to get worse, too. We'll need shelter."

"They're too close for us to stop anywhere other than to let Malcolm rest." Deidre said. "Let's go. I've been wet before."

He gave her an admiring look, but all he did was nod. "Aye. Onward, then."

By noon they were soaked to the skin and even the horse looked miserable, hanging his head to avoid the stinging lash of the wind-driven rain. They were still walking, since Gilead had chosen to try to stick to rocky terrain to avoid tracks. The shoes that Ida had provided for her were too big and Deidre could feel blisters rubbing.

"Do ye want my plaid?" Gilead asked when he noticed Deidre shivering. "It's still dry in the saddle bag."

Deidre shook her head. "It would be soaked in minutes. Save it for later." She hugged her wet arms. "I had no idea it could get so cold here in the summertime." Not even the mistrals that sometimes came hurtling through the south of Gaul were so bad.

"Aye. When the wind switches and blows off the Grampians, it happens." He gave her a sympathetic look and then stripped off his leather jerkin. "Here. Wrap this around. It has no sleeves, but it will keep yer body a wee bit warmer."

"But that leaves you with just a thin linen shirt," Deidre protested, even as she noticed said shirt was plastered to his body, outlining sculpted arms and broad shoulders. Her blood warmed. Maybe if she could just keep looking at him . . .

She stumbled and Gilead caught her. "Careful."

Deidre felt her cheeks redden. This was not exactly a time for her overly active imagination to take over. They were still being pursued.

"Do you think we've lost them?"

"Mayhap. I've been leading them west. I doona know how far they care to wander from their camp or their ships."

"Ida wants the land, Gilead. I—or Elen really, but he thinks I'm her—am his hope. He won't stop so easily."

"That's the game, isna it?" Gilead asked. "How much is he willing to risk? A war band of ten Saxons can do damage to a small village, but if they come upon my father's men or Turius's, they wouldna stand a chance."

"Ida will have no reason to think those armies are out there. He'll be expecting a negotiator, since he thinks I am your mother." Deidre didn't know how Elen had survived, but she was glad she had. "Your father certainly has no reason now to barter or to fight."

Gilead raised an eyebrow. "Just the thought of giving away his land will be enough. Anyway, Da promised his men would be following me. I just didna wait to break my fast."

Deidre felt a lump rise in her throat. He hadn't even bothered to eat first. As soon as he knew his mother was all right, he'd come for her. Maybe the mad magician—or whomever wrote The Book—had been right in concocting those stories. Maybe she was looking at a really noble knight, after all. "That was sweet of you . . . willing to go hungry."

He stopped abruptly. "Not so hungry." He looped the reins over Malcolm's saddle and rummaged through a saddlebag. "I brought this," he said as he drew out a loaf of barley bread, tore some off, and handed it to her. "I've cheese and venison along, too, if ye want to stop for a wee bite."

"We'd better keep moving," Deidre said between mouthfuls of the soft bread. "How did you manage to get this food past Meara?"

He grinned. "She likes me, remember?"

Of course Meara did. All women did. Not only could he stir a female's blood with just a look, he was also unfailingly kind and respectful. The elated feeling that she might have been special just disappeared. Gilead had done no more for her than he would have for any lady who needed help.

"What is it, Dee? Ye don't look well."

She forced a smile. "I'm fine . . . I . . . I'm just tired and my feet hurt, that's all."

Gilead looked down at the big shoes she wore. "Och, lass. I dinna notice. Forgive me."

She found herself up in the saddle, still holding her bread. Gilead swung up behind her and settled her against him as he reached around her and picked up the reins.

"Malcolm can carry us for awhile. Sleep, Sassenach."

Mmmm. He felt so good and warm, even though the rain was still splattering them. She reveled in the strong enclosure of his arms and tucked her head under his chin. She could feel the steady rise and fall of his chest as he breathed. And, for the moment, she could pretend that he was hers. She'd just rest her eyes a bit. This certainly was no time to sleep. Certainly . . . no . . . time . . . at . . . all . . .

She woke with a start. Malcolm had stopped and they were in front of an old crofter's cottage, the torrential rain still pelting them.

"At least the mud should wash clear any tracks we left," Gilead said as he swung down and then lifted her from the horse. "Get inside and let me see to Malcolm."

Deidre lifted the sagging door on its leather hinges. The warped wood scraped the rock sill and stuck about halfway open, but she managed to squeeze through. The place smelled musty, but at least it was dry. Surprisingly, the roof didn't leak anywhere. She looked around. A heavy cauldron hung on a spit rail in the hearth. A table and two chairs were nearby. A small trunk stood at the foot of a bed along the far wall. Deidre walked over and touched the pallet that covered the leather and rope webbing. It was surprisingly thick. She stooped over and sniffed. The straw smelled fresh. That was strange. She moved to the trunk and pried open the lid. Empty, save for a couple of well-worn linen towels. She took them out. At least they could dry themselves later.

Deidre walked back to the cupboard by the hearth. It contained a wooden plate and cup and a ladle, as well a small sack of oat flour and dried beans. Someone had obviously been here, and fairly recently.

She jumped as the door squeaked open and Gilead pulled

himself through. He shook his head, sending droplets of water spewing from his wet hair.

"I don't think Malcolm has ever been so glad to see the inside of a stall, broken down as the shanty might be," Gilead said as he plopped the saddlebags down on the table. "At least he's out of the rain and there was hay."

"Someone is living here?" Deidre asked apprehensively.

"Not likely," Gilead answered. "The shepherds keep stores in deserted crofts here and there to take refuge as they move the sheep. Anyone about, in weather like this, would already be here. I doubt we'll be bothered."

Deidre looked longingly at the tinderbox next to the hearth as she tried to contain her shivering. "Do you think we can risk a small fire?"

"Aye," Gilead replied. "We're a good four leagues away from the Saxon camp. I doona think they'd risk coming this far inland, away from their boats." He pushed open the door again and bent his head to the rain. "I'll be back."

He returned a short time later with a load of small logs. "I took them from the bottom of the woodpile outside. I hope they're not too wet." Quickly, he laid the fire and took some of the straw from the pallet to use as kindling. He struck the flint several times to get a spark, and slowly the wood smoldered and caught, sending a dark plume of smoke upward. He fanned the small flames, coaxing them with more straw until they burst into colors of red and yellow and orange. Satisfied, he stood.

"Take off yer clothes, Dee."

Deidre stared at him. *Now* he wanted to see her naked? She was cold and hungry and tired. Her hair hung in wet strings. For once, her romantic illusions evaded her. She pulled the leather jerkin closer.

"Ye'll catch yer death in those wet things," Gilead said patiently as he went to the saddlebag and pulled out the dry plaid. "Ye can wrap yerself up in this."

She hesitated, suddenly shy, and looked around for a place to change. Gilead frowned and held up the plaid as a screen between himself and her. "If ye doona mind hurrying, lass, I'd like to get out of my wet things, too."

Of course. He was being mindful of their health. Neither of them needed to catch the lung sickness. She was just being silly when she thought he might be personally interested. Deidre pulled off the tunic that Ida had given her, along with the sodden leggings and wet shoes. She dried herself quickly with one of the linen towels and reached for the plaid, wrapping it around her. The soft wool felt wonderfully warm and carried Gilead's spicy soap scent. She handed Gilead the dry towel. "You'll need this."

He took it and stripped his shirt off over his head. Deidre mewled involuntarily at the close proximity of that bare chest with its well-defined muscles, but when Gilead loosened the laces of his trews, she quickly sat down facing the fire and began to dry her hair. Better not to think about—or see—him naked.

"Ye can look now," he said in an amused tone.

Deidre glanced sideways. He had wrapped the towel around his narrow waist, but that only accentuated the sculpted muscles of his thighs and rippling abdominals.

He seemed unaware of the impact he was making, as he arranged their clothes over the spit and mantle. The fire sizzled as water dripped from the soggy clothing. He pulled the wineskin from the bags and laid it in the cauldron while he took their food out. In a few minutes, he poured the warmed wine into the wooden cup and placed it in Deidre's hands, his fingers grazing hers. "Drink."

Just his touch sent heat radiating through her, but she dutifully drank and was surprised at how the hot drink calmed her shivering. She drained the cup. "More."

Gilead poured her a bit more. "Ye need to eat something before ye get drunk."

Drunk? Now, there was an idea. Maybe if she got Gilead drunk, he would lower that shielding wall that he kept so carefully around himself. How could a man who looked like he did be so damnably proper? For sure, he was nothing like his father.

"I've been selfish," Deidre said as she handed back the cup. "Please have some."

He poured a good-sized drink and took several swallows,

closing his eyes as the soothing liquid slid down his throat. Then he opened them and began to eat.

Deidre turned her attention to the food, too, for she was ravenous. They could get drunk later. In truth, she didn't think she'd ever tasted anything quite so good as that simple meal of bread and venison and cheese.

Gilead tended the fire after they had eaten and Deidre was soon drowsing in the warmth of the room and the plaid, not to mention her third cup of mulled wine.

"Ye'd best get some sleep," Gilead said. "I'll keep watch."

Of course he'd keep watch. He was totally sober. She was the one who was a bit tipsy. She sighed as she curled into a ball under the plaid and drifted off to sleep. Now that she was warm and dry and fed—and maybe a wee bit drunk—she wanted to snuggle. It really was a pity that Gilead didn't have just a speck of Angus's unbridled lust in him.

Deidre awakened sometime later to a cold room. The fire had been banked and Gilead was sitting close to the ashes, arms wrapped around his legs. She propped herself up on one elbow. "Why is the fire out?"

"I heard a noise outside," Gilead answered. "I dinna find anything, but decided it best not to take any chances on anyone seeing a fire in here or smelling smoke."

"You're shivering," Deidre said as she noticed he was still wearing only the towel. "Are any of our clothes dry?"

He shook his head and gave the plaid a lingering glance. "I was wondering . . . if I swear to ye that I wilna touch ye improper, would ye consider letting me share that?"

In the dim light of the fading embers, he looked erotically dangerous. His angular face was half-cast in shadow, the one eye a brilliant blue, the other a dark circle. Half of his full sensual mouth was visible, the hidden part seeming to turn up in a boyish smile. His massive shoulders and bulging biceps were silhouetted against the dying glow and Deidre felt a pulsation begin between her legs. The last thing she wanted was for him to be proper. Maybe it was the wine or maybe it was the aftermath of the abduction, but she decided to be bold. She knew they might have regrets in the morning, but just this one night she wanted to have him. She wanted him to be the man who took her virginity.

"It's *your* plaid. Of course, I'll let you share it," she said. "On one condition."

"I've already told ye I'd not—"

Deidre put her fingers across his lips. "But I want you to make love to me."

Gilead stared at her and a long moment of silence hung between them. Finally, he swallowed hard. "Are ye sure, Dee? Ye've had some wine—"

"I'm sure." Deidre took a deep breath of her own and opened the plaid, revealing her body to him. "Come here."

She heard his sharp intake of breath and then his hands were on her shoulders, caressing them as he brought her closer to him and slid under the plaid. It felt pleasantly strange to have her bare breasts pressed against his hard chest.

"Dee," Gilead murmured in her ear as he nuzzled her neck, "I've wanted to do this for so long." His tongue probed her earlobe and she moaned when he drew it between his lips and nibbled gently. He trailed kisses down her throat, his hands stroking the length of her back.

His touch set her skin afire. Deidre wrapped her arms around his neck and ran her fingers through his damp hair. This was as good as she'd always imagined.

Gilead groaned and brushed his lips against her mouth, barely grazing her, teasing. He kept the pressure light, his kisses soft and warm and gentle. The effect was like stoking a fire. Deidre wanted more of him, longed to feel his tongue inside her mouth, and parted her lips. But he was not to be hurried. He caught her lower lip leisurely between his teeth and tugged, then traced her upper lip with his tongue. He rained kisses across her forehead and closed eyelids, along her cheeks and the tip of her nose. All the time his hands moved, gliding along her spine, kneading the indenture where her back curved, tracing the contours of her buttocks. His fingers slid along her ribs, making her breasts suddenly needy. She pressed closer to him and felt the rocky hardness of his shaft against her leg. Now that she actually had him naked and had seen the size of his manhood, she felt a stirring of apprehension. Lord, *that* was going to go inside her?

Gilead growled low and slanted his mouth over hers, capturing her lips with light caresses. Lazy kisses turned into deeply passionate ones as he explored her mouth, their tongues tasting each other, each dueling to take more of the other.

He cupped a breast, kneading it, his thumb flicking over the nipple. It budded immediately, the heat of it searing deep into her belly. Her body began to tingle all over.

Gilead lowered his head to her other breast, teasing the tight tip as his tongue whirled around it, not quite touching. He licked a slow circle around the base of the soft flesh, spiraling upward in concentric circles, making her breast feel hot and heavy and full. She whimpered as that torturous tongue finally flitted across the taunt peak, bringing a bit of relief, and then gasped when his mouth covered it and he began to suckle.

Dear God, the sensation was exquisite. Her breast thrummed in response to the pressure of his lush mouth and a corresponding throb began to vibrate between her legs.

Gilead switched to the other breast, lavishing equal attention on it before trailing wet kisses across her stomach and making abdominal muscles clench deep inside her. Deidre closed her eyes in complete bliss. How could things get any better than this?

She felt his weight shift and when she opened her eyes, he was on his knees between her legs. When had she spread them, anyway? From this angle, his manhood appeared even larger. Huge, in fact. Long and thick, it jutted out at her, the dark red of its head pulsating slightly. For the first time, she wondered how much pain there would be. No one had really prepared her for this. Once she had asked the matron the grim-faced Clotilde had put in charge of her to explain what happened between men and women, but the woman had near swooned. So she had only gleaned bits and pieces from eavesdropping on the maids at Childebert's court. And they had giggled, so maybe the pain wasn't so bad. So far, everything had felt really, really good. She took a deep breath. "Go ahead. Do it."

Gilead raised an eyebrow at her. "I'm not finished."

She *knew* that much. Could *see* that much. She was still warm and glowing from his kisses, so this would be a good time. What was he waiting for?

He took one of her legs and lifted it to rest on his shoulder and began to nibble on her thigh, sending delightful shivers throughout her. Gilead lifted the other leg and did the same, this time his tongue flickering a path closer and closer to her core. His arms slid forward, hands cupping Deidre's breasts as he leaned down.

She uttered a small cry at the feel of his warm, velvet tongue making broad deliberate strokes between her woman's folds. Her body trembled as he slowly licked her, teasing the throbbing little nub at her center, inflaming her until she thought she would burst into a blazing inferno. And then, when she thought she could take no more, he sucked hard and she felt herself explode into flames, every nerve tip on fire.

Before she had time to recover, he slid up the length of her, his mouth ravishing hers in a deep, penetrating kiss. Deidre felt the tip of him nudging at her and then he plunged in, breaking the barrier in one forceful motion. She shuddered against the sharp, sudden pain, and Gilead deepened his kiss, holding his body still within her.

"Let me know when it stops hurting," he whispered and took her mouth again.

The pain was already subsiding, but it felt strange to have something so thick and hard inside her. Deidre could feel her muscles relaxing to accommodate him and then, something else stirred. A deep, longing need, ancient from beyond Time, filled her. She wanted to feel him move. She wiggled her hips a little.

He responded with a slow withdrawal.

"No!" she gasped. "Don't take it out . . ."

Gilead grinned at her. "Och, lass. 'Tis only to put it back in again." He rocked against her slowly, watching her face for signs of pain. She smiled up at him.

"That feels good."

He felt his cock harden even more, if that was possible. She was tight—so tight—and hot and wet. No woman had ever roused him to the extent that Dee did. She might very well be a witch but he no longer cared. He rammed a little harder and deeper. Instinctively, she began to writhe under him, her hips undulating to the natural rhythm of the ages. He abandoned his caution then and ground into her.

Deidre arched her back, taking all of him. The fire that had hardly banked itself reignited, the torrid heat spreading throughout her until her skin felt pricked by a thousand tiny flamelets. Her breathing changed, coming in short, shallow gasps as his thrusts came harder, faster, and deeper. The pulsation in her center increased, building, surging into a prolonged spasm, as deep inside, vaginal muscles contracted and her body convulsed. For a moment the world went black and then she felt something warm squirt inside of her.

Gilead took in great gulps of air, propping most of his weight on his elbows, but keeping himself buried inside of her. His hair was plastered to his head and his body glistened with sweat. The plaid lay discarded beside them.

"You can still share my plaid, if you want," Deidre said with a wicked smile.

He grinned and rolled over, bringing her to lie on top of him. "Mayhap later, Sassenach. Right now, ye are the only blanket I need."

She laid her head on his chest, listening to the slowing, steady beat of his heart. He was still partially inside her and she felt the warm, wet mushiness of their lovemaking. A sigh of contentment escaped her. Gilead was hers now.

Deidre awakened to find the plaid draped over her and Gilead already dressed and packing the saddlebags. He'd left out some bread and cheese for her to eat.

Gilead was quiet this morning. She watched him now as he finished saddling Malcolm. She wanted nothing more than to throw her arms around him and kiss him, but, from the brooding look on his face, she didn't think trying to entice him would do any good. What was wrong with him, anyway? Last night they'd been so close . . . he'd made her feel so good . . .

Deidre felt her face flame suddenly and turned away so he wouldn't see if he looked up. Everything he had done to her had felt good, but maybe she hadn't pleasured him as well. Maybe he'd expected more from her. She bit her lip, wishing she knew more about these things. Even The Book, with all its fanciful notions of love between Gwenhwyfar and Lancelot, stopped short of telling what *happened*. Gilead was, no doubt, used to experienced women who knew how to please him.

"Are ye ready?" Gilead asked.

She nodded and then kept her eyes averted as he offered his hands for a leg up onto Malcolm. She felt his weight settle behind the saddle.

"Ye can take the reins, lass," he said.

So he didn't even want to put his arms around her. She blinked back tears, glad that he couldn't see her face. So much for her dreams.

As Malcolm plodded along the road that led to Culross, Gilead cursed silently. He looked at the back of Deidre's silken hair hanging loose about her shoulders. She looked even more beautiful in the morning sunshine than she had last night in the firelight. A faint muskiness clung to her, evidence of the passion they'd shared. He didn't dare touch her or he'd take her again, right there.

He shouldn't have done it in the first place. He was always in control of his emotions, especially lust. He'd seen what that had done to his mother and father. What had he been thinking? Deidre had been vulnerable after her escape, and a bit drunk. He should have held himself back. The way she had avoided looking at him just now and the way she was holding her back stiffly away from him told him only too well that she regretted their actions, too. She probably thought him an ass for taking advantage of her.

Pounding hooves interrupted his miserable thoughts. They were coming from up ahead, but the road curved through the trees, so it was impossible to see who the riders were. Malcolm snorted as Gilead took his reins.

"Slide down," he said to Deidre, "and hide in the trees. Don't come out unless I call you." He was glad when she didn't argue. He pulled his sword and turned Malcolm to face the party.

Angus and Niall galloped into view, along with twenty of Angus's men. They pulled to a stop, mud clumps churning under stomping hooves.

"Dinna ye find her?" Niall asked.

By the Dagda! He'd forgotten about Niall. "Aye," he answered reluctantly.

"Where is she?" Angus asked. "Is she dead?"

"Nay." The thought startled him out of his mood. "Deidre, ye can come out!"

Slowly she emerged from the forest to come to stand before them.

"Did they rape ye?" Niall asked bluntly.

She turned crimson and glanced at Gilead quickly and then looked at the ground. She shook her head.

Gilead stared at Niall. The man was a lout. He was probably more concerned with whether Deidre was soiled goods now than if she had been hurt. Guiltily, Gilead felt his own face burn. As far as Niall would care, she *was* soiled goods. He, Gilead, had ruined her. Even if she didn't want him, he would have to find a way to stop this marriage to Niall, for if he found out she wasn't a maiden, she'd pay a horrible price. Gilead shuddered. Why the hell had he not stopped once he'd given her pleasure with his tongue?

Angus threw a sharp look at him. "Ye are sure she wasna harmed?"

Gilead shifted in his saddle. "The Saxons dinna hurt her." Angus's face grew thoughtful and Gilead quickly added, "Ida thought she was my mother. He was going to use her to barter for land title."

Niall snorted. "As if a woman is worth land."

Angus raised an eyebrow. "Ye might hold yer tongue in front of yer intended."

Deidre glared at both of them and Niall had the sense to look almost chastised. "Well. If I think on it, mayhap a wee bit of land would be worth trading. I would expect my lady to reward me well in bed for it, though."

Deidre looked away, caught Gilead's eye, and looked at the ground again.

"We'll be getting back, then," Angus said. "Elen is worried about ye, lass."

Gilead nudged Malcolm forward and started to dismount to help her up. Niall stopped him. "She rides with me."

Gilead saw Deidre cringe. "Malcolm's used to carrying two," he said evenly.

"So's my horse," Niall muttered and stepped down. He grabbed Deidre's arm and she tried to pull away, but he was ready for that. He hoisted her into the saddle none too carefully and climbed up behind her. One hand immediately went around her waist. "Mayhap we'll have a wee kiss before we get home, eh?"

Deidre didn't answer, only crossed her arms across her breasts and stared into space moodily as they moved ahead.

"So tell me what happened," Angus said as he held his horse back and came alongside Malcolm. "How did you get her out?"

"She escaped herself," Gilead answered.

Angus's eyebrows rose. "How did she manage that? Or mayhap, if she is a spy, they let her go?"

Gilead gave his father a sour look. "She's not a spy, Da. She said she invited her guard to eat with her. His hands were full when he entered the tent and she banged him over the head with the chamber pot."

"Sounds like something Mori would do," Angus said with a grin.

Gilead's face turned even more dour. Formorian. He didn't need to be reminded of what lust could do. "They chased us for most of the day. I was surprised they'd wander so far from their boats."

"How did ye lose them?"

"The rain washed some of the tracks away. Then I stuck to rocky ground when I could find it."

His father nodded and then glanced over at him. "And where did ye sleep?"

Why would he want to know that? Gilead flicked a deer fly off Malcolm's mane. "We came on an empty crofter's cottage."

"Ah."

'What's that supposed to mean?'

"Ye tell me, son."

Gilead stared ahead of them to where Deidre was riding with Niall. His father's men surrounded them, thank goodness. If Niall tried to take advantage of the situation, he could quickly be stopped. Gilead looked at his father and shrugged. "The cottage was warm and dry; we were cold and wet."

"And ye'd have to get out of those damp clothes and hang them in front of a roaring fire to dry, I expect?" Angus said drily.

Gilead studied his horse's ears.

"Well?" Angus asked. "Did ye tup her?"

He didn't "tup" her. He had made love to her, with his heart and soul, as foolish as that was. He felt his face grow hot. "Is that all ye think about, Da?"

A corner of Angus's mouth lifted. "Mostly. But it isna my love life we're talking about. It's yers."

Gilead turned on his father furiously. "And why would that be of yer concern?"

"Normally it wouldn't," Angus replied, unperturbed by his son's hostility. "Ye have my blessing to tumble as many wenches as ye wish. But this lass is handfasted to Niall, lest ye forget."

"She canna marry him, Da!"

Angus raised a brow. "She canna? She may not want to, but she *can* and *will*. Ye know what a temper Niall has. With Ida this close, I doona need to be watching my back, too. I need Niall's alliance. Deidre will marry him."

Gilead set his jaw. "She canna."

Angus reined his horse closer to Malcolm and lowered his voice. "If ye spilled yer seed in her, Gil, she may already be with child. The quicker she marries Niall, the better the chance he'll think it his."

Gilead stared at his father, horrified. Another stupid mistake on his part. For certes, he'd never let Niall raise *his* child. If Deidre were pregnant—and how she would hate him for that—the babe would be his responsibility. His. If Niall didn't kill Deidre first.

"I wilna not let that happen," he said stubbornly.

"Ye have no choice," Angus answered. "Ye've had yer fun. If ye pleasured her, there should be no regrets. Let done."

"Like ye've 'let done' with Formorian?" Gilead lashed out at him.

Angus eyes smoldered and his hand tightened on the reins. Gilead had no doubt that, had they been dismounted, he'd have found himself lying on the ground, nursing a broken jaw. Still, he glared at his father defiantly. He had carried on a double standard too long.

Angus's voice was surprisingly calm when he spoke. "There are things between us ye would not understand and I wilna explain them to ye. If ye continue to chase after the lass's skirts, knowing she be handfasted, ye'll be as big a hypocrite as ye think me." He spurred his horse forward, leaving Gilead sprayed with muddy droplets.

Gilead stared after him. What he had done was wrong; he knew that. But he still wanted Deidre. Wanted to taste her again, to feel himself clenched by that powerful, warm wet contraction. Lust for someone he couldn't have was a horrible thing, but God help him, he wanted Dee—needed to be with her—again. Even if she was angry with him. He would find a way to win back her favor. Forget Niall. Forget if it meant war.

He had prided himself on controlling his emotions, of staying within his own self-made boundaries. Dee had brought down those walls last night, taken away the defenses he was so proud of.

Didn't his mother's priest say, "Pride goeth before a fall?" Well, he had fallen hard. With a growing sense of mortification, he realized he had become what he always feared. He was as bad as his father.

Chapter Fifteen

THE PROPOSAL

Angus leaned back against Formorian's silk bed pillows the day after they returned and fisted a handful of the fiery curls that spread across his belly. "Ye bolted the door?"

"Uh-huh," she murmured as she cupped his testicles with one hand and alternated squeezing them lightly and kneading them harder. She bumped her buttocks against his shoulder and he groaned as her hot mouth covered the end of his erect shaft. Her tongue began to tease the rim of his head in spiraling circles. His cock jerked and Angus felt the telltale drop spurt. Obligingly, Formorian took him deeper into her mouth.

Swiveling her hips, Angus lifted a thigh and buried his head between her legs, his tongue thrusting deep inside her. She began to tremble as he spread her juices over her core and sucked on the nub. Her mouth and hands were working him frantically now, driving them both into a frenzy. His tip touched the back of her throat and he plunged his tongue into her damp, warm center once more. Her body gave a great shudder as she came and he reveled in the muscles contracting around his tongue. With a groan, he released his own need and felt her swallow.

"Thank ye," he whispered as she nestled against his shoulder a short time later. "I always like it when ye do that."

Formorian looked up and gave him a wicked smile. "We've naught but started. Turius won't be back for hours." She ran a hand through his hair. "What would ye like me to do next?"

Angus sighed and took her hand. "Not today."

"What's wrong, love?"

He sighed again and tugged her toward him, laying her head on his shoulder as he wrapped an arm around her. "It's Gilead."

"What of him?" she asked as she nuzzled his neck.

"The lad has gone and tupped Deidre."

Formorian raised her head to look at Angus. "He told ye that?"

"Nay. He dinna have to. It was in his eyes."

She rolled off Angus and sat up against the headboard. "Well, 'tis natural, I suppose. With the excitement of rescuing her and then being chased and finally getting to safety . . . It's what any young, red-blooded man would do."

Angus pushed himself up, too. "Aye. But Gil thinks differently than most. He barely notices the lasses who all but throw themselves on the ground in front of him. If I didn't know he paid silver coin to a woman or two in the village, I'd worry about him."

"Then mayhap it was time for him to find out what a lass will do willingly, without being paid," Formorian said as she brushed her fingers along Angus's cheek.

Angus kissed her fingertips. "That's what I'm afraid of, Mori. He has that strange sense of honor; he'll think he's responsible for her now."

"She's handfasted to Niall."

"I pointed that out to him," Angus said drily.

"And?"

"He told me he wouldna let her marry the man."

Formorian's eyebrows rose. "Niall will never let her go. It will mean war."

"I told Gilead that, too. He said he dinna care."

She grew thoughtful. "Do ye suppose he loves her? Really, I mean?"

"Bah!" Angus said. "Why would he? Half the time, they avoid each other like the plague. Nay. It's just . . ." His voice trailed off and he stared into space.

"It's just what?" Formorian asked curiously when Angus grew pensive.

Angus grinned suddenly and turned to her. "I know what the lad needs. 'Tis simple."

"I know that gleam in yer eye, Angus. If ye mean to set a different wench at his door every night until he forgets the episode with Deidre, I doona think it'll work."

He shook his head. "It wouldna. That's why I'll set just one."

Formorian looked puzzled. "One?"

"Aye. If Gilead were married, he'd turn that sense of duty to his wife and not Deidre. Ye remember the council meeting where Comgall mentioned that his daughter was of marriageable age?"

Her look turned to one of wariness. "Aye. And Gilead ignored it."

Angus shrugged. "'Twould be a good alliance. Worse matches have been made."

"But what if Gilead doona want to marry her?"

"To hear Comgall tell, the lass is a beauty. Gilead needs to marry someday to beget an heir. Comgall is a powerful laird. Why wait?"

"I can think of a few reasons," Formorian said.

"Ah, Mori, doona fight me on this," Angus said as his fingers caressed the side of her breast lightly. "I'll send a messenger this afternoon. If Comgall doona completely agree with me, I'll drop it. I swear." He leaned down and licked her nipple with the flat of his tongue, causing a satisfying quiver in her. "Let's not argue."

Formorian slipped down and under him and pressed his head against her breast. "No argument from me, Angus. But Gilead will be a different matter."

"Leave Gilead to me," he growled and slipped a thigh between her legs.

"Gladly. We've spent too much time talking about him already," she answered and then smiled as she wrapped her legs around Angus's waist. "Now tell me what I want to hear."

He entered her slowly, allowing her to savor each inch of him. Formorian sighed and tilted her head back, exposing her throat to him. He nipped sharply once, lapping the tiny drop of blood onto his tongue and letting her taste it. "Blood unto blood . . . ye are mine for eternity."

To Deidre's relief, Angus sent Gilead to Lothian to alert the king to Ida's location. It spared her the embarrassment of seeing him and remembering how naïve she had been during their lovemaking. If only she'd known what to do. For one wild, crazy moment, she even considered asking Formorian . . .

This was the fourth morning she'd been back and, as she looked out her window, she saw Gilead riding through the gates. So he was home. She'd better make her time with Elen short because he would be sure to visit.

She was picking up Elen's breakfast dishes when Angus walked in. He set the customary wine in front of Elen and Deidre excused herself to take the tray down.

"Stay," he said.

For a moment, Deidre bristled under that commanding tone. She wasn't a dog, after all. But Elen was nearly cringing and Deidre couldn't leave her like that.

"Sit."

Really. Did he want her to bark next? Why did the man have to be so domineering? She considered defying him, but couldn't see what good it would do, other than to be personally satisfying. With a lift of her head, she sat back down.

"I've news," Angus said, "that should please ye, wife."

Elen looked disconcerted. "News?"

"Ye've wanted a grandson, nay?"

Deidre started. How could he know she was pregnant? *She* didn't even know; it was far too early to tell. Then she felt the blood drain out of her face. Was some other woman with Gilead's child?

Angus's dark gaze swept her face and then he turned back to Elen. "Gilead is four-and-twenty. 'Tis past time for the lad to wed and produce offspring to carry on."

Deidre felt the blood rush back into her face as though a

geyser had sprung from somewhere. Had Gilead told his father what happened? And Angus was actually going to allow her to marry him? She was soiled goods as far as Niall would be concerned. It was the honorable thing to do, after all. Her face grew even hotter as hope plunged to shame and despair. If she hadn't pleased Gilead in bed, she didn't want him to marry her because of duty. Then the thought of his hands on her, where his tongue had gone and what . . . what he'd done to her with his manhood . . . she shivered slightly. Perhaps she could make him love her. She would learn to please him. Do whatever he wanted. She'd even ask Formorian if she had to.

"The messenger got back at dawn. Comgall agreed," Angus was saying.

Comgall? The laird to the west of Niall? What were they talking about? Deidre chided herself for letting her imagination take over again. Daydreaming when she should be paying attention.

"And what of Gilead?" Elen asked weakly.

"I'll talk to him later," Angus answered and looked at Deidre evenly. "Doona ye agree, lass?"

"I . . ." She gulped, wishing she had heard everything Angus had said. She planted a smile. "Yes, my lord."

Angus cocked an eyebrow at her and then nodded at Elen. "Ye'll need to have the two best rooms prepared. Comgall will be bringing Dallis for a get-acquainted visit within a few days." He grinned, obviously pleased with himself. "The soldier said Comgall was so eager for this arrangement, he was ready to come back with my escort, but Dallis needed time to pack." Whistling, he went to the door.

Deidre sat quietly, holding her hands tightly together to keep them from trembling as the full impact of his words drove into her brain. Angus had arranged a marriage for his son. It was done all the time. She should have known the laird would never let his only heir marry a woman of unsure parentage and no wealth. If only she could tell him! And now, this girl was coming here and Deidre had no doubt that once Dallis looked at Gilead she would fall madly in love with him. What woman wouldn't? She didn't want to be here to see that. She had to get away. Now.

"Would you excuse me, Lady Elen?"

"Certes." Elen reached over and took her cold hand. "Are ye ill? Brena should be here in a few moments with my potion. Shall I send her to ye?"

Deidre shook her head, hardly trusting her voice. "No. I . . . I just need to rest a bit. I . . . I didn't sleep well last night."

Elen nodded. "Go, then. I shall be fine."

"Thank-you." Deidre forced herself to walk out the door and not run. This had to be the worst news she had ever heard, other than being handfasted to Niall. Just a few more steps down the hall. Turn a corner. Her room was close. She would make it.

She heard Gilead's steady tread on the stairs. There wasn't any way she could face him now. She sprinted the last few steps and slipped through her door, closing it softly just as Gilead's boots turned the corner. He had not seen her, thank goodness.

Then she threw herself on her bed and wept her rage silently into the pillow until the feathers were flat and sodden. Her fists pounded into the soft mattress and she wished with all her heart that it was Angus's hard body she was hitting.

Her eyes burned, the tear ducts dried up, and still her body heaved in noiseless sobs. The sun had risen high in the sky and she sat hunched in the window seat, her arms hugging her knees, and stared woodenly down at the bailey, seeing nothing.

Surely, Gilead would not agree to this preposterous proposal. Not after their night together. She worried her lip, remembering how somber he'd looked the next morning, like he regretted ever touching her.

How could Angus be so cruel? Could he really force Gilead to marry? She sighed. Yes, he could. He was forcing her to marry Niall, even when he knew what a drunken sod the man was. Well, *that* wouldn't happen. One way or another.

Her door burst open and she looked up to see a distraught Una. Her impeccable snowy apron had streaks of brown on it and her steel gray hair, always tightly knotted in a bun, had loosened, allowing wisps to stand off from her head.

"What is it?" Deidre asked uneasily.

"Lady Elen," Una answered with a crack in her voice. "Someone's tried to poison her again."

Deidre flew off the bench and rushed past the housekeeper. This was her fault! She should have stayed with Lady Elen. Sheila had claimed to be ill this morning and Janet had been sent to gather herbs. Elen should never have been left alone. Hadn't she told Gilead she'd protect his mother?

Brena was already in the room, holding the basin beneath a gagging Elen. She lay curled up on her side, clutching her stomach, her head hanging over the side of the bed.

"What happened, lady?" Deidre asked as she wrung out a cloth and pressed it to Elen's forehead.

Elen sank bank into her pillow and closed her eyes for a moment. "I . . . was feeling fine. Janet returned and showed me the basket of herbs she'd collected." She gestured toward the frightened girl huddled in the corner. "I crushed a bit of snakeroot into my wine to sooth my stomach." Elen looked up at Deidre and managed a weak smile. "I fear I ate too many of those delicious figs this morning. Angus should never have bought them."

Angus. Could he really be trying to poison his own wife so he could be with his leman? After hearing how coldly and ruthlessly he could ruin Gilead's life, Deidre began to believe it. But she'd had several of those figs this morning, even though Meara would probably have beaten her if she'd known that even one of those expensive imported tidbits had gone to a maid. Elen had insisted on sharing, and Deidre tasted her food, anyway. The only thing she hadn't done, because she was too upset to think, was drink any of the wine Angus brought.

She narrowed her eyes. Where was he, anyway? Every time something happened to Elen, he was conveniently away. She turned to Janet, who was still cowering, as though, somehow, this was her fault.

"Go and find the laird. Search all the rooms if you must. Bring him here." Surprisingly, Janet didn't protest. Deidre watched as she scurried away, wondering if the girl would find him with Formorian. She hadn't been seen, either. Interesting.

Gilead looked at his father incredulously. "Ye did what?"

Angus turned away from the solar window. "Ye heard me. I arranged for ye to marry Dallis."

Gilead clenched his fists and then unclenched them. "Doona ye think I can pick my own wife?"

"Mmmm. And who would that be? Deidre?"

"Mayhap."

Angus snorted. "She be handfasted to Niall. Understand that, once and for all. It wilna be undone." He held up a hand as Gilead started to protest. "Even if she weren't, she wouldna suit."

A muscle twitched in Gilead's jaw. "I think I can decide that."

His father's voice barely concealed his growing anger. "She is not Scotti. We doona really know where she comes from or who she is."

If his father only knew. Deidre was more than well-matched for him. But he had promised to keep her secret. "I doona care about her past. I've taken her maidenhead. Niall will beat her for it. I want to do the honorable thing."

Exasperated, Angus slammed down the wine cup he'd been holding, sloshing the watered contents onto the polished oak table. "Ye tupped her, son. That is all. Men tumble wenches every day. Did she fight ye? I wager not. Did she like it? I wager she did. Was she good? Aye . . . or ye'd not be so besotted." He turned and started pacing. "If it werena Niall she is bound to . . . if I didna need him as ally, I'd say go ahead and have yer fill of her. Rut until ye be raw. 'Twould get her out of yer head."

"Rutting hasna gotten Formorian out of yer head, has it, Da?"

Angus swung back, his eyes stormy. "I've told ye, I wilna

speak of it. Mori and I made a pact . . ." Suddenly he reached for the wine and took a huge swallow.

Gilead's eyes widened. "Ye took the Oath? The one that binds for eternity?"

Conflict played across Angus's face and then he set the goblet down. "Aye," he said more quietly. "Now ye know. We'll speak no more of it."

"But—"

"No more." Angus's voice was dangerously flat and low.

Gilead bit back a retort. He'd seen what happened to men who ignored that tone. So his poor mother never had a chance, and Turius probably never did, either. From time beyond Time, and long before the Christians had entered their lands, priestesses had held the Mysteries, much like the secret of the Stone that the magician had taken from Deidre's people. His own grandmother had imparted the knowledge of the love-binding oath, woven from the ancient magics of Brocéliande. But it only worked if the two people were truly each other's soul's mate. He sighed, knowing he could not change that.

"I canna marry Dallis."

"Certes, ye can," Angus said. "The lass is quite comely and Comgall well pleased. I need not remind ye what gross insult it would be for ye to turn down a well-matched offer. And do I need to remind ye that Comgall's lands border Fergus? If he were to turn against us, Niall would most like follow, weasel that he is. Cenel Oengus would be overrun. Even Turius's Roman-trained legions couldn't hold back three powerful cenels *and* the Saxons." He paused and studied Gilead's face. "Sometimes a man—or a woman—has to think beyond what he wants and do what he must."

Gilead knew his father was thinking of the sacrifices he and Formorian had made and the risks they still took, but it didn't make him feel any better. Just the opposite. If Turius ever decided to acknowledge what his siren wife did behind his back and wage war himself, the Scotti would have to stay united to stand even a chance of survival. Gilead knew he would lead the clan one day and he knew, too, that he must marry and produce heirs. His father's logic was solid; marriages were arranged all the time. He had just hoped he could choose a woman he would love. Maybe if he hadn't met Dee—had left her alone and untouched—he could stomach this. But he couldn't change what he had done. Somehow, he must get Comgall to understand.

A rapid knock on the door interrupted them. Angus flung it open and Janet nearly fell into the room. "Come quickly," she gasped, out of breath from the stairs, "someone has tried to harm Lady Elen."

Angus looked tense as he followed Gilead into Elen's room. "What happened this time?" he asked Una.

That stalwart matron paled. "Poison, my lord, we think. Janet came for me just as soon as she'd found Brena."

Angus turned a thunderous look on Janet. "*What happened?*"

The maid cringed and began to tremble so much that Deidre was afraid she'd wet her skirts. "I doona know . . . I showed her my . . . my herbs . . ." she stammered, "and she put some in her wine . . ."

"'Twas only a bit of snakeroot," Elen whispered.

Brena took the basket from the small table beside the bed and sorted through it. "Aye. There be snakeroot here. But there be also foxglove and henbane." She shook her head. "Mayhap ye took the wrong one, my lady."

Angus looked relieved. "A simple enough mistake. I would suggest that in the future, Elen, ye let Brena be in charge of herbs." He went to the door and turned around. "Are ye coming, Gil? We've a discussion to finish."

Gilead shook his head. "I'll stay with my mother for a while."

Brena gathered her supplies and the basket, while Una handed the basin to Janet.

"I'll have Meara fix ye some chamomile tea," Una said as they left.

Deidre sat down on one side of Elen's bed and Gilead on the other. Elen grasped both of their hands.

"It was snakeroot I took," she said. "I'm sure of it."

Gilead turned troubled eyes on Deidre. "Then that would mean someone else tried to poison her with something else."

Another wave of guilt washed over Deidre. She should have been there. "It's my fault," she said softly. "I didn't taste the wine this morning."

Gilead inhaled sharply. "My father brought it?"

Deidre started to nod, but Elen shook her head sharply. "Ye canna think yer Da has anything to do with this!"

Deidre bit her lip. The poor woman was still in love with her husband, even though she must know . . . or suspect . . . Deidre wondered if she could have that kind of loyalty. She could if she were married to Gilead. She stifled a sob. That wasn't about to happen, was it?

"Tell me, both of you," Elen said and her voice was suddenly stronger, "that ye doona suspect Angus!"

She was getting upset and in her condition, that could quite easily bring on a fever. Deidre squeezed her hand. "Of course we don't, Lady Elen."

Gilead nodded. "Doona fash, Mother."

Elen calmed somewhat and then looked agitated again. "Did yer Da talk with ye, Gilead? About the marriage?"

Gilead looked down at the floor. "Yes," he said.

Deidre stared at him. Surely, he hadn't agreed to it! Not that easily!

"And?" Elen asked gently.

He grew pensive. "I need time to think. I've decided to ride north with Turius tomorrow to make sure the Saxons have cleared our shores. I'll be gone several days." He stood and kissed his mother on the cheek. "I have some things to do before then, so I'll take my leave." Gilead avoided looking at Deidre as he left, closing the door softly behind him.

Deidre blinked back tears. Time to think? Did that mean he was actually considering this idiotic plan? To marry a perfect stranger? Even though Angus was forceful, she thought Gilead had more backbone than this. Enough to stand up to his father about choosing a wife, anyway. As tender as Gilead had been with their lovemaking, surely it must have meant something to him. Even if she wasn't experienced. Her stomach churned into a knot. Maybe it didn't. She was the one who had asked him to bed her . . . had wantonly exposed herself. Maybe he had only taken advantage of what she freely offered. Some seductress she was! She couldn't hold a candle to someone he didn't even know. The thought of Gilead holding this Dallis person in his arms, bathing her with hot, wet kisses, their naked bodies pressed intimately into each other, was more than she could swallow. The tears began to spill over.

Elen took her hand. "Do ye love my son, Deidre?"

Deidre wiped at her tears with the back of her hand. Looking up at Elen, she saw only sympathy on her face. Not trusting her voice, she merely nodded.

Elen brushed a wisp of hair out of Deidre's face. "Have ye told him?"

"No," Deidre stammered. Good lord, she'd already made a fool of herself.

"Mayhap ye should," Elen said gently.

"I can't." He'd probably run like a rabbit chased by a fox if she acknowledged that to him. She choked back another sob and turned it into a hiccup. "Besides, would it change things? Your husband seems to get what he wants."

Elen sighed and sank back into her pillows. "Aye. Arranged marriages are the way of things. Love seldom matters. And ye are handfasted to Niall, to boot." She closed her eyes. "Let me think on it, child."

Deidre tucked the sheet around her and tiptoed from the room as Elen drifted into sleep. Angus might be used to getting his way, but this was one time he would meet his match. By all that was holy, including the Stone itself, she would not marry Niall.

"You're awfully quiet," Turius said the next afternoon after they had ridden as far as Loch Leven.

Gilead shifted in the saddle. "I've been thinking."

Turius grinned. "Nervous about meeting your future wife for the first time?"

His future wife. Bloody hell. He didn't even know the

woman. Or girl, actually. She was just fifteen, from what his father had told him.

"Nay. Not nervous. I doona plan to go through with it."

Turius raised an eyebrow. "Have you told Angus that?"

"I tried to. He wouldna listen."

"Ah. Well, it would make a solid alliance for your clan and be a safeguard against Fergus."

"I know that," Gilead said miserably. "It's just that I doona want to marry a perfect stranger."

Turius chuckled. "Ye'll know her well enough once ye've bedded her."

Gilead gave him a dire look. "Unlike my Da, that's not all I think about."

Turius sobered. "No, you don't. You have a sense of duty and responsibility that few men have. I wish my son would be more like you."

Gilead looked at him surprised. Turius rarely mentioned Maximilian, the boy he'd sired by the high priestess of the Iona isle. His mother had told him once that Turius had been deeply in love with the lady and that she was furious when he married Formorian, snapping the child back to her for druidic training. The boy was rebellious and finally was fostered by relatives deep in the South. They were about the same age, Gilead thought.

"How is Maximilian?" he asked, to change the subject.

Turius grunted. "What I hear is that he has made friends with both Cerdic and Aelle. That would be all right, if he meant to keep peace, but Max generally stirs up trouble wherever he goes."

"Do ye see his mother?"

Turius slanted a look at him. "Not often."

There was a note of wistfulness in his voice that made Gilead ask, "If ye could do it over, would ye marry her instead?"

Turius took a deep breath. "If all I had to consider was myself, yes. But I am king of northern Britain and I need my Scotti allies as much as they need me. Marrying Formorian was necessary. You will be leader of your clan one day. You must not only think of yourself, but what is good for your people."

Gilead clenched his jaw. "But what of love?"

Turius signaled his men to stop near the river to water the horses before he answered. Leading his horse away, he paused and turned around. "There is that, I suppose. A sacrifice that I made and Formorian did, as well."

Deidre hauled the digging tools out of the shambles of the crumbling lean-to that had once been attached to the chapel. This was the third day she'd come up here, and today she would finish the job.

The castle was bustling in preparation for the arrival of Comgall and Dallis. Bed linens had been washed and sundried, and fresh rushes strewn on the floors. Shuttered windows had been opened to freshen the air and Meara was in a tizzy preparing sweetbreads and a variety of puddings and sauces. Men were sent on hunting expeditions daily to gather enough meat for several days of feasting.

Deidre wanted no part of it. If Gilead were willing to marry this girl, she wanted to be gone as soon as possible. Lugnasad was looming closer and she had no intention of being here for *that*.

But she had to finish her project. The feeling that she was close to the Stone had persisted, although she had not had the Sight since the vision—or whatever it was—in the circle of stones. If she turned up nothing today, somehow she would try to visit the circle again and draw on its energy.

Without Gilead, though, it was hard to ride out. Angus had been adamant that she and Formorian were only to ride with an armed escort. Formorian had seemed amused by that, but she hadn't defied him.

As she dug, Deidre wondered if Childebert had given up looking for her or the Stone. Frankish soldiers would not be welcome for long on Briton soil, but she had also heard Turius saying to Angus near midsummer that a boat had put ashore and that Maximilian had provided shelter for them.

No, she doubted that Childebert had given up the search. Turning the Stone over to the Roman pope would obligate Vigilius to support Childebert's endeavors to move west and claim more land. Since Clovis's wife had converted them all to Christianity, the Church already favored them, but now they would have the powerful backing of the Church and its wealth. King Merovee probably rolled over in his grave at the thought of the Bloodline turning traitor to the Mother.

Deidre's duty was to find the Stone before her cousin did and to return it to the grotto so the ancient Goddess worship that the Magdalen and her bloodline personified would survive. To that end, Deidre must keep her identity secret, even if it meant that Gilead would marry someone else.

Or so she told herself as her tears mingled with the sun-soaked dirt of the earth.

Chapter Sixteen

THE BETROTHAL

Turius and Gilead returned home only hours before Comgall and Dallis arrived. Deidre carefully avoided Gilead, and pleaded a headache to Elen.

She stood in her room now, looking down at the scene in the bailey. Gilead stood beside his father and Elen as the carriage came to a stop. The driver jumped down nimbly and opened the door.

Deidre's heart sank to the soles of her feet. She had been hoping against logic that the girl would be plain or fat or stupid. Preferably all three. What she saw alighting daintily from the coach was a raven-haired beauty with curves in all the right places.

She watched as Gilead stepped forward and took her hand to help her down. He bowed—rather stiffly, Deidre thought—and then stepped back. Angus thumped Comgall on the back and Elen hugged Dallis. All in all, it looked like a happy family reunion.

Deidre turned away from the window. She didn't want to see Dallis slipping her hand over Gilead's arm or see him smile at her. She'd have to put up with that at dinner. To make her misery complete, Niall would be there as well.

Dinner was worse than she feared. Close up, Dallis was

even more beautiful. Her black hair set off startling pearl grey eyes and her skin looked like freshly poured cream. It didn't help matters that Drustan had taken one look and began composing an ode to her on the spot.

Dallis graciously accepted it as her due, smiling brightly at him and looking positively radiant beside Gilead. Even her voice sounded silken. Deidre wished the floor would open up and swallow her whole.

Miserable, she forced herself to watch as Gilead prepared a plate for Dallis, slicing the most succulent meat from the boar and spooning gravy over it, asking her which puddings and sauces she would like. Beside her, Niall was tearing great chunks of meat off a bone and wiping the grease on the linen tablecloth.

The girl ate daintily, too, taking small bites and dipping her fingers frequently in the small bowl of water that the laverer had poured. Deidre would have given just about anything to see a piece of meat or vegetable lodged between those small, even white teeth. But no. Her manners were impeccable.

Deidre nearly overturned her wine as her vision blurred with unshed tears.

"Careful," Formorian said from her other side as she righted the glass.

Deidre bent her head quickly. Of all people to have to sit beside her tonight. Formorian had the innate ability to see through bravado. She wondered sometimes if the woman were fey, after all.

"Enchanting, isn't she?" Formorian asked.

Umph. Formorian probably recognized a kindred spirit. Two of a kind, the one enticing Angus while the other hooked Gilead with every wile any female had ever been born with.

"I guess she is," Deidre managed to say, "considering no man here can take his eyes off her." The only small thing she could be thankful for was that Niall was included in that count and for once, wasn't trying to grope her under the table.

Formorian arched an eyebrow. "Retract yer claws, young one. It never pays to let them know ye're jealous."

"I'm not . . ." Deidre began and then stopped. She *was* jealous, much as she hated to admit it. And it would do no good to lie to Formorian. And yet . . . what had she just said? It never pays . . . did that mean that even Formorian had experienced jealousy? It was almost impossible to believe, considering that Angus hid his adoration so poorly.

She caught Gilead watching her from across the table and she plastered a smile on her face. She would not give him the satisfaction of knowing that she cared.

"That's better," Formorian whispered, "but ye don't need to bare yer teeth like a she-wolf guarding her den, either."

At that moment, Deidre did indeed feel like emitting a feral growl and then imagined the expressions on everyone's faces if she did. It broke her melancholy mood, anyhow. At least until Drustan reluctantly put his harp away to make room for the pipers.

Turius came to collect Formorian and Angus led Elen to the floor for the first dance. Deidre noticed that she clung to him with shining eyes, although his own glance slipped away toward Formorian more often than it should have. Poor Elen. Angus was doing nothing more than making a show for Comgall. Still, it was better to watch him than his son.

Deidre remembered what it felt like to be dancing with Gilead, one of his arms securely around her waist, the other hand holding hers, his thumb caressing her palm . . . She squinted. She couldn't see if he was doing that to Dallis or not.

"Let's dance," Niall said, belching and pushing his chair back at the same time.

"I'd rather not."

"I dinna ask ye if ye wanted to," he snarled and gave her arm a firm yank. "We'll dance because I want to."

There was no one to rescue her this time. Rather than have another sprained wrist, she followed him.

She didn't think she'd ever spent a more horrible evening and just when she thought it couldn't get worse, with Gilead attending to Dallis and her stuck with Niall, it did.

Angus stopped the festivities to make the betrothal announcement. Deidre gasped involuntarily. Somehow, she had hoped they wouldn't make it official so soon. She had wanted just some sign . . . some small moment of hope. . . .

From where she stood, she could see Gilead go still as a

granite statue. Dallis dipped her head demurely as the room broke into thunderous applause. People hurried to retrieve wine cups and the toasts began.

Deidre listened woodenly, wishing she could make the excuse to attend to Elen. But for once, Elen seemed to be enjoying herself. She had her hand slipped through the crook of Angus's arm and was being a gracious hostess. And Angus—for Comgall's benefit no doubt—almost appeared to dote on her. So Deidre was forced to endure round after round of well-wishing and an occasionally more raucous suggestion of the advantages of being married. Gilead's face was closed, but she could tell he was furious. Dallis only blushed prettily.

Lost in her own agony, Deidre was totally unprepared for what came next. Niall lurched, half-drunk, across the room, to toast Gilead, pulling Deidre along with him. They stopped only a few feet away and Deidre kept her eyes trained on Gilead's chin, refusing to look into his eyes.

Niall raised his goblet. "I think my wife would like to share her wedding day with ye," he slurred.

Deidre felt the blood drain from her face. How could that oaf totally humiliate her like this?

Gilead's jaw set and Angus stepped forward, an angry frown on his face. "What mean ye by that?"

Niall spun around to face him and tottered for a moment, getting his balance. "Why, nothing more," he said slyly, "but to share the day. We could both get married on Lugnasad." He looked at Deidre. "Didna ye want to have Gilead share yer—"

"Enough," Angus said.

Comgall joined him, apparently unaware of any innuendo. "I think it's a wonderful idea. Don't ye agree, Dallis?"

She looked like a startled deer, but she nodded obediently.

"There. Ye see," Niall said, as he raised the cup once more. "No need to keep an impatient bridegroom waiting. Especially with such an eager bride."

The men around them laughed heartily, although Gilead did not join them. He was watching Deidre.

Niall followed his gaze. "Och, I almost forgot me own bride. Such a willing lass." He grabbed her and pulled her against him and smacked her lips with his. "There'll be plenty more of that on yer wedding night, ye can bet on that."

Gilead clenched his fists and Angus stepped between them, put a hand on Niall's shoulder and pulled him away from Deidre. He spoke low enough for no one else to hear. "We had an agreement, remember?"

Niall jerked away from him, glowering. "Aye. I wilna have to wait much more."

Deidre's stomach lurched as she wiped his slimy kiss with the sleeve of her dress. Dallis looked appalled, but Deidre didn't care about proper manners at the moment. She just hoped she could keep her supper down until she could get away.

Elen appeared at her side. "Suddenly, I don't feel well. Would ye come with me upstairs, please?"

Bless her, Deidre thought with relief, as she complied. She didn't look back as they left the room. That would be the last time Niall kissed her. Repulsed, she wiped her mouth again and then sighed.

Gilead's betrothal was formal. She hadn't found the Stone. Her Sight must have been wrong, obviously. There was nothing keeping her here, now. Lugnasad was only a fortnight away. The gates would be open late tonight for all the guests. It was time to leave.

"Come on, Mori," Angus said as he nuzzled her neck in the shadows of the rose garden behind the Great Hall. "It's late. The place is quiet now. Let's go to my chambers." He nibbled the sensitive area just behind her earlobe that he knew she liked, and drew a slow hand across a breast, thumb and fore-finger squeezing the nipple lightly.

"Mmmm," she said as she slid her body across his hand so he could knead her other breast. "I doona know if I'm in the mood."

Angus slanted his mouth over hers, his tongue demanding entry. She teased him, parting her lips only slightly and then moving her head to the side.

He growled low in his throat. "We can play this game better in private."

"Aye. We could. *If* I were in the mood."

He wrapped both arms around her and pressed his hard erection against her belly. "Does that put ye in the mood?"

She smiled benignly. "Mayhap we should talk first."

Angus was suddenly wary. Mori seldom wanted to "talk." They were usually in harmony with each other's thoughts. What had he done? Dance with Elen? Mori couldn't possibly be jealous over that. Could she? His manhood swelled a little proudly.

He sighed and loosened his hold a bit, enraging his cock with the broken contact. "If this is about Elen, that was only for show. To help Gilead."

"I doona think ye helped Gilead much."

"What do ye mean?"

"Ye should have given them some time before ye announced the wedding. They'd scarce met one another."

Angus shrugged. "It's an arranged marriage. Did ye know Turius well before ye agreed to it?"

"I knew what I was getting into, Angus," Formorian said evenly. "I doona think Gilead wants this."

"Nonsense. Dallis is a beauty. He'll learn to love her."

Formorian arched an eyebrow. "Like ye did Elen?"

Angus frowned. Maybe his Mori was jealous after all. "I never loved Elen."

"My point exactly."

She looked somewhat triumphant, but her logic defied him. She didn't have to wheedle an affirmation of love from him. They told each other that regularly. And the growing need in his groin was making him impatient. He moved closer and began sliding his hands up and down her back. By the Dagda, she was tense. Frustrated, he stepped back. "What would ye have me do?"

"Doona force this marriage. If there is any attraction—"

A torch flamed suddenly, its light throwing them into sharp relief.

"I checked your chambers first," Gilead said acerbically.

Angus kept the anger out of his voice at his son's tone. "What is it ye want?"

"I thought ye might want to know that Mother has been attacked. Again."

* * *

Deidre stared at the purple bruises around Elen's neck. Her eyes were closed and her breath still rattled if she inhaled too deeply. Who could have done this?

"What happened this time?" Angus demanded as he slammed through the door and then stopped at the sight of his wife. He bent over the bed. "Elen?"

Her eyelids fluttered and she looked up at him with a wan smile.

"What happened?" he asked more gently.

"I doona know," Elen said weakly. "Brena gave me my potion and I fell asleep. The next thing I knew, Sheila was shaking the near wits out of me."

Angus turned to her. "Did ye try to strangle my wife?"

No one in the room mistook the deadly quiet and dangerous tone in his voice. Still, Sheila managed to look shocked and hurt at the same time. "Certes not, my lord. I was coming up the front stairs to relieve Deidre and I heard footsteps running down the back steps. When the room was empty, I thought it was Deidre who had left."

Angus fixed his gaze on Deidre. "And where were ye?"

It took every ounce of her willpower not to cringe before him. She could feel the anger radiating from him. What was worse, she deserved it. She should have been there, instead of sneaking away to pack a few items for her planned departure that night. Guilt swept over her.

"I . . . I did stay until she fell asleep. Since you barred the passage door, I felt no harm would come to her."

Gilead touched his mother's throat gently. "Ye doona remember anything?"

Elen shook her head. "I shouldna have taken the potion. I dinna want to . . ." Her voice trailed off as she looked at Angus. "I wanted to wait for . . ." she stopped and bit her lip.

For a moment, Angus almost looked embarrassed, but then he jerked his head around. "Where is Brena? Someone fetch her," he snapped. A half dozen servants, crowded in the hallway, bumped into each other in their hurry to obey him.

Deidre thought Brena looked very pale when she arrived, but it had been a late night for everyone.

"Did ye give Elen a stronger potion this eve?" Angus asked without preamble.

The healer shrugged. "A bit, my lord. 'Twas the excitement of the evening. Her face was all red and her breathing fast."

"Because she had actually been moving about this night. Dancing with me," Angus answered. "Did ye see anything suspicious?"

"Nay. Deidre was sitting in yon chair. No one else was here."

Angus looked in Deidre's direction once more and let his gaze travel to her hands. She resisted the urge to put them behind her back, like a naughty child caught with a sweetmeat. She shouldn't have been packing. This wouldn't have happened if she'd just stayed in the room. But Elen slept alone most nights. . . . And then outrage hit Deidre as she realized just why Angus was studying her hands. Did he really think she might try to strangle Elen? She was the one trying to protect her! She glanced at Gilead, hoping for support, but he was frowning at her. Not him, too!

She swallowed a lump in her throat that was threatening to become a sob. "I'm sorry. I should have stayed."

Angus narrowed his eyes and then looked at Elen. "I'll have a guard posted at yer door from now on. And no more bedtime potions for a while." He turned to Brena. "Is that clear?"

Brena started to protest, but apparently thought better of it. She nodded mutely. "I'll stay with my lady tonight."

"No need," Gilead said as he pulled the big stuffed chair nearer to Elen's bed and lowered himself into it. "I'll spend the night. Or what's left of it."

Brena opened her mouth, but before she could say anything, Angus interrupted. "That's settled, then. Everyone, go to bed."

Shaken, Deidre filed out with the rest of them. There was still time for her to try to make her escape, but she knew she couldn't leave now. Whoever was behind this was becoming bolder. The first attack might have been mistaken for food poisoning, and the second incident on the stairs for an accident; maybe the third attempt could even have been misconstrued as Elen having taken the wrong herb, but no one could deny bruises around a person's throat.

Who would want Elen dead? The two logical choices were Angus and Formorian, but that would leave the not-so-subtle problem of Turius still being around. No one had tried to kill him. Yet Angus had looked genuinely concerned this evening and was even posting a guard. Unless he intended to give the man coin to look the other way.

Formorian certainly was strong enough to have strangled Elen and perhaps Angus's attention to his wife that night had spurred the queen on. But there was the matter of the Saxons. Deidre felt the abduction was somehow related to these incidents and she doubted that Formorian would ever treaty with a Saxon. She valued the land even more than Angus did.

Who, then?

The next few days were a blur. Deidre switched her schedule with Janet so she would not be present when Gilead visited his mother, often with Dallis in tow. She couldn't abide seeing them together and Dallis's tinkling laughter set her teeth on edge. Janet was only too happy to oblige, and flirted with Gilead even more in front of Dallis. Deidre hated to admit it, but Dallis acted like a proper lady, not seeming to be concerned about Janet's flagrancy. But then, maybe Gilead had already promised his undying love for the beauty and she had no reason to be jealous. Deidre tried desperately to put down her own green-eyed monster at those thoughts.

Angus, meanwhile, had closed the gates that night and everyone who was inside the walls was questioned the next day. Several times, Deidre heard the lash of the whip and quickly stifled screams from one unfortunate man or another bound to the hitching post by the stables. Men who were supposed to have stood posts that night but apparently had not.

Angus stomped into the Great Hall late that afternoon and threw the whip into the corner. Deidre hastily gathered some fruit from the sideboard at the far end of the hall and wished she could disappear into thin air. She had no desire to incur Angus's wrath, especially if he still thought her a suspect.

He appeared not to notice her and then she saw why. Formorian was leaning against the door frame that led to the rear hallway.

"No one saw anything?" she asked in her low, melodious voice.

Angus looked tired, but he gave her a smile as he shook his head. "Not a thing. 'Tis like some ghost appeared."

"A ghost? Ye'd best be careful where ye say that. The common people are like to believe ye." Formorian walked around behind him and began to massage his shoulders. "I think ye need a good rubdown."

He turned and draped an arm around her shoulders and smiled. "And I know just the place . . ."

Deidre had stared after them as they sauntered away. For all their attention, she had been invisible. A ghost, though? Was that the story they planned to spread?

Gilead couldn't remember a time that he had felt so trapped. The last few days had been nothing short of a brutish nightmare. He was worried over the increasingly violent attacks on his mother and tried to spend as much time with her as he could, both for her safety and to try to discover some clue as to who might be behind this scheme.

He glanced down at Dallis beside him as they climbed the stairs to Elen's chambers. He would much have preferred to go alone, but Angus had made clear that he was to spend time with Dallis and, in a way, this was easier than being with her alone.

He knew he was the envy of all the eligible males around. Drustan had expounded her virtues to him often enough and he'd seen the way the other young men appraised Dallis when they thought he wasn't looking. She only had to begin a request before a dozen wishful suitors would leap to do her bidding. To her credit, she really did nothing to encourage any of it, except to smile benevolently at them. She even blushed charmingly when Drustan presented a new ode to her. Gilead couldn't blame her for that, either. But she wasn't Deidre.

He opened the door to his mother's room and was surprised to see Deidre still there. She leapt up at once, as he knew she would. She had avoided him like he had the pox since Dallis arrived.

"I must be going, Lady Elen. I promised to gather some herbs for Meara."

Gilead raised an eyebrow and leaned against the door frame. To his knowledge, Meara didn't want her anywhere near the kitchen. Ever.

"For certes, ye doona have to go this minute. Meara was boxing the ears of the scullery lad when we came up. Ye might want to let her cool her hand a bit."

With a dismayed expression and one lingering glance at the door that he was blocking, Deidre sat back down. "Well, I'm in no mood to be screamed at."

Dallis looked puzzled. "Screamed at? By Meara? She was so kind to me when I asked for some special tea last eve. Especially when she had already cleaned the pots."

Deidre clenched her jaw and Gilead quickly intervened as he took a chair beside Elen. "Special tea?"

"Aye. I had a bit of a headache," Dallis answered. "'Twas a long evening."

Gilead frowned. It *had* been rather a dreary dinner. Drustan had not returned from one of his solitary hikes, so there was no music while they ate. They sat with Turius and Formorian and, although he and Turius discussed the Saxon threat, he thought that Formorian had kept the lass entertained. In fact, he remembered her plying Dallis with questions. Had she answered them? They danced when the musicians played later. Granted, she had been quiet and retired early. He had actually been grateful for that.

"I'm sorry. I dinna realize ye werena feeling well."

"'Tis nothing to fash about," Dallis said and smiled brightly at Deidre. "I've seen ye, but I doona think we've met. I'm Dallis."

Gilead watched as several emotions warred on Deidre's face. Resentment. Anger? And then a mask slid into place and Deidre nodded sedately. Far too sedately for Gilead's comfort.

"I'm Deidre," she said and glanced at Gilead. "I'm just a lady's maid."

Och, she was reminding him of who she really was. Cousin

to the king of Gaul. At least as well matched for him as Dallis was. Not that he cared if she'd been a cotter's child. All he wanted to do was tangle his hand in the silken strands of pale hair and press Deidre close to him and watch that angry blaze of blue flame in her eyes turn to dark, smoldering passion. He wanted to tell her he loved her and . . .

He sighed. He was in a fine mess, thanks to his father. Gilead fully intended to take Comgall aside and explain that Angus had acted in haste and that it wasn't fair to Dallis to be thrust upon a perfect stranger. That, at the very least, there should be time for them to get to know each other before any future plans were discussed.

But when he tried, shortly after their arrival, Angus chided him for not letting Comgall get the dust off his boots before trying to negotiate a dowry settlement. Both of them knew that was not Gilead's intent. And then, while the three men and Turius were enjoying a strong red wine before dinner, Angus waved off another attempt at serious conversation, saying there was time for all of that later.

Gilead acquiesced, swearing to himself he would speak to Dallis's father before the night was over. But Angus, shrewd planner of battle strategy, had outwitted him. Never had Gilead expected the betrothal to be announced that very night. And now, he would have to figure out a way to save Dallis's pride and salvage a needed alliance with her father. A difficult task, but not impossible.

"Ye have not been spending much time with my mother," he said to Deidre.

Her eyes went cold. "I haven't been needed. She has had much company of late."

Gilead heard the chill in her voice. "Ye have not attended her at dinner, either."

"I gave her permission not to," Elen interjected.

"Well, certes," Dallis said to Deidre. "Ye are betrothed as well, I understand. I think it kind of Lady Elen to allow ye to spend yer time with the man ye love." For a moment she looked a bit wistful.

Deidre grimaced. "Niall can be a demanding man, it seems."

Gilead brightened. For certes! Why had he not thought of

this before? He could at least keep Niall away from her at dinner. "Mayhap this evening, ye would sup at our table with us, Dee—"

The look Deidre sent him could have doused the fires of Bel. She rose and gathered the tray and linen from the midday meal. "I don't think that would be appropriate, my lord," she said and turned to Elen. "If I may take my leave?"

Elen looked at her thoughtfully and then nodded. Gilead could have sworn he felt a blast of cold air as Deidre passed him. Now, what had he done? Did Dee not want to talk to him at all? He really needed to explain what he intended to do.

Deidre pushed wisps of hair out of her eyes and wiped a bead of sweat off her forehead with her shirtsleeve. She had come to the chapel ruins one more time just to make sure she hadn't overlooked anything.

But she knew that wasn't true. There was nothing here. She had come just to get away from the castle. She needed time away from Dallis.

Perfect, charming Dallis. She seemed to have all of the men—save Angus and Turius, perhaps, whom Formorian kept quite beguiled—enamored of her. Drustan had composed countless odes, which he tried to improve on nightly at dinner. And Dallis sat there, like a royal queen, her lips curling in approval. And Gilead, ever the proper suitor, keeping her entertained with different table partners for conversation. And he'd even had the indecency to invite Deidre to sit at their table. She jabbed the shovel heatedly into the ground and hit a rock, jarring her forearm in the process. She winced at the pain and grabbed her wrist with her other hand. *Merde.* He'd better not try again to make her sit at his table.

"What did the rock do to make ye mad?"

She spun around. Gilead stood not far from her, a faint smile on his face.

"What are you doing here?"

He picked up another shovel and started shifting the dirt. "I think ye've been avoiding me."

"Nonsense." Deidre bent over to inspect something, causing

her long hair to hide her face. She couldn't let him know that he sent her blood racing, just at the mere sight of him. He wasn't hers and never had been.

"Dee. Look at me."

When she kept shuffling and sifting the dirt, he reached down and lifted her to her feet, turning her around to face him, arms loosely around her waist. "I want to talk to ye. Please."

Dear God, his arms felt strong and solid. Deidre inhaled the soap and leather scent of him, mingled with the warmth of the sun as the breeze blew his dark hair away from his face. Brilliant blue eyes in a tanned face studied her. Her breathing grew shallow. That sinfully sensual mouth was only inches away from her. All she had to do was lift her head and part her lips and he would kiss her. She knew he would. And she wanted it. She wanted him, wanted to tear off his clothes and hers, and roll in the warm earth they had just dug, having him burrow deep inside her.

But he was betrothed.

She pushed away from him. "I don't think we have anything to talk about."

"Ye know this was naught of my doing."

Deidre circled the old altar stone, keeping it safely between them. If she were going to maintain any kind of dignity, she must not let him near her. His touch would be her undoing.

"Maybe not. But I don't see you protesting too much. Wait," she said and held up a hand. "I know what I see. In the mornings, you bring her to your mother to visit. You both come back in the afternoon. At dinner you pay more attention to her than you do your food. You dance afterward—"

Gilead stared at her in amazement. "I dinna know ye noticed."

Heat flared across her face. How stupid could she be? She wouldn't give him the satisfaction of knowing she was jealous. She tossed her head. "A person would have to be deaf, blind, and mute *not* to notice."

"I'm only being polite," he protested. "Let me explain . . ."

Deidre glared at him. "I heard your father's pronouncement. You are betrothed to Dallis. Do you deny it?"

"No, but—"

"Then there isn't anything left to say." She bit the inside of her cheek to keep the tears back. He was betrothed. The words sliced through her like a cleaving knife. "Just leave me." If he didn't, her heart would be laid open soon.

"If ye'll just hear me out, Dee. Please."

She shook her head. Even if Gilead thought he could get out of the betrothal—and she wasn't really sure he did—Angus would never let him. She had been there long enough to understand that the land and the alliances needed to keep it safe were all that mattered to Angus. Better not to listen to Gilead. Better to make a clean break. She took a deep breath. She had never been good at lying and this was going to be the hardest thing she ever did.

"Save your breath and your dignity, Gilead. You and Dallis are well matched. You can't deny that." She looked past him to fix on a distant tree. "And . . . I . . . I don't love you. So just leave."

"But—"

"Go." She turned and picked up the shovels to return them to the shack. Her legs were trembling so hard she wasn't sure she wouldn't fall down. She knelt and rolled the equipment in old leather skins to keep it from rusting and fought to control her breathing. *Breathe deep. Have courage.*

When she straightened and looked back, Gilead was gone. Only then did she allow the tears to come.

Gilead stomped furiously down the hill. She wouldn't even listen to him! Not even let him try to explain! He was willing to risk clan war to break this vow he had never made. And now she told him she didn't love him!

Did their night of lovemaking mean so little to her? He had taken her virginity, had been her first lover. Bloody hell, that should mean something.

He cringed inwardly, remembering how aloof she had been the morning after. How ramrod stiff she had held her back to him. She had regretted letting him take her.

Gilead broke into a lope, pushing himself harder as if he could outrun his feeling for her. She didn't love him. She had been cool toward him even before Dallis arrived. He had been a fool not to see it.

He slowed, panting a little from the exertion. Maybe he should just go ahead with this stupid plan. Dallis was pretty enough; didn't Drustan remind him that he was a lucky man, every chance he got? War would be avoided. Dallis was also docile and polite and been trained properly to be a lady. He could grow to love her, he supposed, even though she lacked the fire that Dee had.

Dee. He would not call her that again. As far as he was concerned, Mistress Deidre was an imposter. The best thing would be to inform his father who she was and have her sent home. Unfortunately, keeping her secret was a vow that he *had* made.

And Gilead did not break his vows.

Chapter Seventeen

REVELATION

Niall slammed the empty tankard of ale down on the small table beside his bed in the guest quarters of Angus's hall. He cursed as he picked up the empty skin and threw it on the floor. Since Elen's "accident," Angus had kept the liquor locked up and his soldiers sober. Niall had to bribe the chambermaid with pure silver to purloin this one lousy skin.

The damn job had been botched. Again. Elen should be dead. He had outlined, in detail, exactly how it should be done. Could he not count on his accomplice for anything?

He gave a sharp laugh that sounded more like a bark. How ironically different his motives were from those of the woman who had agreed to help him. *She* wanted Elen dead so Angus would be a free man. *He* wanted Elen dead so Angus's rutting with Formorian would finally be exposed—what little discretion they possessed now would vanish into thin air—and Turius would be forced to take action. The Briton's army was mighty and Angus wouldn't stand a chance against them.

And then Turius would need someone to oversee the land in his stead. Niall allowed himself to drift into his favorite dream. Married to Deidre, a distant "kin" of Angus, Niall could assure Turius that he would keep the clan from rebelling. Yes, sir. Niall would be ready to pledge loyalty to Turius. At least until Fergus grew bold enough to lead the Eire raid that was still brewing.

Oh, it would work. And the best thing was, he wouldn't have to do the killing. Not that he would mind slicing Angus through and watching his entrails fall out—he might even relish that, after all these years—but if he had no hand in it, the way would be clear for him to take control.

Gilead would have to die, too, but that could wait. Too many killings would raise suspicion. A convenient arrow in his back during the heat of the eventual battle with Turius should do it. Pity he couldn't make it more torturous, though. Gilead had interrupted his fun with Deidre too many times and he resented the way the young cub was always sniffing around Deidre's skirts, like a dog after a bitch in heat.

He felt his groin tighten and grinned ferally. Mastering *that* little bitch was something he was looking forward to. And he'd be careful that the bruises didn't show.

The thought of all that power nearly overwhelmed him. He was so close to having everything he wanted. So close. If only that damn woman hadn't bungled the job.

He kicked the empty wineskin and cursed. He needed a drink.

With relief, Deidre stood on the steps with Janet and Sheila and watched Dallis and her father depart two days later. The past week was the longest she could remember. Gilead had virtually ignored her after the afternoon at the ruins and even though she knew it was over between them—if there had been anything in the first place—it was still good to know she wouldn't have to watch him lavishing attention on Dallis.

By the time the girl returned for her wedding, Deidre would be gone. Lugnasad was approaching fast; she would have to leave soon. Her big regret was that Elen's attacker was still at large. She would have liked knowing Elen was safe.

Deidre waited until Gilead had disappeared into the stables and then walked to the little partitioned garden that held the roses

Elen so doted on. She'd cut some for her. As she passed the men's quarters, she heard Drustan's harp and stopped to listen.

The music today was slow and mournful, like a funeral dirge. He must be in one of his black moods again. She'd noticed last night while he played that his mouth had been drawn into a tight line and his usually bright eyes had been listless and dull. She knew he didn't drink, and she wished she could ask Gilead what was wrong.

She jumped suddenly as a particularly high-pitched pluck pierced the air like a shriek, and then faded with a long wail that made her hair stand up. Goose bumps rose on her arms and she hurried on. The men of Kernow were known for wildly swinging moods. Meeting up with Drustan in the middle of his angst wasn't something she wanted to do.

But it would have been better than running headlong into Niall, which is what happened as Deidre rounded the corner of the Great Hall, long-stemmed roses in her arms. He took the opportunity to grab her and she turned her head aside at the fetid odor of his breath.

"Ye won't be denying me much longer, lass," he said with a sneer and jerked her head around with one hand. "I'll be taking a wee kiss now to let ye think about it."

Deidre sealed her lips tightly together as he tried to cover her mouth with his. Angrily, he pulled her tightly against him and she felt the thorns from the stems cut into her arms. She gasped in pain and he took advantage to shove his tongue between her lips. Instinctively, she bit down, hard, and he howled in pain. He reared his hand back to strike her.

Gilead caught his arm. Where he had come from Deidre didn't know, but she nearly bent double in relief as she stumbled back from Niall's clutches.

"Ye'll strike no woman on this property," Gilead said.

Niall wiped the back of his hand across his mouth and narrowed his eyes at the blood. "I'm getting real tired of ye coming between me and my betrothed."

Gilead's eyes darkened. "Then mayhap ye best leave."

Niall glowered at him, but before he could answer, Angus came out the front door. He looked quickly from one to the other and then nodded curtly to Deidre. "If those flowers are for Elen, ye'd best see to them."

For once, she was grateful to him. She nodded and glanced at Gilead, but he was still staring down Niall. She decided a hasty departure might prevent a fight.

She nodded to the guard posted at Elen's door and went in, glad to find her sitting in her chair and working on her stitching. Since the attack, Elen had seemed much stronger. Whether it was the extra protection or maybe the little bit of attention Angus was giving her, Deidre didn't know. She was just glad for it.

Elen looked up from the window and smiled. "What lovely roses! Let me smell."

Deidre held them out to her and she sniffed appreciatively and then hissed at the sight of the scratch marks on Deidre's skin.

"How did that happen, child?"

Deidre tried to tug down the sleeves of her dress. "Nothing, my lady." But her fingers trembled as she reached for a vase for the flowers.

Elen stayed her hand. "I want to know."

Deidre crumbled then, sinking into the chair next to Elen and strewing the roses on the table. She hid her face in folded arms and began to sob.

"There. Get it all out. Ye'll feel better." Elen gently massaged her shoulders. "Did Gilead do aught to upset ye?"

Deidre wailed louder. "No," she managed to blubber, "he helped."

Elen stroked her hair softly and eventually Deidre's tears slowed. She hiccupped and accepted the small linen cloth Elen offered and wiped her nose.

"It's Niall, my lady. He tried to force himself on me. I bit him and he was about to hit me when Gilead stopped him." Tears brimmed at the corners of her eyes again. "I cannot marry that beast. I cannot."

Elen made soft, soothing noises as she embraced her. "Ye poor child. I will try talking to Angus, but I doona know if it will help."

Deidre raised her head and swiped at a tear dribbling down her cheek. "Thank-you, my lady."

Elen picked up two roses and studied them. "Pink is for

love and red is for passion. I doona think ye are the only one who does not feel that."

Deidre sniffled and dabbed at her nose. "What do you mean?"

She sighed. "I doona think my son loves Dallis."

In spite of herself, a little spark of hope flared in Deidre's heart. Could it be possible that Gilead really wasn't as smitten with Dallis as every other male? How she wanted to believe that! She hesitated. "What . . . what makes you think that?"

Elen brushed the silkiness of the rose along her cheek. "It's not in his eyes," she said softly. "When a man loves a woman, there is a burning depth in them. A longing never to look away."

Deidre stared at her. Was it possible that Angus had felt that love for Elen once? And if so, how on earth had Formorian come between them? She took Elen's hand in both of hers. "May I ask, my lady . . ." She stopped.

"What is it?" Elen asked when Deidre remained silent.

"It's none of my business, my lady," Deidre replied, "but . . . but was that the way it was for you and your husband once?"

Elen fingertips caressed the rosebud before she laid the flower carefully down on the table. "Nay," she said sadly. "Ours was a thorny road."

Deidre sat quietly while Elen gazed off into the distance, seemingly lost in memory. Then the woman turned to her and smiled gently. "Would ye like to know the way of it? Mayhap it's time I told someone."

"If you like, my lady. My lips will be sealed."

Elen arranged the plaid over her knees and crossed her hands. "I had adored Angus even as a child. My father and his were strong allies and the Mac Erca helped the three cenels settle here. I would accompany my father on the trips two or three times a year." She paused, with a little smile on her face. "Angus was all boy, never without his wooden practice sword and usually sporting a bruise or two from a recent fight. He had not time for girls—certes, not me, who could scarce stand my slippers being dirty. There was only one he tolerated back then and she was as willing to get into scrapes as he was."

"Formorian," Deidre said softly.

Elen nodded. "Even then, I should have known. But as we grew out of childhood, I saw less of her on our visits.

Whether Gabran was keeping her away—Ambrose had already come to his aid a time or two—or whether it was just timing, I doona know. I was just glad I had Angus to myself."

"He courted you?" Deidre asked.

"I thought he did," Elen answered. "He was always polite and attentive to me and paid no mind to the wenches who chased him endlessly. I can't blame them . . . Angus had a wild, unbridled look about him and if ye got close, ye could actually feel some sort of force radiating from him. He drew lasses to him like snakes following St. Patrick."

There was an image Deidre could imagine. As arrogant as Angus was, she could see him piping away, leading women astray. Only she could also see tiny horns sprout from his head and a tail whipping behind him.

"But he paid attention to you?" she asked.

Elen grimaced. "I was young and besotted. Now I can see that the attention was because of who my father was. Even at four-and-ten, Angus valued the land more than anything." She dabbed at tears. "It was five years later that I did my foul deed."

Deidre waited quietly while Elen composed herself. She took several shaky breaths and then continued.

"We had come on a visit in the fall, shortly after the harvest was in. I was surprised to see Formorian there, and even more surprised to learn that she had wedded Turius. Angus was awfully quiet on that visit and he kept watching Formorian when he thought no one saw him. Remember the look I said a man had? I dinna recognize it as love then. Not until I accidentally found them in the walled garden later, kissing."

"What did you do?"

"Oh, they split apart immediately and Formorian pretended that something was wrong with her slipper and Angus acted as though he were merely helping her balance. But I knew what I had seen. I just smiled and left."

"Neither of them followed you? Or tried to explain?"

"Nay. They both have too much pride." Elen paused. "But the thought of them—his strong arms around her and her fingers twined in his hair, their mouths hungry for each other—stayed with me. I wanted that. I wanted to know how it felt to be

pressed against Angus, to have him caress me like he did her."
She looked away, blushing. "And then the wicked idea hit me."

"I can't believe anything you'd do would be wicked,"
Deidre said.

Elen shook her head and continued. "Formorian was married. He could never have her. And I had never wanted anyone besides Angus. So I thought, 'Why not me?' I would bring a good dowry and a powerful alliance. I was sure that, once he got to know me, I could make him forget Formorian."

"So what happened?"

Elen dropped her gaze to the floor and her voice was nearly a whisper. "I . . . I sent a note to Angus saying that I was going to tell Turius, unless he could explain himself. I told him to meet me in the barn just after moonrise. The hay was fresh cut and soft and smelled sweet. A perfect spot for tumbling a maid. I thought—oh, it was wrong—that if I could get him to kiss me, to do to me what he did to her . . ." Her voice trailed off.

"He came?"

Elen nodded and a teardrop fell on her hands. "He was angry; certes not in the mood for what I had in mind. He asked how I dared to ensnare him like that. That I had no idea of how he and Formorian felt about each other."

Deidre frowned. "But he married you?"

Another tear splashed down. "My evil trickery wasn't over. I had arranged for my maid to find my father and tell him I was not abed. That I had mentioned wanting to go for a moonlight ride alone." She wrung her hands pathetically. "When I heard footsteps approaching, I threw my arms around Angus's neck. He caught my arms—more to push me back than anything—and my father found us like that."

"Didn't he try to explain?"

"Aye. My father roared like a bull. Said I would never have met him in a barn if he hadn't filled my head with promises he didn't intend to keep. That Angus was not going to compromise his daughter. I could feel Angus seething beside me, but he contained his anger. He just looked at me, waiting for me to explain and make things right." Elen covered her face with her hands and wept. "I lied. I told my Da that Angus had promised to marry me."

"Ah," Deidre said as she tried to soothe Elen, "and he did the honorable thing."

Elen straightened and dabbed at her eyes with a napkin. "Only after he talked to Formorian. He wanted her permission, I guess."

"What?" Deidre asked in surprise.

She sniffed and wiped at her nose. "For her, it was perfect. She didn't have to worry about losing him to someone he would love. And I," she said morosely, "was naïve enough to think I could change his mind."

"He must have cared about you some," Deidre said. "You have Gilead."

Elen gave her a watery smile. "I thought he would love me then. When I gave him a son." Her face turned wistful. "Once he had his heir, he never touched me again."

Gilead brushed Malcolm's coat with more vigor than usual. The stallion turned his head in the stall and gave his master a reproachable look.

"Sorry," Gilead muttered and ran his hand lightly over the satiny neck. "I didna mean to take it out on ye." Malcolm nickered and went back to munching his hay.

Gilead was angry with himself. He'd just spent five days in Dallis's company and he felt no more for her than he had when they met. She was unerringly respectful in her replies to him, but he sensed emptiness with her. She dinna know how to ride a horse nor did she wish to learn. She had looked totally shocked when he asked if she'd ever shot a bow. He'd tried to jest with her once, only to have her feelings hurt when she took him seriously. He sighed. About the only thing she did like, from what he could tell, was music. Her eyes always took on a dreamy look when Drustan strummed his harp. Or maybe it was the odes he sang to her. All women loved flattery.

Except Deidre, he realized with a start. Oh, she had her strange ideas of something called "chivalry" from that book the mad magician had left, but she was straightforward and honest. He knew where he stood with her. He winced. Aye.

She had told him bluntly enough that she dinna love him. He would do well to remember it.

But she confused him. Seeing Niall about to strike her had nearly undone him. He had to call on every inch of willpower he had not to knock the man down. How could he let that beast marry her? How could he prevent it? Bloody hell, he couldn't even stop his own marriage from occurring, it seemed.

Well, if he were going to marry Dallis, he would have to put Deidre from his mind. If his father had only done that when Formorian married Turius, his mother might have had a chance at finding happiness. Gilead would not do that to Dallis. He would not emulate his father. He would not.

With a last stroke, he finished grooming Malcolm. What a mess his life was.

Deidre sat in Elen's chambers in shocked silence. She had never expected Elen to be capable of such deceit. She was seeing Angus's behavior in a new light. Perhaps he wasn't so cold and overbearing after all. And poor Elen. She had gotten what she wanted, but how horrible to have to face the fact that the only reason Angus was with her was because he had done the honorable thing and not compromised her. Not called her a liar. How horrible to realize that the man you loved could barely tolerate your presence.

It wasn't supposed to be that way. And yet, even in her beloved book, life was not destined to go smoothly. Had Gwenhwyfar been happy? Really? Not with Arthur. When she and Lancelot had the chance to marry, they didn't take it. How sad. Deidre was so lost in her thoughts that she actually jumped when the door opened suddenly and Gilead walked in.

"Am I interrupting something?"

Deidre stood. "I was just leaving."

"Wait," Elen said as she turned toward the door. "Ye've been cooped up with me all morn. Let Gilead take ye for a ride."

"That's not necessary," Deidre hastened to say.

"I've got things to do," Gilead added, without looking directly at Deidre.

"Nonsense," Elen said and pushed aside the plaid. "I'll

walk with ye. And I promise I'll take some fresh air and sun-shine while ye're gone."

Gilead looked at his mother helplessly and Deidre was equally dismayed. Elen hated being outdoors. She was brib-ing them! But why? Maybe Gilead didn't love Dallis, but he had demonstrated his obvious devotion to her.

Una hurriedly dragged a large comfortable chair out to the side of the vegetable garden when she learned that Lady Elen was actually going to sit outside a bit. Gilead and Deidre left her tuck-ing the plaid around Elen to insure that she stayed warm.

"You don't really have to go through with this," Deidre said when they were out of earshot.

Gilead raised an eyebrow. "Why do ye think my mother would come outside on a cool day and choose a spot to sit where she can plainly keep us in sight if she werena deter-mined to see us ride off together?"

A tiny little spark leapt in Deidre's heart. "Why would she want that?"

He sighed. "I doona know. She doona like to see people angry."

The spark ignited into a glowing ember. "Are you angry?"

"Nay. Ye made yer feelings clear enough."

The spark died, doused with ice water. "You are be-trothed," she flared.

"So are ye!" Gilead glowered at her.

She opened her mouth and then snapped it shut. She didn't have to be reminded that Lugnasad was just a short time away. A cunning thought struck her. Perhaps riding wasn't such a bad idea, after all. If they rode far enough, perhaps she could claim to need rest. And, if Gilead were to doze off too, she could make her escape this very day. It was worth a try. But what she needed was some of Brena's sleeping herbs.

"If your mother is determined that we not be angry at each other, let's make a day of this. You go saddle the horses and I'll get some bread and cheese and wine."

Gilead almost grinned. "Ye'll face Meara?"

She had forgotten that. Then she brightened. "I'll ask your mother to do it."

He shook his head and went inside the barn. Deidre went back to the garden.

Elen was delighted at the prospect and Deidre soon found herself with a satchel of fresh bread, a small crock of warm honey, soft cheese, and a skin of wine. Although she had managed to secure her small bag of coin inside her boot, she hadn't been as successful with the herbs. Brena kept her cabinets locked. All Deidre could find was a small packet of woodruff lying on the table. Coupled with the wine, its hypnotic effects should make him sleepy, at least.

"Ye take yer time and enjoy yerselves," Elen said.

Impulsively, Deidre hugged her. She would miss Elen, even knowing now that she wasn't the innocent victim of a hapless marriage after all. Then she hurried across the bailey to where Gilead was leading out Malcolm and Winger.

As Gilead stuffed the parcel into a saddlebag, Deidre started to mount. Since she was wearing trews, she didn't need the stump, even though it was still a high step to the saddle. She placed one foot in the stirrup and pushed off with the other. Just at that moment, a hissing cat streaked out from the barn, followed by a pack of yapping hounds. The whole assemblage flew under Winger's hooves, causing the gelding to rear in fright. Deidre landed in a crumpled heap on the ground as the horse cantered away.

Gilead dropped to his knees beside her. "Doona move. Let me see if anything is broken."

With the wind knocked out of her, Deidre had no trouble complying with his directives, but as his fingers carefully stroked down her arms and up her legs, she realized her breath was shaky for quite a different reason. His hands glided slowly across her rib cage, checking each one. She was sure her heart was going to thump right out of her chest.

"Nothing seems to be broken," Gilead said as he traced her collarbone.

Did she imagine it or did his fingers seem to linger at the pulse in her throat? His touch was doing strange things to her stomach. The battalion of butterflies that she thought was permanently roosting had taken flight again.

"Can ye sit?" Gilead put an arm beneath her shoulders and lifted her gently.

"I'm fine," she stammered. "I should have had a better grip."

"The dogs should have been in the runs, not loose," Gilead answered as he helped her stand. "If you still want to ride, I'll fetch Winger."

Still want to? She had to. This was her escape. And, she admitted to herself, it would give her one last chance to be with Gilead. Whether he was betrothed or not, the fire she thought was banked had rekindled. What harm could it do to spend one last afternoon with him?

Winger watched them dolefully from the gate where he had stopped with drooped head. As Gilead set off after him, Deidre found herself facing an angry Niall.

"Did ye do that on purpose?" he asked suspiciously.

She frowned at him. "I hardly arranged to have a cat chased by hounds."

"Ye know what I mean," he said. "Ye pretended to be hurt so that son of a bitch could put his hands all over ye."

Deidre raised an eyebrow. "I don't think the laird would appreciate your referring to Lady Elen as a dog."

He scowled. "Doona be fresh with your words. I'll not have it."

She reined in her temper. "And I'll not have you telling me what to do."

His face reddened and a vein popped out in his forehead. He clenched his fists and then shot a look toward Gilead. He stepped closer to Deidre and she tried to step away, but he caught her wrist and gave it a hard twist as he pulled her closer. She clenched her jaw to keep from crying out.

"Once we're wed, ye will obey me in everything. Every single thing that I might want ye to do." He bared his teeth wickedly. "And that includes bed. Aye, I look forward to that lesson. Ye'll soon learn what happens to lasses that doona obey quickly." He dropped her hand and stepped back as Gilead approached. "And there'll be no more riding with *him*," he hissed.

Gilead glanced from him to Deidre and back again. "I thought ye were leaving."

"I was," he growled, "but Angus wants to draft a treaty of peace with Fergus and asked me to stay. But I'll not have my betrothed riding off with ye." He turned to Deidre. "Get back in the house."

"She's not married to ye yet, Niall. 'Tis for the lady to decide if she wants to ride with me."

Niall gave her a murderous look. "Ye'll do as I say."

Deidre lifted her chin. "I will not." She brushed past him and the depth of his rage nearly seared her, giving her even more incentive to make this escape good. "Would you help me mount, please?" she said to Gilead.

He grinned and lifted her easily into the saddle, and then vaulted onto Malcolm. He gathered the reins and looked down at a furious Niall.

"My father doona like to be kept waiting."

Niall glanced toward the Hall steps where Turius and Angus stood waiting. He turned back to Gilead. "We haven't finished this."

Gilead gave him a mock salute. "Any time ye're ready, Niall. Any time."

Chapter Eighteen

FOILED

"Where to?" Gilead asked as soon as they had cleared the gate.

"To the circle of stones," Deidre answered. It was a place she wanted to go one more time before she left. Possibly, just possibly, the Sight would return to her there and she would know where to continue looking for the Stone.

Gilead frowned slightly. "It's a long ride."

"Then let's not waste time," she said and spurred her horse into a gallop.

Malcolm's hooves thundered behind her and Gilead came abreast, the sash from his plaid flying behind him. "I'll race ye to the tree at the mile marker." He left her in a cloud of dust.

Winger strained at his bit, not wanting to be left behind. "All right," Deidre laughed and leaned forward, easing the reins. "Go get him."

Eventually they slowed to a rocking canter and then alternated between trotting and walking. Neither of them spoke much. Gilead scanned the land for possible danger and Deidre was intent on planning her escape.

They arrived at the circle near Nones. Gilead squinted up at the sun as he dismounted. "We'll have about an hour or so before we have to head back."

Deidre felt momentary guilt as he helped her dismount. If her plan worked, she'd not be going back.

They walked to the stones and Deidre took a deep breath before she stepped inside. Immediately, she felt light-headed and a slight tingle raced through her, as though she had tapped an energy source, but no woman in white appeared.

"Do you feel it?" she whispered to Gilead.

"Feel what?" he asked.

"There's power here."

He looked at her quizzically. "Do ye think the Stone ye're seeking is here?"

Deidre paused, tuning her senses to the circle. Gilead's aura was pulsating with such vibrancy that she stepped away from him. She began to feel a gentle, humming presence, vaguely peaceful, as though the universe was suddenly totally balanced. The Philosopher's Stone's divine "geometry" *was* perfect harmony, but her Sight remained benignly quiet.

Finally, she shook her head. "Not the Stone . . . but something . . . compelling. Like inside this circle there can be no lies. Only truth. I know that sounds odd."

"Not so odd," Gilead said. "These circles were built for a reason and, undoubtedly, centuries of pagan rituals have taken place in them. Mayhap it's that magic ye feel."

Magic. She certainly needed all the help that she could get. Maybe whatever it was she felt would help her put Gilead to sleep and protect him until he woke. She looked up at him, admiring the strong, clean line of his jaw and the way his blue eyes mirrored the sky. It took all of her willpower not to throw herself at him and feel his arms holding her tight one last time.

"You may be right," she answered. "I'd like to stay inside the circle as long as possible. Why don't we have our meal in here?"

Gilead nodded and went to the saddlebags. When he returned, he handed her the food bag and started to pour wine into two tin cups.

"Wait," Deidre said. "Would you mind getting me some water instead? I'm really thirsty after all that dust we stirred up."

"Certes. I'll be right back."

As he walked down the small incline toward the burn,

Deidre quickly pulled the small packet of herbs from her boot and stirred them into the wine that he had poured. She hated doing this to him, but she had to escape. And the place was perfect. Gilead would be safe inside the circle while he slept. She was already a good two hours away from Niall. By the time Gilead woke and returned home, she'd be almost a day's ride ahead. The woodruff smelled a little like new-mown hay, not unpleasant. She hoped the wine would hide the taste.

Deidre had broken the bread and opened the crock of honey by the time Gilead returned. She handed him the cup of wine. "I'll have some as soon as I finish this," she said and drained the cool, clear water before Gilead could ask to dilute his wine.

He took a long swallow of wine before he began to eat. Deidre poured a little wine in her cup and refilled his as soon as it was empty. When she looked up to give it to him, his eyes were glittering strangely.

Gilead smiled at her lazily as he reached to take the cup. His fingertips brushed over hers, the pad of his thumb slowly stroking her knuckles.

Heat seared through Deidre's arm and flared throughout her body. Every pore of her skin opened for him. His touch stimulated her. Even more so because she wasn't expecting it. Was he getting drunk already? Did the herb affect the wine that much? He didn't look drunk. His eyes had turned a deeper blue, the pupils dilated somewhat, but the look he gave her was intense. Sexual. Apprehensively, she tried to release the cup, but his hand closed over hers.

"Why doona ye come closer, Dee?" The fingers of his other hand gently traced the outline of her cheek and slid lightly down her throat. His gaze drifted to the roundness of her breasts beneath the lightweight linen shirt she wore.

Too late, she remembered another side effect of woodruff. She should have recalled it earlier, but it had a different name. The Romans called it woodrowel and used it as an aphrodisiac. Good Lord, how much had she put in that drink? As much as she would have liked for Gilead to make love to her—would have loved to feel herself naked against his bare skin—she knew he would hate her for deceiving her when the herb wore off.

"I don't think you should be drinking any more wine," she said and reached for the cup.

He held it tantalizingly out of her reach. "If ye want it, ye'll have to take it."

She stretched her reach, careful not to touch him, and then felt his warm breath as he dipped his head to nuzzle her neck. She tried to sit back, but his arm went around her and he pulled her to him.

"Ah, Dee, is this not what ye want, too?" He nibbled her earlobe enticingly.

By the Goddess, this was exactly what she wanted. To feel his big, hot hands caressing her entire body, bringing every nerve fiber alive in her skin, making her insides go all mushy and her knees weak. She wanted to feel herself being stretched by his thick shaft entering her and then feel the length of him fill her completely. Involuntarily, deep internal muscles contracted and she ached for him to be inside her. She began to pant as he undid the laces of her shirt. She must stop this. She knew how he felt about his father's lustful urges. Gilead would want to kill her once he found out he had been a victim of her deceit.

She tried to push away from him, but he rolled over with her, one thigh pressed between her legs, his torso pinning her to the ground. Gilead slanted his mouth over hers, kissing her deeply, his tongue probing for more. With a groan, Deidre parted her lips and tasted him. He sucked her tongue into his mouth and what little strand of sense she had took flight like a bird from an open cage.

Hands fumbling in haste, they divested each other of their clothes. Gilead leaned up on his elbows to look down at her. "Ye are beautiful, Dee." Then he glanced at the remnants of their meal lying close by and gave her a wicked grin.

He dipped two fingers into the honey pot and let the golden liquid dribble on her breasts. He bent his dark head and began teasing a breast with his tongue, licking long, slow, broad strokes underneath and around, the tip of his tongue teasing the aureole, causing the nipple to tighten into a hard bud as he lapped up the honey.

Deidre pressed his head to her breast, begging him to suck.

Obtusely, he flicked his tongue over the tip and then blew cool air on it as he began to ravage the other breast. She wanted to scream in frustration and she didn't want him to stop. What exquisite torture it was waiting for that moment when he would take it in his mouth and the pressure of the suckling would send a jolt that vibrated to her very core.

Already she was pulsating there and when he shifted his weight and she felt his velvety steel sword press against the softness of her female sheath, her body shuddered.

With a growl, Gilead plunged into the hot wetness of her, burying himself to the hilt. Deidre wrapped her legs around his buttocks and arched her back to receive him.

He thrust wildly, ramming her and grinding himself into her over and over. She clung to him and cried out for more. If he were going to hate her for this, she wanted to at least savor the moment.

Her body tingled. The thrumming that had begun in her hardened, throbbing nub, built and spread itself like a wave building in momentum, threatening to pull up the very bottom of the ocean into its vast curl as it rushed forward, cresting in an orgasm that racked her very soul in its intensity. She screamed as her body contracted and erupted, sending the wave crashing back into the turbulent sea of her emotions.

With a mangled shout of his own, Gilead butted the wall of her womb and she felt the strong spurt of his seed hot and juicy inside her.

He collapsed on top of her, their bodies sweaty, their wet hair clinging to their faces. Deidre kept her legs locked around his, holding him inside. For a long time, neither of them said a word and the only sound was the rasping of their breath as their hearts slowed.

Gilead eventually propped himself up and kissed her softly. "There is an oath, Dee, that the Scotti take when they find the one mate they love. If the vow is taken inside a standing circle, it binds them for eternity. Do ye want to take it with me?"

Deidre looked into his chiseled face, at the sinfully sensual lips that had kissed her with such savage, passionate desire and just now with such gentle caring. She looked into his brilliantly blue eyes, still dilated, but filled with tenderness and love. Feelings that weren't real because of the woodrowel. He only thought they were. She bit her lip.

"I cannot."

He frowned. "Why not? After this, ye surely doona think I will let ye marry the likes of Niall?"

Dear Gilead. So gallant, so noble. "You are betrothed, too."

He hesitated just a fraction of a second. "I doona think Dallis will be overly disappointed. Somehow, I'll get Comgall to understand."

She smiled and traced the corner of his delectable mouth. He would soon hate her. "You would not be saying these things if you were yourself, Gilead."

He grinned. "Who would I be, if not me?"

Gently, she wiggled out from under him and sat up, bringing her knees to her chin and putting her arms around them. "I slipped something into your wine."

He looked puzzled and then the dawn of understanding appeared. "Ye wished to arouse me?" He narrowed his eyes when she didn't answer. "Ye wanted me to be unfaithful so ye could have yer sport? Is that it?"

"No!" He was already angry and he didn't even know the real reason. And she couldn't tell him. Not if she wanted to have a horse available to her as a means of escape. She desperately needed to escape.

"What, then?" Gilead demanded and when she just shook her head, he made a disgusted sound and dressed quickly. He gathered up the cups and wineskin. "Since ye've had yer fun, ye best get dressed. 'Twill be dark by the time we get home."

Deidre tried to keep the tears from brimming over as she hurriedly dressed. She hated having him think she was a wanton who had deliberately lured him into breaking his betrothal vow. She should have stopped him. She stumbled over to Winger and mounted before Gilead could assist her. Not that he looked like he wanted to. She swiped at her eyes and kept her head averted.

She should have stopped him. But, Goddess help her, it had been good.

By the Dagda! He was a fool. Gilead shoved the cups and wineskin into the saddlebags. How many times had the Sassenach beguiled him? And now she had spelled him with her witchery. He couldn't blame the herbs alone for what had taken place. The entire ride over here he had pushed thoughts that they were alone together out of his mind. He had tried not to notice how her golden hair caught the sun or how silky her hair looked as it streamed wildly behind her when they galloped. And the tight trews showed off every delectable curve of her body.

Gilead cursed silently. She had told him she dinna love him. Said it in so many words. Why could he not comprehend that? And yet she had put those herbs in his wine. She had *planned* to seduce him. But why? If she had not been a virgin when he had first taken her, he would think that she was a skilled courtesan of the Gaulish court. Her hands alone kindled a fire that set his whole body ablaze. He knew his father would laugh at him for resenting being used—if he ever found out—and tell him to lie back and enjoy it. But Gilead was not his father. The act meant more than just tupping a lass to seek his own release. He wanted it to mean something. He wanted to make love. To Deidre, who wasn't his.

The thought of Niall actually having access to Deidre's naked body did little to settle his temper. And it angered him further that he had not been able to convince his father to break the handfast. He would try again. Whether Deidre loved Gilead or not, she dinna deserve to be doomed to a life with a cruel brute who would beat her into submission. He thought about what Niall had said when they left. He wished he could call the man out, duel with him one-on-one for Deidre's hand. But he couldn't champion her while he was betrothed to another.

He had one foot in the stirrup when the wind stirred the grass and he saw his sash fluttering against one of the standing stones. He'd forgotten it in his haste to get dressed.

"I'll be right back," he said.

As he approached the circle, the sash caught on the wind and sailed into the circle. Gilead stepped through and bent to retrieve it. For a moment he felt dizzy and when he straightened, his eyes widened in wonder.

A mist gathered, shielding him from the outside world, and he could barely make out the looming forms of the stones. An eerie silence invaded the place. Birds should have been chirping and he should have been able to hear the horses stomping and the jingle of harness. But there was nothing. Only stillness and a fog so dense he felt as though he were in a cloud.

The Cromlech began to glow. A subtle light, like a candle behind a shaded window, at first. Then it grew brighter, until its luminescent brilliance overpowered him. He sank to his knees, his arm shielding his face from the radiance.

"Look, Gilead."

The voice, soft and melodious as it was, sounded like thunder in the evasive quiet of the swirling mist. He lowered his arm slowly.

A maiden with golden-red hair sat on the altar stone, holding something oblong in her hands. Tendrils of fog curled around her with an otherworldly air and obscured his view.

"Are ye real?" Even as he asked, he knew she wasn't. He was having some kind of illusionary vision because of those herbs. Or the faerie world really existed and he had walked into it.

She smiled and held out the object. "Seek the gar-al, Gilead."

The stillness deepened and a feeling of complete serenity and tranquility washed over him. He blinked. The maiden, dressed in white, blended in with the vapors that danced around her. Whatever the object was, he couldn't get a clear glimpse of it.

Gilead tried to think. He was probably temporarily mad, but if this really were the Philosopher's Stone that Dee sought . . . He reached out. "I will take it to her."

The maiden shook her head. "Ye must quest for it."

"But I'm looking at it . . . I think." Even as he said the words, the image faded and the mists lifted, baring the surrounding landscape to him again.

He heard Malcolm snuffle even as Deidre called to him. Unsure exactly of what had taken place, he picked up his sash and walked slowly toward his horse.

Deidre was watching him. "You've seen her, haven't you?"

He feigned ignorance. "Who? There's no one here but us."

"The woman," Deidre said. "The one in white with the red-gold hair."

Gilead stared at her. If he thought that they were sharing

the same illusion, that probably meant that he was completely crazy. Deidre hadn't been with him in the circle.

"I've seen her too," Deidre said quietly. "The last time I was here. I told her I was seeking the Stone." She leaned down in her saddle and put her hand on his shoulder. "Please. What did she say to you?"

The warmth of Deidre's hand felt real enough and there was definitely the smell of horse and leather. Birds chirped again and the sun was sinking low in the afternoon sky. He was back in his world. But if Dee had seen the lady too . . . He took a deep breath. "She said that I must seek the gar-al if I am to help ye." When Deidre looked puzzled, he added, "'Gar-al' means 'stone cup' in Gaelic."

She knit her brows together. "I'm searching for a Stone, probably a tablet, not a cup. I wonder why she's said the same thing to both of us."

It didn't make sense to him, either. He shrugged, hoping to appear nonchalant, and vaulted onto his stallion's back. "I think it would be better if neither of us spoke of this when we get back." His father would truly think he had gone daft.

Deidre nodded, but he could see the excitement in her eyes. As they rode along, Gilead tried to tell himself the herbs had taken effect, but he could not deny the feeling of absolute peace that had descended on him when the object—whatever it was—had been extended to him.

And Deidre . . . he glanced over at her. She had a look of calm contentment on her face. Whatever he thought of the incident, there was no doubt that Deidre believed it. Now the question was: could he?

Niall had gone by the time they returned and Deidre gratefully slipped up the back stairs to change hurriedly for dinner. Even so, everyone was already seated by the time she got to the dining hall.

Formorian glanced from her to Gilead, whose hair was still damp from his quick cleanup, and smiled. Deidre hoped she wouldn't make one of her pointed comments, since Gilead's friendship with Deidre was dubious, at best, right now.

"Did ye have a good ride?" Elen asked as the meat was passed.

"Yes," Deidre answered, "we rode to the circle of stones." She was aware of the quick look Gilead shot her. "It's interesting to see."

"Ye should have taken an escort to ride that far," Angus said. "Even if we've cleared the area of Saxons, there could be highwaymen lurking about." His dark glance raked over Deidre. "Ye are familiar with that, are ye not?"

Deidre knew he still didn't quite believe she might not be a spy. She doubted that Turius had mentioned capturing her guard, for Angus would have made a connection and she wasn't about to enlighten him now. He'd probably think a Frankish spy as bad a Saxon one. "I felt safe with Gilead, my lord." When she saw Gilead's ears turn pink and Formorian grinning at him, she quickly added, "I like to look at old ruins."

Angus's smoke-colored eyes turned darker. "Aye. Ye've been digging at the old church, too. What are ye looking for?"

Deidre inhaled sharply. She had been so careful to slip away unseen. Now that she knew the Stone wasn't here—and how had her Sight been so wrong?—she still had to keep secret that the Stone was missing. "It's just a hobby of mine. Once I found an old Roman coin and another time some silver."

"And I would think, if ye found the same on my land, it would belong to me."

"What harm would it do if Deidre found a coin or two?" Elen asked in a rather strong voice. "Ye have no need of it."

Angus looked at her in surprise and Formorian arched an eyebrow, but Elen seemed not to notice. "In fact, I've decided I want Deidre to come with me."

Deidre didn't think Elen could have stunned them more if she had suddenly jumped on the table and begun dancing like the biblical Salome. But Deidre was proud of her; Elen's health had been steadily getting stronger and she doubted Angus had ever expected her to talk back to him at all.

"And where is it ye want to go?" Angus asked.

"Eire," Elen answered. "I want to visit my father."

Deidre's heart leapt. A perfect way to get away from Niall.

Maybe Elen would help her escape. She felt bludgeoned by Elen's next words.

"Eire has the finest lace in the world," Elen continued and looked at Deidre. "Ye must have some for yer wedding dress, and I'll order some for Dallis, as well."

Angus exchanged a furtive look with Formorian. "When would ye be leaving and how long will ye be gone?"

Elen glanced at Formorian, too, and then back at Angus. "Not long. The weddings are in ten days. If we leave day after tomorrow, we should be back a good four days before. Enough time for the seamstresses to attach the lace." She turned to Formorian. "Should Dallis and Comgall arrive before we return, I'm sure ye can entertain her?"

"I'm sure Gilead can entertain her," Angus said.

"Why, no, husband, he canna."

Angus frowned. "And why not? 'Twould be most proper."

Deidre almost laughed. Angus had never been concerned with propriety before. If only they knew just how improper Gilead had been . . .

"I'm sure it would," Elen said demurely, "but Gilead will accompany me."

Deidre felt her mouth drop open and she quickly closed it. What was Elen about, giving her a chance to spend nearly a week with Gilead?

Angus's frown deepened and Gilead looked dismayed. Deidre chewed on her inner cheek. Was he upset with leaving Angus to Formorian's embraces or was he upset about having to spend time with her? His anger had lessened somewhat after his experience in the circle, but Deidre was only too aware that he still thought she had used him. He was probably the only man in the world who would be offended by that.

"I'll send a strong escort with ye, Elen. Ye'll be well protected. Gilead doona have to go."

"He does," Elen said firmly. "Have ye forgotten my father's treasury? When Gilead was born, he asked for our pledge that our son would come and choose his own pieces of silver for his bride."

Another knifelike pain slashed through Deidre. So Elen

wasn't trying to play matchmaker, after all. And Gilead would be thinking of his bride the whole while.

Still, she would be going to Eire. Away from here. Away from Niall. Away from the wedding from Hades.

Angus was quiet for several minutes and Formorian resolutely studied her well-tended fingernails. Finally he nodded. "Ye may take Gilead with ye."

In spite of herself, Deidre's heart quickened and she felt her blood racing through her veins. She could at least spend his last days as a free man with him. Maybe he would even talk his grandfather into letting her stay in Eire. He knew how much she dreaded the thought of being anywhere near Niall, let alone married to him.

So why was Gilead looking so angry? She knew he hated leaving Angus alone with Formorian, but Turius would be there. They would still have to exercise caution. She looked around. Turius had not put in an appearance at dinner.

"Where's the king?" Deidre asked suddenly.

"Maximilian is stirring up trouble again. This time he's aiding some Franks who are accusing Turius of harboring some cousin of Childebert's who's a fugitive," Formorian answered, giving Deidre a lingering glance. "A messenger came this afternoon. Turius sent a man to tell Max he wanted to meet with him and then he rode to Luguvalium."

Deidre turned pale. So Childebert was still looking for her. Another reason to get to Eire before someone discovered her.

Elen interrupted her thoughts. "I was not aware that he had gone."

Formorian smiled. "Ye were having yer nap at the time."

"When will he return?" Gilead asked sharply.

Angus gave him a level look, his dark eyes inscrutable. "Not for at least a week."

"Then I—"

"Will go, as your mother wishes," Angus said.

Formorian gave Gilead a wide-eyed look and folded her hands sedately in her lap. "Doona fash. We'll be just fine."

Deidre stared at her in amazement. Did she mean she and Angus would really behave themselves or was she openly admitting that they would have a fine time together? Formorian was the perfect picture of respectability at the moment, but Deidre knew there was no innocence in her soul. The woman had dauntless nerve.

Elen looked like a small, trapped bird, caught between a gyrfalcon and a feral cat. Deidre could almost hear Formorian purring. Poor Elen. If her intent was to help Deidre, she had been outfoxed by her husband once again. Much as Deidre wanted to get away, she must try to mend this.

"It might be a little late to travel to Eire and back, so close to the wedding date." Deidre managed to keep her voice from trembling. "I'm sure that Gilead could pick out his silver after the wedding."

He threw her a grateful smile. It was a bittersweet victory for her that he wasn't angry any longer, but was he looking forward to picking out the silver for Dallis? With Dallis? And now, she would have to plan a different escape. But it would be worth it if Elen's staying home kept Angus and Formorian apart.

So she was as surprised as everyone else when Elen lifted her head and took a deep breath. "We are going, lass." She gave Angus a long look. "Gilead must fulfill the rite of passage that his grandfather wished."

His pieces of silver. Deidre suddenly felt as betrayed as the Christian Jesus had been. Gilead's wedding would take place.

She blinked back tears. At least she wouldn't be here to see that.

Chapter Nineteen

EIRE

It took a day of land travel to reach the port of Dumbarton. Deidre was amazed at the amount of activity on the docks. She watched as the crew on an unwieldy merchant vessel threw lines to dock hands and maneuvered the broad beam of the ship alongside the pier. The gangplank lowered and, to her surprise, some twenty bawling calves were herded out, contained only by shouting men yielding long whips. The calves balked and bellowed as they stumbled through the narrow alleys away from the water.

"Where are they taking them?" Deidre asked.

"North, probably," Gilead answered. "Gabran told my father he wanted to try raising cattle, but I never thought he'd do it. Sheep are so much easier."

Farther along the dock, longshoremen hauled bales of wool aboard the bulky cargo vessels for shipments south. Beyond them lay the sleek, narrow galley that would take them to Eire. Deidre looked up at it in awe as they approached.

She had crossed the Narrow Channel on a small fishing craft barely capable of holding her and her escorts. Thankfully, the wind had been light and the water calm, because the little boat had pitched and bobbed even in gentle swells. They had all been slightly green around the gills by the time they touched land.

But this was a galley. Over a hundred feet long, it had a narrow hull and the bow extended gracefully into a prow ram shod in bronze. The freeboard's wood was oiled until it glistened in the morning sun. Once on board, Deidre also noticed a difference from her cousin's warships. Instead of having two or three banks of oars for the rowers below deck, this ship had two dozen benches on deck, each of which could hold three men, and their oars passed over the wales instead of through holes at different levels.

"Does this arrangement make the boat more maneuverable?" Deidre asked.

Gilead nodded. "Faster, too. If the winds are fresh, it should take us a little more than a day to reach Eire." He held out his hand to help her down the ladder. "I'll show ye where ye and my mother will quarter."

The stern of the boat held four staterooms, two to port and two to starboard. The captain and first mate used two of them, and the boatswain had a small cabin in the forecastle, near where the food stores were kept.

"Where do the archers and soldiers sleep?" Deidre asked.

"On deck, so they'll be ready for battle," Gilead answered. "And they shift out as rowers. It keeps them conditioned and we're never short of crew or soldiers if many are battle-wounded."

"Do you expect trouble on the crossing?" For the first time, she realized that there were nearly a half century of men on board, all of them carrying weapons.

"Nay. The pirates stay busy south of us most times."

"What about Saxons?"

Gilead shrugged. "They've been known to sail through the Hebrides from time to time. The one thing that we should thank Fergus for is that his ships usually intercept them before they can get far." He opened a door to the nearest stateroom. "Ye'll be sharing this with my mother. We'll set sail immediately, while the ebb is still with us."

After he'd gone, Deidre looked around. The cabin was rectangular and paneled in pine that left a slight cedar scent. Two bunks were securely plated to opposite walls and had high fiddles along their outer ridges. To keep occupants from falling out in rough seas, she guessed. Between the beds, a table with the same type of fiddles was also fastened to the wall. The chamber pot in the corner hung from a hook and chain, allowing it to gimbal with the movement of the ship. The water pitcher and basin were of tin and fit neatly into holes that had been drilled in a shelf. A small porthole opened above the table, allowing some light. All in all, a practical arrangement.

Elen's trunks and hers were brought down, but Deidre didn't bother to change from the trews she'd been traveling in. Wind and waves made a gown impractical and she wondered why Elen insisted on staying on deck wearing one.

Deidre joined her a few minutes later as she heard the thud of lines landing on the deck. Toward the stern, and slightly off-center from the huge tiller that a beefy sailor manned, was a bolted-down bench with a backrest. Unfortunately, there was no canopy for shade, and Elen's pale face was already looking flushed.

Deidre was too excited to sit down. This was her chance to be free from Niall. She joined Gilead midship and craned her neck to look up the tall mast where a sailor was cursing roundly, one leg wrapped around the mast while he dangled from the yardarm, apparently trying to loosen a caught line.

"Get her loose, ye blithering fool!" one of the other sailors shouted. "We be heading into the current and the tide's turning."

Even as he spoke, Deidre could feel the pull of the boat as it yawed to starboard, almost brushing the rocks of the natural jetty. More curses rang out from the straining rowers as they pulled together on the port side to bring the boat back on course.

"I thought you said we were on an ebb tide?" Deidre asked.

Gilead glanced down at her before returning his attention to the man at the spar. "Ye need to get back," he said. "The deck's no place for ye while they're hoisting sail."

"But answer me, first." Her cousin had been meticulous in planning attacks by sea. She was sure she wasn't wrong.

He sighed in frustration. "Ye are too stubborn, lass. We are late and the tide is backing, but the next ebb won't happen until dawn. I'll not have ye and my mother spending the night on the docks. 'Tis too rough. Now go."

Suddenly, the rope came undone and the huge square canvas came crashing downward. Gilead grabbed Deidre and rolled with her on the deck, just as one of the sheets attached to the sail whipped in a lethal backlash to where she had been standing.

She felt Gilead trembling as he lay on top of her, protecting her head with his arms. She sensed he was angry again, since she been foolish enough to get in the way, but his body felt so good against the length of hers that for a moment she didn't care.

"Ye could have been killed," he said harshly as he propped himself on his elbows.

"Then I thank you for saving me," Deidre said as she looked up at him and smiled. Did she dare try a little wiggle? She shifted her weight slightly and was gratified to feel a distinct swelling against her thigh.

He took a sharp breath and then rolled off her, lifting her as he stood up. "Go back to my mother, Dee, and stay there. I have work to do here."

She decided not to argue, still a little shaky from the close call or maybe from being close to Gilead. Elen patted her hand when she joined her. "Are ye all right? I never have liked sailing."

Deidre nodded and watched as the sailors caught the sheets and wrapped them around cleats, pulling the line taut on the port side and allowing the square sail to fill with the northeasterly breeze. High up on the spars, sailors unfurled two triangular sails and adjusted them. The ship found herself and rolled smoothly into the outlet that led to the Firth of Clyde.

Deidre waited until all things had been tidied on deck and the galley was gently plying the waters of the Firth before she approached Gilead in the bow of the boat. He was leaning on the rail, watching sea lions playing in the bow's wake. He glanced at her and then turned back to watching their antics. "Some people say they're really selkies," he said, "and that they take human shape and dance on the beach. My old nurse used to tell me the males are very seductive."

She peered down into the frothing water. One particular creature had lighter fur than the rest and nearly jumped out of the water, her eyes curiously appraising Gilead. Deidre laughed. "I think that one is a girl. Do they lure men, too?"

"The story goes that if a man can capture the fur skin, the selkie female will remain in human form and be his forever." He smiled as the sea lion cavorted playfully in the waves.

"Whether she wishes it or not?" Deidre asked.

Gilead gave her a sharp look. "Ye feel like a captured selkie?"

"In a way," Deidre answered and then looked directly at him. "I'm not returning with you and your mother."

He looked troubled. "What do ye plan to do?"

"I want to stay in Eire. I'll be glad to work for your grandfather if he'll have me."

"'Tis doubtful, lass. Niall's father is a neighbor and his holdings vast. The Mac Erca will not want to risk civil war."

"War, war, war!" Deidre exclaimed heatedly. "That's all I ever hear! Your father spreads word that I'm distant kin and binds me to Niall so Niall will be bound to your clan as an ally. Even when Angus *knows*—and he does—that this union will be disastrous, he will not break the handfast. He doesn't want war. And you have the same problem. I know the herbs I gave you were speaking in the circle when you said that Dallis would not mind, but your father won't risk war with Comgall, either. You're as stuck as I am. The only difference is that Dallis won't be in mortal danger from you." She clenched her hand into a fist and pressed it against her mouth to keep from crying.

Gilead stared at her. "Ye really think Niall might kill ye?"

"Yes!" She held out her arm and rolled up the sleeve of her shirt to show him the fading yellow-green marks Niall had left the last time he had grabbed her. "He wasn't as careful this time. My wrist was so swollen once, I thought it broken. What do you think he's going to do once I'm his legal property?"

He placed a hand under her elbow, the fingers of his other hand gently sliding over the bruise. Then he wrapped his arms around her and brought her close to him. "Ah, Dee, I knew he was cruel. But I had no idea this was going on."

He was so solid and comforting. Deidre buried her head under his chin and against his shoulder, breathing in his scent mixed with salted air. For the moment, she felt safe, as his large, strong hands stroked her back. Finally, he leaned back from her.

"I'll talk to my grandfather," he said.

She gave him a grateful, watery smile. "Thank you."

For a moment, she was sure he was going to kiss her. He started to bend his head to hers when they were interrupted by the first officer.

"Ye'd best be moving to the stern, my lord," the man said. "We just passed Holy Isle and will be coming off Whiting. 'Twill get a bit rough up here then."

The man was right. As soon as they rounded off the peninsula and hit open water, the seas started churning, the waves quickly doubling and then tripling in height, foam spewing from the crests. The galley sluiced through the troughs and rose with the swells. The pitching soon had Elen below deck, green as the water and ill.

Deidre spent the rest of the day bathing Elen's forehead with a damp cloth, wishing that they could have stayed on deck where the air was fresh and she could see the horizon. The rolling motion below made even *her* stomach queasy. By nightfall she had no appetite either, although when Gilead came to relieve her, she managed to climb the ladder and munched on some dry bread.

The night was black and thick clouds scudded across the sky, obscuring the waning moon. Deidre wondered how the captain knew where to steer, with so few stars to guide him, but she supposed he'd made the trip often enough to know what he was about.

She grabbed the rail as the wind picked up in intensity and whipped through the rigging like the sound of a dozen harpies wailing. Big droplets of rain splashed down on the deck around her, and she heard muttered curses as sailors struggled to reef down the big sail while others climbed the mast to bring down the smaller sails.

Deidre scurried down the ladder just as the heavens opened and the rain poured down. She shook her damp hair and shivered as the storm roared its fury and the ship buried her nose in a deep trough, causing green water to wash the deck.

Riding it out wasn't going to be easy. She just hoped this wasn't an omen of what was to come.

The storm passed and by the time they docked the next morning the skies were clear and the water had calmed. The rain, though, had made the emerald-colored hills of Eire even greener and the grass sparkled with diamond dew drops.

Elen, although still pale, managed to walk ashore unassisted. The Mac Erca himself was waiting for her. Although the man must have been past seventy, he stood ramrod straight and had a solid build. His steel grey eyes matched his full head of hair. Deidre was afraid he'd break Elen's ribs from the force of the hug he gave his daughter.

"Ye're much too thin, child," he admonished. "If Angus is not treating ye well, he'll answer to me."

Deidre exchanged looks with Gilead. Angus was continually worried about warring factions, yet he was taking the biggest risks with the two most powerful kings since the Romans left. All because of Formorian.

But Elen was already denying that. "Nay, Father. He treats me well and with respect. I have naught to complain about."

Gilead frowned and Deidre tried not to gape. She knew Elen had accepted her plight because of her own treachery, but she was also trying to protect Angus. This business of avoiding war apparently ran deep in Scotti blood. Deidre thought about all the skirmishes that had occurred after Clovis died and his four sons tried to divide Gaul. Luckily, Childebert, the most rational of the group, laid claim to Paris, which was the strongest fort. Lothar ruled Soissons with a lethal hand and Chlodomir enjoyed strong spirits and young women too much to be a good leader in Orléans. Theuderic, at Metz, was generally ineffective. Still, a lot of blood had been uselessly shed before the four of them agreed to an uneasy truce.

"Well, let's not stand out here," Mac Erca interrupted her thoughts. "Yer mother will be glad to see ye and Gilead, too." He thumped Gilead on the back so hard that any other man would have been sent sprawling.

The Eire king took no notice of Deidre as they walked up

the hill from the dock and toward the fortress. She squelched
a hysterical bubble of laughter. In Gaul she would have been
the one escorted. But ladies' maids were invisible and as far
as her search for the Stone had gone, that was a good thing.
Even now that she had no idea where to continue looking,
she still didn't want her identity known. She would most certainly be put on the next ship home, which would solve her
problem with Niall, but Childebert was an unforgiving man,
for all that he expressed to be Christian. She would either be
locked away in a convent or the castle dungeon. She didn't
know which would be worse.

Elen spent most of the day resting and by the time the
castellan announced dinner, color had come back into her
cheeks and she walked with a determined gait. Eire air was
good for her, Deidre thought, or maybe she was just relieved
to be away from Angus and Formorian. God only knew what
they were up to, left alone.

They passed the Great Hall where Deidre could hear the
clinking of cups and the loud talk of soldiers, but they were
shown into a private dining room. When they entered, she
gasped in delight.

Richly embroidered tapestries covered the walls, threads of
silver and gold catching the light of dozens of sweet-smelling
beeswax candles embedded in niches between the hangings.
The table was ash, its light wood polished so that the surface
glowed in the candlelight. Twelve tall straight-back chairs
were well stuffed and brocaded with fine silk. But it was the
table runner that held Deidre's fascination. Intricately crocheted roses delicately met with entwining vines in the most
exquisitely fine piece of lace that she had ever seen.

So this was the lace that Elen had spoken of. Even Clotilde,
who prided herself on the fine altar cloths made for the
Church, had never had anything so beautiful. No wonder Elen
wanted Dallis to have some of it for her wedding to Gilead.
Deidre swallowed a lump in her throat at the thought.

Then she looked more closely. Roses and vines. From time
beyond Time, the five petals of the rose had symbolized the
five stages of womanhood, but the rose was also symbolic of
the movement of Venus. The astronomer at Childebert's court

had taught that the goddess star crossed in front of, or behind, the sun five times every eight years. The pentacle-shaped path the star took across the heavens traced the five petals of the rose. What Deidre had found fascinating about the lectures was that Venus was either the morning or the evening star, depending on what part of her transit she was in. Deidre missed the kindly old man who had patiently explained so much about the hidden Wisdom masked in the night sky. Clotilde had him exiled from court because she thought his teachings were too pagan, but not before he confirmed to Deidre what her mother had taught her about looking for the rose in carvings and paintings as a concealed symbol of feminine power.

And the vines, twisting and winding around the rose stems with the fluidity of snakes. Another symbol of womanhood and wisdom. Deidre grimaced as she traced the graceful line of one vine and thought of how maligned the snake was. But the vines connected the roses in a fascinating pattern. One large rose spread across her end of the runner. Vines branched out from that rose in different directions, always with a rose at the end of the intricate swirls. Nine medium-sized roses bordered the other end. She bent and peered at one of the roses intently. A small initial, almost indiscernible, was crocheted below a petal. She looked at another rose. Another initial, but different. Now she could see that each flower had an initial beneath it. The last rose had an "E."

Deidre paused in thought. The magician's book had said there were nine holy priestesses on mystic Avalon. The ancient crone who had passed the Mysteries to her mother had ingrained in her that descendents of the Magdalen would someday bring about the true awakening of the loving, peaceful Goddess power of Isis. Could the two be connected in this design? Could she possibly be looking at a hidden code of the Bloodline? The familiar light-headedness buffeted her and she grasped the back of a chair until it passed.

"This is a beautiful piece of work," Deidre said as her vision cleared and the rest had taken their seats. "It almost seems to tell a story."

Elen gave her a strange look. "My grandfather made it for me when I was but a tiny bairn."

"Your grandfather's seamstress was highly skilled."

She shook her head. "Nay. My grandfather did this himself."

"Your grandfather?" Deidre was confused.

"Aye. He took a nasty wound to his thigh in battle that never did really heal. At first he was content to spend his days fishing and let my father take charge, but he grew bored. He told my grandmother he wanted to do something with his life that would last."

"So she taught him how to stitch lace?" Deidre asked and looked at the design again. "It must have taken years!"

"It did," Mac Erca answered. "My mother would closet herself with him for hours. No one was allowed to interrupt them. All we could hear, if we dared to approach that closed door, was the murmur of her voice as if she were telling him stories, and an occasional curse by him. The soldiers took bets that he couldn't do it, with his scarred and calloused warrior hands, but he persevered." He paused. "I was afraid the men would make him a laughingstock, but he told me—in that mild-mannered voice he always used—that perhaps men had forgotten how to contemplate beauty if it wasn't lying beneath them in bed."

Elen and her mother both gasped at his bluntness and even Gilead looked startled.

"Your grandfather sounds like a strong man who knew his own mind," Deidre said quickly to Elen. "How could you bear to leave this behind when you married?"

Pain flashed across Elen's face. "I had hoped to come for it one day and then . . . it seemed better to leave it here, where it can grace a fine room."

Suddenly Deidre knew. Elen wouldn't tarnish a gift that had been made with so much love by taking it to a marriage that was such a farce. She had hoped to make Angus love her, and if he had, no doubt this lace would be with her in Culross.

But the story in the design . . . had Elen's grandmother told her grandfather the legend of the Bloodline? Was it possible that the Stone itself was here? On Eire? She felt a sudden wave of dizziness. If the "E" stood for Elen, then she was at the end of a long line of Goddess power. Since she had no daughter, Gilead must be destined for something big. But what?

* * *

"So will ye help her?" Gilead asked his grandfather the next morning as the two of them sat off to one corner in the Great Hall breaking their fast.

Mac Erca spread a still-warm bannock with freshly churned butter before he answered. "Niall is hotheaded, just like his father. He'll come for her."

"But ye are high king here. She would be under yer protection."

"She's nothing to me. Why should I risk an uprising?"

"Niall is a cruel man. He uses women badly. Once Deidre's married to him, we canna protect her."

Mac Erca gave him a sharp look. "We?"

"Da and me," Gilead answered. "When Da drew up the hand-fast pact, it said Niall was not to bed her until the wedding night."

Mac Erca snorted. "Surprising, coming from Angus. I dinna know the man had any compassion in him."

Gilead shifted uneasily. His grandfather had spies everywhere. How much did he know about the situation at home? "Deidre would earn her keep and she'd be safe here."

His grandfather waved a hand at that. "If ye are so concerned for her, why doona ye send her home? Armorica, dinna ye say?"

Gilead nodded, miserable to mislead his grandfather, but he had promised Deidre to go along with her story. "Her parents are dead. She has nowhere to go."

"She claims to be kin to us?"

"In a way. Through Caw."

"Thin blood there," his grandfather said, "but apparently enough that Angus is willing to claim it to bind Niall. Ye know blood ties canna be broken."

Gilead felt as though one of his grandfather's prize stallions had just kicked him in the stomach with both back hooves. The Mac Erca was turning him down.

"I'm sorry," the old man said as he rose to leave. "I wilna be risking war."

Gilead watched him walk away. There must be something he could do. Maybe the idea of sending her home—well, not to

Childebert—but perhaps to his grandmother in Brocéliande. He wished he'd thought of it sooner. The lake was secluded, deep within the forest; Childebert would think twice about looking for Deidre there. To protect her privacy, his grandmother had been careful to spread stories of spirits that haunted the woods and faeries full of mischief. At least he thought they were tales; his grandmother had something of an otherworldly air about her.

He could arrange passage as soon as they docked in Dumbarton; there were always trade ships moving wool to Kernow in exchange for tin, and from there on to Armorica. Angus would be furious with him, and he'd probably be flogged for it, but, Deidre would be safe.

Feeling better, he took himself off to look through the silver that Mac Erca had sent to his room that morning.

There were three large trunks waiting for him. He opened them and removed several serving platters and wine goblets that Dallis would probably like. He didn't really care if he drank from wooden tankards or not, but his mother had insisted that he go through this.

Gilead pulled out several smaller plates and bowls and set them aside. Deidre could take those with her and sell them, if she needed to. He was just about to close the third trunk when something caught his eye at the bottom. He reached down and his hand encountered something hard and smooth.

It was a marble chalice, streaks of green cutting through the grayish white stone. Etched runes covered the bronze rim and side handles. He turned it over, but no carver had made his mark on the bottom. It was a beautiful piece. Gilead wondered where it had come from. He lifted more pieces of silver, but there was nothing else made of marble in the trunk.

He would give it to Deidre as a parting gift, something to remember him by. If he ever saw her again, he still wouldn't be able to kiss her warm lips or touch a soft breast, for he'd be married to someone else and honor-bound to uphold those vows.

Yes, the cup would be just the thing for Deidre. Maybe they could drink a toast together before she set sail to Armorica.

* * *

Deidre was aware at dinner that night that Gilead was watching her covertly. He seemed edgy. Several times, Elen had to repeat her questions before she got his attention. They would be leaving tomorrow morning on the turn of the tide and Deidre wondered if he really was that excited to get back. Dallis would probably be waiting.

Deidre tried to conceal her own nervousness, too. Since Gilead had not sought her out, she could only assume that Mac Erca had turned down her request to stay in Eire under his protection. Well, Eire was a big place. Gilead's grandmother had taken her and Elen for a carriage ride that morning and Deidre had probed both of them about villages and roads and the lay of the land. She felt a little guilty, thinking of how much Elen had enjoyed answering her questions about places she had gone as a child. But now Deidre had a plan.

She would slip away tonight, on foot. Unlike Angus, Mac Erca did not keep his gates bolted, for Eire was at peace. There was a guard posted, but if Deidre kept to the shadows, she could make her way out. By dawn, she should be near the larger village that Elen had told her held a market every day. There, she would purchase a horse with her coins and make her way south and inland to Tara.

Elen had told her of a trip she had taken there once to see the fabled Lia Fáil—the Stone of Destiny that had been Jacob's pillow when he'd dreamed of the ladder to heaven that was the symbolic generation of the holy Bloodline. Sadly, it, too, had been stolen, but perhaps another Stone awaited her there. The light-headedness had affected her strongly this afternoon. Deidre knew she had to try.

But tonight . . . tonight was the last time she would see Gilead. She tried not to think about that, even as the servants were clearing the dishes.

Elen had left with her mother, and Deidre was about ready to retire to her chambers when Gilead approached.

"Would ye care to go for a walk with me?" he asked.

Deidre nearly overturned her chair, getting up. A corner of his generous mouth quirked up and he offered his arm. She slipped her hand through, thinking how good and warm and strong he felt.

The night air was balmy and they walked toward the sea. "Your grandfather turned you down, didn't he?" Deidre asked when they stopped near the snug little boathouse that doubled as quarters for a guard when trouble was brewing. It was empty tonight and only the small glow of a crescent moon hung over the gently lapping water.

"Aye. My grandfather has no wish to disturb the peace that has settled on Eire since Fergus left." Gilead turned to her and took her hand. "I've another plan, though. One that will save ye from Niall."

Deidre was filled with a different kind of dizziness at his touch. Sharp little tingles pulsated all the way up her arm. "A plan?"

Gilead nodded. "When we dock in Dumbarton, I'll get ye on a ship heading south. I've written a letter to my other grandmother, explaining who ye are. Ye can take it along with ye. She'll give ye refuge at the Black Lake. Ye'll be safe."

Deidre drew in a sharp breath of salt air. To actually live in that forest . . . Even her mother's people held that it was magical, that people went in and never came out. Deidre had even heard about a lady who lived at the Black Lake. People said— not that anyone had actually seen her—that she was ageless. But if she couldn't find the Stone, it would be a perfect place to hide forever. Then another thought struck her.

"What about your father? Won't he be angry if you thwart his plans?"

Gilead shrugged. "Probably."

"What will he do to you?"

"Doona worry about it. He won't kill me."

The sounds of men screaming while being flogged at the whipping post seared Deidre's mind. Angus could easily be ruthless. "He'll beat you, won't he?"

"Doona fash, Deidre. Ye'll be safe. That's what counts. Wounds heal."

She looked into his midnight-blue eyes. He was willing to make this sacrifice. For her. She must mean something to him after all . . . or maybe he didn't want her death by Niall's hand on his conscience. Either way, she couldn't accept his offer. Her way was better. He couldn't be blamed if she ran off on her own.

Besides, she had to get to Tara. Her own Stone was somewhere near. She could sense it. But better that Gilead didn't know.

"Thank-you," she said. "If you're sure your grandmother is willing to defy your father, I accept."

Gilead grinned. "Da won't risk being enchanted by the Gwragedd Annwn."

"The who?"

"Faerie maidens who once dwelt beneath the lakes in the dark mountains of Gwynedd, but were banished by St. Patrick because they'd insulted him. So they crossed the sea to Brocéliande." He paused. "According to my grandmother, they are most beautiful and either drive men mad or take them down to the depths of the lake, never to be heard from again."

"You jest!"

"Nay! 'Tis the story I grew up with." Gilead answered. "Whether or not it be true, Da won't risk losing Formorian." His eyes darkened for a moment and he turned away. "We'd better start back."

Deidre put her hand on his arm and stopped him. "Make love to me?"

Gilead looked startled. "Dee—"

She shushed him with her fingertips. "This is going to be our last night together."

He hesitated and then took a deep breath and she thought she heard him mutter something about not being married yet. "Please," she said.

She could see desire warring with propriety on his face. A muscle clenched in his jaw as he grimaced. His damnable gallantry was winning. She sighed in defeat and took a step toward the path that led to the castle.

Then she felt his hand on her shoulder. She turned to look up at him.

"This way," he whispered hoarsely and led her to the boathouse.

He bolted the door and Deidre had just a glimpse of a snugly furnished room and a cot in the corner covered by a plaid before Gilead claimed her mouth.

His kiss seared her mouth as his hands deftly divested her

of her clothing. The feel of his warm hands caressing her bare skin made her shiver.

"Are ye cold? I can light the fire in the brazier," he said as his lips nibbled her earlobe and then pressed down to her nape.

Deidre twined her fingers through his hair and drew him closer. "You've already done a good job of lighting my fire—" She broke off as Gilead tongued her breast and teased the nipple of the other with the pad of this thumb. Blood surged to the tips, making them heavy and achy for more of him. She moaned softly.

Gilead lifted her and carried her to the bed. He stripped quickly and slipped beneath the plaid, pulling her to him.

It felt good, having their bodies pressed together as they lay on their sides facing each other. Deidre felt his member harden and thicken as she pressed her abdomen to his flat stomach. A very interesting sensation there . . . the energy center that from ancient ages had spurred desire between a man and a woman. She rotated her hips against his to increase the pleasant yearning deep within her belly.

Gilead groaned and brought her thigh over his, his shaft probing the wet heat at her center. He inserted the head slowly, stretching her and allowing her swollen folds to claim him.

"I want you inside of me," she whispered.

He nudged another inch inside and then paused.

"*All* of you. Now."

He withdrew to her entry, the tip of him lingering there.

Deidre took a ragged breath. "Gilead. Please."

He obligingly filled her halfway.

Dear Lord, why was he torturing her? She wrapped her raised leg around his buttocks and pressed herself onto him.

He pulled back, teasing her.

"Gilead . . ."

"Shhh," he said as he slanted his mouth over hers. "We've all night ahead of us."

His tongue thrust in and out of her mouth in a tantalizing imitation of what she wanted his penis to do. She caught his tongue between her teeth and sucked on it. She felt him quiver and then whimpered when she felt him leave her. In the next instant, she was gasping in ecstasy.

Gilead slid the tip of his iron-hard rod between her folds and along the sensitive hood that protected her nub, which pulsated wildly in anticipation. He dipped his cock inside her again and began lubricating the whole area in slow, deliberate strokes, sending Deidre to the near edge time and again as he tormented her bud. Frenzied passion built with every stroke, stoking her very core with a fervor she didn't know she could possess. The drawn-out bedevilment inflamed her whole body, making every nerve ending tingle. She began to shudder and then Gilead impaled her, filling her fully and completely, the thickness of him a welcome relief for internal muscles to grasp, his thrusts hard and deep. She felt her body rack as he pressed against her womb and with a cry, she felt the welcome relief of her body exploding.

Lazily, Gilead's hand slid across the pillow the next morning as dawn began to break in the eastern sky, sending soft shades of pale coral through the open window. Deidre had felt so good in his arms, her satiny skin soft and smooth . . . His hand fumbled for her silky hair and felt only the pillow.

He opened his eyes to an empty bed and swung his legs over the edge to sit up. Where had she gone? To attend to private needs? He wanted her beside him, all warm and desirable, one last time before they sailed.

He frowned when he saw the note on the table. He quickly pulled on his trews and boots and went to pick it up. With a curse, he crushed the note, grabbed his shirt, and raced up the path toward the castle.

His foolish little Sassenach had gone to ground in a wild country that she knew nothing of. She wanted to spare him a flogging, she'd said. As if he cared whether he got beaten for helping her against his father's will. After last night, he knew beyond any doubt that he loved her. He had been sure that day in the circle, but last night had proved it had nothing to do with the herbs she'd used.

He loved Dee and she was gone.

Chapter Twenty

SHIP OF THE FOOL

"What do ye mean, she's gone?" Mac Erca glowered at Gilead as he stood by the table where his grandfather had been breaking his fast.

"She left a note," Gilead said glumly and turned to his mother who was still seated. "This is Da's fault. Deidre wilna marry Niall."

Mac Erca took in Gilead's disheveled appearance and wrinkled clothes. "Would ye have anything to do with that?"

"Nay. Aye." Gilead swallowed hard. "Regardless of me, the lass dinna want to marry Niall."

"Since when did coinless lassies with no land holdings have a say in the matter? She ought to be grateful to Niall—and yer father—for making her future solid."

Gilead squared his shoulders. "I've seen the bruises he's left on her. What kind of a future do ye think she'll have?"

Elen gasped. "Bruises? Again? I knew her wrist was swollen once, but she has said naught more. If Niall has hurt her, once more, even Angus must agree—"

Mac Erca snorted. "Yer husband should have thought of that before he agreed to handfast her. As far as the law's concerned, she's all but the man's property already. And I'll not have Niall and his hotheaded father come raiding my lands in retaliation for harboring her." He turned to a waiting servant. "Summon Colin. Have him bring the hounds. Then find Duncan. Have him bring that wolf of his." He turned back to Gilead. "She must be found and sent back, one way or another."

Gilead stared at his grandfather. He didn't know about the wolfman, but hounds, in a pack, could bring Deidre down and tear her to shreds before their keepers would catch up to them. He turned and walked quickly toward the door.

"Where are ye going?" Mac Erca thundered.

"To get a horse and go look for her," Gilead answered. "Ye see, I love her."

He didn't hear his mother's whimper of despair or see the sad expression on her face, and he ignored his grandfather's order to stop. He only prayed that Deidre had enough sense to have stolen a horse.

It might just help her survive until he found her.

The sun had just sent its first warming rays filtering through the tops of the trees along the riverbank when Deidre heard the baying of hounds. They were still distant, but she knew they were on her trail.

Had Gilead set dogs on her? After their incredible night of lovemaking, she hated to think that he would. She had hoped he would believe her note when she said she had coin and could arrange for passage to Armorica from Dun Laoghaire. But would he suspect that Dun Laoghaire was not the direction she was headed? She felt a bit of guilt over that deception and then pushed the thought away, holding close the memories of the many times and different ways that they had made love just hours earlier.

It was that lovemaking that had cost her time, she knew. She had planned to leave Gilead after the first time and gather her things to be gone well before midnight. But he had felt so comforting and strong, not to mention the imaginative erotic places he took her to, that she was exhausted and had finally fallen asleep in his arms. She had awakened just before dawn.

The barking was closer now. She would have to take to

water to erase her scent. She had stayed on dry ground to make quicker time, but now she stepped into the swiftly flowing current. The water oozed over her boots, soaking her feet immediately with its chill. She grimaced as she sloshed through the shallows, trying to keep her balance against the pull, and not stumble over the many small rocks in the river. She held high the small knapsack that she had packed the previous day with cheese and bread. It might be her only food for days. Her original plan to buy a horse at the nearby village was impossible with the dogs behind her. They'd catch up to her if she stopped now. Ruefully, she wished she'd taken the chance of stealing a horse, but she hadn't wanted to give Mac Erca any reason to look for her.

Deidre plodded on, forced to leave the river when it wound seaward. She chose the rockiest ground she could find, climbing boulders, rather than walking around them, to confuse the dogs. She fell twice, bruising her legs on sharp ledges.

Sometimes the baying was so faint she could hardly hear it. Once, when she tripped over a root from near exhaustion, she stopped for a minute to tear off some bread and a hunk of cheese, but she didn't dare sit down to eat. Whenever she found a stream, she waded through it, her feet nearly numb with the icy cold of the water, even though it was summer.

She had blisters on both feet by the time it turned dusk, but she hadn't heard the dogs in a long time. Either they had lost the trail or their keepers had secured them for the night. She was almost too tired to care. Sleep had been scanty last night and she must have walked at least seven—maybe even eight—leagues today. Her feet felt too heavy to lift off the ground.

Wearily, Deidre forced herself around another boulder, far too tired to try to climb it, and was delighted to see a small cave of sorts. Actually, it was just a ledge overhang, but the ground beneath it was dry and smooth and would afford enough shelter from wind or rain. She sat down and pulled off her sodden boots and wished she could build a small fire, but the smoke and the light would be a dead giveaway if someone were still trailing her, to say nothing of bandits. She ate a few bites of her small store of food and then curled up beneath the crag, asleep before she'd finished a huge yawn.

She awoke the next morning to brilliant sunshine and the smell of roasting fowl. For a moment, she was disoriented, thinking she was back at the castle. Then, slowly, she opened her eyes to find a huge bear of a man watching her.

Her note said she'd headed south toward Dun Laoghaire, but Gilead had ridden only a league or two when he began to have doubts. None of the horses in his grandfather's stable had been taken, and he'd checked with the smithy in the village as well. No one had seen her and no one had purchased a horse.

He reined in and shifted in the saddle, surveying the terrain. The land was hilly and studded with large rocks and small boulders. Hard walking unless she'd followed the road. Yet, he should have caught up with her by now, since he was mounted. Gilead hadn't even seen footprints in the soft dirt. In the distance, he heard the hounds but they were neither coming closer nor fading. If they were on a parallel course, she was somewhere between him and them.

He nudged his grandfather's palfrey forward, his eyes scanning the forest that had been cleared a safe arrow shot from the road. Deidre might very well seek the cover of trees, but he doubted she'd venture far in. It was too easy to get lost. Gilead shuddered suddenly, thinking of her moving in circles while the dogs closed in. Yet, the underbrush was too dense to take the horse through. At least here. He'd have to proceed farther south to where the trees thinned.

He stopped at the next village to inquire. "Does anyone here have a horse for sale?" he asked the smithy.

"Aye. I've a fine mare." The man ran an appreciative eye over the bay. "Would ye be looking to trade?"

Gilead patted the gelding's neck. "Nay. I just thought someone might have purchased an animal this morn."

The smithy shook his head. "A band of gypsies passed through this morn, but they only stopped because one of their horses had slipped a shoe. Seemed to be in a hurry to reach Loaghaire."

Gilead felt a glimmer of hope. Could Deidre have met up

with them and offered coin to them to take her south? "Did ye notice if there was a woman with them?"

The smithy grinned. "There's always women with them. Comely lasses, too, with their dark eyes and hair—"

"How about a woman with light hair?" Gilead clarified.

The man shrugged. "Canna say. One wagon kept its curtains pulled tight, but I heard female voices in there. One sounded angry."

Fear stabbed at Gilead. Most of the gypsy bands that roamed the countryside in Eire caused no harm, but there weren't many blond, Saxon-looking women here, either. If they thought Deidre might fetch a good price . . .

"Thanks," he said and spun his mount around, setting off at a canter that liberally spewed dust over two men stepping out of a tavern. He hardly noticed. If the gypsies were in a hurry, he had to reach the port of Dun Loaghaire before they put Deidre on a ship bound for Saracen country and the slave trade that bought young women.

Deidre stared at the huge man sitting on his haunches, calmly turning the spit. His massive hands were like bear's paws and the wild, shaggy, black hair and bushy beard only enhanced that picture in her mind.

Where had he come from? Obviously, he had been there long enough to build a small fire and roast the hare that he must have caught. How long had he been watching her? All night? She trembled at the thought. Stupid of her to fall so sound asleep.

Did he mean to rape her? Somehow, she thought not. He'd have had the opportunity if he'd wanted to. She slowly pushed herself to a sitting position.

"Are ye hungry?" the man asked, and his voice, in contrast to his fierce appearance, was pleasantly low and steady. Almost mesmerizing.

"Who . . . who are you?" Deidre stammered. His midnight eyes seemed to glow as he watched her. For a moment, she felt panic seep in. Had she wandered onto a faerie mound in her exhaustion last night? If legends were to be believed, the

Tuatha dé Danaan were said to appear to mortals now and then. Only those people usually weren't seen again.

"The name's Duncan," the man said and tore off a chunk of meat and handed it to her. "Ye'd best eat, lass."

Deidre accepted it tentatively and took a small bite. The hare was succulent and tender. Only then did she realize how ravenous she was. She devoured it nearly without chewing and the man laughed, a definitely human sound, and handed her more.

"What are you doing here?" she asked.

He lifted a thick eyebrow. "At the moment? Protecting ye. 'Tis not wise to sleep without a fire to protect ye from the wild beasts."

She considered him. Perhaps he lived nearby and would help her. "I'm trying to get to Tara," she said. "I got separated from my escort . . ." She hesitated, thinking of how true that had been when Gilead had first found her, so this was just a little lie. If she could buy a horse, she'd be fine, but could she trust this man to know she had coin?

"Why do ye want to go to Tara?"

"I . . ." How much should she tell him? "I . . . want to make a pilgrimage. To see the shrine of the Lia Fáil."

"It's gone, ye know. Some say Fergus Mor took it."

Deidre frowned. She hadn't heard that Fergus may have been the one to steal it. The Stone of Destiny was a powerful relic. If the Scotti actually had it, he would be nearly unbeatable. Was that part of the reason Gilead's father was so adamant about retaining allies?

"Still, I'd like to see the place. Could you help me get there?"

He seemed to think about it. Then he shook his head. "The Mac Erca would be put out if I did that."

"The Mac Erca?" Deidre felt a jolt that turned her stomach to lead. Had she been found out? She swallowed the lump in her throat and decided to bluff. Maybe he didn't know who she was. "Why would the high king mind if a simple woman wanted to pay tribute at the shrine?"

Duncan arched his brow again. "He wouldna mind a *simple* woman doing that. But he wants ye back. *Deidre.*"

The lead weight thudded to her feet, rooting her to the spot.

He knew! Her shoulders slumped. "How did you find me? I threw off the hounds yesterday."

The man smiled, revealing surprising canine eyeteeth, and jerked his thumb toward a spiny gorse shrub nearby.

Deidre turned her head and then gasped, scooting back under the protection of the crag in her near panic.

The wolf raised his massive head from his huge paws, his golden eyes penetrating even as his tongue lolled to the side in a cynical grin.

"He'll not hurt ye," Duncan said and whistled. The wolf slunk forward on its belly and pushed his nose under his master's hand. Duncan gave him what was left of the meat. ". . . unless I tell him to."

Deidre could believe that. Now that she saw them together, and especially after seeing those sharp teeth, the man looked more like a wolf than a bear. She shivered.

"We'd best be getting back," he said as he stood. "I think, if it's the same to ye, I'll be getting us some horses to ride back. I nigh wore my boots out, tracking ye." He gave her a grudging look of respect. "I'll say this for ye. I dinna think ye would last this far. Whatever ye are running from, it must be bad."

She looked at him dismally as they started along a deer path that would lead to the road and a village. "I'm running from my death, most likely."

Duncan frowned, but was silent as they walked on, the wolf placidly padding by his side.

By the time Gilead reached Dun Loaghaire the following day, the gelding was nearly blown. He didn't dare push his stouthearted horse any faster that a walk, yet every fiber in his being was screaming that he would be too late.

There were only two ships tied to the wharf, one a fishing vessel and the other a small sailing craft. There were no signs of gypsies anywhere. Gilead breathed a sigh of relief as he made his way to the harbor master's shanty. But the relief was short lived.

"Aye," the man said when Gilead asked if any ships had

sailed in the last day. "The *Ahman* left at dawn, loaded with cargo."

"Did she take any passengers?" Gilead asked.

The dock master rubbed the stubble on his face. "Strange thing, that. A gypsy came in and bought two tickets."

Gypsies. So they were here. Gilead hesitated and then asked, "Was there a blond woman with him?"

The man frowned. "Canna rightly say, lad. They boarded while it was still dark."

"Where were they headed?"

"Constantinople."

Gilead's heart thudded. *Right in the middle of a nest of wealthy sultans.* He pulled out some coin. "Get one of those two boats at the pier ready to sail."

Greed shown on his face, but the harbor master shook his head. "The sail's mast is cracked, if ye dinna notice. The fish-boat has been taking on water and needs the hull tarred. It'd not last in the high seas but an hour or two."

Gilead bit back a retort. It wasn't the man's fault that Deidre might be on board a vessel bound for white slavery. All he could do was ride back and take command of his father's warship and hope the galley was fast enough to catch up to the bulkier cargo vessel.

He traded the horse he'd ridden for a young, half broken stallion. The gelding had served him well, but he couldn't ask the horse to put up with the strain of a fast ride back north. The younger animal would have the stamina for it.

The horse reared when he mounted, but Gilead swung him around and dug his heels into the flanks, causing the stallion to whinny shrilly and plunge into a full gallop.

He took only brief periods to rest the horse and continued on through the night, wearily climbing the hill that led to his grandfather's castle as the sun shot its first brilliant rays of red and orange across the sky.

Even as early as it was, his grandfather and mother were both up, breaking their fast. Packed trunks stood in the entrance, waiting to be loaded.

"Ye'll be needing those to stay here a while longer, Mother,"

Gilead said when she'd jumped up to hug him, as Mac Erca glow-ered at him. "I'm taking the ship to Constantinople."

Elen's eyes widened. "Ye are so set on not marrying Dallis that ye'd run off?"

Dallis. He hadn't even thought about her or that his mar-riage was less than a week away. "Nay. Deidre has been ab-ducted, I think, and may be on a ship that sailed yesterday morning. I must intercept before she . . ." He couldn't bring himself to go on.

"Before I what?"

Gilead froze, sure that he was hearing things. Slowly, he turned to see Deidre standing in the doorway. He crossed the room in three strides and gathered her into his arms. "Ye're here! And safe!" He inhaled the light fragrant scent of her hair and clean skin and realized he probably smelled worse than his horse. But for just a moment longer, he wanted to savor the way she clung to him, soft breasts pressed against his chest, arms clasped tightly around his neck. He knew he would still lose her, for the only place she would be really safe from Niall was at the Black Lake, but right now, this felt so good. So right.

A shadow rose from a far corner of the hall. Duncan whis-tled to his wolf and left the room, shaking his head.

"I still don't understand why ye dinna tell me," Gilead grumbled as they sat on the stern deck of the pitching ship.

Deidre grasped the edge of the bench to avoid flying off it as a rogue wave lifted the bow of the galley and sent it crash-ing deep into a trough, washing the foredeck with green water. Elen had retired below deck as soon as the ship made the turn into open water and a confused sea, but Deidre was determined to stay above deck where she could breathe fresh air and try to keep an eye on the horizon. It made her stom-ach less queasy.

"If I had told you, would you have let me go?" She had ad-mitted to Gilead earlier that something about the empty shrine at Tara had pulled her toward it.

"Not by yerself."

Deidre raised an eyebrow. "You would have come with me? Your grandfather would have been furious."

He shrugged. "Mayhap. But it would have been too late for him to do anything about it."

"And what excuse would you have given when we returned? You've vowed to keep my search for the Stone a secret."

Gilead scowled. "I'd have thought of something." He hesitated a moment. "Do ye really think yer Stone is there?"

"I don't know," she said honestly. "When your mother spoke of the Lia Fáil, I felt dizzy, just like I did the afternoon you'd had the talk with Mac Erca. There's *something* that pulls me. Yet, the closer I got to Tara . . . I felt nothing."

The ship heeled over sharply to starboard as a strong gust caught the square sail fully. Deidre slid along the seat, stopped only by Gilead's hard thigh. He wrapped an arm around her waist, his other leg braced on the deck, holding them in place. He felt so warm and solid in the damp chill of the sea. She snuggled against his chest and felt him take a sharp breath.

"Once I have ye safely off to Armorica, I'll come back and see if I can find anything at Tara," he murmured into her hair.

Deidre looked up at him, warmth spreading through her as gratitude flooded her. Gilead believed in her cause—that the Stone belonged with the Goddess—and was willing to help, even if she couldn't be here. And she trusted him. If he found the Stone, he'd make sure she received it. Maybe he'd even bring it himself to Brocéliande.

"Thank-you," she said and sat up reluctantly as the captain walked by and gave them both a knowing grin. Gilead had bribed the captain to keep the sailors on board, without liberty, until he could make sure another boat was available to take her south to Kernow. If there wasn't one, his father's galley would turn at once and set back out to sea. Gilead had refused to tell her the story he'd given the captain, but by the man's lecherous smiling, she could only imagine that he thought Gilead was hying a leman away to a remote spot for personal sport before he got married. It galled her to think she could not set the man straight, but in truth, she almost wished that it were true. She longed to have Gilead make love to her once more before . . . Resolutely, she pushed from her head the image of the beautiful Dallis enjoying Gilead's embrace and kisses. She'd go mad if she thought about Gilead doing to Dallis what he'd done with her.

"Tell me how I'll find your grandmother."

He smiled. "Doona fash. She will find ye. She'll know ye're coming."

Deidre stared at him. "How? Does she have the Sight?"

"Some say that. Others . . ." His voice trailed off.

"What?" Deidre persisted. "What do others say?"

"The water faeries I told ye about. Some folks feel they still watch for ships from their homeland to bring their people safely ashore." He shrugged. "'Tis probably some nonsense my grandmother started herself."

His grandmother was sounding more intriguing with each thing that Gilead had told her. That her home was really a large cave—well furnished he had assured her—hidden behind a waterfall. Once, long ago, a person wandered far enough into the forest to the Lake—and returned—to tell the story of a young woman who disappeared into the water and presumably drowned. Yet, when someone else made the journey, albeit it on a dare, the maiden had been there again. That girl had been his grandmother.

Gilead also told her other stories of how mischievous his grandmother had been when she was younger, appearing with a white brachet to startle hunters and then fading into the growth of the forest with no trail to follow. As a child, Gilead told Deidre, his grandmother had found a series of hollows throughout the forest that led to hidden burrows, deserted, at least temporarily, by whatever animal inhabited them. She enjoyed hiding in them and popping out unexpectedly. When Deidre had asked him if she wasn't scared that the animal might return, he'd grown more serious. She had a way with the forest creatures, he'd said, and Deidre should be prepared to see tame wolves and bears resting alongside hart and hind.

Deidre broke out of her reverie. "So she'll be waiting for me when I disembark?"

Gilead shook his head. "Nay. She'll not venture as far as the dock. She dislikes the noise and bustle."

"Then how will she find me?"

"Hire a cart man to take ye to the forest. To the edge of it anyway, for few will go farther than that. Doona be afraid. Walk in about ten paces and stand still and listen. Once the birds begin to chirp again, ye'll hear one that sounds different from the rest. Follow that sound. Doona be surprised if my grandmother seems to appear from nowhere. She's done it oft to me when I was a bairn."

Deidre smiled. "If your grandmother has such a sense of humor, why is your father so stern and intimidating?"

Gilead thought a moment before he answered her. "Da told me once that when he was learning to fight, the other boys would gang up on him and call him a water boy since he lived by the lake. He had to prove he was stronger than all of them."

"His father didn't live with him?" Deidre asked in surprise.

"Nay. He had a castle to run in Eire and warriors to keep trained. Twice a year my grandfather would visit my grandmother: in the spring when he'd come for my father and take him back to Eire, and in the fall, before the winter turned, to bring him back. The only way my grandmother would agree to that relationship was if she didn't have to give up her home."

"She sounds like a unique woman," Deidre said quietly. "I'm looking forward to meeting her."

"Aye. She'll like ye, too," Gilead said. "Ye remind me of her sometimes. Ye're willing to dream of what no one else will."

The captain returned and almost succeeded in wiping the smile off his face. "Sorry to interrupt, but the boatswain has spotted a ship to port. Another galley."

"Pirates?" Gilead asked as he got up.

"Too far off to tell," the man said, "but I've altered course and let out more sail. Ye'd best come forward."

"Wait!" Deidre called after them as they started off. Gilead turned around.

"So I'll know . . . what's your grandmother's name?"

"Vivian. I've got to go." With a wave of his hand, he followed the captain.

It couldn't be. Deidre's skin tingled like a thousand needles had pricked her skin. The old magician's book had mentioned Vivian. But so much of what had been written in The Book didn't exist. There was no Camelot or King Arthur. The dreams of knights in shining armor rescuing damsels in distress were a far cry from anything she'd experienced, much as she wanted to believe in that perfect world. But the name of Vivian . . . it couldn't be true. Was Gilead's grandmother really the Lady of the Lake?

The seas had calmed considerably by the time they spotted the shores of Dumbarton early the next morning. The captain had kept them close-hauled all night, hoping to outrun the other ship, and his ruse worked, for there was naught but a line of blue upon deeper blue on the horizon. Whatever the ship had been, it was gone now.

Deidre had no chance to ask Gilead further questions about his grandmother, for he stayed with the captain throughout the night. Elen had seemed distraught when Deidre asked her, so she'd dropped the subject.

Deidre had trouble hiding her excitement, though, as the sailors started to lower the sail and the rowers took their places to bring the ship alongside the pier. Not only was she going to escape Niall, once and for all, but she might just be venturing into the real truth from The Book. She began to feel light-headed, a sure sign that something was lurking at the edge of her consciousness.

Gilead joined her by the rail. "I think ye're in luck," he said. "Two ships in dock and they both look like they're preparing to sail. Ye just wait here until I make arrangements and I'll come back for ye."

The ship thumped against the pilings and threw Deidre into Gilead's arms. She felt his arms tighten around her momentarily and his lips brushed her forehead lightly. "I love ye, Deidre. Ye know that."

She wanted to cling to him and never let go. What a bittersweet moment. To be safe, she had to part from him. "I love you, too, Gilead."

Elen joined them, a worried look on her face as the gangplank was lowered. "I doona think yer plan will work, Gilead."

"Mother, we've talked this through. What's important is Deidre will be safe. I'll face Da's wrath."

"It's not yer father that is the problem," she answered and pointed. "Look."

Deidre turned her head and her blood turned to ice, freezing her to the spot. Standing on the dock, looking up at them with an evil, twisted grin, stood Niall.

"Welcome back," he said.

"Mmmm," Formorian murmured as her last bit of clothing fell to the floor in her chamber and Angus dipped his dark head to lap at a nipple. She arched into him and threw her head back, exposing her throat.

He nibbled his way up her neck, his hard phallus pressed firmly into the soft roundness of her belly as he sidled toward her bed. "I like these midday delights."

Formorian rubbed her breasts against his bare chest and sucked his lower lip into her mouth. He caught her upper lip with his and for a moment she challenged him before he claimed her, their tongues frantically entwined. Angus's large hands caressed the silkiness of her skin, kneading her buttocks and drawing her closer. With a contented sigh, she ran her fingers over the smooth, hard muscles of his shoulders and then laced her fingers through his hair, pressing the kiss deeper.

The sound of horses' hooves approaching the gate interrupted them. Angus lifted his head to listen. "That must be the escort Niall took to bring Deidre home."

"And Elen." Formorian leaned back from him, but kept her arms linked around his neck. "Shall we get dressed?"

"Nay. She'll think me working somewhere and go straight upstairs to rest. Sailing tires her." He turned his attention back to Formorian and nudged the juncture of her thighs with his cock. "Unless ye doona want this."

Formorian purred deep in her throat and lifted a thigh to wrap around him. Angus caught it and gently pushed it down, causing a look of surprise to flit across her face.

"Not that way today," he said as he encircled her waist with his hands and turned her around. "Bend over for me and hold unto that bedpost."

Formorian chuckled and bent low, thrusting her rump up, but

Angus merely leaned over her and cupped the fullness of her hanging breasts, squeezing them gently and rolling the nipples between forefingers and thumbs. She closed her hands over his and pressed. "Harder."

Angus placed her hands back on the bedpost. "Doona let go of that again or I'll stop what I'm doing."

She groaned. "Ye ken I can't bear to be still."

"I ken it well," he whispered in her ear and resumed his slow torture of her engorged, needy breasts. "'Tis why I ask it."

Formorian gasped as his warm, velvet tongue licked broad strokes down her spine, one hand now sliding down her ribs and across her belly while the other still teased her breast.

"Spread yer legs for me, Mori. Wider."

She began to pant when a probing finger dipped into the hot, wet well of her womanhood and then spread that juice between her folds and began to circle her nub. His fingers flicked expertly over its tautness, then massaged the nether lips in flat strokes, returning to inflict more pleasure at her throbbing center. She bucked wildly against his hand, mewling softly as she felt the tip of his shaft at her entrance.

Angus quickened his finger movements, not sparing the wildly pulsating nib a second of respite. With his other hand, he pulled on her nipple the way she liked and was rewarded to feel her trembling as her body began the rippling shudder that culminated in a giant contraction as she screamed out.

He drove himself into her, then, taking her hard and deep with strong thrusts. Formorian gasped again and held to the post while her hips undulated against his thighs, matching his fierce plundering of her body with an intensity of her own. Her body convulsed again in a series of spasms as he ground into her with a feral growl and released his seed.

Totally sated, Angus leaned over her again, his head resting on her back, hands cupping her breasts softly. Formorian clung to the post, her head down between her arms, wet hair hanging loose, while she took in great gulps of air. Neither of them heard the door open.

"Mayhap I should come back," Turius said.

Chapter Twenty-one

DOOM

Deidre clutched the rail and stared down at the wharf where Niall stood. "Dear God, what am I going to do?" She gave Gilead a wild-eyed look. "Can we turn the ship around? The men are still aboard . . ."

But it was too late. Even as the last lines were cleated, the heavy gangplank was lowered and Niall sprang onto it, coming aboard.

"This is the last time ye'll be going anywhere without me." He grabbed her arm and glowered at Gilead. "Ye'll be leaving my wife alone."

"She's not yer wife yet," Gilead answered with a steady look. "And she doesna look too happy to be a bride, either."

Deidre jerked her arm away from Niall. "Why are you here?"

He smiled sardonically. "I wanted to be sure my . . . property . . . arrived at its proper destination. I dinna want anything happening to ye."

She glared at him. "Gilead has enough men to protect his mother and me."

He gave her a cold-eyed stare. "I dinna want ye getting . . . lost, if ye ken my meaning. I canna marry ye if ye were not to make it home."

Merde. How had he known? Or was it just a lucky guess? Deidre lifted her head and walked past him, down the gangplank and over to where Winger waited patiently. Angry as she was, Deidre softened a little as the gelding nickered a welcome. She stroked the satiny coat. "It's good to see you too, boy."

"Ye'll ride beside me," Niall said as he approached her and offered a leg up.

Deidre ignored him, thankful that Winger wasn't as huge a horse as Malcolm. Once mounted, they set off at a brisk pace, leaving the lumbering wagons behind with some of Gilead's men.

Deidre stole a furtive glance back over her shoulder at Gilead. He was looking almost as miserable as she felt. Their plans were foiled—there would be no possible way of getting back to Dumbarton to catch a ship—and all because of this lecherous oaf who rode beside her.

"Ye might be looking a bit more cheerful," the oaf said. "Ye'll be my bride in three days."

She looked at him sullenly. "I don't want to marry you."

He shrugged, seemingly unfazed, but she noticed that his fist tightened on his reins. Deidre knew that it wasn't wise to make him angry, but at the moment she didn't care. She had only seventy-two hours to escape. Somehow.

Elen had said she'd talk to Angus one more time and Deidre had felt a ray of hope from the determination in her voice. Clearly, being at her father's had given Elen a renewed strength of will, but as they drew nearer the castle, Deidre could see Elen retreating back into her timid self. Damn the laird. Why could he not be brought down a peg or two and realize what he was doing to others around him?

Gilead nudged his horse forward, abreast of hers. "Looks like Turius has returned," he said as they rode through the gates.

Deidre hardly noticed the extra twenty or so horses that were being unsaddled. Then she frowned. "I thought he was going to the south of Britain to meet his son."

"Nay. Turius summoned Maximilian to come to Luguvalium. I wonder how it went . . ." He broke off as a grim-looking Turius came out of the Great Hall and headed for the stables in long, hard strides. "Apparently, not well. He doona look happy."

They dismounted and handed their horses over to the waiting stable boys. Elen was climbing the steps to the Hall when the door burst open and Angus rushed through, nearly toppling her. Gilead caught her and glared at his father. "Have a care!"

Angus hardly glanced at any of them as he hurried toward the barn. Deidre opened her mouth to comment and then closed it again at an almost imperceptible shake of Gilead's head. Niall was staring after Angus with open curiosity on his face. Gilead was right to stay silent. Whatever was wrong, it wasn't any of Niall's business.

"I'll take you up to your rooms," Deidre said to Elen.

Deidre wondered where Formorian was as they went through the entrance and into the back hall that led to the guest rooms and the stairs. It was unusually quiet, except for the distant sound of pots and pans banging in the kitchen. If Meara was in one of her rages, no wonder no servants were about.

Deidre got Elen settled and was about to brave the downstairs in search of Una and a hot bath for Elen when the castellan burst through the doors.

"Aye and it's glad I am to see ye home, Lady Elen," she said as she swooped like a great grey hawk and gathered the fragile woman in her large arms. "Things will be just fine now. They will."

Deidre knitted her brows. "Has something happened?"

Una glared at her. "Nothing that's any of yer business. 'Tis a family matter. There, there," she said to Elen as she started to speak. "Doona fash yerself. I'll fetch ye a hot bath and then ye should rest from yer long trip."

As she left, she muttered to Deidre. "The lady is not to leave this room. Ye stay with her until ye're summoned. Do ye hear me?"

Deidre nodded, puzzled. If Elen needed protecting, she would do it. From what, she didn't know, but she was more than happy to stay hidden away from Niall. She picked up the fragile, hand-bound Bible that Elen kept beside her bed.

"Shall I read to you?"

Elen sank down in the great chair by the window and nodded, her face pale.

Deidre sat down across from her and carefully opened the

book. "The Gospel of John, Chapter Eight. 'He that is without sin among you, let him first cast a stone . . .' Does this sound good to you?"

Elen closed her eyes. "I fear it may be appropriate."

Gilead finished fastening the brooch to his sash as he slipped into the chair beside his mother. His father hated for anyone to be late for the evening meal. Gilead squared his shoulders to take the verbal rebuke, but Angus just looked at him mildly and cut some slices of capon for his mother.

He was grateful that his father was paying attention to her, for he needed to think. His wedding—and Deidre's to Niall—were in three days. Comgall and Dallis would be arriving on the morrow. He knew he didn't love Dallis, although, docile as she was, life would be tolerable. Boring, more like. She had none of the fire and spirit that Deidre had. Deidre . . . he had failed miserably in his plan to help her escape. There must still be something he could do. *Had* to do, to keep Niall from hurting her.

He let his gaze wander to one of the lower tables where Deidre sat with Niall. She was hunched over her trencher, arms close to her sides, as though she was trying to curl herself into a ball well away from Niall. Gilead watched in disgust as Niall took a long draw on his tankard and then slammed it down on the wooden table, bellowing for more. He lurched toward Deidre, hand reaching to turn her face to him, but she shrugged him off and pushed his hand back with her shoulder. He fisted a hand and Gilead saw the look of anger flash in his not-quite-drunken face, but he must have remembered where he was because he slithered a look at the high table. Gilead stared him down and he sat back, muttering.

Gilead lost his appetite. If he were a free man and not betrothed, he could call Niall out. Challenge him for Deidre's hand. But there was Dallis. To call off the wedding when some of her clansmen had already arrived and were camped outside the walls would tarnish her honor. Comgall would have every right to go to war with Cenel Oengus. Just then he noticed Niall's hand lecherously reaching for Deidre's thigh and saw her shift her weight away. By the Dagda! He must halt this. Gilead took a deep breath. War or not, he would speak to Dallis and her father on their arrival. And then he would prepare to face his father's fury.

He glanced at his father. Angus was being unusually attentive to Elen. Had he actually missed her? Looking at his mother, he noticed that she was paler than usual and seemed about ready to burst into tears. Why? Formorian, for once, wasn't vying for Angus's attention. His mother should be happy.

His gaze slipped to Formorian. She was uncommonly subdued this evening and Turius had not lost the grim look from earlier in the day. Even her attempts at drawing her husband into a conversation were met with silence. Gilead saw a small look of annoyance flit across her perfect face and wondered what had happened that both men would ignore her.

Then, suddenly his blood chilled and he knew. What he had feared and what he had tried to prevent for the last several years had happened. Angus and Formorian had been caught. In the act, judging from Turius's demeanor.

Gilead's bubble of hope for calling off his nuptials burst like a tied wineskin speared with a knife. Turius would leave in the morning—his men had made preparations all afternoon, much to Gilead's puzzlement—but Gilead had no doubt he would return in force once he'd rallied his northern troops. Damn his father's indiscretions. Angus would need Comgall allied with him if it came to war. There wasn't any way Gilead could risk a breach right now. Unless . . .

Unless he could get the men to sit down and treaty before Turius left. Gilead held title to land in Lothian, bequeathed to him at birth by King Loth as a gesture of permanent alliance with Cenel Oengus. He would offer that. And it might cost his father some pride to part with part of their prized stock, but Turius had a weak spot for good horses.

The meal seemed to extend into infinity. Finally, as the servants gathered the remnants of the meal, Gilead leaned across the table. "Might I have a word with ye, King Turius? In the family room." He looked at his father. "I'd like ye to be there, too."

Both men looked uneasy, but Formorian gave Gilead a steady look. "I'd like to attend also."

Gilead hesitated. It would be easier to get the men to agree if neither of them had to salvage their pride in front of Formorian. But how could he stop her? She always attended council meetings. Reluctantly, he nodded.

"Then I'm coming as well." Elen pushed back her chair and stood. "Deidre! I need ye to come with me."

Gilead groaned. He didn't need a full audience for what he was trying to do, but Deidre nearly overturned her chair in her eagerness to get away from Niall. He turned to his mother. "This is men's business. Have Deidre take ye to yer room."

Elen looked as though she might faint, but her voice was surprisingly strong. "What concerns my husband, concerns me. I will go."

With a small sigh, Gilead waited for Deidre and then led the party down the back hallway to the end room that was used for private company.

He poured wine for all of them, which everyone accepted rather stiffly, but no one drank. When they were seated, he looked around the room. "Something has transpired while we were gone. I doona need to know what it is." He made the briefest of gestures toward his mother while he glared at his father. "But the tension is so palpable, I could slice the air with my dirk and eat it." He set his goblet down and looked at Turius. "I would that ye not be angry when ye leave. How can we make amends?"

He saw Turius clench his jaw and then glance at Elen and force a smile before he looked back at Gilead. "You are mistaken. I am troubled that Maximilian refused to meet with me and that he continues to aid the Saxons. I only came to fetch the rest of my troops so we can march south and meet *him*. I won't have my . . . son . . . defy me."

"Thank ye, Turius, for being so kind." Elen smiled at him, but the smile left her face when she turned to Angus. "Is there something ye wish to tell me?"

For a long moment Angus was silent and Gilead thought he saw pain pass fleetingly in his father's eyes. At an almost imperceptible nod from Formorian, he took a deep breath.

"Turius found us in a . . . rather compromising situation."

Elen's face paled, but her eyes remained steadily trained on Angus. "Go on."

He stared at her. "I would spare ye the details."

Turius reached over and took her hand in both of his. "I agree. Let me say that Formorian is leaving with me tomorrow and when I return from the South, I will see that she's admitted to a convent for the rest of her days."

Formorian slammed her goblet down, sloshing the contents onto the table. "I have no intention of entering a convent."

"You have no choice," Turius replied calmly as he sat back. "I have been cuckolded far too long as it is."

Formorian laughed. "Ye are a fine one to talk. Maximilian isn't *my* son. I am well aware of yer trips to the Holy Isle to see yer priestess, still."

"I am your king."

"In name only," she retorted. "We were both aware that the marriage was to bind our lands. Ye promised me, if I crossed the Wall with ye, ye'd never deny me the woman's right of thigh freedom. Have ye forgotten?"

Elen gasped and Turius stood up, his anger barely veiled. "Enough! We are finished here." Turning to Elen, he said, "I am sorry you had to be brought into this. You deserve better." He gave Formorian a slight shove toward the door, Deidre and Gilead falling in behind them.

Gilead hoped his mother would finally give his father the tongue-lashing he deserved, but what he heard as he closed the door softly behind them, shocked him.

"I never meant to hurt ye, Elen. Please believe that."

"Aye. I knew ye had taken the Oath with her." His mother started weeping. "I have gotten exactly what I deserve."

Something was going on. Niall didn't like it. All afternoon, Turius's troops had been making preparations to leave. Marching south to subdue Maximilian, they said.

If Niall's plan to have Turius get rid of Angus for him was to work, something would have to be done tonight before Turius left. Niall just wished he could have arranged for Angus to have been caught with Formorian. Then Turius would have had to call the Scotti out. Either trial-by-combat, one-on-one, or full-scale war that would be distracting enough that Niall could convince Fergus Mor to swoop down from the north and take advantage of the turmoil.

He would have to move on to his other plan. He shook his head to clear it, wishing he hadn't had so much to drink at dinner. But Deidre vexed him. She made him drink too much. And she would atone for all those times he'd gone to bed with no female relief. He grinned, thinking of the ways he would make her pay and then forced himself back to the present. Turius was leaving half a century of his men behind. No doubt Formorian would stay as well while he was engaged in the south. By law, the queen would be in charge of his troops. That suited Niall's plans perfectly.

If Elen were found dead before Turius left, that would leave Angus dangerously single. Formorian had always considered herself Gaelic and not Briton; she would draw to Angus like a finely notched arrow to a bowstring. Turius would realize the risks of losing his wife, especially if Niall could add a little fuel to the particular fire-thought. He certainly would not put up with being openly cuckolded. With luck, Turius might even call Angus out before he left; certainly when he returned and found out the queen was an adulterer, he'd take action. Niall would need documentation, though. One way or another, Turius needed to be persuaded to destroy Angus.

Elen would have to die tonight.

Whistling off tune, Niall went to find his coconspirator. This time, he would make sure she succeeded. The devil help them both.

"How did Mother sleep last night?" Gilead asked Deidre the next morning as they stood on the steps outside the Great Hall, waiting for Turius's troops to leave.

"Brena fixed her a potion," Deidre answered and looked up at the charcoal-colored clouds scudding low. "It's such a dreary morn, I thought I'd let her sleep a while longer."

"Aye. 'Tis better she not have to see Formorian again," Gilead agreed. "I'll make her excuses."

"There's no need for that," Formorian replied as she stepped through the door, pulling on her riding gloves and apparently unfazed by last night's conversation. "I think yer mother and I understand each other much better than ye think."

"Where's Turius?" Gilead asked to change the subject.

Formorian shrugged. "With yer father, I imagine. There are details to be worked out about the soldiers Turius is leaving behind."

Deidre studied her. How could the woman be so calm after what transpired? Like Helen of Troy, she could very well be launching a war, even if the men were trying to pretend that nothing really happened. How long would that last?

"I am so sorry that we won't be at yer weddings," Formorian said brightly, "but Turius is still a bit upset and I do need to appease him before he leaves for battle. I wouldn't want him making a strategic mistake because he's not thinking straight."

"Ye aren't going with him to the south?" Gilead asked coldly.

"I never have anything to do with his son," Formorian answered and tilted her head to one side, looking at Gilead. "Regardless of what ye may think, I do respect my husband's military prowess. I'll not be the one who brings him down."

Niall stumbled out to join them on the steps. He looked at Formorian blearily. "Are ye waiting to see yer husband off?"

"I'm riding with him," she replied.

He looked startled. "Ye can't!"

Formorian arched an eyebrow. "I can't?"

Niall began to sputter. "I mean . . . well, ye should be here . . . uh, for the wedding."

She sounded amused. "I doubt that Gilead will miss me."

"But yer . . . presence is needed for Deidre and me. Isna that right?" He tried to put an arm around Deidre, but she drew away from him and Gilead stepped between them. Niall cursed and then looked around belatedly. "Where's your mother?"

"Sleeping," Gilead answered. "Why?"

A sly look crept over his face. "Yer mother is not a rude lady; she always sees her guests off. Mayhap ye should check on her."

"She's fine," Deidre snapped. "She needs her rest. Comgall will be riding in later. She'll have to see to those arrangements."

Niall leered at her. "And Dallis. Don't forget our fine Gilead's bride. Just two more days, eh, lad? Then ye'll be able to bed that beauty and I'll be making Deidre my very own."

Deidre tried to suppress a shudder and Gilead clenched his jaw, but Niall went on. "I'm sure yer mother wouldna want to insult the king of Britain, would she?"

He might have a point, Deidre thought. After the confrontation last night, the last thing anyone here needed was to have Turius feel slighted in any way. "I'll go see if she's awake," she said to Gilead and then was interrupted as Angus and Turius came out the door.

Judging by their conduct, last night might never have happened. Deidre knew that Angus had determination as hard as steel, but beneath it she could feel tension seething from him as he approached Formorian. Turius, on the other hand, appeared calm and serene. Maybe it was that cool composure that made him such a great leader.

Turius's foot soldiers had fallen into rank outside the walls and his cavalry filled the bailey, filing into formation for the journey to Luguvalium.

Niall appeared edgy. "If ye'll wait, my lord, Deidre was just going to fetch Lady Elen. I'm sure she'll be disappointed if ye leave without her farewell."

"I believe the lady said her good-byes last night," Turius said quietly.

"But . . . ye know how she feels about good manners . . ." Niall protested.

Angus raised an eyebrow. "Aye. Yet she tolerates ye at the table. If Elen wishes to rest this morn, she will. She has a full day ahead."

Niall fell back, grumbling to himself as he walked into the house. "I wonder why he's so concerned about manners all of a sudden," Gilead said.

Deidre shrugged. "He probably thinks it will impress me. Which it won't . . . and *never* will," she added as she glared at Angus.

He ignored her and held the mare's head for Formorian to mount. Then he bowed formally to both her and Turius. "May yer dispute with Max be settled quickly."

Turius nodded and the procession began its slow march from the fort. As Deidre watched Turius and Formorian's horses round the bend and disappear from view, the first large, cold splats of rain began to fall from the darkened sky.

Una detained Deidre as she walked back into the Hall and put her to work with a grumbling Janet and sulky Sheila, making up Formorian's former room for Dallis.

"I doona ken why *we* have to do chambermaid's work," Janet muttered as she stripped the bed of used linen. "We attend Lady Elen."

"Aye," Sheila answered and slid a glance toward Deidre. "But Lady Dallis will also need a maid once she's the laird's son's wife, wilna she?"

Deidre swallowed hard. Having to serve Gilead's new wife would be almost as bad as marrying Niall, but not quite. She had less than forty-eight hours left in which to make an escape. But she had no plans to wait that long. She would be gone today. With all the furor of Dallis's arrival, no one would notice if she slipped to the stables. She'd leave some of her coin to pay for Winger. She was just sorry that she had failed in her mission to find the Stone because the feeling had returned—strongly—that the Stone was *here*.

"The maid won't be me," she said.

Janet gave her a sour look. "Aye. Ye'll be a grand lady, too, wilna ye? Servants of yer own and all."

"If she can stand the pain," Sheila snickered. "Remember what the servant that came with Niall's wife once said about how he takes his pleasure in bed?"

Janet's face lightened, but Deidre was spared a reply by the sound of horses and wagons approaching. She ran to the window and looked out.

"By the saints! It's Comgall already! And Lady Elen isn't even up!" She threw the towels she had gathered in a heap on the floor. "I told her I'd wake her in plenty of time! Will one of you send Una with hot water?" She didn't give them time to answer as she bolted for the door.

And nearly ran into Meara in the back hall. The cook's face

was a livid red and she had a kitchen maid by the arm and a scullery lad by the ear. The tirade was enough to make Deidre want to cover her own ears.

"It's a fine morn for ye to be havin' yer sport with her, laddie! The laird and Lady Dallis are here, and we've nothing prepared to break their fast. If I dinna need the use of yer hands this day, I'd thrash yer skin bare. And ye . . ." She turned to the frightened girl and gave her a shake. "I'll not be havin' ye making bairns instead of bread in my kitchen! Are ye going to keep yer skirts down or do I send ye on the road?"

Deidre flattened herself against the wall as the trio swept past her, Meara still in a fine fit of rage. Perhaps this was not the best time to try to get food for Elen.

She bounded up the back stairs and paused to catch her breath and smooth her hair before she knocked on the door. Elen liked for her to look at least somewhat tidy.

No one answered. Deidre turned the knob gently and the door swung open squeaking a hinged protest. She'd have to get one of the servants to oil it.

Elen was still asleep, curled on her side, back to the door. Deidre approached the bed and laid her hand softly on Elen's shoulder.

"It's time to rise, lady. The company's come early."

There was no response. Deidre shook Elen's arm. "Please, lady." She brushed back the blond curls that covered part of Elen's face. Her skin felt so cold. Deidre took her shoulder to turn her over and then stepped back, mouth open in a silent scream.

Elen stared blankly up at her, eyes unseeing.

She was dead. Deidre grasped the bedpost and gasped for air, fighting the wave of dizziness and nausea that swept over her. Somehow, though she wouldn't remember it, she found her vocal cords and split the air with a piercing, keening wail.

Chapter Twenty-two

LAST CHANCE

Gilead's head snapped up as the hair-raising shrieking from his mother's room rent the air in the bailey. He had just helped Dallis down from her carriage, but now he quickly handed her over to Drustan, who nearly dropped his harp in his hurry to offer her his arm.

"Take care of her," Gilead said and raced toward the entrance. He pounded up the stairs two at a time, slid around the corner to his mother's room and then stopped abruptly, his mind not willing to absorb what his eyes saw.

Deidre sat crumpled on the floor beside his mother's bed, tears streaming down her face. His mother's glazed eyes looked into emptiness, her face twisted in an expression of pain. Her hands, curled like a bird's, clawed at the sheet.

"My God," he said softly as he stumbled toward the bed and leaned over, gently closing his mother's vacant eyes. He reached down and lifted Deidre into his arms where she clung to him frantically.

"What's happened?" Angus burst into the room and then froze at the sight of Elen lying on the bed. "What . . . who . . . ?"

Behind him, others were clambering up the steps. Janet and Sheila began wailing when they discovered Elen dead and a grim-faced Una shouldered her way through the throng that gathered in the hall. She crossed herself and then lifted the sheet in a precursory exam.

"There are no marks," she said to Angus. "No wounds. Nothing."

Her voice had the effect of unfreezing him. "Find me the guard from last night," he thundered. "I want an accounting of everyone who entered and left this room."

The guard arrived, sleepy and tucking his shirt into his trews as servants were removing Elen's body. His eyes widened and he snapped to attention. "What happened, my lord?"

Angus's eyes darkened. "That's what I want to know. Were ye at yer post the entire time?"

The soldier flinched a little, but returned the look. "Aye, sir."

"And ye were awake? Ye dinna take a wee nap?"

The intimidating sarcasm would have squelched most men, but the guard squared his shoulders. "Nay, sir."

"Then tell me who came in."

The man frowned slightly. "The lady's maid," he said and pointed to Deidre. "Brena, with the lady's usual potion. You, sir. And Queen Formorian—"

"Formorian?" Deidre and Gilead asked together.

"Aye. She said she wouldna stay long and she dinna."

Gilead gave his father a level look. "Any idea why she might invade Mother's privacy?"

"Aye." Angus turned to the guard. "Find Brena for me. If ye remember anyone else, come and find me." He waited until the man's footsteps sounded in the hall and then turned back to Gilead.

"It's not what ye're thinking. Mori wanted to apologize."

"Why? She's never been sorry for her dalliance before."

Angus's eyes smoldered, but he held his temper. "She dinna mean to hurt yer mother. It was never our intent. Ye doona know how it is—"

"I know ye took the Oath," Gilead interrupted, "but I would think Formorian would have the decency not to rub my mother's face in yer foul mess."

Angus reached Gilead in two strides, his fists clenched. "That's *why* she wanted to apologize. I told her to leave be."

"But would she poison your wife?" Deidre asked.

Both men turned to her, their anger momentarily harnessed. "What?"

"It had to have been poison," Deidre said, "just like the other times. There were no bruises, no marks, just a look of pain and, from the way her hands clenched the sheet, she might have been clutching her stomach."

Deidre walked over to the dresser where stood a wine cup, along with a basin and ewer of water. A drop of residue remained in the cup. She lifted the goblet and sniffed. A slightly piney odor wafted past her nostrils. She began to dip a finger, but Angus snatched the cup away.

"Are ye daft?"

Deidre lifted her head, refusing to be intimidated. "Are you afraid I'll suddenly fall ill if I taste what's in that cup?"

Angus narrowed his eyes at the implication. "I'd not kill my own wife. But ye . . . ye are a stranger here. Gilead says ye are no spy, but I havena been so sure. Ida found ye quickly enough. Was it information he was wanting?"

"Da! She was kept a prisoner," Gilead interjected.

"Or mayhap that's what they wanted us to think," Angus answered, not taking his eyes off Deidre's face. "It seems to me that ye have been present every time something has happened . . . the first time Elen fell ill and ye claimed poison . . . it would be very clever of ye to bring that up and cover yer own trail."

"I didn't—"

"And ye were right behind Elen on the stair," Angus continued. "Did ye push her? Or did ye just loose the rug when ye looked for the jewel from her brooch?"

"Da! Deidre could never hurt my mother!"

"No?" Angus looked at Gilead. "Wasna it Deidre who discovered Elen with the bruises around her neck? No one else was seen." He turned back to Deidre. "If ye are going to be accusing me, or Mori, ye might do best to look into the tin and see yer own face."

Deidre began to tremble, in spite of her bravado. "I swear I did not—"

The door flew open and the disheveled guard appeared.

"What is it?" Angus asked in agitation.

"It's Brena, sir. We canna find her anywhere."

Angus swore. "Have Una go through her room. See what's missing." As the guard left, he turned back to Gilead. "If ye are as sure of Deidre's innocence as I am of Mori's, that leaves only Brena."

"I am sure of Deidre, Da. But . . ." He hesitated and then said reluctantly, "Remember that Brena was Formorian's healer when she came here. And that she offered to stay after our own physician suddenly died."

Angus looked at him thoughtfully. "Go on."

"Well, if Mother were poisoned, then mayhap our medic was, too, so Brena could volunteer to stay . . . and . . ."

Angus's eyes darkened. "Say what ye mean."

Gilead glanced at Deidre and then back to his father. "Mayhap, she wasna working alone. Mayhap someone else—"

"Like Mori?" Angus's voice was deadly calm, a sure sign of his anger.

Gilead recognized it and took a deep breath. "Who else would want Mother—"

"Ye listen to me," Angus said as he advanced and stood almost nose-to-nose with his son. "It be true that Mori and I have always loved each other and intended to marry. But Fate was not kind. Mori accepted that. And I didna have to marry yer mother. I could have let her honor be tarnished for the trickery she used. I dinna. But this is what's important and I'll only say it once. When Mori and I took the Oath, we also made a pact. That if the gods were kind and let us be together, neither of us would seek to destroy the other's marriage. And we've both honored that."

"Might I make a suggestion?" Deidre asked.

Angus stopped glaring at his son and looked at her. "What?"

"While Una is checking Brena's room, could we have a look at the herb closet? Maybe we can find the poison."

Without bothering to answer, Angus spun on his heel and walked out, Deidre and Gilead at his heels. The closet was locked when they got there. Angus didn't bother sending for Una and a second key. He stepped back and then rammed his shoulder forcefully against the door, splintering the frame.

Pungent aromas assaulted their nostrils: the mustiness of

herbs hanging upside down from the ceiling for drying, the sharp smell of eucalyptus from a corner of the tiny room, the muskier scent of sandalwood on a countertop. Deidre rummaged through small packets of herbs, sniffing each one, identifying only common garden varieties of rosemary, basil, bay leaf, and fennel. She picked up various small jars from a shelf, undoing the stoppers. Nothing seemed to be out of the ordinary. Even the motherwort that Brena used for her sleeping potion and the snakeroot for stomach upset were neatly labeled. Deidre sighed in disappointment.

"I don't see anything that could have caused such a quick and painful reaction."

Gilead looked up at a shelf near the ceiling, wondering why a shelf had been placed that high where a woman as small as Brena would need a stool to get up there. The wood looked to be somewhat newer than the other shelves, too. He stretched his hand along the top, encountering nothing but dust until he came to the very end. He touched something smooth and cold and pulled down a small vial of liquid.

He undid the stopper and the smell of pine filled the room.

Deidre's eyes widened as she took the vial from him. "Hemlock!" She turned to Angus. "I've not had much training in herbals, which is why I didn't ever think of hemlock, but I know it can kill within the hour and death is painful. It can also," she continued, frowning as she remembered her own mother's healer speaking to the priestesses, "be administered a drop here and there to make a person weak and appear to be wasting away over time."

"Which is what happened to Mother," Gilead exclaimed. "And it started happening shortly after Brena joined us!"

Angus stared at them both for a minute and then bolted out the door, yelling for Adair and Calum as he strode into the bailey.

"Ride after Turius," he told his captain of the guard. "See if she somehow slipped out with them." He turned to Calum. "Ride to Gabran. Tell him what we suspect and that Brena may likely try to return to her own clan on his lands. Tell him to take her captive if he finds her."

When his men rushed off to do his bidding, Angus laid a

hand on Gilead's shoulder. "I swear to ye, son, I will avenge yer mother. I owe her that." He turned to Deidre. "Ye were her favorite. Would ye do her the honor of being with her while the body is prepared?"

Deidre glanced askance at Gilead and he gave her a faint nod. "Mother would like that," he said.

Somewhat numb from shock, Gilead walked slowly back into the Hall. Comgall, Dallis, and Drustan were seated at a table in the far corner and he joined them there.

Comgall clasped his shoulder. "Ye have our condolences," he said gruffly.

"I'm so sorry," Dallis said in her sweet voice and put a soft hand on his arm. "Drustan and I were trying to compose a fitting funeral dirge for Lady Elen."

"One that we could sing together," Drustan added. "Dallis has a pretty voice and 'twould be fitting for her to honor her mother-in-law thus."

Gilead nodded miserably and out of the corner of his eye, he saw Niall enter and head toward them. He turned his back hoping the lout would take the hint and go away.

"About the wedding," he began, "I doona see how I can marry now."

"Certes not," Dallis agreed almost too quickly. "Ye are upset and need time to heal. I understand."

Gilead gave her a grateful look. Ironically, he had gotten his freedom. His mother's death was an awful price to pay, but, in her passing, she had helped him avoid a war. *Mother, ever the peacemaker, even in death.*

"What's this?" Niall asked as he sat down, uninvited. "I hope ye doona expect me to postpone my wedding as well?"

Gilead clenched his fists under the table while Dallis gasped and both Comgall and Drustan frowned at Niall. The man's insensitivity knew no bounds, obviously. "There will be no marriages taking place anytime soon," Gilead said in the same flat voice that spelled danger in his father.

"I'll be in charge of when I decide to marry!" Niall said

furiously. "I can marry Deidre on my own property, ye know. Just have her be ready to leave on the morrow."

"Surely not, sir," Dallis said softly. "She'll want to attend the funeral."

"Aye," Comgall added. "And if Gilead is willing to postpone his wedding, ye should be, too." He looked at Gilead. "Lugnasad is day after today. How about Mabon, when the apples be ripe for good cider? Dallis loves the drink and 'twould give ye time to grieve." When Gilead hesitated, he narrowed his eyes. "Unless ye doona want to wed my daughter at all?"

"For certes, he does!" Angus said from behind Gilead.

Gilead nearly jumped and then swore silently. He hadn't heard his father approach, but that was one of Angus's talents when he chose. And this would have been the perfect time to tell Comgall that he wasn't ready. And yet, Niall had a gleam in his eye that told Gilead if he didn't agree to a joint postponement, Niall just might make good on his threat to take Deidre. He sighed. He'd have to bide his time and try to reason with Comgall later.

"I'll think on Mabon."

At least he'd bought Deidre some time.

Niall cursed roundly as he saddled his horse to leave Cenel Oengus later that day. Elen was supposed to have been found dead before Turius left. He had counted on Formorian staying behind, in charge of the half century of soldiers Turius was leaving behind. Something had gone wrong there. Still, if that stubborn bitch, Deidre, had obeyed him and gone to check on Elen, he might have persuaded Formorian to stay and help settle the household. That was a woman's job. He gave the cinch an extra hard pull and his horse laid its ears flat, but he ignored it. That little bitch would pay—and pay hard—once he was wedded to her.

Having to wait for that pleasure infuriated him. Another two months! But short of abducting her—damn her, she always kept herself surrounded with people—there wasn't much he could do. He pulled the stopper from the wineskin

hooked on his saddle and took a healthy swig, wiping the
back of his dripping mouth on his sleeve.

A thought niggled at him, growing in intensity as he took
another draught. Turius had taken four and a half centuries
with him, leaving Angus with only fifty Britons and his own
five hundred or so warriors. And Elen's death would be un-
settling as well, if not to Angus himself, certes to his ever-
honorable son and the people who had cared about the
woman. Even Niall couldn't find much to dislike, except that
she was weak and mealymouthed, in his opinion.

The time was right for Fergus Mor finally to make his move.
And Niall, while pretending to aid Angus, would be right behind
him.

He'd send the messenger tonight.

Gilead wasn't surprised to learn, a sennight later, when
Adair returned with the news, that Brena had indeed stowed
away in one of Turius's wagons. The bad news was that she
had left the party shortly after, heading northwest.

"She told Formorian that her mother ailed and she had to
go home," Adair said. "Doona fash. I've already dispatched
another man to Gabran. He'll be waiting for her."

Somehow, Gilead didn't think she'd be captured so easily.
She was wily. For the thousandth time since his mother's funeral, he condemned himself for not seeing through the ruse
before it was too late.

At least Comgall had returned to his lands and taken Dallis
with him. She had offered no protest when Gilead told her he
would not be good company for a long while. And indeed, he
had hardly spoken to her, trusting Drustan to escort her to the
funeral and the feast that followed it. Thank the gods for
Drus; it allowed him to wallow in his grief while appeasing
her father.

Deidre was the only one he wanted near, but Una kept her
busy all day and most evenings, too. Janet and Sheila had returned to their own clans after Elen's death, and Una had
handed their responsibilities over to Deidre with Angus's

blessing. She'd have to learn to run a household, his father had said.

So Gilead was already in a foul, black mood several days later when a rider from Comgall came flying through the gates, his horse near foundering.

The man half-jumped, half-fell off his horse before it had even stopped. "Fergus Mor," he burst out. "He's moving through the outlands of Gunpar's territory. I'm but a scarce day or two ahead of him."

Deidre watched in dismay the hustle and bustle of men preparing for war. The jingle of harnesses and the creaking of leather mingled with the clanging of metal as swords were sharpened and maces and spikes hung on to saddles. So soon after Elen's death, she didn't think Gilead was mentally prepared to fight and she feared for him. Angus, on the other hand, was driven as though possessed by demons. War seemed to give him a sense of purpose. He was everywhere, inspecting weapons, encouraging the youngest of soldiers to buck up and heartily slapping the veterans on their backs. The men roused to him, bragging on how many kills they'd make and how quickly Fergus would be subdued. How many would not be returning? She prayed Gilead would not be among the fallen.

Deidre sighed and wandered into the walled herbal garden. She and Meara had made a sort of peace, or truce, perhaps, and Deidre had taken to gathering herbs daily for the evening meal.

A shadow fell across her path as she leaned over a row of sweet basil. She looked up to see Niall standing in the small doorway, blocking the entrance. She straightened, keeping a wary eye on him. He had ridden over this morning, all assurances that his troops were ready to ride with Angus, but she had been able to ignore him successfully. Until now.

He moved forward, keeping himself between her and the door. Deidre took a step back.

"That's no way to treat yer betrothed," Niall said with a sneer. "Here I am, going off to fight and it's only a wee kiss I'm wanting."

"No. Please leave, I have things to do."

"Aye. Things to do. Like kiss me," he said and lunged toward her, grabbing both arms and drawing her against him. He rubbed his chest against her breasts and laughed. "Ye feel good. I canna wait to bed ye."

The odor of his unwashed body nearly overcame her. Deidre pushed against him. "Let me go!"

"Nay! Not until ye've kissed me. Proper, too."

"No!" Deidre raised her knee but he swerved and she only caught his hip. But his grip had loosened momentarily and she jerked her arm away, tearing the sleeve in the process.

He grabbed at her dress, catching the bodice and ripping it down the front. "Mayhap I will take more than a kiss, at that."

She struggled, turning her head away, lips firmly closed, fighting with all her might to keep him from kissing her. With all the noise in the bailey from the preparations, no one would even hear her scream, and besides, she wasn't about to open her mouth.

"Ye're taking yer sweet time out here," Meara grumbled as she entered the garden and then stopped and gaped.

Surprised, Niall whipped his head around and Deidre broke his hold, stumbling for the safety of Meara's skirts and the door.

The cook held up the slender, lethally sharp paring knife that they used to cut herbs. "Ye'd forgotten this," she said to Deidre, "but it looks like ye might need it for another purpose." She glared at Niall and he fell back. "Do ye want to take me on?"

Niall glowered at both of them and clenched a fist. For a moment Deidre thought he would actually try to strike them, but Meara adjusted her stance and held up the blade. He let out a string of curses and pushed past them toward the bailey.

"Thank you," Deidre said when he had gone.

Meara grunted, an unbecoming pink color seeping upward from her neck. "A man doesna have the right to force ye." And then she turned without another word and walked back to the kitchens.

Deidre clasped the pieces of her torn bodice together and brushed back the hair that had come loose from her braid. She skirted the edge of the garden wall, staying in the shadow of the main Hall until she came to the rear entrance. Thankful that no one had seen her in this unkempt state, she reached for the door handle just as it opened and Gilead stepped through.

He took in her disheveled appearance—the torn sleeve and ripped gown that nearly exposed an entire breast—and wrapped his arms around her, one hand smoothing her hair and the other stroking her back gently.

"Niall did this?"

Deidre nodded and buried her face on his shoulder, her knees suddenly jellied. Gilead's clean scent of soap and spice mingled with the leather of his hauberk was such a contrast to Niall, and Gilead felt so solid and warm and safe. Tears began to fall as she clung to him, fingers entwined in his hair.

"I'll finish this," Gilead said as he soothed her. "I'll call the bastard out."

"You can't." Deidre sniffled in an attempt to stop crying and leaned back, bringing her hand to his cheek. "It would be an affront to Dallis."

"I doona care," Gilead answered. "Niall has gone too far. Let me get ye into the house and then I'll find him."

"No, Gilead. Please. Your father has said often enough how he needs the alliances. He'll need Comgall to protect his flank and fall in behind him. You can't insult the man by offering for me. Not now."

Gilead looked unconvinced.

"Please," Deidre said and stood on tiptoe to kiss him. He gathered her tightly to him, his mouth slanting over hers, passion building as she parted her lips and invited him in to explore her mouth fully. Their tongues swirled round each other and Gilead deepened the kiss until they were both panting and gasping for air.

Their private little world was shattered by the blowing of a ram's horn. Gilead eased himself from Deidre with a slow, sultry kiss. "That's the signal to mount up," he said as he nuzzled her neck. "I've got to go."

Deidre clung to him for one last kiss and then stepped back. "May the Great Mother protect you."

She watched until he rounded the corner and was lost from

view. Holding her torn dress together, she prayed silently that he would return and, knowing it was wrong, that Niall would not.

As they rode north, Gilead kept an eye out for Niall, but the man kept his troops well back of Angus. At first, Gilead thought it was to avoid a confrontation, but by the second day, he questioned his father on whether Niall meant to fight or not.

His father looked back at the distant cloud of dust when Gilead came up alongside him with the question. "Aye," Angus confirmed, "he'll fight, but he'll not lead."

"Coward," Gilead muttered. 'Chicken-livered bastard."

Angus glanced over at him. "Ye seem a mite put out with the man."

"He tried mauling Deidre in the herbal garden ere we left."

"Mauling? Do ye jest? More like he tried to take a kiss and she felt insulted."

Gilead lifted an eyebrow. "The man tried to tear her clothes off. I mean to call him out as soon as we're through fighting."

"Ye ken ye'll be tarnishing Dallis's honor by doing that and making an enemy of Comgall?"

"Deidre doesna deserve a fate at Niall's hands," Gilead replied stubbornly.

Angus was quiet for several moments as they rode along. Then he sighed. "I doona trust Niall either. We will see how the battle goes. Mayhap the gods will see fit to help ye and Niall won't be going home."

Gilead took a deep breath. "Are ye saying to kill him?"

"Nay." Angus gave him a reproachful look. "That would make us the cowards. But I can move his army to the fore, instead of behind us, like he wanted. That would put him in the thick of it." He shrugged. "Who knows what pleases the Old Ones?"

Word came that Gunpar had stopped the passage across his lands, but that Fergus had turned south and laid siege to Gabran's fortress. But now, several more weeks had slipped by without any word from Angus. During the day, Una kept Deidre too busy to fret overmuch, but she spent her nights worrying about Gilead being wounded or worse. She tried walking the battlements to ease her mind, but Gavin, the man Turius had left in charge of the fifty soldiers that had remained, had men posted every dozen strides, which made any kind of solitude impossible.

Grateful as she was that neither Niall or Dallis was in residence, the Great Hall seemed empty at night, Elen's seat conspicuously vacant. Deidre didn't miss the snide remarks and sly glances that Sheila and Janet had been wont to make, either, but she did miss having someone to talk to. Drustan had sunk to low depths, his music increasingly wild and mournful, like the death-keening Meara and Una had done for Elen.

Strangely, Deidre missed—and was startled to realize it—Formorian's company. Although she still did not approve of the entanglement that had caused Elen such sorrow, she was beginning to understand the why of it, having been with Gilead. No other man would ever come close to him. And, if Formorian were here, they might just be able to ride outside these confining walls.

Deidre sighed as she folded fresh sunshine-scented linens the servant had brought in from the drying line. She had a desperate urge to visit the circle of stones, to draw on that energy once more to aid in her quest. If she sensed nothing, she would abandon the search for the Stone and ride toward Dumbarton, hoping to catch a ship to Armorica.

The one day that she had saddled Winger, she'd been stopped at the gate. Angus had left orders that no woman venture out until they returned. Neither fuming nor flirting had worked. Gavin had been Roman-trained by Turius and remained staunchly oblivious to her attempts to wheedle him into changing his mind.

The sounding of the horn at the gate, announcing an arrival, made her drop the sheet she was holding and hurry outside.

Her shoulders drooped in disappointment when Dallis's carriage rolled through the gate. Deidre had completely lost track of time. Mabon—the fall equinox—was almost upon them. Gilead's wedding date. *Her* wedding date, if she didn't manage to escape.

Drustan rushed out into the bailey to help Dallis step down. "You're as lovely as the first sight of heather after a winter's snow," he said with a flourish.

She gave him her dimpled smile and laid a small hand on his arm. "'Tis good to see ye, Drustan. I've missed yer music."

Ha! Deidre thought as she reluctantly approached them. Dallis would hardly like what had passed for Drustan's music lately. But his mood seemed to have lightened considerably.

"I'll compose something for ye tonight," he said with a slight bow.

"And I'll show you to your room," Deidre announced.

"Certes," Dallis replied politely. "I would appreciate that."

"This way, then." As they turned and walked into the Great Hall, Deidre added, "Gilead and his father aren't back yet."

"I ken," Dallis answered and tossed a look back at Drustan. "I thought to arrive early and get settled. My Da wanted me here to welcome back my betrothed."

Deidre tried to ignore the clutching of her stomach. Gilead's bride-to-be. Wife. Settled. This would be her home. There wasn't any way she wanted to be here to witness that. Or to marry Niall.

Several days later and only two days before the weddings, Deidre retreated to the herbal garden, supposedly to gather fresh leaves for dinner, but more to avoid contact with Dallis. The girl's sweetness left a sour taste in Deidre's mouth. It was blissfully quiet and peaceful within the vined walls.

The sound of thundering hooves approaching the gate brought her out of her reverie. Deidre ran outside and scrambled up a ladder to the parapet and peered over. Angus's familiar red lion banner waved over the head of the standard-bearer. The men were home!

She rushed down the steps, only to collide with Una at the far corner of the house. "Where are ye going in such a rush?" the castellan asked.

"To welcome back . . ." Even as she said the words, her heart plummeted. It was not her place to greet Gilead. That honor went to Dallis. Deidre wanted nothing more than to throw herself into his arms and feel his warm, strong embrace.

"Go back to the garden, lass, and finish yer work."

So it wasn't until the evening meal that Deidre was actually able to see Gilead. The sight of Dallis seated next to him at the high table in what had been Elen's chair was almost too much to bear. The only relief Deidre had was that Niall had stopped at his own holdings and hadn't accompanied Angus home.

When the dancing started and she saw Gilead offer his arm to Dallis, the few morsels of food Deidre had managed to swallow threatened to return to her plate. She pushed away from the table in haste and bumped into Drustan.

He steadied her. "Would you like to dance?"

The last thing she wanted to do was dance. The sight of Gilead's arm around Dallis's slender waist was threatening to make her embarrass herself and be sick in front of everyone. "I don't think—" but Drustan was already leading her onto the floor.

"Gilead asked me to dance you over. He wants to talk," Drustan whispered.

Hope surged through her like a spring bubbling through a crevice in a rock.

As they circled near Gilead, Drustan said grandly, "If you'll excuse me, might I claim a dance with your betrothed before she is fully claimed by you?"

Gilead made a small bow and handed Dallis over. Then he turned and held out his arms. Deidre stepped into them and was immediately inundated by his unique scent and the strong, hard maleness of him.

He was careful not to hold her too close, since Angus was watching from the dais, but she felt his arm tighten as he turned her. "I tried to convince my father to let ye go."

"And he said 'no.'" It was a statement, not a question.

"Aye." He looked into her eyes, his own dark with worry. "We managed to turn Fergus Mor back, but it wasna easy. All the cenels together could bare contain him. At one point, Da even thought Niall had turned."

Deidre raised an eyebrow. "Why?"

"Niall's army was lagging behind, so far that we lost sight of them once until my father finally called a halt and waited for them to catch up." Gilead drew her closer as they spun. "He ordered Niall's troops to advance in front of us, then."

Deidre frowned slightly. "Wouldn't Niall be in a more dangerous position, then?"

A corner of Gilead's mouth lifted. "That was the idea."

Her eyes widened. "Your father did it on purpose?"

Gilead nodded. "But it dinna work. The next morn when we were to march, Niall claimed to have eaten foul meat and lay about the food wagons all day."

By the saints! If the man had died in battle, he could have been a hero and she would have been free. "What a sniveling coward that man is!" she said indignantly.

"Aye. My thoughts exactly." He brushed her cheek lightly with his fingertips and then took her hand again. "But living cowards know they're weak, which makes them dangerous. Da canna afford to leave Niall unencumbered."

Deidre's legs suddenly felt wooden and nailed to the floor. She stopped dancing and stared at Gilead. "Which means that your father needs to bind Niall to him and to do that, I have to marry him."

"Aye, lass," Gilead said hesitantly, "but I—"

Deidre pulled away from him and bolted to the hallway door, not wanting to hear any more excuses.

Deidre refused to come out of her room the next day, the day before the wedding. She had no wish to see the look of pity in Gilead's eyes and she certainly did not want to take part in any of Dallis's preparations, either.

Una had come up to get her, but took one look at her red, swollen eyes and puffed-up face and shook her head, returning downstairs. Deidre heard some muffled roaring—Angus probably—at her refusal to leave her room, but he hadn't come thundering up the stairs, either. Instead, they'd given her this day. Her last day of freedom.

Deidre had spent the night praying to Isis, whom the Magdalen had served; to the Scotti Brighid; and even to the

Christos. In desperation, she had even tried to conjure up the ancient magician who had left The Book with her mother so many years ago. He'd told her mother that he had lived for ages. Deidre felt hysteria rapidly rising in her throat, threatening to spill over into some heart-wrenching scream of laughter at her foolishness. An immortal man? No doubt, a braggart. The whole book had been a bunch of lies. If any damsel had ever been in distress, it was she and there was no knight in shining armor to rescue her. They didn't exist.

And then, to add insult to rapidly weakening faith, when she had finally fallen into a fitful state of semisleep, the red-haired woman from the stone circle, still dressed in white, appeared to her, holding out a cup for her to drink from, and smiling benignly.

Deidre woke in a rage. She'd probably been offered poison in her dream, but she was not about to kill herself. She lifted her night shift and fingered the smooth leather scabbard tied to her leg, which shielded the sgian dubh Formorian had taught her to use.

Never would she allow Niall to become her bridegroom. *Never.*

Chapter Twenty-three

THE CUP OF LOVE

Deidre sat by her window looking down at the crowded bailey, roiling with activity. Soldiers' leather hauberks had been oiled until they glistened in the sun, women of all ranks appeared wearing their finery, and Gilead's clansmen sported their softly woven blue formal kilts and sashes.

It was Gilead's wedding day. Deidre bit her lip to hold the tears back. It was her wedding day, too, *may all the saints curse it!*

She had made one more attempt at escape last night, but when she opened the door well after midnight, a solemn Gavin stood guard. She'd considered knotting her sheets and sliding down the wall, but when she leaned out her window, Adair looked up at her. Frustrated, she had cried herself into an exhausted stupor, haunted by nightmares of a fiendish Niall showing her no mercy.

As taut as her nerves were, she nearly fell off the stool when the doorknob turned and the door squeaked open. Saints, she felt like she was being led to her execution.

Angus frowned when he saw her wedding dress crumbled on the bed, the Dubb Lein with its gossamer veil on the floor. "Dinna Una come in to help ye dress?"

Deidre lifted her chin. "She did, but I took it off as soon as she left." Purposely, she had chosen the plainest work garment she had, a grayish homespun that had seen better days.

His eyes narrowed as he strode into the room and picked up the fine silk with the Irish lace overlay and handed it to her. "Put it on. Now."

"I will not."

"Ye will do as I say."

"No." She glared at him, too angry to be frightened of his barely controlled temper. "Hit me if you want. In fact, knock me cold. Then I won't have to—"

"Silence!" he roared. "I've ne'r hit a woman and ye'll not be my first." He took a deep breath and his eyes darkened. "But I have disrobed women and clothed them again, too." He took a step closer. "It's yer choice, lass."

"You wouldn't dare."

Angus arched an eyebrow. "Wouldn't I?"

And she knew he would. If he stripped her to her shift, he'd see the little dirk strapped to her leg. As defiantly as she could, she snatched the dress from him, crushing the soft fabric, and stepped behind a dressing screen. For a moment, she considered tearing the fragile gown in two. That would show him.

"If I doona hear the sound of clothing rustling, I'm coming back there," he said.

Deidre pulled the working dress over her head quickly and struggled into the tighter-fitting gown. Unfortunately, its laces wound round her bodice and tied in back.

"Doona tarry. I'll not have everyone be kept waiting because of ye," he warned.

Deidre stepped out from behind the screen, her arms crossed in front of her to hold the dress up. "I need Una."

"Nonsense." Angus crossed the room in three strides and turned her around, his fingers deftly running the lacings through the eyes and tugging the dress lightly to her form. His touch was surprisingly gentle and Deidre bit her lip again to keep from crying. Would his son's hands be so smooth and adept with Dallis's dress tonight?

"There." He stepped back and inspected her hair, some of

which had come undone. "I canna do much about that," he said and brushed a strand back behind her ear. "Would that Mori were here." He sighed and his voice was softer when he spoke. "She'd make ye understand the importance of clan alliances."

"You're throwing me to the wolves and you know it."

He was silent as he stooped and picked up her headdress. "Here."

"No. I will *not* wear it." She would rip it off if he tried putting it on. "I'll not make a total mockery of this day."

Something flickered at the back of his dark eyes. Abruptly, he threw the veil back on the bed. "As ye wish, then. Let us go." He took her elbow to escort her, but Deidre knew if she even tried to pull away, that light hold would turn to a steel grip.

The carriage was waiting for her and she and Angus were both silent for the short trip to the village. Only when they entered the kirk yard, did Deidre give a slight involuntary gasp. Her worst nightmare had become very, very real.

Had Angus not been supporting her, she was sure she would have squiggled to the ground like a bowl of jelly, for her knees shook and her legs had no strength.

Inside the crowded, stone-walled church, Gilead waited at the altar, pale and still, the lights of a hundred flickering candles playing across his strong features, making him seem a Roman god. Beside him stood an equally pallid Dallis, her hands clasped tightly. Deidre hardly noticed Niall grinning evilly at her from the other side of the altar.

The little priest that Elen had so respected cleared his throat and nodded to Gilead and Dallis to step forward. "We are gathered here today . . ."

Deidre shut out the words. She didn't want to hear Gilead promise to love and honor Dallis until death should them part. Her eyes sent daggers toward Niall. Forget that she was in a church. If he were fool enough to try and rape her, he'd be dead by tonight. The Goddess would understand.

"Do ye, Gilead, take Dallis to be yer lawfully wedded wife . . ."

Only slowly did Deidre realize that Gilead had not responded. She tore her attention away from her murderous thoughts.

"I canna do it, Dallis," he said quietly. "Please forgive me. I should have stopped this much sooner." Ignoring his father's enraged look, he turned to Comgall. "There need be no war between the clans on account of this. Ye may seek your vengeance on me alone. Have me flogged, if ye like. I will also turn over my lands in Lothian—"

"Nay," Dallis interrupted and both Angus and Comgall stopped glaring at Gilead. "'Tis not Gilead's fault. There is no love between us." She hesitated, dipping her head. When she spoke her voice was barely above a whisper. "Not when I love another."

Dumbfounded, Gilead lifted her chin with a finger. "Whom do ye love?"

Her face flushing a bright pink, she pointed at Drustan.

He leapt from his bench, nearly knocking the confused priest over as he hastened to them. "I've loved ye since the first time I set eyes on ye! Ye are the sun, the moon, the stars in the heavens—"

"Now see here," Comgall began gruffly and then looked into his daughter's smiling face. "Is this want ye've wanted, sweetheart?"

Dallis nodded and wiped a tear from her eye.

Comgall turned to Angus and gave a slight shrug. "It seems we fathers have been bested on this."

Angus was silent while he studied Gilead and then glanced at Dallis and Drustan. Finally he nodded. "Ye have my permission as well."

Almost giggly now, Dallis looked up at Drustan, her eyes luminous as she fit her small hand into his and repeated her vows firmly.

And then it was Deidre's turn.

Niall grabbed her arm and yanked her toward him.

"Not so fast," Gilead said.

"Get out of my way, lout."

"Nay." Gilead removed his gauntlet and threw it on the floor in front of Niall. "I am free to challenge ye for Deidre's hand, now. I'm calling ye out."

Niall's eyes narrowed and his hand went to his sword hilt. "Ye miserable cur, I'll kill ye where ye stand."

The priest blanched and clasped the edge of the altar. "This is a house of God!"

"Outside," Gilead said.

Niall sneered at him and pushed Deidre out of the way as he stalked down the aisle into the bright sunshine of the kirk yard.

Guests poured out of the church and a throng formed around the two men as they drew their swords and began circling each other warily. Niall lunged suddenly, but Gilead sidestepped him and his momentum sent him crashing into one of the onlookers, who pushed him back into the circle. Several ladies tittered.

Gilead waited for him to return to guard position. Furious, Niall thrust, cutting low. Gilead parried and did a quick riposte, driving Niall backward. The crowd parted for them. Niall thrust again and this time they engaged, flats of swords pressed against each other until Gilead broke away. He feinted left and Niall cut left, giving Gilead enough time to step forward and draw first blood. The crowd cheered.

Enraged, Niall bellowed like a bull and lunged again. Gilead met his blows with agility, light on his feet and moving the older man in circles. Niall began to pant heavily, his movements slowing.

"Do ye yield?" Gilead asked as he disengaged from Niall's blade.

"Never! Ye'll rot in hell before I give up that bitch!"

Several people booed and some of Niall's men began to slink away from the outer circle of the fight.

"Fight on, then," Gilead said grimly.

Niall feinted and as Gilead moved to counter him, the ball of his foot caught on a loose cobble. For a mere second, he unbalanced.

It was all Niall needed. He leaped onto Gilead, plunging his sword into his groin. Gilead dropped to one knee, blood gushing down his upper thigh. Niall pushed him to the ground, deliberately grinding dirt into the open wound. Gilead gasped in pain and went still. Niall laughed and stood, holding his dripping sword high. "She's mine now!"

He never saw the dirk flashing through the air from Deidre's hand, finding its target directly in his heart.

* * *

"Ye are exhausted, lass," Angus said quietly. "I'll watch him for a while."

Deidre shook her head stubbornly, almost too tired to hold it up as she sat beside Gilead's bed. He had passed out from loss of blood and, for the past two days, had lain in a feverish semicoma in the infirmary, due to festering. The medic had said only time would tell if he would regain enough strength to recover. The wound had sliced through muscles and nearly severed an artery.

"I want to be the first person he sees when he wakes up."

"If he sees ye half dead yerself, what good will that do him?" Angus asked as he started to lift her out of her chair.

"Doona . . . do . . . that . . ." Gilead moaned.

Deidre bent over him, her hand caressing his cheek. "You're awake!"

"Aye." He groaned again. "My leg feels afire."

"Ye've a nasty wound," Angus said. "With no healer, it festered."

"I told the medic to stuff the wound with sphagnum moss to draw out the infection, but he wouldn't let me apply it myself," Deidre said as she brushed Gilead's hair off his forehead. She wasn't about to tell him that, when she'd tried to convince the medic that she'd seen male anatomy before, he'd said the damage was not a pretty sight and he only hoped Gilead would still be able to use his manhood.

Gilead managed a wan smile. "Something's down there. I can feel it." He tried to move his leg and winced in pain.

"Lie still," Deidre said.

Gilead closed his eyes and then snapped them open. "I lost the fight. Are ye . . . are ye wed to Niall?"

"Nay," Angus said, "the bastard dinna fight fair. You were right. I should ne'r have trusted him."

Gilead looked relieved and then he frowned. "Will there be war, ye think?"

Angus's mouth twitched. "Not unless the man rises from the depths of hell."

"He's dead?" Gilead asked. "I'd ne'r have thought I'd wounded him badly."

"Ye dinna," Angus replied, trying not to grin. "Yer bonny lass put a dirk through him, straight and true to his heart."

Gilead's eyes widened as he looked at Deidre. She grasped his hand. "I thought he'd killed you. I don't really remember doing it . . . I only saw the dirk leave my hand."

Angus nodded. "The fighting frenzy. It emboldens some men in battle, giving them the strength of a dozen." He looked at her with something like respect or maybe even admiration. "Formorian was right, then, when she told me we could make a warrior out of ye."

Deidre shuddered. "No thanks. I don't want to do any more killing." She paused and lifted her chin. "But I'm not sorry he's gone."

"Aye. He wilna be missed by most. His men have already pledged their allegiance to me," Angus said. "The priest took his body back to Lugaid and will explain what happened."

Gilead nodded and looked at Deidre. Then he hesitated.

"What?" Deidre asked.

He took a deep breath. "I doona ken if I have the right to ask, not knowing how fully recovered I'll be . . ." He held up a hand when Deidre tried to speak. "The medic told me I might not . . . er, might not be able . . ."

"Shhhh." Deidre soothed him. "What do you want to ask?"

"Will ye marry me?"

Tears sprang up in her eyes. "Yes! A thousand times yes, even if you never leave this bed! I love you, Gilead."

He tugged her head down and gave her a gentle kiss that was quickly met with moist open lips and an inviting tongue. He deepened the kiss into a passionate soul quest, arms wrapping around her as she pressed her breasts against his chest.

Angus chuckled and closed the door quietly behind him.

"I think you should know who I am."

Angus turned from the solar window and studied Deidre. She forced herself not to fidget under his scrutiny. His face was impassive and she could not even fathom what he was thinking. He sounded resigned when he finally spoke.

"Sit down, then."

She slipped into a chair across the table from where he now poured a goblet of wine. He offered her some, but she shook her head.

"I'm not Saxon," she began, and thought she saw a fleeting glimpse of relief in his eyes before he masked his face again. She took a deep breath. Being Frankish might not be any better.

"I am cousin to King Childebert of Gaul."

Angus raised an eyebrow. "And why would the king of Gaul send his . . . cousin . . . here? And alone without escort or coin?"

She shook her head again and told him of her mother and the Beltane ritual that had made Caw her father. And how, after her mother's death, Childebert had all but kept her prisoner, for her dowry was large and he didn't want it spent. She even told him of her unsuccessful search for the Stone and her somewhat undependable gift of Sight.

Angus stood and began to pace when she finished. "'Twould almost be better if ye were Saxon, lass. I've seen the foolishness of Turius's men searching for that damn grail. If yer cousin thinks ye have the gift to find this Stone, he will want ye returned."

She stared at him, feeling her heart thudding in her chest. "You're going to send me back, aren't you? Because you don't want war with the Franks."

Angus paused and then sat down abruptly, elbows on the table and put his head in his hands. He was quiet for so long that Deidre was about ready to scream at him.

He looked up, and, again, she saw the resignation on his face. She became aware that she was holding her breath and forced herself to exhale.

"Nay. I wilna send ye back." He gave her a lopsided grin when he saw her surprise. "I will not let Gilead make the mistake I did by sending away the one woman he loves. I will send a letter to Childebert and explain the situation. Since ye have not found the Stone, it probably isna here and he will let ye be."

"And if he doesn't?" Deidre hated to ask, but she didn't want her hopes dashed by return courier.

Angus lifted his head and squared his shoulders. "If he wants war, then he will have it. 'Tis time I look at something more important that binding the clans. Doona fash, Deidre. I've seen the look in Gil's eyes when he gazes on ye. 'Tis the same with me and Mori. I wilna take that from him."

In that moment, Deidre understood what Angus had given up and that there truly was a compassionate side to him. She could have hugged him, then. Well, almost.

Gilead was mending in the warm sunshine of a late autumn day, his leg propped up on a bench along the wall near the herbal garden. Deidre sat beside him, reading the letter that had just arrived by messenger from Gabran.

"He says they finally found Brena." Angus had felt sure she would head straight back to her clan, but no one there had seen her. Or would admit it.

"Where?" Gilead asked.

"In a Highland crag." Deidre scanned the writing. "She seems to have saved the life of a laird there when she was young and he gave her refuge. Only when Gabran threatened Mac Erca sailing across the sea with full force to avenge Elen's death, did the man let her go. Gabran sent her to Eire for Mac Erca to mete out justice." She paused. "Brena named Niall as her accomplice."

Gilead's face tightened. "It's a good thing the bastard is dead."

"Your poor mother," Deidre said softly.

Gilead drew her back to lean against him, arms around her waist. "Does Gabran say why Brena did it?"

"Ummm, it seems that Brena is the fraternal twin to Formorian's fanatical nanny. They were worshippers of the Old Ways and the Mother Right. A warrior queen had the right to choose her escort. And they knew Formorian had always loved Angus, so they hatched up a plan to get Elen out of the way." Deidre let the letter slip to the ground and turned to Gilead, tears in her eyes. "What an insult to the Great Mother, who seeks for peace in the world instead of violence."

He reached up and wiped a tear away with the pad of his thumb and smiled at her. "Like that holy grail ye told me about? The one that would bring peace if Turius's men but found it?"

"But they've given up looking, haven't they?"

"Aye. He's recalled them to strengthen his ranks and bring his son to heel." He nuzzled her neck. "But let's think of pleasant things. I'm nigh well, and Samhain is but a fortnight away. The beginning of a new year and a new life with ye as my wife."

His wife. She definitely liked the sound of that.

Two days before Samhain, Formorian unexpectedly arrived, wearing widow's black. "Maximilian killed him," she told a shocked Gilead and strangely quiet Angus in the solar that afternoon.

Deidre handed Formorian a goblet of wine and then poured some for Angus and Gilead. The queen's hand shook slightly and she was a little paler than usual, but her green eyes burned with intensity as she watched Angus. A look quite different from the subdued parting they'd had three months ago.

"When . . . How . . ." Gilead and his father both spoke at once.

"There was a battle near a small river. Maximilian was riding with Aesc . . . they were supposed to parley, but something went wrong." She sighed. "I found out a fortnight ago. It took the messenger near a sennight to reach me." She looked at Deidre. "Did ye not wed Niall, after all?"

"Nay," Angus said and told her what had transpired. She gave a satisfied nod. "I told ye throwing a dirk would be a good thing to know." She glanced sideways at Angus. "It keeps a man in line."

He grinned at her. "Aye. Where in line would ye like me to be?"

The look on her face left no doubt in anyone's mind.

Turius had been dead nearly a moon. Elen was gone. Nothing would stop Angus and Formorian now. Deidre wondered how long it would take before they would be in bed together.

And then she smiled. They had both done their duty. Maybe the Goddess was finally smiling on them.

Deidre's smile broadened. Tomorrow was her wedding day and Gilead would be bedding her tomorrow night. She shivered a little in anticipation, the tingling in her swelling breasts jolting through her belly to gently pulsate at her core. She could wait. But just barely.

Their wedding was a quiet and subdued affair on the day before Samhain. To honor Elen's wishes, they were married by the priest in the little kirk in the village. So soon after his mother's death, neither Gilead nor Deidre wanted a festival atmosphere. They would wait and hold the great feast come Beltane, when enough time had passed. He hoped, Gilead had told Deidre, they would be celebrating a pregnancy, too. To Deidre, though, the important thing was to slip away to the circle of stones this eve and say the Oath that would bind them for eternity.

Gilead closed the door to their chambers at twilight and helped her out of the silk dress she had once refused to wear. Tiny flames pricked her bare skin wherever his hot hands touched. His fingers caressed her shoulders and breasts, stroked down her back and cupped her buttocks, lifting her against him.

"We have waited nigh three moons," Gilead whispered as he backed her toward the bed. "I doona want to wait any longer."

Deidre tightened her hold around his neck and pressed her breasts into his chest. "I want you inside of me. Now."

It was all the invitation he needed. Settling her beneath him on the bed, he spread her legs wide with his thighs and ravaged her mouth with his, his tongue mimicking his other movements as he plundered her hot, wet sheath, ramming his sword to the hilt, butting against her womb in long, hard thrusts.

She arched her back to receive him more fully, seconds later feeling the pulsing at her core quicken until her body racked in one great shudder. Gilead growled, lifting her partially off the bed, and spilled his seed deep inside her.

They lay panting for some moments and then Gilead gently

turned her on her side, facing him. "This time we'll do it slow," he said as he nibbled a trail from her ear to her nape, his tongue lightly flickering across the damp skin.

Deidre shivered in delight as he licked circles around her breasts, teasing the nipples with his breath, but not quite touching them. They hardened immediately into perky little nubs, and the more time he took in tonguing across her belly and then back up to the mounds of her breasts, the more swollen and achy they became. Softly, he rolled one tight peak between his forefinger and thumb, stirring desire that jolted straight through her. Deidre moaned as the tip of his tongue flitted across the other one. She mewled helplessly as he continued to lave at her damp breasts, titillating her in ways she didn't think possible. When he finally, mercifully, began to suckle fully, her whole body convulsed.

Gilead slid himself lower, his lips mouthing the throbbing little bud between her swollen folds, and sending her body into new, rippling waves of sensation. He entered her slowly this time, inch by inch, letting her feel the thick fullness of him before he began an easy rhythm, allowing the delicious warmth spreading through her to kindle into flames that soon roared through her blood like wind-driven fire over dry brush. Muscles deep inside contracted as her body spasmed, and she cried out in pleasure as they melded together.

Gilead held her close, his fingers playing with the strands of her hair. "I have looked forward to this night since the day I woke up in the infirmary."

"Mmmm," Deidre murmured sleepily. "The first times were wonderful, but tonight has been . . . fantastic. I had no idea I could be so satisfied."

"Well, doona go to sleep yet, Sassenach. We're not through." He rolled over on his back and pulled her on top of him. "'Tis yer turn to ride me and do as ye will."

Shy at first, she ran her hands across the broad width of his shoulders and down his chest, pinching gently at his nipples until he groaned. "Do you like this, too?"

"Aye, lass. It pierces straight through to my shaft." He swiveled his hips under her and grinned. "Canna ye feel it?"

She widened her eyes as his once relaxed member began to

grow again and she wiggled her own hips, sliding her juices across the length of him. Obligingly, his manhood jerked upright, prodding her.

"Ah, Dee, what ye do to me," he said as she impaled herself on his now granite shaft and he felt the hot, tight clenching of her muscles grip him. He rocked upward, driving himself deeper. To her surprise, she found she could control his movements with hers. She concentrated on experimenting, angling herself forward, rocking backward, and then lifting and slowly lowering herself again onto his shaft. He groaned as she ground against him, her hips gyrating until he was full bucking under her. Their arousal grew into a torrid frenzy and they exploded together, Deidre collapsing on top on him, their breathing ragged, their hearts pounding. Not wanting to separate, they lay like that for some time.

Well sated, Deidre snuggled into the warm bend of Gilead's arm and rested her head on his shoulder. "We should probably leave for the circle soon," she said, "but I'm not sure I can move."

His hand brushed against the side of her rounded breast as he planted a kiss on the top of her head. "Nay, Sassenach, can ye be worn out already?"

She slapped his chest playfully. "If I'd known you had so much staying power, I'd have insisted we practice several nights before this."

Gilead laughed. "'Tis exactly why I wanted to wait. I wanted to claim yer body, yer heart, and yer soul, just like the Oath says." Gently, he pulled his arm from under her and sat up. "And if we're going to be there for the Samhain dawn, we'd best get going."

He walked in all his glorious nakedness to the bureau and Deidre smiled at the way his tight buttocks contracted with each step. Fifty years from now, she would still not get tired of looking at him.

He reached into the drawer that held his second-best plaid and then stopped, a mildly surprised look on his face. "By the Dagda! I had forgotten this."

Deidre watched as he held up a cup made of an odd cast of green stone, the bronze rim reflecting the firelight from the softly glowing braziers. As he brought it closer, Deidre could see that it was actually marble.

"This is for you," Gilead said as he handed it to her. "I found it in my grandfather's treasures. It was the only piece like it."

She was surprised that the marble had none of the cool feel that the stone usually did. In fact, a faint, warm vibration hummed between her hands. Deidre ran a fingertip over the rim and withdrew it quickly. The metal was almost hot, as though it had been placed over flames. She squinted and held the cup up to the firelight to look at the rim. One row of runes was etched above a fine engraved line. Another identical set of runes ran below the line. Two circles, cut through with a square, the square divided into triangles, the theme repeating itself around the rim. No beginning and no end.

The handles were a labyrinth of entwining vines embedded with roses. Deidre paused. Vines and roses, in much the same pattern she had seen on the tablecloth at Eire. The vine representing the bloodline of Jesus and the rose that of the Magdalen, uniting the old religion with the new. Deidre's fingers began to tingle and she looked closer. Tiny rosebuds interplayed with large, open flowers. Innocence and childhood combined with maturity and knowledge.

Knowledge. Wisdom. Deidre felt the familiar light-headedness begin to settle and she struggled to see through the misting haze in front of her eyes. The runes . . . each shape was a symbol of sacred geometry, repetition of the life force, divided by a line. "As above, so below." The sum of all knowledge for those who had eyes to see.

The image of the red-haired woman from her vision floated in front of her, the cup that the maiden held out transposing itself over the cup Deidre held in her hands.

She stared down at it, trying to shut away the gray shadows. Slowly, the cup began to glow, growing warm in her hands again. She leaned against a bedpost.

"Are ye all right?" Gilead had hold of her arm, a look of concern on his face.

She looked up at him. "More than all right. You've found it."

"What?" he asked in a puzzled voice.

"The cup," she said and held it up. "This is the gar-al . . . the cup of stone. Or more precisely," she added, as she looked at it in awe, "the Philosopher's Stone."

They neared the circle of stones just before dawn. The night had been mild and a fine mist lay on the grass, tendrils gently rising here and there. Deidre had the cup carefully wrapped in a saddlebag. What was supposed to be a wondrous finish to their wedding nuptials had now turned bittersweet.

"I will have to sail to the Languedoc as soon as a ship is available," Deidre said as Gilead helped her dismount and they unwrapped the cup. "It must be returned."

"I know," he said, "and ye've told me ye must travel alone so ye wilna be spotted by Childebert's troops, but I doona like it. Yer cousin's reply to Da's letter was not over-happy. If ye get caught, ye will be held hostage. At least let me and our men sail with ye as far as Béziers."

"We've been over this," Deidre said in a patient voice. For the long ride, they had discussed little else. "If—and they will—Childebert's men see a Scotti armed galley come sailing in, they'll think you're coming to take back the lands that I gave up as part of the settlement. And you'd have war. No," she continued, without letting Gilead respond, "it's better if I sail on a cargo ship. Shhh," she said as he tried to speak again. "Let's not mar our happiness with argument. I would have the Oath sacred."

Gilead put an arm around her waist, his warm, strong fingers comforting. Deidre held the cup in front of her. Rays of bright orange and red slanted through the spaces between the stones as the sun's rim peeped over the horizon, casting the circle in eerie light. Deidre smiled at him as they stepped through the stones.

"So you've come at last."

Startled, they looked around. The circle was empty, but the voice had been full, luminous with melody. Slowly, fog rose from the ground, enfolding them in gracefully twisting spirals of vapor becoming dense enough to obscure the stones from their view, leaving them in a soft cloud of gray mist. The ethereal music that Deidre had heard before emanated from the stones again, oft and more melodious than even Drustan's harp.

The maiden took form, her red-gold hair floating out from her head, her gossamer gown of white flowing gently around her. She smiled at them and held out her hands. "I will take the cup."

Deidre handed it to her. "I thought I was supposed to return it to the grotto in the Languedoc so women will once again come to power."

"The time is not yet," the maiden replied and the music suddenly stopped, leaving them in total stillness. "Great Darkness is coming. In the wrong hands, the power and knowledge of this cup would bring utter destruction. Better that it remain safely hidden until mankind once more emerges into the Light." The vision smiled and the music began again. "Then, women will be treated with utmost courtesy and respect. The wisdom of the Goddess will be allowed to shine. And I think," she said rather mischievously as her form began to fade, "you have come here for something else. I'll not keep you from it."

The fog dissipated as quickly as it had appeared, leaving them standing in the midst of a sun-drenched circle, a brilliant blue sky overhead.

Gilead wrapped his arms around Deidre's waist and drew her close. "The Oath has two parts," he said. "When we made love earlier, the first time, we joined our bodies, the second time, we connected our hearts. The third time, our minds opened to each other. And now, this," he said as he slipped his dirk from its sheath and pulled a fresh strip of linen from his pocket, "will entwine our souls."

Carefully, he nicked Deidre's wrist and then his own. He pressed the small wounds together and wrapped the bandage around them. "As this strip of cloth binds us physically, the exchange of my blood for yours binds our souls. Blood unto blood, soul unto soul, ye are mine, and I am yours, for eternity."

He bent to kiss her, and time, stretching endlessly forward, really did stand still.

Epilogue

Deidre surveyed the preparations in the Great Hall for the feast that would be held that evening, the bulk of her pregnancy not yet encumbering as she moved to supervise the pewter settings on the tables just below the dais. Elen's lace table runner graced the high table. Mac Erca had sent it, for, he said, he knew this love was true. Deidre smiled as she laid a hand on her stomach and felt the baby move.

"My lady," Una said as she approached, a little breathless from trying to be in three places at once. "There is a Druid at the gate who requests an audience."

"A Druid?" Deidre asked. There were few of them left since Christianity had taken over and the ones who remained usually stayed on the holy isle of Mona far to the south. But this was Beltane, after all, and news of this celebration had spread far.

"Show him into the family solar," Deidre said and tried to smooth her skirt and tuck stray curls away as she hurried to the kitchen to request that wine be brought.

It took a bit of time to capture Meara's attention with all the bustle going on. Even though Deidre was now the lady of the holding—there had been peace in the land since the cup was returned, and Angus spent more and more of his time in Luguvalium with Formorian—it was still wise not to rile Meara.

So the Druid was already standing near the hearth, his back to her, when she entered with the warmed wineskin and two silver goblets. His long, white hair blended into the white robe he wore, banded with a rope of gold, designating his status as High Druid from wherever he came.

He turned around, his uncanny golden eyes piercing through her and rooting her to the spot. "You!" she said and almost dropped the tray.

He moved with suprising agility for an old man and steadied the tray. "I did not mean to startle you, child. I've come for The Book."

Deidre tried to steady her hands as she poured his wine. This was the man who had pilfered the Stone from its hiding place deep within the sacred grotto, leaving in its place *Locus Vocare Camulodunum*. A magician, most had called him, for though his person and belongings were searched, not a trace of the Stone could be found, and they had to let him leave. And his robes had been blue, then.

She wasn't sure she could trust him. "What makes you think I have The Book?"

He raised one shaggy white eyebrow, but his eaglelike gaze didn't waver. "I only come to claim what is mine. The Stone has been returned, hasn't it?"

"How did you know about that?" she asked in surprise.

He looked mildly amused. "It is my way to know of . . . things."

Something in his gaze held her almost spellbound. Without her willing it, she found herself unlocking the small cabinet where she kept the book and handing it over.

He caressed the smooth leather as a lover would. "In another eight hundred years a young man named Thomas Mallory will have need of this."

Deidre eyed him suspiciously, the fine hair on her arms beginning to stand on end. "How do you know this? Are you a sorcerer?"

He shrugged. "Some have called me that."

"And is that when . . ." In spite of the glowing coals in the brazier, a chill crept through her. "Is that when all this is supposed to happen?"

"Oh, no, dear. It's already happened. Mallory will just write of it."

"Nothing in that book was true," she said. "None of it. There is no King Arthur or Camelot for that matter. The behavior of the men I've witnessed is far from noble."

The mage smiled. "Except for Gilead, I assume." He appeared deep in thought and then he nodded, more to himself than to her. "Mallory will embellish the story, to be sure, but it is a woman, several hundred years past him, who will make the connection."

Deidre was beginning to wonder if the old man was truly mad. He had already behaved strangely when he took residence at the shrine so many years ago. This talk of the future was something he couldn't possibly know. Yet, her curiosity got the better of her. A woman . . . could she be the bearer of the wisdom the maiden had spoken of?

This time the Druid did laugh. "Nay, the woman is not the Goddess that you think," he said, although she hadn't spoken, "but a learned woman, nonetheless."

In spite of the light-headed haze that was beginning to form around her head, Deidre pressed on. "You wanted me to read The Book. Why? Tell me what you know."

He set his wine down and began to pace, his stride sturdy and his back straight for one apparently so advanced in age. "As I said," he began, "the stories in the book are true, but mayhap not where history has placed them. A woman named Norma Goodrich will decipher that Lancelot was actually an inaccurate translation from the Latin language into Old French. It should have been spelled "*l'Ancelot.*" An infamous mistake, as it turns out."

Deidre furrowed her brow. "So his name is misspelled. There is no Lancelot—or l'Ancelot—here."

"Are you sure?" The old man paused. "The Latin name was Anguselus."

"Anguselus?" Deidre asked and then gasped. "Angus? Angus is Lancelot?" When he nodded, she frowned again. "But what of Gwenhwyfar? No one by that name—"

"Ah. 'Gwenhwyfar' means 'white shadow' in the western part of this isle," the Druid said as he folded his hands behind him. "Here in the North, she would be called 'Findabair,' or 'white phantom.'" He eyed Deidre. "You know her as 'Formorian.'"

Deidre felt her knees go weak and she sank down into a chair. That would explain the compelling and overpowering attraction they had to each other. "And Arthur? Was he Turius?" she asked weakly.

The mage nodded, a look of sadness in his eyes. "Arturius left much to be done," he said softly. "If only he had listened to me. . . ." His head snapped up, his eyes suspiciously bright. "But pay no mind to me, child. I am but an old man. I will take my leave of you now." He picked up the book and moved toward the door.

"Wait!" Deidre called as he reached the doorway. "You're Merlin, aren't you?"

For a moment his eyes glowed yellow as a hawk's and then he smiled. "It's one of the names I go by." Before she could ask anything more, he was gone.

She sat very still, her hands trembling as she tried not to shiver. So it was all true, even if the story didn't turn out the way she thought it would.

But then, perhaps it had. In The Book, Lancelot had been forced to marry Elaine, the daughter of the wounded Fisher King. Gilead's grandfather had received a sword thrust to his leg that wouldn't heal. Even though the legend clearly showed that Lancelot did not love Elaine, she had borne him a son named Galahad. Elaine. Elen. The woman whose rose on the table runner indicated she was a descendant of the Holy Bloodline.

Galahad. Gilead. Deidre had found her noble knight at last. The one man pure enough of heart to have helped her find the Philosopher's Stone.

But maybe Galahad had found the real Holy Grail, after all.

Author's Note

The origin of Lancelot's identity has always lured me. Was he the mythic French knight, descended from the holy bloodline of Vivian II, Lady of the Lake; or was he, in actuality, an Irish king equal to Arthur in stature?

Dr. Norma Lorre Goodrich (*King Arthur,* Harper & Row, 1989) claims the latter. History shows that there was an Irish Angus ruling in the sixth century. Dr. Goodrich explains that Geoffrey of Monmouth's (*History of the Kings of Britain,* Penguin Classics, 1977) Latin name for Angus would have been "Anguselus." When Chrétien de Troys translated the text into Old French, the middle syllable would have been dropped, leaving the name as An+sel+o or Anselot. De Troys referred to him as "l'Ancelot" ("the" Angus), indicating that he would have been a clan chieftain in Scotland. She believes that in a clerical error in transcription, the definite article "the" got attached to the proper noun "Ancelot" and became "Lancelot."

Gwenhwyfar's origins are also a mystery. Some historians claim she was Welsh, others that she was of Roman descent, and still others that she, too, was Irish-Scotch. In P.F.J. Turner's *The Real King Arthur* (Quality Books, Inc., 1993) he states that the name "Guinevere" was Celtic in origin, derived from the Irish "Findabair" meaning "white phantom," possibly because she was pale-skinned and blond. In *Celtic Myth & Magick* (Llewellyn Publications, 1995) Edain McCoy argues that "Findabar" comes from the same roots in the Giodelic language as Guinevere does in the Brythonic. Findabar was the daughter of the powerful Queen Maeve and helped to slay a water demon, a symbol of the battle with the Formorians.

About the Author

An avid reader of anything medieval, Cynthia Breeding has taught the traditional Arthurian legends in high school for fifteen years and owns more than three hundred books on the subject.

She lives on the bay in Corpus Christi, Texas, with her bichon frise, Nicki, and enjoys sailing and horseback riding on the beach.

Readers can reach her through snail mail at: 3636 S. Alameda, B116, Corpus Christi, Texas 78411, or visit her Web site: www.cynthiabreeding.com.